CITY OF BURBANK
Public Library

NOTE DATE DUE APR 1 6 2002

EACH BORROWER is required to sign an application and is responsible for books drawn in his name.

FINES are charged for each book kept overtime (including Sundays and Holidays.)

The Rotters' Club

The Rotters' Club

JONATHAN COE

Alfred A. Knopf   New York   2002

THIS IS A BORZOI BOOK
PUBLISHED BY ALFRED A. KNOPF

www.aaknopf.com

Originally published in Great Britain by Viking,
an imprint of the Penguin Group, London, in 2001.

Knopf, Borzoi Books, and the colophon are
registered trademarks of Random House, Inc.

Owing to limitations of space, all acknowledgments for permission to
reprint previously published material may be found on pages 417–19.

Library of Congress Cataloging-in-Publication Data
Coe, Jonathan.
The Rotters' Club / Jonathan Coe.— 1st American ed.
    p.   cm.
Contents: The chick and the hairy guy—
The very maws of doom—Green coaster.
ISBN 0-375-41383-9
1. Birmingham (England)—Fiction.   2. Male friendship—Fiction.
3. Teenage boys—Fiction.   I. Title.
PR6053.O26 R68 2002
823'.914—dc21
2001042523

Manufactured in the United States of America
First American Edition

For Janine, Matilda and Madeline

Contents

The Rotters' Club

On a clear, blueblack, starry night, in the city of Berlin, in the year 2003, two young people sat down to dinner. Their names were Sophie and Patrick.

These two people had never met, before today. Sophie was visiting Berlin with her mother, and Patrick was visiting with his father. Sophie's mother and Patrick's father had once known each other, very slightly, a long time ago. For a short while, Patrick's father had even been infatuated with Sophie's mother, when they were still at school. But it was twenty-nine years since they had last exchanged any words.

—Where do you think they've gone? Sophie asked.

—Clubbing, probably. Checking out the techno places.

—Are you serious?

—Of course not. My dad's never been to a club in his life. The last album he bought was by Barclay James Harvest.

—Who?

—Exactly.

Sophie and Patrick watched as the vast, brightly lit glass-and-concrete extravagance of the new Reichstag came into view. The restaurant they had chosen, at the top of the Fernsehturm above Alexanderplatz, revolved rather more quickly than either of them had been expecting. Apparently it had been designed that way back in the 1960s, to demonstrate the superiority of East German technology.

—How is your mother now? Patrick asked. Has she recovered?

—Oh, that was nothing. We went back to the hotel, and she lay down for a while. After that, she was fine. Another couple of hours and we went shopping. That's when I got this skirt.

—It looks great on you.

—Anyway, I'm glad that it happened, because otherwise your dad wouldn't have recognized her.

—I suppose not.

—So we wouldn't be sitting here, would we? It must be fate. Or something.

It was an odd situation they had been thrown into. There had seemed to be a spontaneous intimacy between their parents, even though it was so long since they had known each other. They had flung themselves into their reunion with a sort of joyous relief, as if this chance encounter in a Berlin tearoom could somehow erase the intervening decades, heal the pain of their passing. That had left Sophie and Patrick floundering in a different, more awkward kind of intimacy. They had nothing in common, they realized, except their parents' histories.

—Does your father ever talk much about his schooldays? Sophie asked.

—Well, it's funny. He never used to. But I think it's all been coming back to him, lately. Some of the people he knew back then have resurfaced. For instance, there was a boy called . . .

—Harding?

—Yes. You know about him?

—A little. I'd like to know more.

—Then I'll tell you. And Dad mentions your uncle sometimes. Your uncle Benjamin.

—Ah, yes. They were good friends, weren't they?

—Best friends, I think.

—Did you know they once played in a band together?

—No, he never mentioned that.

—What about the magazine they used to edit?

—No, he never told me about that either.

—I've heard it all from my mother, you see. She has perfect recall of those days.

—How come?

—Well . . .

And then Sophie began to explain. It was hard to know where to start. The era they were discussing seemed to belong to the dimmest recesses of history. She said to Patrick:

—Do you ever try to imagine what it was like before you were born?

—How do you mean? You mean like in the womb?

—No, I mean, what the world was like, before you came along.

—Not really. I can't get my head around it.

—But you remember how things were when you were younger. You remember John Major, for instance?

—Vaguely.

—Well, of course, that's the only way to remember him. What about Mrs. Thatcher?

—No. I was only . . . five or six when she resigned. Why are you asking this, anyway?

—Because we're going to have to think further back than that. Much further.

Sophie broke off, and a frown darkened her face.

—You know, I can tell you this story, but you might get frustrated. It doesn't end. It just stops. I don't know how it ends.

—Perhaps I know the ending.

—Will you tell me, if you do?

—Of course.

They smiled at each other then, quickly and for the first time. As the crane-filled skyline, the ever-changing work-in-progress that was the Berlin cityscape unfurled behind her, Patrick looked at Sophie's face, her graceful jaw, her long black eyelashes, and felt the stirrings of something, a thankfulness that he had met her, a flicker of curiosity about what his future might suddenly hold.

Sophie poured sparkling mineral water into her glass from a navy-blue bottle and said:

—Come with me, then, Patrick. Let's go backwards. Backwards in time, all the way back to the beginning. Back to a country that neither of us would recognize, probably. Britain, 1973.

—Was it really that different, do you think?

—Completely different. Just think of it! A world without mobiles or videos or Playstations or even faxes. A world that had never heard of Princess Diana or Tony Blair, never thought for a moment of going to war over Kosovo or Iraq. There were only three television channels in those days, Patrick. Three! And the unions were so powerful that, if they wanted to, they could close one of them down for a whole night. Sometimes people even had to do without electricity. Imagine!

The Chick and the Hairy Guy

WINTER

I

Imagine!

November the 15th, 1973. A Thursday evening, drizzle whispering against the window-panes, and the family gathered in the living room. All except Colin, who is out on business, and has told his wife and children not to wait up. Weak light from a pair of wrought-iron standard lamps. The coal-effect fire hisses.

Sheila Trotter is reading the *Daily Mail:* " *'To have and to hold, for better for worse, for richer for poorer, in sickness and in health'—these are the promises which do in fact sustain most married couples through the bad patches."*

Lois is reading *Sounds:* "*Guy, 18, cat lover, seeks London chick, into Sabbath. Only Freaks please."*

Paul, precociously, is reading *Watership Down:* "*Simple African villagers, who have never left their remote homes, may not be particularly surprised by their first sight of an aeroplane: it is outside their comprehension."*

As for Benjamin . . . I suppose he is doing his homework at the dining table. The frown of concentration, the slightly protruding tongue (a family trait, of course: I've seen my mother look the same way, crouched over her laptop). History, probably. Or maybe physics. Something which doesn't come easily, at any rate. He looks across at the clock on the mantelpiece. The organized type, he has set himself a deadline. He has ten minutes to go. Ten more minutes in which to write up the experiment.

I'm doing my best, Patrick. Really I am. But it's not an easy one to tell, the story of my family. Uncle Benjamin's story, if you like.

I'm not even sure this is the right place to start. But perhaps one place is as good as any other. And this is the one I've chosen. Mid-November, the dark promise of an English winter, almost thirty years ago.

November the 15th, 1973.

Long periods of silence were common. They were a family who had never learned the art of talking to one another. All of them inscrutable, even to themselves: all except Lois, of course. Her needs were simple, defined, and in the end she was punished for it. That's how I see things, anyway.

I don't think she wanted much, at this stage of her life. I think she only wanted companionship, and the occasional babble of voices around her. She would have had a craving for chatter, coming from that family; but she was not the sort to lose herself in a giggling circus of friends. She knew what she was looking for, I'm sure of that; already knew, even then, even at the age of sixteen. And she knew where to look for it, too. Ever since her brother had started buying *Sounds* every Thursday, on the way home from school, it had become her furtive weekly ritual to feign interest in the back-page adverts for posters and clothes (*"Cotton drill shirts in black, navy, flame-red, cranberry—great to team with loons"*) when her real focus of attention was the personal column. She was looking for a man.

She had read nearly all of the personals by now. She was beginning to despair.

"Freaky Guy (20) wants crazy chick (16+) for love. Into Quo and Zep."

Once again, not exactly ideal. Did she want her guy to be freaky? Could she honestly describe herself as crazy? Who were Quo and Zep, anyway?

"Great guy wishes groovy chick to write, into Tull, Pink Floyd, 17–28."

"Two freaky guys seek heavy chicks. 16+, love and affection."

"Guy (20), back in Kidderminster area, seeks attractive chick(s)."

Kidderminster was only a few miles away, so this last one might have been promising, if it weren't for the giveaway plural in parentheses. He'd definitely blown his cover, there. Out for a good time, and little else. Though perhaps that was preferable, in a way, to the whiff of desperation that came off some of the other messages.

"Disenchanted, lonely guy (21), long dark hair, would like communication with aware, thoughtful girl, appreciate anything creative like: progressive, folk, fine art."

"Lonely, unattractive guy (22), needs female companionship, looks unimportant. Into Moodies, BJH, Camel etc."

"Lonely Hairy, Who and Floyd freak, needs a chick for friendship, love and peace. Stockport area."

Her mother put the newspaper aside and said: "Cup of tea, anyone? Lemonade?"

When she had gone to the kitchen, Paul laid down his rabbit saga and picked up the *Daily Mail.* He began reading it with a tired, sceptical smile on his face.

"Any chick want to go to India. Split end of Dec, no Straights."

"Any chick who wants to see the world, please write."

Yes, she did want to see the world, now that she thought of it. The slow awareness had been growing inside her, fuelled by holiday programmes on the television and colour photos in the *Sunday Times* magazine, that a universe existed beyond the confines of Longbridge, beyond the terminus of the 62 bus route, beyond Birmingham, beyond England, even. What's more, she wanted to see it, and she wanted to share it with someone. She wanted someone to hold her hand as she watched the moon rise over the Taj Mahal. She wanted to be kissed, softly but at great length, against the magnificent backdrop of the Canadian Rockies. She wanted to climb Ayers Rock at dawn. She wanted someone to propose marriage to her as the setting sun draped its blood-red fingers over the rose-tinted minarets of the Alhambra.

"Leeds boy with scooter, looks OK, seeks girlfriend 17–21 for discos, concerts. Photo appreciated."

"Wanted girl friend, any age, but 4 ft. 10 in. or under, all letters answered."

"Finished."

Benjamin slammed his exercise book shut and made a big show of packing his pens and books away in the little briefcase he always took to school. His physics text book had started to come apart, so he had re-covered it with a remnant of the anaglypta his father had used to wallpaper the living room two years ago. On the front of his English book he had drawn a big cartoon foot, like the one at the end of the *Monty Python* signature tune.

"That's me done for the night." He stood over his sister, who was sprawled across both halves of the settee. "Gimme that."

It always annoyed him when Lois got to read *Sounds* before he did. He seemed to think this gave her privileged access to top-secret information. But in truth she cared nothing for the news pages over which he was ready to pore so avidly. Most of the headlines she didn't even understand. *"Beefheart here in May." "New Heep album due." "Another split in Fanny."*

"What's a Freak?" she asked, handing him the magazine.

Benjamin laughed tartly and pointed at their nine-year-old brother, whose face was aglow with amused contempt as he perused the *Daily Mail*. "You're looking at one."

"I know that. But a Freak with a capital 'F.' I mean, it's obviously some sort of technical term."

Benjamin did not reply; and he somehow managed to leave Lois with the impression that he knew the answer well enough, but had chosen to withhold it, for reasons of his own. People always tended to regard him as knowledgeable, well-informed, even though the evidence was plainly to the contrary. There must have been some air about him, some indefinable sense of confidence, which it was easy to mistake for youthful wisdom.

"Mother," said Paul, when she came in with his fizzy drink, "why do we take this newspaper?"

Sheila glared at him, obscurely resentful. She had told him many times before to call her "Mum," not "Mother."

"No reason," she said. "Why shouldn't we?"

"Because it's full," said Paul, flicking through the pages, "of platitudinous codswallop."

Ben and Lois giggled helplessly. "I thought 'platitudinous' was an animal they had in Australia," she said.

"The lesser-spotted platitudinous," said Benjamin, honking and squawking in imitation of this mythical beast.

"Take this leading article, for instance," Paul continued, undeterred. " *'That precise pageantry which Britain manages so well keeps its hold on our hearts. There's nothing like a Royal Wedding for lifting our spirits.'* "

"What about it?" said Sheila, stirring sugar into her tea. "I don't agree with everything I read in there."

" *'As Princess Anne and Mark Phillips walked out of the Abbey, their faces broke into that slow, spreading smile of people who are really happy.'* " Pass the sick bag, *please!* " *'The Prayer Book may be three hundred years old, but its promises are as clear as yesterday's sunlight.'* " Pukerocious! " *'To have and to hold, for better for worse—'* "

"That's quite enough from *you*, Mr. Know-All." The quiver in Sheila's voice was enough to expose, just for a second, the sudden panic her youngest son was learning to inspire in her. "Drink that up and put your pyjamas on."

More squabbling ensued, with Benjamin making his own shrill interventions, but Lois did not listen to any of it. These were not the voices with which she longed to surround herself. She left them to it and withdrew to her bedroom, where she was able to re-enter her world of romantic daydreams, a kingdom of infinite colour and possibility. As for Benjamin's copy of *Sounds*, she had found what she was looking for there, and had no further use for it. She would not even need to sneak down later and take another look, for the box number was easy to remember (it was 247, the same as the Radio One waveband), and the message she had seized upon was one of perfect, magical simplicity. Perhaps that was how she knew that it was meant for her, and her alone.

"*Hairy Guy seeks Chick. Birmingham area.*"

2

Meanwhile, Lois's father Colin was sitting in a pub called The Bull's Head in King's Norton. His boss, Jack Forrest, had gone to the bar to get three pints of Brew XI, leaving Colin to make halting conversation with Bill Anderton, a shop steward in the Longbridge underseal section. A fourth member of the party, Roy Slater, was yet to arrive. It was a great relief when Jack came back from the bar.

"Cheers," said Colin, Bill and Jack, drinking from their pints of Brew. After drinking in unison they let out a collective sigh, and wiped the froth from their upper lips. Then they fell silent.

"I want this to be nice and informal," said Jack Forrest, suddenly, when the silence had become too long and too settled for comfort.

"Informal. Absolutely," said Colin.

"Suits me," said Bill. "Suits me fine."

Informally, they sipped on their Brew. Colin looked around the pub, intending to make a comment about the décor, but couldn't think of one. Bill Anderton stared into his beer.

"They brew a good pint, don't they?" said Jack.

"Eh?" said Bill.

"I said they serve a good pint, in this place."

"Not bad," said Bill. "I've had worse."

This was in the days before men learned to discuss their

feelings, of course. And in the days before bonding sessions between management and workforce were at all common. They were pioneers, in a way, these three.

Colin bought another round, and there was still no sign of Roy. They sat and drank their pints. The tables in which their faces were dimly reflected were dark brown, the darkest brown, the colour of Bournville chocolate. The walls were a lighter brown, the colour of Dairy Milk. The carpet was brown, with little hexagons of a slightly different brown, if you looked closely. The ceiling was meant to be off-white, but was in fact brown, browned by the nicotine smoke of a million unfiltered cigarettes. Most of the cars in the car park were brown, as were most of the clothes worn by the patrons. Nobody in the pub really noticed the predominance of brown, or if they did, thought it worth remarking upon. These were brown times.

"Well then, you two—have you worked it out yet?" Jack Forrest asked.

"Worked what out?" said Bill.

"There's a reason for this evening, you know," said Jack. "I didn't just pick you out at random. I could have got any personnel officer, and any shop steward, and set this evening up for them. But I didn't do that. I chose you two for a reason."

Bill and Colin looked at each other.

"You have something in common, you see." Jack regarded them both in turn, pleased with himself. "Don't you know what it is?"

They shrugged.

"You've both got kids at the same school."

This information sank in, gradually, and Colin was the first to manage a smile.

"Anderton—of course. My Ben's got a friend called Anderton. They're in the same form. Talks about him from time to time." He looked at Bill, now, with something almost approaching warmth. "Is that your boy?"

"That's him, yes: Duggie. And your son must be Bent."

Colin seemed puzzled by this, if not a little shocked. "No, *Ben*," he corrected. "Ben Trotter. Short for Benjamin."

"I know his name's Benjamin," said Bill. "But that's what they call him. Bent Rotter. Ben Trotter. D'you get it?"

After a few seconds, Colin got it. He pursed his lips, wounded on his son's behalf.

"Boys can be very cruel," he said.

Jack's face had relaxed into a look of satisfaction. "You know, this tells you something about the country we live in today," he said. "Britain in the 1970s. The old distinctions just don't mean anything any more, do they? This is a country where a union man and a junior manager—soon to be senior, Colin, I'm sure—can send their sons to the same school and nobody thinks anything of it. Both bright lads, both good enough to have got through the entrance exam, and now there they are: side by side in the cradle of learning. What does that tell you about the class war? It's over. Truce. Armistice." He clasped his pint of Brew and raised it solemnly. "Equality of opportunity."

Colin murmured a shy echo of these words, and drank from his glass. Bill said nothing: as far as he was concerned, the class war was alive and well and being waged with some ferocity at British Leyland, even in Ted Heath's egalitarian 1970s, but he couldn't rouse himself to argue the point. His mind was on other things that evening. He put his hand inside his jacket pocket and fingered the cheque and wondered once again if he was going mad.

Perhaps it had been a mistake to invite Roy Slater along. The thing about Slater was that everybody hated him, including Bill Anderton, who might have been expected to show some solidarity with his putative comrade-in-arms. But Slater was the worst kind of shop steward, as far as Bill was concerned. He had no talent for negotiation, no imaginative sympathy with the men he was supposed to represent, no grasp of the wider political issues. He was just a loudmouth and a troublemaker, always looking for confrontation, and always coming out of it badly. In union terms he was a nobody, way down the hierarchy of the TGWU's junior stewards at Longbridge. It was all Bill could do to be civil to him, most of the time, and tonight he was expected to do more than that: honour demanded that the two of them put up some sort of united front against these alluring management overtures. It was enough to make him suspect calculation on Jack's part. What, after all, could be more effective than to divide the opposition by pairing up two shop stewards who famously couldn't stand each other?

"Bit of all right, this, isn't it?" said Roy, nudging Bill fiercely in the ribs as they studied the menus in their red leather wallets. They had adjourned, by now, to a Berni Inn on the Stratford Road.

"Don't wet yourself, Slater," said Bill, taking out his reading glasses. "There's no such thing as a free lunch in this business, in case you hadn't noticed."

"On this occasion," said Jack, "that's exactly where you're wrong. You're all here as my guests, and you can order anything you like. The tab for this is being picked up by the British Leyland Motor Corporation, so expense is no object. Go for it, chaps. Let your imaginations run wild."

Roy ordered fillet steak and chips, Colin ordered fillet steak and chips, Bill ordered fillet steak, chips and peas and Jack, who went to the South of France for his holidays, ordered fillet steak with chips, peas and mushrooms on the side, a touch of sophistication that was not lost on the others. As they waited for the food to arrive, Jack tried to instigate a discussion about the marital prospects of Princess Anne and Captain Mark Phillips, but it failed to catch fire. Roy seemed to have no strong views on the subject, Bill wasn't interested ("Bread and circuses, Jack, bread and circuses") and Colin's attention was beginning to wander. He stared out at the night, beyond the car park, into the charcoal distance, the cars winking past on the Stratford Road, and it was impossible to know what he was thinking. Worrying about Ben, and his school nickname? Missing Sheila, and the hiss of the coal-effect fire? Or perhaps longing to go back to those days in the design room, before he had taken this job, this stupid job that had looked like a step up the ladder but turned out to be a nightmare of human complication.

"You know, this won't work, Jack," Bill was saying, his tone friendly but combative, his fifth pint of Brew now having a decidedly mellowing influence. "You can't wipe out social injustice by taking the enemy out for steak and chips every so often."

"Oh, this is nothing, Bill. This is just the beginning. In a couple of years' time, employee participation is going to be codified. It's going to be government policy."

"Which government?"

"It doesn't matter. Doesn't make a blind bit of difference. I'm telling you, we're going to be entering a whole new phase. Management and workers—elected representatives, that is—are going to sit around the table and take decisions *together.* Looking at the forward plans of the company *together.* Mutual interests. Common ground. That's what we're looking for. And it's got to happen because at the moment confrontation is crippling the industry."

"This," said Slater, suddenly and irrelevantly, "is a bloody good steak." His meal had arrived first, and he hadn't waited for the others before starting. "Give me something like this every day of the week and we might be talking, do you know what I'm saying?"

Bill ignored him. "The point is, Jack, that it's not confrontation for the sake of it. That's what you people never seem to understand. There are grievances, you see. Real, proper grievances."

"And they'll be addressed."

Bill paused for a while, sipping his beer, his eyes narrowed. A waitress arrived with their food and he was distracted, momentarily, by the sight of his steak and then, more extensively, by the sight of her calves and slender thighs encased in sheer nylon, the promise of an untried body insinuated by the fall of her white blouse. The old habit. Never shaken. He forced his gaze away from her and towards Jack, coating his chips with salt and tomato ketchup as if there were no tomorrow. Bill cut off a wedge of steak, chewed on it with undeniable relish (you didn't get this at home) and said:

"Of course, I can see where this is leading."

"How do you mean?"

"It's the usual tactic, isn't it? Divide and rule. Take a few shop stewards, invite them upstairs, sit them round the conference table, make them feel important. Let them in on a few secrets—nothing too sensitive, mind, just a few little titbits to make them think they're in the know. And suddenly they're feeling very full of themselves, suddenly they're beginning to see things from the management's point of view, and as for their members . . . Well, they're beginning to wonder why these guys are spending half the day up in the boardroom, why they're not around on the shop floor any more when there's a problem to solve. Isn't that the way it'll be, Jack?"

Incredulous, Jack Forrest laid down his cutlery and said to Colin, "Do you hear that, though? Do you hear the kind of thing we're up against? That typical trade-union paranoid mentality."

"Look, mate," said Roy to Bill, speaking indistinctly through a mouthful of chips, "if these two gentlemen want to treat us to a nice dinner every now and again, put their point of view across, what's the problem, eh? You've got to take what you can in this life, mate. It's every man for himself as far as I can see."

"Spoken like a true pillar of the Labour movement," said Bill.

"What do you think, Colin?"

Colin glanced at his boss nervously. He had a hatred of confrontation, an undoubted drawback for someone saddled with a job in industrial relations.

"It's the strikes that are holding this company back," he said at last, talking into his plate, giving voice, reluctantly, to a firm conviction that nevertheless had to be dredged up from somewhere remote and unvisited, in his profoundest depths. "I don't know if this is the way to stop them, but they've got to be stopped somehow. It doesn't happen in Germany or Italy or Japan. Only here."

Bill stopped eating, and held Colin in a thoughtful, penetrating gaze. Of all the things he could have said, he chose only: "I wonder what your son and my son talk about on the bus home."

Jack saw the chance to inject a note of levity. "Girls and pop music, I expect," he said, and after that Bill gave up, turning his attention to the food and his sixth pint of Brew. A steak was a steak, after all.

Bill and Roy, their paths lying in the same direction, were obliged to share a minicab home. Roy pulled a face when he saw the turbaned driver sitting behind the wheel, and turned to his companion, ready to share some blokey, insulting witticism. But Bill wasn't having any of it. He let Roy get into the back and then pointedly made for the passenger seat, where he chatted to the driver for most of the twenty-minute journey. He learned that he and his wife were second-generation immigrants, living in Small Heath; that they liked Birmingham because it was full of parks and you didn't have to drive far to get out into the hills; that his eldest son was training to be a doctor, but the youngest was having trouble with bullies at school.

Overhearing this last fragment, and sensing a lull in the conversation, Roy leaned forward and said to Bill:

"That thing you said to Trotter, about your kids talking on the bus home: what was that about?"

"It was just a comment, that's all," Bill answered.

"Your kids go to the same school, then? Is that it?"

"What's it to you, Slater?"

"Trotter's boy goes to King William's, doesn't he? That fucking . . . toffs' academy in Edgbaston."

Bill snorted. "You don't know what you're talking about. We don't pay anything for him to go there. It's a direct-grant school. He's a bright lad and he passed the exam. All I'm doing is giving him the best start in life."

Roy didn't reply to this, but sat back, satisfied, believing apparently that he had located some chink in his colleague's armour. They said nothing more to each other that night, apart from the most cursory goodbyes.

When Bill got home he found that Irene had already gone to bed. He scowled at the heap of paperwork waiting for him on the dining-room table and decided that he would leave it for another day. It was almost midnight. But he took the cheque out of his jacket pocket one more time and examined it again by the light of his reading lamp.

It continued to puzzle him. A cheque for £145, drawn on the Charity Committee account, made out to a name he didn't even recognize. Signed not by Harry, the chairman, or by Miriam, the highly fanciable secretary (and was it his imagination, by the way, or had she been staring at him through most of the meeting the other night?) but by himself. And yet he could remember nothing about it. What was more, the bank had returned this cheque because the amount had only been written out in words, not figures: again, a mistake he was very unlikely to make. Unless he was cracking up. Unless the pressure was getting to him.

He filed the cheque away in his bureau and poured himself one more beer before going to bed.

Jack Forrest and Colin had said goodnight in the restaurant car park. Jack seemed ambivalent about the evening, not sure that it had been worthwhile. "Was that a success, d'you reckon?" His breath was cloudy in the winter air. There would be frost before morning.

"I think so," said Colin, who always wanted everything to be for the best. "I think it was, well . . ."

"Constructive?"

"Yes. I think so."

"Good. Yes, I think you're right. I think it was constructive." He rubbed his hands, clicked back the knuckles of his long fingers. "There's a nip in the air tonight, though, isn't there? Hope the wife's remembered to put the blanket on."

They shook hands and parted. Their cars were on opposite sides of the car park. Colin tutted, then allowed himself a few mild swear words as he wrestled with the lock of his brown Austin 1800, struggling to free the obstinate catch he had personally designed, a few years ago, with such confidence.

3

On Wednesday afternoons they had double English, taken by a Scotsman called Mr. Fletcher who slurred his words and whose accent was hard enough to understand in the first place and who they all suspected of being an alcoholic. Most of them were frightened of Mr. Fletcher, because he shouted whenever he lost his temper and lost his temper every lesson, sometimes twice or even three or four times. The only person who never seemed to be frightened of him was Harding. But then everybody—especially Benjamin—had been known to wonder exactly what it would take to frighten Harding.

Double periods were different. When the bell went after forty minutes you just had to sit there, as if nothing was happening. More often than not, the master would actually make a point of talking through it, as if to emphasize that this was nothing special, only a halfway point, but it was hard to hold the boys' attention for those few minutes, with the corridors outside roaring beneath the impact of hundreds of youthful feet, as the rest of the school thundered from classroom to classroom. Slowly the rumble of footsteps, the banging of doors would fade away, silence would settle again, and you had no further excuses for not listening to the queasy fits and starts, the lurching monotone of Mr. Fletcher's voice.

"That was a masterpiece, Spinks, a veritable masterpiece," he said, as three red-faced boys returned to their desks. Sarcasm, unleavened by humour or playfulness of tone, was a fixed habit of mind for Fletcher. "When Hollywood comes to make the inevitable film of *Catcher in the Rye*, you will undoubtedly be called upon to play Holden Caulfield. You've got him perfectly, right down to the Brummie accent. Peter Fonda won't get a look-in. Right—" he raised his voice to quell an upsurge of laughter which never materialized "—who's next? Trotter, Harding, Anderton, Chase. Sounds like a bloody legal conglomerate. Solicitors and commissioners for oaths. What have you got for us?"

The three of them stood up (Harding had asked to be excused, a few minutes ago, and was expected back any moment) and Philip Chase, as unofficial spokesman, announced: "We're doing the trial scene from *To Kill a Mockingbird*, sir. Dramatized by Trotter and I."

"Trotter and *me*, Chase. Trotter and me."

"Yes, sir. I play Atticus Finch, the defendant."

"The defence *lawyer*, not the defendant."

"Yes. Sorry, sir. Anderton is playing Mr. Gilmer, the, er . . . the prosecuting lawyer. Trotter is going to play Judge Taylor, and Harding—"

At which point the door was flung open and Harding re-entered the classroom, to howls of laughter and delight.

"—Harding plays Tom Robinson, sir."

This explanation was already superfluous, for Harding's make-up told its own story. His face was more or less unrecognizable beneath a black coating of ink. He must have hidden the bottle in his pocket when he went to the toilet. The effect was astonishing, not least because of the rings of translucent whiteness that circled his eyes, and because he had also, for some reason or other, failed to apply any ink at all to his nose, so that it now stood out preposterously like a little white punctuation mark. His classmates went berserk. The room ricocheted with trebly laughter, like an aviary at feeding time, until this gave way, after nearly half a deafening minute, to what sounded like a wall of machine-gun fire as twenty-two boys pounded the lids of their desks up and down in a frenzy of gobsmacked approbation. Fletcher, unsmiling, waited for the uproar to subside, his patience only running out when Harding lost his cool and began to surf the wave of his audience's enthusiasm, parading back and forth in front of the blackboard with flapping hands and extended fingers in an impersonation which owed less to Al Jolson than to weekly viewings of *The Black and White Minstrel Show*. At which point the master stood up and thumped his desk imperiously.

"Quiet!"

Afterwards, in conference at the bus stop, Chase, Trotter and Anderton agreed that this had probably been one of their friend's sillier ideas, and they should never have let him attempt it. The joke had backfired on all of them, and they were now saddled with the task of writing six sides each on the subject of "racial stereotyping," to be deposited in Fletcher's pigeonhole by nine o'clock the next morning: a particular humiliation for Benjamin, who was famous for never incurring punishments of any kind. As for Harding himself, he had been put, inevitably, in Saturday-morning detention. They could see him now, waiting at the bus stop on the other side of the road (Harding lived to the north of Birmingham, in Sutton Coldfield), surrounded by fans and still bearing the battle scars of his adventure, for his face had been thoroughly scrubbed but retained a spectral residue of ocean blue. At least half of his audience was female, Benjamin noticed. King William's School for Girls stood on the same site as its male counterpart, and while there was very little official contact between the schools—until you got to the sixth form, anyway—a good deal of nervy, spellbound fraternization would take place on the buses home, and Harding already had no shortage of female admirers. He looked gleefully unbowed, basking in the heat of his growing notoriety.

Benjamin and his friends were savagely envious. The girls in their bus queue talked only among themselves, perhaps throwing an amused glance in their direction once in a while, but otherwise indifferent to the point of hostility. Lois, of course, would not have dreamed of talking to her brother on these occa-

sions, even though they were standing only a few feet apart. The
edgy fondness which they sustained at home collapsed into hideous embarrassment whenever their schoolfriends were around.
It was bad enough that they were known, collectively, as "the
Rotters," an epithet dreamed up when somebody noticed that
their names could be pronounced "Bent Rotter" and "Lowest
Rotter." What made it worse was that Benjamin still had to wear
school uniform while Lois, as a sixth-former under the Girls'
School's more liberal regime, could dress as she pleased. (Today
she was wearing her long blue denim coat with thick white fur
collar, over a ribbed acrylic roll-neck jumper and embroidered
denim loons.) Somehow this created another barrier, the firmest
of all, so that normal contact was out of the question until they
had reached the impenetrable privacy of the family tea table.

"Busy evening ahead for you boys, then?" said a plummy,
prematurely broken voice behind them. They turned to see
their old enemy Culpepper: junior rugger captain, junior cricket
captain, would-be athletics champion and long-standing object
of derision. As always, he was carrying his books and his PE kit
in the same bulky sports bag, from which the handle of his
squash racket protruded like a permanently erect penis. "Six
sides apiece, wasn't it? That should have you burning the midnight oil."

"Fuck off, Culpepper," said Anderton.

"Ooh," he gasped, in mock-admiration. "Most amusing.
Such dazzling repartee."

"It was only a joke, anyway," said Benjamin. And he pointed
out: "You were laughing with the rest of them."

"You've only yourselves to blame," said Culpepper, wiping
his nose and thereby revealing, to less than general astonishment, that even his handkerchiefs had name-tags attached.
"Fletcher's a dreadful old liberal softie. He wouldn't let anyone
get away with impersonating a nigger."

"You shouldn't use that word," said Chase. "You know you
shouldn't."

"What—nigger?" said Culpepper, enjoying the effect these

two tiny syllables were having upon them. "Why not? It's in the book. Harper Lee uses it herself."

"You know that's different."

"All right, then. Wog. Coon. Darkie." Having failed to provoke them, he added: "It's a rotten book, anyway. I don't know why we have to read it. I don't believe in it at all. It's propaganda."

"No one's interested in you or what you think," said Anderton, and to prove the point they turned away from him, knotting themselves into a tighter group. The conversation drifted, as it always did, towards music. Anderton spent nearly all his pocket money on records and had just bought *Stranded* by Roxy Music. He was trying to persuade Chase to borrow it, insisting it blew the socks off his poxy Genesis albums. Benjamin was listening, but half-heartedly. Both bands left him cold: so did the Eric Clapton tape his parents had given him for his birthday. He was growing out of rock music, looking for something new . . . And besides this, something very distracting was going on at the bus stop on the other side of the road. Harding now seemed to be talking—this was unbelievable, but true: actually talking—to Cicely Boyd, the willowy goddess who ran the junior wing of the Girls' School Drama Society. How was this possible? Her aloofness was legendary, and yet there she was, staring wide-eyed and open-mouthed as he recounted and pantomimed the recorded highlights of his latest prank. Ben watched in amazement as, even more incredibly, she licked her finger and rubbed at his cheek, attempting to wipe off some of the inky traces.

"Look at that," he said, nudging his friends and pointing.

The musical spat was quickly forgotten.

"Bloody hell . . ."

"Shit . . ."

Even Anderton, whose sexual politics were rather more sophisticated than the others', was reduced to speechlessness by the spectacle of Harding so casually hitting this particular jackpot. There seemed to be nothing they could do, except gawp; until, after a few moments, the 62 bus arrived, and with a series of wistful backward glances they piled on to the front of the top deck.

"He's got a nerve, you know," said Chase, as the bus swayed into motion again and rattled with the din of schoolkids' chatter. "It was all his idea. Now we get into trouble and he gets all the glory."

"It was a crap idea anyway," said Anderton. "I said so at the time. You never listen to me, you people. There's only one person who should have been allowed to play that part, and that's Richards."

"But he's not in our form."

"Exactly. So we should have dropped the whole thing."

Richards was the only black pupil in their year: the only one in the entire school, in fact. A tall, sinewy, somewhat melancholy Afro-Caribbean, he lived on the outskirts of Handsworth and was a new arrival at King William's; he had joined in the third year, and his form was upper-middle D. Anderton, incidentally, was unique in referring to him as Richards. The other ninety-five boys in his year called him "Rastus."

"But we worked for hours on that scene," Chase protested, "and we never even got to perform it."

"That's life."

The bus had squeezed its way through the Selly Oak traffic and was making its way along the faster, leafier carriageways of the Bristol Road South. Chase's stop was the first, just before Northfield, and a strange thing happened when he got up to leave. The girl who had been sitting behind them—a girl they had all seen countless times before, but barely noticed—followed him down the stairs, but just before she disappeared from view she threw a glance, unmistakably, in Benjamin's direction. It was an eloquent glance: sidelong, surreptitious, but at the same time not exactly quick. Her eyes, peeping out from an unruly fringe of dark hair, lingered on Benjamin for two or three seconds, almost appraisingly, and there was the clear intimation of a smile in her full lips. In a couple of years' time, Benjamin might have recognized this smile as flirtatious. For now, it merely stupefied him, setting in motion a wild complex of different feelings which had the effect of rooting him helplessly to the spot. Before he could make any kind of response, she was gone.

"Who was that?" he asked.

"Her name's Newman, or something. Claire Newman, I think. Why, d'you fancy her?"

Benjamin didn't answer. Instead, he looked curiously out of the window, watching as Chase followed her along St. Laurence Road. He was walking at an unnaturally slow pace, probably because he was too shy to overtake her on the pavement. At this point it would have been hard to imagine that one day they would become friends or even, briefly and unsuccessfully, husband and wife.

The girl's name was indeed Claire Newman, and she also had an elder sister called Miriam, who worked as a typist at the British Leyland factory in Longbridge.

When Claire got home that afternoon she found that the house was empty, and she let herself in using a key hidden in the watering can in the back porch. Her mother, father and sister were all still at work. She dumped her schoolbag on the kitchen table, took some cream crackers out of a biscuit jar and spread them with butter and Bovril. She put the biscuits on a plate and went upstairs. Before going into her sister's room, she paused on the landing. The house was wonderfully quiet and still. A good atmosphere for mischief.

Miriam kept her diary hidden beneath a chest of drawers, along with a man's purple nylon shirt presumably of some mysterious sentimental value, and a good supply of the Pill. Claire had discovered this treasure trove two weeks earlier and was now well up-to-date with her sister's private life, which had become rather exciting of late. She reached for the diary, put the plate of food down on the floor and sat cross-legged beside it. Impatiently, she thumbed through to the latest page, licking the Bovril off her fingers as she went.

Her eyes darted across the most recent entry, which turned out to be disappointing. No further progress, then: Miriam's current *amour* was still stuck at the fantasy stage. But the details at least were getting more colourful.

20 November

Went to another meeting of the Charity Fund Committee last night. All the usual people there (including Vile Victor). Mr. Anderton not in the chair, this time, but sitting opposite me. I took the minutes as usual. He kept looking at me, just like before, and I kept looking back. It couldn't be plainer what he was thinking, I'm amazed nobody noticed anything. He is rather old I suppose, but so dishy, I couldn't concentrate on a thing and must have missed half what was being said. I really, really want him to kcuf me and I know that he wants to as well. Spent most of last night thinking of the ways he could kcuf me and what it would feel like. It would have to be at the factory but there are lots of places like the showers where the men clean themselves off after the shift. I imagined him taking me in there and lifting my skirt and licking my tnuc until I came. Somehow I have got to speak to him and get him to have me but I don't think it will be difficult, he wants it just as much as I do if not more. I don't think I will be the first either but that doesn't matter. It has got to happen soon or I will go spare with fancying him.

Downstairs, the kitchen door slammed. Claire shoved the diary back into its hiding place and scrambled to her feet. It would be her mother, probably, back from the solicitor's office where she worked. She would have stopped at the supermarket on her way home. She would need some help with the unpacking.

SPRING

4

Some weeks later, on the afternoon of Wednesday, 13th February, 1974, all was quiet at the Longbridge plant. The Bristol Road, normally ribboned with parked cars at this time of the day, was almost empty. Irene Anderton savoured the strange tranquillity as she walked back from the shops, the basket of groceries weighing heavy on her arm. Shifting it from one hand to the other, she waved to the cluster of men standing on the picket line at the entrance to the South Works, and some of them waved back, recognizing her. A proud little fire glowed within her. Her husband meant something to these men; he was a hero to them. If it wasn't for him they would be lost, leaderless. She walked on up the hill towards the 62 bus terminus, past the rows of prefabs. It was a long walk but sometimes she didn't feel like taking the bus, and today it was nicer than usual, with this silence hanging snugly over the whole area. You didn't realize how much noise the assembly track made, shuddering all day behind the factory gates; you got used to it; didn't notice, until it stopped.

She dropped in at the newsagents' to pick up the *Evening Mail*, and looked through it quickly on a bench in Cofton Park as she took the short cut home. She didn't linger; the day was darkening already, and getting cold. This had been a bitter winter. Bill was mentioned, but there was no picture, which was probably how he would have wanted it.

When she got home, he was sitting at the dining-room table, papers spread everywhere. He was keeping himself busy, like he always did. That was one of the things she hated most about the newspapers: they always seemed to imply, whenever there was a strike, that the workers headed straight off to the pub, or sat around at home watching the racing. She had never known Bill do anything like that. As Convenor of the Works Committee he fought a constant battle against paperwork. There was never any getting the better of it. He was up until midnight, two or three nights a week, sometimes, and always staying late for meetings. She didn't believe that most of the bosses worked nearly so hard. They had no idea what it was like. True, he didn't do much work on the track any more, but nobody could begrudge him that. He had responsibilities now, huge responsibilities. No wonder his hair was beginning to whiten, just a little, around the temples.

He was still a handsome man, though. Not bad, for pushing forty.

"Cup of tea, love?" she offered, kissing him on the forehead.

He sat back, stretched, threw his fountain pen down. "That'd be grand." Then, gesturing at the unread correspondence: "God, it never ends."

"You'll get through it," she said; confident, supportive, as ever. "Is Duggie home yet?"

Bill made a face: a scowl, tinged with indulgence. "About a quarter of an hour ago. Went straight upstairs. He's been to that record shop again. He tried to sneak it past, but I saw the bag."

On cue, a drumbeat began pounding through the floorboards from Doug's bedroom. Reggae, although neither Bill nor Irene would have been able to identify it as such. Bob Marley, in fact.

"I'll get him to turn it down. You can't work with that going on."

Disappearing upstairs on this errand, she left Bill to contemplate the letter he had slid guiltily out of sight just before her arrival. A needless action, really, provoked not so much by

its contents, but by the more generalized guilt that came to him
so readily these days, whenever Miriam's name was mentioned,
or whenever she was in his thoughts. A bad business, all round.
But still: the amazement of that supple body, those lovely breasts
so eagerly offered . . . And she was the—ninth, was it? The
tenth? A terrible record, after eighteen years of marriage. Most
of them from the factory, the typing pool, the sewing shop; that
redhead in the canteen, God knows what happened to her . . .
There was that trip to Italy two years ago, the week at the Fiat
factory in Turin they'd wangled by hooking up with the WEA,
and the girl he'd met in the hotel bar, Paola her name was, she
had been lovely . . . But there was something different about
Miriam, some quality of intensity that made it both better and
worse than any of those other, quicker affairs. She frightened
him, at some level. Some level he hadn't quite acknowledged yet.

He read the letter again, with the same clenched annoyance.

Dear Brother Anderton,
 I am writing to complain to you about the
work of Miss Newman in her capacity as
Charity Committee Secretary.
 Miss Newman is not a good Secretary. She
does not perform her duties well.
 There is a lack of attention on the part of
Miss Newman. At meetings of the Charity
Committee, you can often see her attention
wandering. I sometimes think she has other
things on her mind than performing her
duties as Secretary. I would prefer not to
say what these other things might be.
 I have made many important remarks, and
addressed many observations, which have not
been recorded in the minutes of the Charity
Committee, due to Miss Newman. This is true
of other Committee Members, but especially

```
of me. I think she is discharging her duties
with total inefficiency.
   I draw this matter to your urgent
attention, Brother Anderton, and personally
suggest that Miss Newman be removed as
Secretary of the Charity Committee
forthwith. Whether or not she continues in
the Design Typing Pool is of course at the
firm's discretion. But I do not think she is
a good typist either.
   Yours fraternally,
   Victor Gibbs.
```

Bill wiped his brow, and yawned: an action which often signified tension with him, rather than fatigue. He didn't need this. He could do without this busybody making life even more difficult for him, with his insinuations and his venomous innuendo. What had Miriam done, what had they both done, to inflame these suspicions? Doubtless exchanged one smile too many, held one of those gazes for just a fraction of a second too long. That was all it need take. But it was interesting that Gibbs, of all people, should have been the one to notice it.

The Charity Committee included members from all parts of the factory, who met to channel a small proportion of their respective union funds into worthy local causes, chiefly schools and hospitals, and Victor Gibbs was its treasurer. He was a clerk in the accounts department, a white-collar worker, so his whee-dling use of "Brother Anderton" and "Yours fraternally" was lit-tle more than affectation—bordering on affront, in Bill's view. He was from South Yorkshire; he was sour and unfriendly; but more important than any of these things, he was an embez-zler. Bill was almost certain of this by now. It was the only way he could explain that mysterious cheque which the bank had returned three months ago, and which he could not remember signing. The signature had been forged: rather expertly, he had to admit. Since then Bill had been making regular visits to the bank to inspect the Committee's cheques and he had found three more made out to the same payee: one with the chairman's signature, and two with Miriam's. Again, the forgeries were good, although the felony itself was hardly subtle. It made him wonder how Gibbs was expecting to get away with it. He was glad, in any case, that he had followed his instinct, which told him to say nothing at first, bide his time and wait for the evidence to mount up. This had put him in a strong position. If Gibbs was planning to make trouble about Miriam, he would not find Bill a very sympathetic listener. His malice would be turned back on him; repaid with interest.

Bill filed the letter carefully among his papers. He would not dignify it with a reply, but nor would he destroy it. It would come in useful, he was sure of that. And besides, he made it a point of principle not to destroy any documents. He was building up an archive, a record of class struggle in which every detail was important, and for which future generations of students would be grateful. He already had plans to donate it to a university library.

The music upstairs had been turned down. He could hear Irene and Doug having an argument; nothing too serious, not one of their slanging matches, just a bit of bickering and teasing. That was all right. They got on OK, those two. The family was secure, for the time being. No thanks to him, it was true . . .

Next on the pile were a couple of related items: a scrap of paper he had found last week, pinned to the notice board in the works canteen and a crudely printed leaflet that had lately been in circulation among his members.

The notice said:

IRA BASTARDS KILLED 12 PEOPLE
ON MANCHESTER BUS YESTERDAY
REFUSE TO WORK WITH
IRISH BASTARD MURDERERS

The leaflet was the latest effusion from something called "The Association of British People," a far-right offshoot, more cranky and less organized even than the National Front. Bill found their propaganda pathetic, and would have been tempted to bin it without a second glance. But there were rumours that these people had been behind a recent attack in Moseley on two Asian teenagers, who had been found beaten half to death outside a chip shop, and he didn't want anything like that spreading to the factory. There was plenty of scope for violence in a big workplace. All sorts of stuff could go unnoticed.

Reluctantly, then, he glanced through the opening lines.

Workers of Britain! Unite and wake up!

Your job is at risk. Your home and livelihood are at risk.

Your whole way of life is threatened as never before.

Neither Heath nor Wilson nor Thorpe has the will to stop the tide of coloured immigration into this country. All are slaves to the liberal establishment way of thinking. These people do not just tolerate the black man, they think he is actually superior to the true-born Englishman. They want to fling the gates of this country wide open to the black man, and do not give a damn for the jobs and homes of the white Englishman that will inevitably be lost as a result.

Look around you at your place of work and you will find that the number of black men in the workplace has increased tenfold. You are being told to work alongside them but note that you are being **TOLD** *not* **ASKED***.*

*If this has also happened to you, you may be interested to know some of the following scientific **FACTS:***

1. *The black man is not as intelligent as the white man. His brain is genetically not so well developed. Therefore, how can he do the same job of work?*

2. *The black man is lazier than the white man. Ask yourselves, why the British Empire conquered the Africans and Indians, and not the other way around? Because the white races are superior in industry and intelligence. Historical **FACT.***

3. *The black man is not so clean. And yet you are being asked to share a place of work, perhaps eat in the same canteen, perhaps even use the same toilet seat. What are the implications for health and the spread of disease? More scientific research needed.*

Bill did not bother to read any further. He already spent too much of his time organizing lectures and meetings to counteract this sort of nonsense, making sure the union put out its own anti-racist pamphlets, most of which he ended up having to write himself (and he was no writer). Today, taken together, the scribbled message and this putrid leaflet served to depress him profoundly. It was so easy, so stupidly easy, for the workforce to find reasons for hating each other when they should be uniting against the common enemy. For all that effort to mean nothing.

These gloomy thoughts—made darker by the clouds of conscience-stricken anxiety that his reflections upon Miriam had gathered together—were scarcely relieved by what he saw on the television a few minutes later. Irene had brought him his tea, strong and sugared, and together they went to watch *Midlands Today*, sitting side by side on the sofa, her hand resting fondly on his knee. (She persisted in these gestures, either not minding or not noticing that he never returned them.) The Longbridge strike was the third item on the programme.

"The telly people turned up, then," said Irene. "Did they talk to you? Are you going to be on?"

"No, they'd all gone home by the time I came out. I don't suppose they bothered to—"

He broke off, and was suddenly swearing at the television screen, driven to fury by the spectacle of Roy Slater—yes, Slater, the bastard!—addressing some reporter with a microphone thrust before his face. How in God's name had *he* managed to get to the cameras before anyone else today? And what gave him the right to start mouthing off about the dispute before they'd had a chance even to agree on an official line?

"They're doing it again, the management," Slater was saying, in that coarse, hollow voice of his. "Every time they go back on their promises, they chip away at the workers' pay packets. It's not good enough. It's—"

"It's not about pay, you fool!" Bill was shouting, cutting across the rest of Slater's answer. "This strike is not about pay!"

"What is it about, then?" said Doug, who had appeared in the living-room doorway, drawn by the sound of the television.

"This ignorant . . . pillock!" For a moment Bill was speechless with anger. "It's about right and wrong," he then explained, ostensibly to his son but more, you might have thought, to an imagined audience of television viewers. "They've been docking workers' pay because of the time they've been spending cleaning themselves up in the last half hour of the shift. It's about the right to . . . cleanliness, and hygiene."

". . . just as long as it takes," Slater was insisting, on the screen. "We want this money. We have a right to this money. We're going to get—"

"*It's not about bloody money!*" Bill shouted, a hand coursing frantically, now, through the thinning hair above his forehead. "You didn't even call this strike, Slater. You know nothing about it. You don't know what the bloody hell you're talking about."

"Is he the one that was so rude to me," Irene ventured, "down at the club that time? When you were buying drinks?"

"He's rude to everybody. He's a nasty piece of work. And he's got no *right*, no right at all, to get up on the television and start—" The telephone rang, shrill and excitable. Bill scarcely

missed a beat as he went to pick it up. "Here we go, then. This'll
be Kevin. He'll have seen it. He'll be screaming blue murder."
He grabbed the receiver and snapped: "Hello?"

It wasn't Kevin. It was Miriam.

"Hello, Bill. Is this a good time?"

He still retained, occasionally, the capacity to surprise himself: it took only a second or two to recover, and take the measure of the situation.

"Oh, hello, Kev. Yes, I saw it. What's . . . what's your view,
then? How do you think we should proceed?"

Miriam, too, was accustomed to this kind of subterfuge.
"Listen, Bill, I was ringing about tomorrow night. I wondered if
you might be free."

"Always . . ."—he glanced at his wife, whose attention was
concentrated on the television—"always difficult, that, isn't it?
Always a bit of a problem."

"But Bill—*darling*—" (was the word calculated, or had it
come naturally? She would surely know the effect it would have
on him) "—it's Valentine's Day."

"Yes, I'm aware of that. Well aware. But—"

"And I've got the house to myself. All evening."

Bill was silenced, for a moment.

"Claire's going to some disco, you see. And it's parent—
teachers. Parent—teachers night at King William's. Mum and
Dad'll be out."

And so will I, you fool, Bill said to himself. *Had you not thought
of that? I've got to be there too.* And yet, at the same time, a heav-
enly vista opened up to him. An hour alone with Miriam; maybe
two. Privacy. *A bed.* They had never made love in a bed. Every
time so far had been rushed, fumbled, in some corner of the factory, always the threat of someone disturbing them, never the
chance to do it properly, to take their time, to undress. And this
way they could undress. He could see her naked. For a whole
hour; maybe two.

But it was parent—teachers night. Irene would expect him
to go. She had a right to expect that. And he owed it to Doug.

"Can you not find an alternative, Kev?" he said loudly into the phone. "I have to say that of all the nights you could have chosen, that has to be the worst."

"Please try to make it, Bill. *Please.* Just think what it would be like . . ."

"Yes, all right, all right." He cut her off, not wanting to listen to her pleading. The picture was quite vivid enough as it was. He sighed heavily. "Well, if that's when it has to be, then . . . that's when it has to be." He could hear her relief at the other end of the line. An emotion swelled inside him: pride, or gratification. A tender feeling; there was almost something paternal in it. "So what time are you calling the meeting?"

"Seven-thirty? Can you make it by then?"

A final sigh: thick with weariness and resignation. "OK, Kev. I'll be there. We'll sort this thing out once and for all. But after this, you owe me one—OK? I mean it."

"'Bye, Billy," said Miriam, using an endearment he would never have tolerated from Irene.

"Ta-ra then," said Bill, and replaced the receiver.

They had tea together, the three of them, sausage, beans and chips, and it wasn't until Doug had gone back upstairs to do his homework and listen to the new record again that Irene broached the subject.

"Do I gather that you won't be coming tomorrow night, then?"

Bill spread his hands in apology. "This has got to be sorted out, love. We'll have a proposal on the table from the management tomorrow morning. We've got to get together to discuss it, and we've got to decide what we're going to do about Slater. Disciplinary action." He wiped his mouth with a piece of kitchen towel. "It's a bugger, I know, but what can I do?" More softly, as if to himself, he repeated: "What can I do?"

Irene looked at him for a few seconds, the light in her eyes warm but oddly inscrutable. She stood up and kissed him, gently, on the top of his head. "You're a slave to the cause, Bill," she murmured, and drew the curtains against the thickening night.

5

On the morning after the parent—teachers meeting, Chase came into their form room, threw his briefcase down beside his desk, went over to the window where Benjamin was sitting and made a dramatic announcement.

"I'm going to come to dinner round at your house."

Benjamin looked up from his book of French verbs (they had a test later that day) and said: "I beg your pardon?"

"My parents are going to dinner at your parents'," Chase said, pleased with himself. "And I'm coming too."

"When?"

"Next Saturday. Didn't they tell you about it?"

Benjamin was quietly indignant at not having been consulted or even informed about this startling proposal. He quizzed his mother about it that evening, as soon as he got home, and found out that everything had been arranged the night before, at King William's, where Chase's parents and his own had met for the first time.

Benjamin had, incidentally, been nursing fond hopes for this particular parent—teachers session. Not because he expected to receive glowing reports from the masters, but because it meant his mother and father would be out for most of the evening, and there was every possibility that Benjamin might have the living room—and more importantly, the television—all to himself for some of that time. This was a fantastic stroke of luck, because there was a film on BBC2 at nine o'clock that evening, made in France and billed as a "tender and erotic love story," which was almost certain to contain some nudity. Benjamin could hardly believe his good fortune. By dint of reasoned argument and persuasion—backed up, as always, by the threat of physical violence—Paul could easily be packed off to bed by 8:30 at the latest. His parents would not be back until ten o'clock. That allowed a whole hour in which one—surely, at least one—of the three lovely young actresses featured in this "intense, provocative and revealing study of *amour fou*" (Philip Jenkinson in the *Radio Times*) would have the opportunity to strip off for the cameras. It was almost too good to be true.

And Lois? Lois was going to be out. Lois was doing what she did every Tuesday, Thursday and Saturday night. She was having a date with the Hairy Guy.

They had been going steady now for almost three months. His name was Malcolm, and although he had rarely been allowed by Lois to cross the threshold of the Trotters' home, her mother had seen enough of him to form a distinct impression, and found him shy, courteous and appealing. He kept his thick, vinyl-black hair at a respectable length, his beard was well trimmed and his wardrobe ran to nothing more outlandish than a rust-coloured corduroy jacket worn over a fawn cheesecloth shirt and flared denim loons. He called her "Mrs. Trotter" and his intentions towards her daughter seemed entirely honourable. To the best of her knowledge (and the best of Benjamin's), her daughter's dates with Malcolm comprised nothing more racy than a few hours down at The Gun Barrels or The Rose and Crown, huddled in smoky conversation over pints of Brew and halves of bitter shandy. Very occasionally, they would branch out by attending musical events to which Malcolm referred—indecipherably, at first—as "gigs," and which sometimes conjured up, to Sheila's worried mind, images of pot-crazed teenagers gyrating to the thrashings of hirsute guitarists and drummers in an atmosphere thick with sexual abandon. But her daughter

seemed to return from these fancied orgies well before midnight, and looking none the worse for wear.

The sing-song chime of the doorbell announced Malcolm's
arrival shortly after seven o'clock. Lois was running late, detained
in the bathroom by the mysterious ablutions which invariably
occupied the three-quarters of an hour before one of her dates,
and her parents were busy too, smartening themselves up for
their visit to King William's. It fell to Benjamin, therefore, to
entertain the hopeful suitor as he hovered awkwardly by the
living-room fireplace.

They nodded at each other, and Malcolm's muted greeting—
"All right, mate?"—was accompanied by a reassuring smile. A
fair start, on the whole. But Benjamin still couldn't think of anything to say.

"Who's the axeman?" Malcolm asked. He pointed at the
nylon-string guitar which had been left leaning up against one
of the dining chairs. It was Benjamin's, a birthday present: his
mother had bought it two years ago, for nine pounds.

"Oh. I play, a little bit."

"Classical?"

"Rock, mainly," said Benjamin. Then added, hoping that it
would sound impressive: "Blues, as well."

Malcolm chuckled at this. "You don't look much like B. B.
King. Are you a Clapton fan?"

Benjamin shrugged. "He's all right. He was one of my early
influences."

"I see. You've gone past that, have you?"

Benjamin remembered something he had read in *Sounds*, a
quote from some willowy prog-rocker. "I want to push back the
boundaries of the three-chord song," he said. He didn't know
why he was suddenly confiding in this person, sharing ideas
about music which he normally kept under close wraps. "I'm
writing a sort of suite. A rock symphony."

Malcolm smiled again, but said, without condescension:
"This is the right time for it. The scene's wide open." He sat on

the sofa, his hands clasping at the knees of his loons. "You're right about Clapton, though. No real ideas of his own. Apparently he's doing Bob Marley covers now. That's pure cultural appropriation, if you ask me. Neo-colonialism in a musical setting."

Benjamin nodded, trying not to appear baffled.

"Are you in a band?" Malcolm asked.

"Not yet. I want to be."

"If you're serious about this," said Malcolm, "I could lend you some records. There's some pretty far-out stuff being laid down out there. Freaky times on the event horizon."

Benjamin nodded again, more and more fascinated the less he understood.

"That would be great," he managed.

"There's a guitarist called Fred Frith," Malcolm continued. "Plays with a band called Henry Cow. Does amazing things with a fuzzbox. Imagine The Yardbirds getting into bed with Ligeti in the smoking rubble of divided Berlin."

Benjamin, who had no experience of The Yardbirds, Ligeti or indeed the smoking rubble of divided Berlin, might well have found his imagination taxed to the limit by this task; but Lois now arrived to rescue him.

"Blimey, love," said Malcolm, rising promptly to his feet. "You look cracking." He seemed to be able to switch between these different modes with some agility.

They kissed on the cheek, and Malcolm said, "Happy Valentine's Day," handing her a box of Cadbury's Milk Tray, in a plain brown newsagents' wrapper. When she opened it, Lois's face glowed, incandescent with pleasure and gratitude. Benjamin, who tended to watch his sister more closely than he realized, noticed her reaction and shared in it, so that for a moment a flame rose between the three of them, and Benjamin felt a sudden, unexpected surge of fondness for the man who could bring such happiness into their household. He and Malcolm exchanged tiny, conspiratorial smiles.

"Remember," said Malcolm, as he helped Lois with her coat. "Henry Cow: I'll bring it round next time."

"Yes," said Benjamin, "please do."

Lois looked at them both, fleetingly puzzled. Then she shouted goodbye to Sheila, and they were gone.

Benjamin went up to his brother's bedroom, intending to lay down some early ground rules about how their evening together should develop, and found Paul sitting by the window, overlooking their scrappy front garden and the street beyond. From this vantage point, they could see Malcolm and Lois waiting at the bus stop, she clinging to the lapels of his greatcoat, her face tilted towards him, the two of them wrapped in a haze of intimacy, haloed by the amber streetlamps. The two brothers watched this scene with equal concentration: Benjamin, perhaps, because it crystallized some ideal of romantic fulfilment for which he, too, was beginning to yearn; Paul, for more prosaic reasons.

"What do you think?" he said.

Benjamin surfaced. "Mm?"

"Have they, or haven't they?"

"Haven't they what?"

Paul spelled it out, slowly, as if to a younger, more dimwitted sibling. "Have they had sexual intercourse yet?"

Benjamin drew back in horror. "Do you mind?" he said.

"What?"

"You're a filthy little pervert, do you know that? You're not to speak about your sister that way."

Paul sniggered delightedly. "I'll say what I want."

Benjamin made for the door. There was no point in arguing with this little monster. "I want you in bed by eight-thirty tonight," he said, "or I'll mash your willy with a rolling pin."

In the half-light of Paul's bedside lamp, it was hard to see whether he looked intimidated by this threat or not.

King William's main assembly hall, known as Big School, had been radically transformed for the occasion, with all the benches removed and a number of beechwood desks placed at regular intervals throughout the echoing space. Behind these, the masters sat, awaiting the inquiries of anxious parents with expressions of trepidation, mild amusement or ferocious contempt, according to temperament. Long queues formed at some desks, either because of the perceived importance of the subject, or because of an inability on the part of some masters—Mr. Fairchild (modern languages), for instance—to deliver their opinions in anything less than five or ten minutes. There were others—such as Mr. Grimshaw (divinity)—who couldn't attract a crowd for love nor money. Conversation was loud, and the whole occasion seemed to be forever teetering on the verge of a benign chaos.

Clutching a list of masters' names, Sheila led the way between the desks, the more hesitant Colin trailing behind her. Colin was looking around for a glimpse of Bill Anderton. More than half of the Longbridge plant was still closed down because of that stupid strike, and he had a good mind to take him to task for calling his men out over something so trivial. He had already rehearsed a few scathing lines to this effect, although in his heart, gloomily, he knew full well that he would never have the nerve to deliver them. It was beside the point, in any case: Bill was nowhere to be seen.

Sheila's first call was on Mr. Earle, the head of music, who racked his brains frantically when she confronted him about her son's progress. The name "Trotter" was familiar to him, vaguely, but he couldn't match it to a face.

"But you must know him," she insisted. "He's ever so musical. He plays the guitar."

"Ah." This gave him a useful let-out. "Well, here at King William's, you see, we don't regard the guitar as a real instrument. Not a real classical instrument, that is."

"How ridiculous," said Sheila. She stomped away, pulling Colin with her, and they took their places behind five or six couples waiting to talk to Miles Plumb, the school's head of art. "What does that mean, 'Not a real instrument?' That's the one thing I object to about this school. It doesn't half give itself airs and graces."

"You're right," said the woman in front of her, turning. "You know what really annoys me? The way they don't let the boys play football. Only *rugby*." (With a disdainful emphasis on the word.) "As if it was trying to be Eton or something."

"Our Philip was a cracking inside right, too," her husband added. "Broke his heart when he found out he wasn't going to play for the school."

"It's Sheila, isn't it?" said the woman, holding out her hand. "Barbara Chase. Your Ben and my Philip were both in the play last term. That dreadful Shakespearean thing."

She was referring to Mr. Fletcher's crushingly lacklustre production of Ben Jonson's *The Alchemist*, which had reduced successive audiences of doting parents to a state of glassy-eyed catatonia for three nights in a row shortly before Christmas. Sheila had kept her copy of the programme, however, and filed it away lovingly along with her son's school reports. The names Chase and Trotter could be found at the bottom of the cast list: they had played two mutes.

Once this introduction had been made, the foursome rapidly divided along gender lines. Sam Chase noticed that there was nobody waiting to talk to the games master, so he and Colin went to take issue with him on the vexed issue of football vs. rugby. A lively, ill-tempered argument broke out at once. Meanwhile, Barbara and Sheila waited in line for their audience with Mr. Plumb. His queue was moving slowly. Sheila looked ahead and was at once intrigued by his body language. He was addressing his remarks exclusively to the boys' mothers, never making eye contact with the fathers and indeed barely seeming to acknowledge their existence. He was wearing a bottle-green corduroy jacket with leather patches at the elbows, over a cotton shirt with thick blue checks, the whole ensemble being set off by a brilliant cravat, in vermilion with greenish spots. A moustache of sorts drooped limply on either side of his lips, which were thin and dark as if wine-stained. When talking to the women in the queue, he held their gaze with an embarrassing directness, compelled them to return it. As for his voice, they were soon to discover that it was reedy and high, almost to the point of effeminacy.

"My word," he exclaimed, when they appeared at the front of the queue. He was staring at them with the startled, fixed intensity of an electrified ferret. "And whom do I *now* have the pleasure—the most unexpected pleasure—of addressing?"

The two women looked at each other briefly, and giggled. "Well I'm Barbara, and this is my friend Sheila."

"I see." Addressing Barbara now, he said abruptly: "Are you familiar with Morales?"

"I don't think so," she answered, nonplussed.

"You don't know *The Virgin and Child*?"

"We don't get out to pubs much," said Sheila.

"You misunderstand me. It's a painting. It hangs in the Prado. I only mention it because—" (tilting his head, now, to look at Barbara even more closely, appraisingly) "—the resemblance is quite striking. From a certain angle, you're her very image. The likeness is quite uncanny. Positively . . . thaumaturgic."

After another nervous glance at her companion, as if to seek confirmation that this was really happening, Barbara ventured: "I wanted to ask about my son. My son Philip. I wanted to know how he was coming along."

"Then you must be . . ." Mr. Plumb paused, as if to savour the taste of the words on his palate ". . . Mrs. Chase. Mrs. Barbara Chase: how it trips off the tongue. The thrill of the Chase, ha, ha!" Following which note of near-hysteria, his tone grew suddenly serious. "Your son, Madam, is a child of most singular gifts. A dexterity with the brush which can only be described as prodigious. An imagination both antic and phantasmagoric. And above all, he evinces, in my view, the most refined aesthetic sense; the most profound responsiveness to beauty in all its myriad forms. Whence he acquired this unique sensitivity has always been a mystery to me. Always, that is, until tonight." His voice acquired, at this point, a kind of tremulous urgency which could hardly be other than comic, and yet Barbara still found herself staring deep into his eyes, captivated. "But of course, now everything becomes clear. How could Philip not respond to beauty, when he must have been surrounded by it, in the shimmering form of Mrs. Barbara Chase, every day of his short, but happy—oh, so very happy—life?"

The brief, uncomfortable silence which followed this remark was broken by Sheila, who asked: "What about Benjamin? Benjamin Trotter."

"Competent draughtsmanship," said Mr. Plumb, coming swiftly down to earth. "A fair facility with light and shade. He tries hard. That's about all there is to say."

Barbara became conscious, for some reason, of the other parents still waiting in line behind them.

"I suppose we mustn't keep you," she stammered. "I'm glad Philip's doing so well. I would have liked to talk some more."

"We will," said Mr. Plumb, his stare growing ever more piercing and earnest. "We will meet again. I'm quite, quite certain of it."

For a delirious instant, Barbara thought that he was going to kiss her hand. But the moment passed, and she hurried away, turning only once, involuntarily, to catch another glimpse of him as he began talking to the next anxious mother.

Sheila was snorting with amusement. "What a creep! Who does he think he is, Sacha Distel or something?"

She looked at Barbara, expecting her to share the joke. But her new friend seemed remote, lost in thought.

"D'you fancy coming to dinner on Saturday?" Sheila asked, on a sudden impulse.

"Dinner?"

"Yes. Come round to our place. All of you. I'm sure Ben would like it. He's always talking about your Philip. Does he have any brothers or sisters?"

"No, Philip's the only one." Barbara swallowed; her voice, which had become cracked, was returning almost to normal again. "That sounds lovely. I'll have to ask Sam first."

They found him still talking with Colin and Mr. Warren, the games master, but no longer about sport. Somehow they had progressed to politics, and were railing against the incompetence of Edward Heath's government. They shook their heads at the scandal of a nation held to ransom by obstreperous, strike-happy miners, the shame of a once-great country reduced to measures more often associated with Eastern Europe or the Third World: power cuts, petrol rationing, three-day weeks. There was to be a general election soon, on February 28th, and Sam Chase and Mr. Warren had already made up their minds: Heath would have to go. He had proved himself unfit to govern.

Colin was horrified. "You're voting for Wilson? You're going to let the socialists back in? You might as well just give the miners the keys to the ruddy country and let them get on with it."

Mr. Warren told him that, given the chance, the only Tory he would vote for—the only one with any integrity—was Enoch Powell. But Powell had by now publicly distanced himself from the party, in protest at Britain's entry into the EEC, and would not be standing in the election.

"That man should be listened to," said Mr. Warren, emphatically. "He's a scholar and a visionary."

Sam nodded. "And a Brummie to boot."

Half an hour later, in the car home, Colin Trotter was still fuming silently at this new evidence of the British electorate's terminal fecklessness. "Wilson!" he would mutter, every so often, half to himself, half to his wife, but she took little notice. She was wondering why Benjamin, a bright enough boy in her opinion, had made so little impression on any of his teachers. The subject preoccupied her so thoroughly that they had almost reached Longbridge before she thought to tell Colin: "Oh: I invited the Chases to dinner next Saturday."

"That's nice," he said, barely registering.

As they drove through the last few streets, he noticed that the windows of the grey, somnolent houses were uniformly darkened.

"Another power cut," he said, his voice quiet and bitter with incredulity. "I don't believe it. I don't bloody believe it."

Neither did Benjamin, who they found a few minutes later reading back issues of *Sounds* by candlelight in his bedroom, combing them for references to Henry Cow. The electricity had failed at 8:45, shortly after he had packed his brother off to bed, a quarter of an hour before his film was due to start.

6

On the night of the dinner party, Lois was in a bad mood. It was the first time for many weeks that Malcolm had not taken her out on a Saturday, and although she could hardly find fault with his excuse (it was his best friend's stag night), she still took it upon herself to feel poutingly, irrationally aggrieved. Now she would have to spend the evening sitting around the dinner table making polite conversation with two total strangers, not to mention this awkward, gangly friend of her brother's who never seemed to take his eyes off her.

And Philip was, without doubt, behaving rather oddly. The truth was that for several weeks he had been nursing a minor crush on Lois, and the sight of her this evening, in a sleeveless orange dress which could only be described as low-cut, was putting him under a lot of strain. He had been placed opposite her at the dinner table, so that her breasts loomed large, white and goosepimpled, exactly in his line of vision. He knew that he was staring fixedly in their direction, his lips moist and parted, a look of besotted fascination etched on his face, but was powerless to do anything about it. As for conversation, his abilities in that area—always limited when there were girls around—had tonight deserted him altogether. He appeared to have forgotten most of the words in the English language. A simple request for the salt cellar had already emerged as gibbering nonsense, and he was terrified at the thought of attempting anything else. Now he and Lois had lapsed into a sepulchral silence compared to which, down at the other end of the table, the atmosphere seemed riotous. In what amounted, for him, to a fit of extravagance, Colin had bought not one but two bottles of Blue Nun to accompany the meal. Add to this the fact that the Chases, by some happy chance, had arrived with a gift of the very same wine, in a litre bottle no less, and the stage was set for a scene of almost orgiastic excess. All of which was small consolation to Philip, confined as he was to orangeade and unable to think of a single comprehensible remark to address to his dining companion, who was by now chatting quite freely with Sam Chase. Straining to overhear a few fragments, Philip glimpsed, at last, the prospect of an entry into the conversation, and took his courage in both hands.

"What is the name of your goldfish?" he asked.

Lois stared at him. Although nobody else had stopped talking, it seemed to Philip that a new silence had descended, even colder and deathlier than before, and quite irrevocable. After what felt like aeons, she repeated:

"What is the name of my goldfish?"

Philip stared back, and swallowed hard. He had misjudged the situation; he had misheard; something, anyway, had gone terribly wrong. In a few moments Lois had turned away, with a contemptuous toss of her head, and he was left to contemplate, once again, the pallid gorgeousness of her breasts, in the now absolute certainty that this was as close as he would ever get to them.

(Typically, Paul had witnessed the whole incident, and would later inform Philip with demonic glee that the word he had mistaken for "goldfish" was in fact "Colditz," since Sam and Lois had been discussing the popular TV series of that name. This explanation, by the time he heard it, was somewhat beside the point as far as Philip was concerned. Lois clearly regarded him as some kind of simpleton, and they were to exchange no more words, not only for the rest of that evening, but for the next twenty-nine years, as it happened.)

Lois excused herself and disappeared up to her room after dinner, which eased Philip's tension slightly. He began at last to be infected by the grown-ups' high spirits. Sheila and Colin in particular were on sparkling form, fired by the success of the meal which had, they quietly admitted to themselves, been a gastronomic triumph. After *hors d'oeuvres* of salt and vinegar and cheese and onion crisps, served in tupperware bowls, they had moved on to a course of melon slices, topped with glacé cherries and washed down with generous glassfuls of Blue Nun. It was followed by sirloin steak—each portion charred, with exquisite calculation, almost but not quite to the point of unrecognizability—served with chips, mushrooms, salad and unlimited dollops of salad cream, while the Blue Nun, needless to stay, continued to flow in a Bacchanalian torrent. Finally, fat wedges of Black Forest gâteau, doused remorselessly with double-cream, were thrust before the swollen bellies and glazed eyes of the satisfied diners, and the Blue Nun began to flow faster and more freely even than before, if that could be considered possible. Places were swapped so that Sam and Colin moved next to each other, and soon they began to supplement their wine with what was indisputably the Trotter household's alcoholic *pièce de résistance*: Colin's homemade light ale, which he brewed in a forty-pint plastic keg in the cupboard under the stairs, using a kit from Boots the Chemist. The cost, as he was always ready to point out, worked out at a little under 2p per pint: an astonishing price to pay for a drink which differed hardly at all from the commercially manufactured beers, except that this one tended to come out of the keg looking cloudy and green, with a head that took up at least two-thirds of the glass and an afterburn like fermented WD40. Stoked up by a couple of glasses of this lethal concoction, the men fell to discussing the Irish question, dividing their contempt equally between the supine Northern Ireland Secretary, Francis Pym, and the "bloody Catholic killers" who had caused all the trouble in the first place. Their voices began to take on a vengeful, exasperated edge. Naturally enough, the women ignored this discussion. They had more pressing, more personal things to talk about.

"You know your art teacher," said Sheila, leaning confidentially towards her elder son. "The one with the moustache?"

"Mr. Plumb?"

"Is there anything . . . Is there anything strange about him at all?"

"We call him Sugar Plum Fairy," Philip volunteered. "That's his nickname."

Barbara's face fell. "What, you mean he's . . . one of them?"

"No, of course not," said Benjamin, laughing. "We only call him that 'cause he's such a pansy. He's randy as an old goat, actually."

"He's having an affair with Mrs. Ridley," Philip stated, with great authority.

"And who's Mrs. Ridley?" Barbara asked, in an offhand way.

"She teaches Latin at the Girls' School. She and Plumb went on a school trip last year and that's when it started."

"They went to Florence with the sixth form," Paul added. His knowledge was second-hand, but he had no intention of being left out. "And they had it off in the hotel every night."

"Language!" said Sheila, turning a furious gaze on her son. "In front of guests."

"It's only what Lois told me."

Philip had begun to laugh irresistibly, at the return of some priceless memory. He turned to Benjamin and said:

"D'you remember what Harding did? The night of the Girls' School Revue?"

"Oh yes!" Benjamin's eyes shone, as they always did when recounting a Harding story. He savoured the rooted attention of his mother and Mrs. Chase. "At the Girls' School Revue last term, Mr. Plumb and Mrs. Ridley were in a sketch together. And when they got up on the stage, Harding stood up in the middle of the audience, and shouted . . ." He paused, looked to Philip for confirmation, and they both exclaimed in unison:

"Homebreaker!"

Their mothers were gratifyingly shocked.

"What happened?" said Sheila, her hand to her mouth. "Surely he could have been expelled."

Benjamin shook his head. "Nobody said anything about it."

"Harding always knows what he's doing," said Philip. "He always knows just how far he can go."

His father's voice, meanwhile, was getting louder and louder as the alcohol continued to work its unsubtle magic.

"I'm not one for making predictions," he bellowed, and Barbara groaned inwardly, for this was his invariable prelude to making predictions. "But I'll tell you this, and I'll stake my life on it: the Irish business'll be over—over and done with—two years from now."

"Anyway," Benjamin was asking his mother, "why do you want to know about Sugar Plum Fairy?"

"Oh, he just seemed a bit of a character, that's all."

"Shall I tell you why?" Sam continued. "Because the IRA haven't got the guts for a real fight."

"He's certainly got the gift of the gab, hasn't he, Barbara?" said Sheila, reluctant to drop the subject of Mr. Plumb. "A bit of a way with words."

Barbara nodded, distantly. Her eyes were on her husband as he thumped the dining table with the palm of his hand and said: "Scratch the surface of one of those bastards and d'you know what you'll find? A coward. C—O—W—E—R—D."

"A way with words," Barbara repeated, in a thoughtful, abstracted way. Then she rose to her feet, and her manner was suddenly brisk. "Come on, Sheila: let's make a start on these dishes."

Benjamin and Philip quickly became bored with their fathers' conversation. Itching to play Philip some of the records Malcolm had lent him a few days earlier, Benjamin took him up to his bedroom, which he had spent much of that afternoon tidying in readiness. He had hidden away the Letts Desk Diary in which he faithfully recorded the excruciating minutiae of his daily television-watching and homework schedule, and removed, too, all evidence of his unfinished comic novel, not yet daring to admit to anyone, even his closest friend, that he had undertaken this ambitious project, or that in doing so he believed he might have found a vocation, an area of creative obsession which seemed likely to rival or even to overtake his tentative musical activities. A poster of his erstwhile hero, Eric Clapton, remained in pride of place on the wall, next to a picture of Bilbo Baggins's house at Bag End, drawn by J. R. R. Tolkien himself, and another Tolkien illustration, a detailed map of Middle Earth, whose geography both he and Philip knew far more intimately than that of the British Isles.

"Have a listen to this," Benjamin said, watching with some anxiety as the stylus of his portable mono record-player crashed heavily on to the spinning vinyl. "Maybe if we ever get the band started, this is the sort of thing we ought to be doing."

"That reminds me," said Philip. "I've thought of a brilliant name." He pointed at the wall-map, his finger skimming expertly across the Misty Mountains and coming to rest a few hundred elf-leagues south-east of Fangorn. "Minas Tirith."

Benjamin pursed his lips. "Not bad, I suppose." They were thirty seconds into the first track on the album: an angular, two-part melody was being stated on guitar and saxophone, while the rhythm section kept delicate hold on some tricksy time-signature Benjamin had still not been able to identify. The music was confident, brainy, slightly deranged. "What do you think of this, then?"

"It sounds like they're tuning up," said Philip. "Who are they?"

"They're called Henry Cow," said Benjamin. "I got it from the Hairy Guy."

"Who?"

"Malcolm. Lois's boyfriend."

"Oh," said Philip, glummer than ever. "I didn't know she had a boyfriend." He looked in puzzlement at the album cover, where the stark, unexplained image of a chain-mail sock gave little indication of the contents. "Is it like this all the way through?"

"It gets weirder," said Benjamin, proud of his new discovery. "You have to open your ears, Malcolm says. Apparently they're very influenced by Dada."

"And who or what," said Philip, "is Dada?"

"I don't know," Benjamin admitted. "But . . . Well, try to imagine The Yardbirds getting into bed with Ligeti in the smoking rubble of divided Berlin."

"Who's Ligeti?"

"A composer," said Benjamin. "I think." He picked up his guitar and made a deeply abortive attempt to play along with the violin's atonal counter-melody.

"Why *is* Berlin divided, anyway?" Philip asked. "I've always wondered that."

"I don't know . . . I suppose there's a river through the middle of it, isn't there? Like the Thames. I expect it's the Danube or something."

"I thought it was something to do with the Cold War."

"Maybe."

Benjamin put down his guitar, restless. From downstairs, there was a muted roar of laughter, and then another, more insistent noise: the thud of a crassly inflexible drumbeat. His father had switched on the music centre, and was playing that appalling James Last album again. He clenched his teeth with contempt.

"What's it all about, though, the Cold War? I mean, why's it called the Cold War in the first place?"

"Well," said Benjamin, struggling to raise some interest in this topic, "I expect it *is* very cold in Berlin, isn't it?"

"But it's all to do with America and Russia, I thought."

"Well it's definitely cold in Russia. Everybody knows that."

"And why's it called Watergate? What's President Nixon supposed to have done?"

"I don't know."

"Why's petrol got so expensive?"

Benjamin shrugged.

"Why do the IRA go round killing everybody?"

"Because they're Catholics?"

"Why are we having power cuts?"

"Because of the unions?" He turned up the volume, sensing the approach of what was already a favourite passage. "Listen to this bit—it's brilliant."

Philip sighed, and began to pace the room, seemingly not at all satisfied with their collective grasp of current affairs. "We don't know much about the world, do we?" he said. "Really, when you think about it?"

"So what? What does it matter?"

Philip pondered this question, and failed, for the moment, to think of a response. Perhaps Benjamin was right, and it didn't matter, after all. Perhaps it was more important that they did well in their Latin unseen on Monday morning. Perhaps it was more important that they succeeded in some of their shorter-term ambitions: getting an article published in the school newspaper, catching the attention—somehow, even for a moment—of the beautiful Cicely Boyd, or starting the band, the band they had been talking about for months now, but whose instrumentation still extended no further than Benjamin's guitar and Philip's mother's piano. Perhaps all of this was more important.

"So you like the name Minas Tirith?" he said.

"I told you," Benjamin answered, "it's all right. I think it's more important to decide what we're going to sound like."

"Well, what about Yes? Mum and Dad got me *Tales from Topographic Oceans* for Christmas. It's fantastic. I'll lend it you on Monday."

Benjamin didn't answer. He may already have known, deep down, that the venture was doomed; but he wouldn't admit it yet, even to himself. He was still an optimist in those days.

7

Thursday, March 7th, 1974, was an important day, a memorable day. It was the day Philip made his first foray into journalism, and it was the day Benjamin found God. Two events which were to have far-reaching consequences.

It was also the day on which Benjamin's worst nightmare seemed about to come true.

For many days now, Philip had been hard at work on an article which he hoped to see published in the school newspaper. *The Bill Board* appeared once a week, on Thursday mornings, and he was one of its most avid readers. The title betrayed its humble origins as a loose collection of typewritten essays and notices which used to be posted on a bulletin board in one of the upper corridors; but this had proved an inconvenient format, in most respects, and the previous year an enterprising young English master called Mr. Serkis had overseen its transition into print. The paper now extended to eight stapled sheets of A4, put together on Tuesdays by a cartel of sixth-formers in the glamorous secrecy of an office tucked away in the rafters above The Carlton Club. It was rare, very rare, for someone as young as Philip to have anything accepted by this uncompromising crew; but today, somehow, he had managed it.

Shortly before nine o'clock that morning he was to be found

sitting in the school library, reading his article for the twelfth time through eyes misty with pride and excitement. The front page of the paper contained a long editorial penned by Burrell of the upper-sixth, lamenting the indecisive outcome of last week's general election, and the reappointment of Harold Wilson as Prime Minister. Philip couldn't possibly aspire to writing such a piece, at this stage; the front half of the paper would remain unreachable, beyond imagination. But at least his review came before the sports results, and Gilligan's cartoons. And how comfortably it nestled on the page, between Hilary Turner's magisterial discussion of *The Caucasian Chalk Circle*, which had just opened at the Birmingham Rep, and a few lines of appreciation— penned by Mr. Fletcher himself—about the poet Francis Piper, in advance of his keenly anticipated visit to King William's (a visit scheduled for that very morning, Philip almost-registered in his trancelike state). To see his own efforts slotted in between the work of these senior practitioners was more than he would have dared hope for.

And yet, thought Philip, reading his piece again for the thirteenth time, and now with something like objectivity, there was no doubt that he deserved it.

"Tales from Topographic Oceans" [he had written] is the fifth album from Yes, without doubt the most musically talented and advanced rock group in Britain today, if not the whole world. Without doubt it is their masterpiece.

The concept behind the album was created by Jon Anderson, Yes's brilliant lead singer and songwriter. Hailing from Accrington, Lancs., Anderson has always had an affinity with Eastern spiritualism and philosophy. Inspired by Paramhansa Yoganda's "Autobiography of a Yogi" (nothing to do with Jellystone National Park!) the album is a double album with four sides, each containing only one long song, comprising four long songs in total. The shortest of these songs is 18 minutes 34 seconds long, while the longest is 21 minutes 35 seconds long. Only Mike Oldfield's "Tubular Bells" has longer pieces of music on each side, to the best of my knowledge. But this album has four, whereas "Tubular Bells" only has two.

Some songwriters, e.g. Roy Wood, Marc Bolan etc., just write pop lyrics, but it would be nearer the truth to say that Jon Anderson writes poetry and sets it to music. Take this couplet of lines from his song "The Memory":

"As the silence of seasons on we relive abridge sails afloat
As to call light the soul shall sing of the velvet sailors course on."

What does this mean, the listener wonders? Who are the velvet sailors, and where is the bridge that sails afloat? Jon Anderson is too profound a poet to give us pat answers and soapbox slogans. In the enigma lies the message.

Musically all five members of the band are virtuoso's. Anyone who has heard Rick Wakeman's brilliant "Six Wives of Henry VIII" (based on real Events from history) will need no introduction from me. Steve Howe is perhaps the greatest rock guitarist of his time, bar none, although really to heap special praise on any one of these band members would be insidious.

Side Three of the album's Four sides tells of The Ancient Giants Under The Sun, who are "atuned to the majesty of music." These words could equally apply to Yes themselves. They too are "atuned to the majesty of music."

In conclusion, if someone was to ask me who this album was by, and whether or not it was a masterpiece, I would be able to give the same answer:

YES!!

Flushed with self-congratulation at the ingenuity of those final lines, Philip was not aware of Benjamin's presence until he felt the tap on his shoulder. Even then, he failed to notice how distressed he was looking.

"Have you seen this?" he said, in a triumphant whisper. "They printed it. They actually printed it."

Then he realized, suddenly, that his friend's cheeks were pallid, his hands trembling, his eyes rheumy with tears.

"What's the matter?"

And when he learned the awful truth, it provoked a horrified intake of breath. It was far worse than he could have imagined.

Benjamin had forgotten his swimming trunks.

King William's had an outdoor swimming pool, tucked away behind the chapel, adjacent to the main rugby fields. It came into use halfway through the spring term, after which Benjamin's form would have two swimming periods a week, on Monday and Thursday mornings, directly after break. Benjamin dreaded these periods at the best of times. He was not a good swimmer, he did not like exposing his body to the other boys, and he disliked, intensely, Mr. Warren, the PE master, a laconic sadist popularly known as "Rosa" on account of his passing resemblance to the mannish villainess in *From Russia with Love*.

It was not just his penchant for driving the boys to the point of exhaustion that made Mr. Warren universally feared. Where his swimming periods were concerned, there was also one notorious rule, responsible over the years for any amount of humiliation and psychological damage. This rule was perfectly simple, and admitted of no exceptions: if a boy forgot to bring his swimming trunks, he had to swim in the nude.

It's true that there existed some schools, at this time (and perhaps still), where all boys were required to swim naked as a matter of course, either in the mistaken belief that it was character-building or simply in order to gratify the none-too-private enthusiasms of the sports teacher. But that, in a way, would have been different. It might at least have created a kind of beleaguered camaraderie, a redeeming sense of everyone-in-the-same-boat. The awful thing about the King William's arrangement was its malign, inexorable divisiveness. Any unlucky pupil caught in this situation would not only have to run a gauntlet of sniggers and pointing fingers on the day itself, but from then onwards could look forward to weeks, terms, even years of relentlessly single-minded taunts about his deficiencies in the genital area, whether he had them or not. This was the sort of treatment more likely to destroy character than to build it, and there were one or two cases (shy, defensive Pettigrew of the fourth form; taciturn but sexually obsessed Walker of the remove) where this already seemed to have happened.

Of course, there were the occasional showmen—freaks and exhibitionists, for the most part—who could cope; who even revelled, out of some perverse bravado, in the attention they might generate. Chapman, for instance, had forgotten his trunks so often that most people were now convinced he did it on purpose. But it goes without saying that he was the proud owner of a quite colossal member, which on the many awestruck occasions it had been exposed to public view had been compared variously to a giant frankfurter, an overfed python, a length of lead piping, the trunk of a rogue elephant, a barrage balloon, an airport-sized Toblerone and a roll of wet wallpaper. And it was Chapman, in fact, who one memorable morning had brought embarrassment upon the school by combining two misdemeanours: forgetting his trunks, and talking during a swimming lesson. For a second offence the culprit was traditionally punished by being made to stand on the top diving board for five minutes; which Chapman duly did, only for Mr. Warren to realize, after a minute and a half, that the naked felon was clearly visible from the Bristol Road to anyone travelling on the top deck of a 61, 62 or 63 bus. The sight of that legendary instrument, glimpsed suddenly and without warning on a routine shopping trip to central Birmingham, must have impressed itself deeply on the passengers' consciousness. During the course of that day the Chief Master had received four complaints, and one request for Chapman's telephone number.

But Benjamin was no Chapman. For the whole of his school career he had been dreading that this might happen. That morning his father, summoned to deal with an ineffectual foreman at the Castle Bromwich plant, had offered to drop the children at school on his way. How eagerly, with what thoughtless delight had Benjamin leaped at the chance of a lift, an escape from the bus, an extra ten minutes in bed! But the treat had been his undoing. Somehow, through some catastrophic oversight, he had left his kit bag on the back seat of the car. He could see it now, picture it, lying redundant against the upholstery in some distant car park, unnoticed by his father; unreachable. The towel, the freshly laundered rugby shirt, the scuffed plimsolls, and the all-important swimming trunks: those few square inches of terylene which alone had the power to shield him from disaster. All gone. There was nothing that could save him now.

Chase was consoling, sympathetic, but there was little he could offer in the way of practical help. The obligations of even the closest friendship (and Benjamin could see this, had absolutely no illusions or expectations in this area) stopped well short of any kind of sacrifice: Chase would be swimming in the same period, and wearing his trunks throughout. A loan was out of the question. Had Benjamin asked around, to see if anybody had a spare pair? Apparently he had, and it had only made the situation worse. No one had been willing or able to help, and the only effect of asking had been to spread the news throughout the third form, so that now his entire class was anticipating the swimming lesson with an impish, neurotic hilarity, and could talk of nothing else. A few minutes earlier he had slouched shamefacedly into the form room, only to find Harding entertaining a circle of his usual admirers with a dramatization of the scene they could expect to witness in two hours' time.

"And now, emerging from the changing rooms," he was saying, in the kind of plummy whisper a BBC commentator might adopt for a wildlife documentary, "we see a magnificent specimen of manhood in all its glory. Naked as nature intended, the great-crested Trotter creeps out from his nest, blinking into the sunlight, a hand clasped, protectively, over the genitalia which no man, woman or child, is ever permitted to see; or indeed capable of seeing, without the use of a powerful electron microscope. Invisible to the human eye, in fact so small that a team of biologists, working around the clock, are still struggling to prove its existence, the Trotter penis cannot be measured on any scale so far—"

Harding had broken off when he realized that Benjamin had

entered the room, when he saw the wounded look, the wordless accusation of betrayal. The audience dispersed, but the only person to say anything to him was Anderton, who had been lurking at its fringes, half-listening. "Just leg it, mate," he advised. "Head off into town for the morning. Don't let the bastards grind you down." As for the others, their giggles and sidelong, ribald glances persisted, following Benjamin as he performed a brief, forlorn circuit of the room, before he regained the corridor in his search for Chase, and the sanctuary of unconditional friendship.

He had wanted simply to offload his panic, to unburden himself. He wasn't expecting salvation, or anything like that. But suddenly, as he sat beside his friend in the library, head in hands, contemplating the end of tolerable school life as he knew it, salvation was exactly what Chase appeared to find.

"Wait a minute," he whispered, snatching up the magazine. "There's no swimming today."

The clouds parted. A ray of fragile, impossible sunlight. "What?"

"There are no lessons this morning after break. They've been cancelled."

"Why?"

"Because this guy's coming to read to us. This old poet."

Chase handed Benjamin his copy of *The Bill Board*, already open at the page where his review squatted presumptuously alongside the rolling Johnsonian cadences of Mr. Fletcher's article. He pointed at the closing sentences. "There."

Benjamin craned forward, weak with hope. *"Mr. Piper's reading will take place at approximately 11:45 in Big School,"* he read. *"Thursday morning's timetable will be amended accordingly."*

"There you go," said Chase, triumphant. "No swimming. You're saved."

Benjamin still had his doubts. It was too good to be true. "It doesn't actually say that," he pointed out. "It only says 11:45 *approximately.*"

"So?"

"Well, swimming ends at ten to twelve. They're never going to cancel the whole period just so we can get there five minutes earlier."

"They'll have to. I'm sure that's what it means. Just you wait and see."

It was easily said, but less easily managed. Benjamin dragged his way through the next sixty minutes in an agony of unknowing. There was no school assembly on Thursdays, only form meetings, and no definite information was forthcoming there. Benjamin's form master, Mr. Swallow, was hazy about the revised arrangements: either the last three periods of the morning had been cancelled, or only the last two; he couldn't be sure, and didn't appear to consider it very important. Benjamin was left to drown in uncertainty, his innards churning with apprehension, light-headed, unable to concentrate even for a few seconds on Mr. Butterworth's account of the restoration of Charles II, which occupied the first forty minutes of the teaching day. Then, during the English lesson that followed, the issue was finally resolved. At the beginning of the lesson (devoted, inevitably, to the work of Francis Piper), Mr. Fletcher announced that the great poet's reading would now take place at twelve noon, and the third period of the day would proceed as usual. On hearing which, Benjamin froze in his chair, and then clutched his stomach, convinced for a moment that he was going to be violently sick. He looked across to where Chase was sitting, in the adjacent row, and caught his concerned eye, but was obliged to turn away at once, too ashamed to hold his gaze.

So it was real. It was happening. There was to be no reprieve. That fleeting possibility, which Benjamin had never really trusted anyway, had been snatched away as whimsically as it had been offered.

Dark terrors began to crowd Benjamin's brain, and at ten to eleven he could remember nothing of what had passed in Mr. Fletcher's lesson.

. . .

As it happened, he had missed a good one. Or at least, he had missed a confrontation between Fletcher and Harding which found them both on vintage form.

"Can I ask you a question, sir?" Harding had asked.

Mr. Fletcher, fresh from explaining Francis Piper's tangential association with the Bloomsbury group, and sketching out an analysis of *The Unkindness of Birds*, one of his most famous verse cycles, looked up warily. He could sniff trouble a mile off.

"Yes, Harding, what is it?"

"Well, there's something about these poems that puzzles me."

"Go on."

"It's just that . . . I mean, it's a little hard to understand, with all these allusions and metaphors you've been talking about—but these are meant to be love poems, aren't they?"

"Of course they are. What about it?"

"Well, I only wondered, because nearly all the, er . . . the personal pronouns, and what have you—they all seem to be male."

Mr. Fletcher took off his glasses.

"Very observant of you, Harding. And so?"

"So this bloke Piper, sir—I assume he must be a bit of an old shirt-lifter."

Mr. Fletcher rubbed his eyes tiredly. Was it really worth rising to the bait?

"His sexual orientation, Harding, is frankly neither here nor there."

"But I am right, aren't I?"

"Right?"

"In thinking that he . . . well, takes it up the Hershey Highway, as our American cousins say."

"The Hershey Highway?"

"Yes, sir. Bournville Boulevard, I suppose you'd call it round here."

This got a good laugh from the rest of the class. Mr. Fletcher, deadpan as ever, stared out of the window for a while, pensive, unflinching. His words, when they came, seemed heavier than ever with fatigue and indifference.

"Your basic problem, Harding, is that you have a grubby and ultimately rather *banal* little mind. I suggest—in fact, why be coy about this—I *insist* that you report to me in this classroom at five minutes before twelve today and instead of attending Mr. Piper's reading you write an essay of not less than twelve sides entitled 'Why the artistic temperament has no gender.' And since this will be at least the fiftieth imposition I've set for you this year, I imagine that by the time you've finished it you will have enough for a book and I personally recommend that you send them all off to Faber and Faber with a covering letter and a self-addressed bloody envelope!" His voice, which had risen to a pitch of something like irritation, if not actual fury, subsided into its regular monotone. "All right, the rest of you. Gidney here is going to read from one of Mr. Piper's most affecting *villanelles*. Page seventy-five of the anthology, please: 'The sweat of the young working boy stiffens my resolve.' "

Morning break was at ten to eleven, at which time most of the boys would sprint off to the tuck shop and stand in an unruly queue, scrambling for the processed meat pies and warm baps filled with sausages that passed for delicacies to this undiscriminating clientele. Normally, Benjamin would have joined them, but there could be no question of food today. This particular condemned man would not be eating a hearty breakfast prior to his hanging. Nor could he tolerate the company of his so-called friends, whose teasing and unconcealed anticipation grew more gleeful by the minute. He could think of nothing to do except crawl to a remote corner of the locker room, where he sank to the floor and assumed a foetal position, solitary, forsaken, pulling his knees tightly beneath his chin in fierce despair.

He was in the furthest corner of the locker room. There

were three rows of empty lockers here (for there were more lockers than boys in the school), and it was rarely, if ever, visited. The silence was absolute. Benjamin settled in for a long dark fifteen minutes of the soul.

He thought about the advice Anderton had given him. Should he just make a run for it? It was a measure of his desperation that Benjamin even considered this prospect, since he was by nature almost pathologically conformist, and had never once, to his knowledge, broken any of the school rules. All the spirit of youthful rebellion which animates most boys at this age was channelled, in his case, into admiration for Harding and his devilish, anarchic humour. Benjamin would only ever be a dissident by proxy. Besides, there were serious obstacles to any plan of escape. If he were to head off along the school drive at this hour of the day, or across the playing fields, he would almost certainly be spotted by a master. The only realistic alternative was to find a quiet spot somewhere in the school—one of the music practice rooms, for instance—and cower there for the duration. Or even wander into the library and pretend to have a free period; sit reading the newspapers, and brazen it out. That's what Harding himself would have done. Probably Anderton too, for that matter.

The simple fact was that he didn't have the courage. But what he decided to do instead—or rather, found himself doing—was, in its way, even more radical. And certainly more surprising.

Afterwards, he would not remember getting to his knees, or starting to talk aloud like a mad person in the silence of that empty locker room. He would not remember how his first involuntary moans, his mechanical repetition of the phrase "Oh God, Oh God, Oh God," had somehow evolved, cohered, and begun to assume the character of a prayer. He had never spoken to God before. Never needed him, never looked for him, never believed in him. Now, it seemed, within the space of a few rapturous seconds, he had not only found him but was already trying to strike a bargain.

"Oh God, Oh God, send me some swimming trunks. Send me some swimming trunks in thy infinite wisdom. Whatever it takes, whatever you want from me, just send me some swimming trunks. Send them to me now. I'll do anything for you. Anything at all. I'll believe. I promise that I'll believe. I'll never stop believing in you, trusting in you, following you, doing whatever you want me to do. Anything. Anything in the world that's in my power to do. I don't care. I don't mind. Just please, please, *please*, in the name of the Father, in the name of the Son, in the name of the Holy Ghost, please, God, just grant me this one wish. Send me some swimming trunks. I beg of you. Please.

"Amen."

Benjamin's eyes were screwed tightly shut as he repeated the word.

"*Amen.*"

And then there was silence.

And then there was a sound.

It was the sound of a locker door slamming open and shut in a breeze which Benjamin had not even noticed before. In fact, as he would discover during the swimming lesson, it was an absolutely windless day, so this could not have been an earthly breeze at all. It was the breath of God. The sound came from the next row of lockers, and when Benjamin stumbled to his feet and walked there with quaking, reverent footsteps, he knew what he was going to find. The door slammed open and shut again, and as Benjamin approached it, all points seemed to converge on this locker, as if he were seeing it through a distorting lens. It spoke to him. It beckoned him.

He opened the door and found what he knew was there. A pair of navy-blue swimming trunks. Damp, recently used, and many sizes too large. But they had a drawstring, so that didn't matter. Nothing mattered. Nothing would matter from now on, ever again, for as long as Benjamin lived.

· · ·

By everyday standards, it was an exceptionally disastrous swimming period. Benjamin was chosen to be part of a relay team captained by Culpepper, and was clearly the weakest link in the chain. By the time he had completed his two purple-faced, asphyxiated, floundering lengths of butterfly stroke, their lead had been all but erased, and they were later beaten at the post by the number two seeds, a more consistent line-up headed by the tenacious and ruthlessly competitive Fit Eddy. Benjamin's colleagues were furious. They piled scorn and abuse on him without mercy.

"You arsehole, Bent," Culpepper hissed, as they changed back into their uniforms. "You fucking useless pathetic little arsehole weakling tosser. You let us all down. Every one of us. We would have won if it wasn't for you. You wimpy sherring tosspot arsehole."

But Benjamin simply smiled back, and that seemed to infuriate him even more. He wasn't even doing it to antagonize him, either. He was smiling because he loved everybody and everything, including Culpepper, and from now on nothing could shake his faith in humanity or the essential rightness of things. And the same smile—beatific, serene—was his only response when Chase grabbed him by the arm on their way to Big School and demanded, "What happened? Where did you get them?" Later on he would tell him, "They were a gift," but that was the closest he would ever come to explaining the mystery of those knee-length, ill-fitting, navy-blue swimming trunks. They entered, for a while, the arcane and changeful mythology of King William's School, and then were quietly forgotten. Other wonders took their place.

Benjamin listened with great attention to Francis Piper's reading. Not to his words, exactly, but to the pleasing tremolo of his seventy-year-old voice, a fragile woodwind playing melodies which sounded, to Benjamin's newly devotional ears, like the distant echoes of some psalm or hymnal. He gazed intently, too, at the old man's kindly, placable face, scored deeply with laughter-lines, and felt that he was seeing not—as Mr. Fletcher might have hoped—a little piece of twentieth-century literary history, but an emanation, a vision of perfect clarity that was for his eyes alone; something not unlike the face of God.

Dustclouds swirled in the beams of gold around Francis Piper's dove-white, angel-white hair, and it was all Benjamin could do to stop from laughing out loud. It was everywhere. Divine Grace was everywhere.

WINTER

8

The track had been stopped for about an hour and a half. Nobody seemed to know why. Bill Anderton stood out in the yard beneath the loading bay, surrounded by workers from the underseal section and the machine shop; surrounded by them, but not joining in any of their laconic banter, or the game of football a dozen of the men had begun to improvise. He was smoking his fifth or sixth cigarette, tipping the ash into the sludge of cold tea at the bottom of his plastic cup. Every so often he would exhale deeply, blowing out rigid columns of smoke which mingled in the freezing air with the breath steaming from the chapped lips of his colleagues. It looked as though everybody was smoking, that raw November afternoon.

A familiar scrawny figure walked by, wearing a dark grey suit and also sucking fiercely on a cigarette. It was Victor Gibbs, looking more than usually sallow and cadaverous. He nodded at Bill, who nodded back, relieved that they weren't going to attempt a proper conversation. But this relief was short-lived. After a few more steps Gibbs stopped and turned in his tracks. He approached Bill with a sly, insinuating smile on his face.

"I've got a bone to pick with you," he said, "Brother Anderton. Some months ago I wrote you a letter. Do you remember?"

Bill remembered perfectly well, but answered: "I get a lot of letters."

"It was about Miss Newman. *Miriam*, to you and me."

Bill didn't want to talk about this. Not here. Three feet away, on the other side of the machine-shop wall, was the shower block where he and Miriam had made love the day before. The usual feverish, clumsy business. The more entangled they became, emotionally, the more joyless and inadequate these fumbled occasions started to feel. He couldn't discuss her with someone else. Not in this place. Not anywhere, with Gibbs.

"Your complaint was investigated thoroughly," he said, "by a third party. They concluded there was nothing in it."

"I never had a reply."

"That was remiss of me. Sometimes the system breaks down."

Gibbs looked away, sensing an impasse.

"Lovely girl, that Miriam," he said, after a while. "Very . . . fetching. A lot of blokes round here got their eye on her. But I bet they'll never get anywhere." He frowned, as if the thought had just occurred to him, although Bill could tell that this was all part of some rehearsed strategy. "D'you know what I think the chicks find attractive? D'you know what turns them on?"

"Chicks?" said Bill, contemptuously.

"It's power, Brother Anderton. That's what it is. They go wild for it. It drives them crazy."

Bill forced a glance at him. He didn't even want to meet his eye, if he could help it. "Can we just drop this subject, Gibbs? I'm not interested in your opinions, to be honest."

"Fair enough." He held up his hands, acquiescent. "I just thought it would be good news to a man like you. After all, power oozes out of your every pore. These men"—he gestured at the football players—"they do pretty much everything you want them to, don't they? What's going on this afternoon, anyway? Have you called them out again?"

There were several ways Bill could have responded to this goading. He could simply have walked away, or he could have played his trump card and dropped some sort of hint about the

Charity Committee theft, which he had still not mentioned to anybody. For the time being, though, he decided to keep his cool.

"Sledgehammer fell on the track a while ago. We're waiting for someone to come and sort it out."

"You know, it's funny," said Gibbs, "I've noticed, every time something like this happens—and it seems to happen a lot, every couple of weeks—it always happens just before lunch, so they can't get an engineer out before two, and half the day's gone before the thing's up and running again. Meanwhile, the company's lost how many cars? Sixty? Seventy?"

"I don't know what you're implying," said Bill, turning on him as fine droplets of rain began to splatter the tarmac, "but I do know that your knowledge of working practices is exactly nil. Nobody who spends all day sitting on his arse pushing figures around is going to criticize *my* men for the way they do their job." He stubbed out his cigarette, screwing it angrily into the ground. "Come and spend a day or two on that track, Gibbs, and then tell me you begrudge these blokes a few minutes kicking a ball around. There's a mate of mine called Ian, Ian Bateman, was laid off last week aged *forty-eight*, with a back that's killing him and six months in hospital to look forward to. That's what ten years as an undersealer does for you."

He began to walk off, but Gibbs stopped him with the words: "No chance of your son ending up like that, then, is there?"

"My son?" repeated Bill, turning.

"Not after that fancy school he goes to. That toffs' academy. Too good for the local comprehensive, was he?"

Advancing towards him, Bill seemed suddenly to grow in stature. The hostility between the two men was immediately charged, physical.

"What *is* your problem, Gibbs? Eh? What is it?"

"I know about you and Miriam Newman," he answered, calmly.

At which point, Bill couldn't help smiling. He was glad, finally, that the thing had been mentioned at last. It made everything very straightforward.

"You shouldn't have said that," he said. "And you shouldn't have forged those cheques, either." He didn't even wait to watch Gibbs's expression change. "I've a terrible feeling that one of us," he said over his shoulder, ambling away, "is going to be out of a job on Monday morning."

And for the rest of the afternoon, whenever he thought about that moment, Bill found himself glowing with pride. The sort of pride that comes before a fall.

That evening, he met Miriam at The Black Horse in Northfield, and they drove out to Stourbridge in his brown Marina. They checked into The Talbot Hotel as Mr. and Mrs. Stokes (a little tribute Bill had decided to pay to the current chairman of British Leyland). Irene was under the impression that he was in Northampton, staying overnight for a TGWU dinner. And indeed, that's where he should have been. But he had phoned the regional office that afternoon, and called off sick. It had all been arranged more than a month ago. It was to be their first whole night together.

They sat in the hotel's cavernous lounge bar, Bill drinking pints of Brew, Miriam drinking Dubonnet and bitter lemon. He rested his hand on her knee beneath the table. It was proving surprisingly hard to sustain a conversation.

"Wouldn't it be lovely," Miriam said, "if we could spend every evening together like this?"

Bill wasn't sure that it would be lovely at all. It was beginning to dawn on him that he and Miriam didn't know each other very well. Yes, they knew each other's bodies—knew every inch of each other's bodies, knew them inside out—but they had never done much talking; had never had the time. The affair had been going on for eleven months but tonight, quite unexpectedly, Bill felt that he was sitting with a stranger. He thought about Irene and found himself aching for her company: not for anything in particular she might say or do; just for her wordless, kindly presence. He thought about his son, about how he would feel if he could see his father in this ridiculous situation. And then he watched Miriam as she went to the bar for more drinks, and his body was galvanized, yet again, with the knowledge that he had somehow won the affection of this beautiful woman— this beautiful *young* woman, more to the point—and that tonight she was going to give herself to him, willingly. To him: not to any of the young designers she worked for, or the fitters who were always trying to chat her up in the social club, but to him, Bill Anderton, pushing forty, losing his hair. Other girls had fallen for him in the past, often enough, so clearly there was something about him, something they must have liked: but the thrill never quite went away, the thrill of knowing that he could still inspire those feelings, even with Miriam, even after eleven whole months . . .

If only she would stop looking at him that way.

"Cheers," he said, raising his glass.

"To us," she said, raising hers.

They smiled at each other, and drank, and then just a few seconds later she put her glass down and let out a convulsive sob and said: "I can't go on like this, Bill, I just can't."

Soon afterwards she composed herself and they went in to dinner.

The dining room was vast, and empty. A waitress led them through the gloom to a far corner, lighting their way with a candle which she carried before her as if it were a torch, and which was then set down to flicker bravely on their table, partly no doubt as a romantic gesture but also, perhaps, in a futile attempt to ward off the swathes of funereal darkness that surrounded them. Buried somewhere in the walls was a speaker system through which John Denver's "Annie's Song" dribbled out like primeval musical ooze. The base of the candlestick was encrusted with lumps of molten wax which Bill initially mistook for ice, so Arctic was the room temperature. They took it in turns to warm their hands at the flame of the candle, thereby finding a third use for it. Neither spoke much as they perused their menus, which were printed on enormous sheets of card, some two feet by eighteen inches, but seemed to offer only three choices, one of which was off.

Bill went for the mixed grill. Miriam chose the chicken-in-a-basket.

,"Do you want chips with that?" the waitress asked.

"What's the alternative?" asked Miriam.

"Just chips," said the waitress.

"Chips is fine," said Miriam, fighting back tears.

"I'm sorry about that," said the waitress, concerned. "Do you not like chips?"

"It's all right," said Miriam, reaching for a tissue. "Really."

"She loves chips," said Bill. "Adores them, in fact. We both do. This is a purely personal matter. Please go away." Just as she was about to disappear into the encroaching shadows, he added: "And bring us a bottle of Blue Nun while you're at it."

He took out his own handkerchief and dabbed tenderly beneath Miriam's eyes. She pushed him away.

"I'm sorry," she said. "I'm sorry. I'm being stupid."

"Don't worry. It's this place. I know how you feel. It's so depressing."

"It's not that," said Miriam, sniffing. "It's Irene. I want you to leave her. I want you to leave her and move in with me."

"Oh, Jesus Christ," said Bill. "I don't believe this is happening."

This was not a response to Miriam's declaration—which he had been anticipating anyway, with growing dread—but to the arrival of a party of twelve men and a ferocious, tweedy woman at a nearby table. The men were a sullen-looking bunch: middle-aged for the most part, too poorly dressed to be businessmen, too weedy and unathletic to be rugby players. They were noisy but there was no boisterousness, no high spirits about them; and they all seemed to be terrified of the woman, who, after sitting down at the table, took out a monocle and clamped it over her right eye. It would have been an unprepossessing assembly, at the best of times. But this was the worst of times: for among their number, quite unmissably, was someone Bill recognized only too well. Someone he saw every day of the working week, and usually went out of his way to avoid. His brother-in-arms in the labour relations war, and personal *bête noire:* Roy Slater.

"Don't move," said Bill. "Don't look around, and don't say anything. We're going to have to leave."

"What are you talking about?" said Miriam. "Did you hear what I just said to you?"

"Of course I heard," said Bill. "And we'll discuss it. I promise we'll discuss it. But right now"—he glanced over his shoulder, taking note, with some relief, of a velvet-wallpapered door in the wall behind them—"it's time for a quick getaway. You know who Roy Slater is, don't you?"

Miriam nodded, confused.

"Well, he's right behind you. And if we don't get out of here in the next ten seconds, he's going to see us."

The dimness of the lighting was on their side, this time, and it was easy enough to leave their table and slip out through the door. They found themselves walking down a deserted corridor, past a number of dark, unused public rooms, until a fire exit gave them access to the hotel car park. The cold night air assaulted them brutally, without warning. Miriam actually cried out: a brief, uncontainable wail of distress. It was the shock, mainly, but also a hint of her despair at the way this longed-for evening was turning out.

They hurried round to the front of the hotel, ducked inside, then paused uncertainly in reception.

"Let's go upstairs," said Bill. "Let's go to bed."

"*Bed?* It's only eight-thirty."

"We can't stay down here. It's too risky."

"What about my chicken and chips?"

Bill didn't seem to have heard her. "What's he doing here, anyway?" he was saying to himself. "Who are those people?"

He went to the reception desk and asked for details of the large party which had just arrived for dinner. Were they guests at the hotel? The receptionist checked her register and told him that they were members of something called the Association of British People, and they were holding a training conference and would be there for the whole weekend. Bill listened to this information impassively. He was silent for a few moments, then remembered to say thank you to the woman behind the desk. When he returned to Miriam, his face was transformed, marked by some grim new knowledge.

"What is it?" Miriam asked. "What's the matter?"

Bill took her arm and led her towards the stairs. "The bastard's a fascist," he said.

Post-coitally, they lay side by side in the centre of the bed, their bodies pressed tightly together, Bill's hairy, white, thirty-nine-year-old legs bristling against the smoothness of Miriam's newly waxed calf and thigh. They lay like this not for the sake of intimacy, but because their double mattress sagged heavily in the middle, and gave them no choice in the matter. For preference, they would have been lying with a foot or two of space between them. They had made love effortlessly, mechanically, neither of them feeling like it, but both knowing that this whole disastrous excursion would seem even more of a fiasco if they didn't at least go through the motions. And now, while they remained physically conjoined, their thoughts had already begun to run along separate paths.

"You don't understand what these people are about," Bill was saying. "At least with Enoch Powell you've got some thought behind it, something you can argue with. Christ, even the National Front's got an ideology. Of sorts. But these people . . . It's just an instinct with them. It's just hatred. Hatred and violence."

"D'you think he saw us?" Miriam raised herself on one elbow, her thick brown hair falling across one shoulder. Bill couldn't help but run his finger along her skin, the immaculate softness of it. "D'you think Mr. Slater saw us?"

"I don't know, love. I just don't know." He laughed, contemptuously. "Did you ever see such a bunch of wimps, eh? Such a bunch of bloody runts. No wonder they have to get other people to do their dirty work for them. And as for that . . . harridan! Did you ever see anything like her?"

"What would you do, though?" Miriam persisted. "I mean, if he saw us, if he spread it all over the factory, if Irene found out about it—what would you do?"

"He didn't see us," said Bill. "*I* saw *him*—that's more to the point. So now I know. Now I know who's been spreading that stuff around. Those stupid bloody leaflets."

"It probably doesn't matter, anyway," said Miriam, her voice far-off, dreamlike: until it suddenly acquired a sharper tone. "I think there's someone who knows already."

Bill looked up. "Eh?"

"In fact I know there is. Mr. Gibbs, from the Charity Committee." She watched him, hoping, apparently, to see some sign of panic, or surprise. When there was none, she said: "Doesn't that worry you?"

"Oh, I know all about Gibbs. In fact, we had words about it this afternoon."

"Words? What sort of words?"

Bill shook his head, skirting the question. "He's a little sod, that one. An interfering little bastard. What's it to him, anyway? Why can't a bloke like that mind his own business?"

"Because he's got it in for me," said Miriam. She lay back against the pillow, her arms folded behind her head. The pose was languid, provocative. It was somehow as if she relished the subject, took an almost sensual pleasure in it. "He hates me, you know. He hates me because I wouldn't sleep with him."

"What?" said Bill, shaken this time. "When was this?"

"Oh, months and months ago. He came up to me in the committee room one evening, after you'd all gone home, and he asked me out for a drink. I said, No thank you—politely, you know, in a pleasant sort of way—and he said why didn't we skip the drink then and just go for a nice screw back at his place." She glanced at Bill, checking to see that he was suitably agitated. "So naturally I was . . . horrified, and I told him so in no uncertain terms, and he said that I needn't act all innocent, he knew just the kind of girl I was, he knew all about me and you, he could see it in the way we looked at each other, and then he started calling me all kinds of names like slut and whore and dirty piece of stuff, and then I told him that even if I was a whore I'd have to be paid more than a million pounds to do it with a creep like him, and then he just stared at me, stared at me for ages and ages, I don't think I've ever seen anyone look so angry, I was sure he was going to belt me in the face or something—"

"I would have belted him back, if he had, I can tell you that."

"—but instead he just walked out of the room, without saying another word, and in a way that was the most scary thing of all, that silence, that not saying anything, and ever since then, every time he sees me, I can see it in his face, the same thing, this . . . hatred. This total hatred he has for me."

Bill raised himself, leaned over her, brought his face close to hers. He willed himself to smile, wanting to reassure her, but even as he did so, some cloud was gathering at the corner of his memory. How strange it was, how very strange, that he should have encountered both Gibbs and Slater on the same day. And going back all those months to the day before Valentine's Day, the time Miriam had phoned him at home . . . Yes, that was the afternoon he read Gibbs's letter, and saw Slater on the television, and read the foul leaflet that Slater, it now seemed, must have been putting around the factory. They always seemed to crop up together, those two; as if there was some sort of connection between them. And there was something else, something else weird, something that Gibbs had said to him this afternoon. He hadn't really taken it in at the time. "Toffs' academy" . . . that's right. That was how he had described King William's. But that was the phrase Slater had used, as well, exactly a year ago, when they shared that minicab home from the restaurant. Why should they have used the same expression? And come to think of it, how did Gibbs know which school Doug went to in the first place? They must have been talking about him: that was the only explanation. And so they must know each other. They must be friends.

"Don't worry about it, Bill," Miriam was saying, running a hand across his stubbly cheek. "I don't care if he's got it in for me."

But no, he thought, there was more to it than that. Something worse, some kind of dread came over him, when he thought about those two: something in relation to Miriam. Like a premonition . . .

He did his best to shake this feeling off, to think of his responsibilities. He'd got Miriam into this mess in the first place. It was his job to protect her.

"I'm not worried," he said, almost managing a smile. "Not about Gibbs, at any rate. He's history."

"What do you mean?"

"I'm going to have him sacked."

Miriam's eyes widened, and then she was smiling too; not just with pleasure but also with some amusement, it seemed, at this unexpected display of macho resolve.

"You can't sack someone just like that," she said. "Can you?"

"He's a crook. He's been filtering money from the charity account."

"Can you prove that?"

"Yes. I've got the cheques back from the bank. All with forged signatures."

"Whose signature has he been forging?"

"Tony Castle's. Mine." He paused for emphasis, before admitting: "Yours."

Miriam said: "Why haven't you done something about this before?"

"I've been waiting for when the time's right," said Bill. "Which is now." He kissed her gently, and suddenly an irresistible wave of emotion washed over him. Words began pouring out, and he heard himself saying things, knowing even as he said them that he shouldn't be saying them, that they were the worst things he could be saying. "I love you, Miriam. I'd do anything for you, you know. Anything to make you happy."

And now he expected her to reach for him, to feel the kiss returned. But instead, she answered:

"I've got someone else as well, Bill. You're not the only one."

He drew away.

"What?"

"Perhaps Mr. Gibbs is right," said Miriam, her voice quite toneless now. "Perhaps I am a slut. A whore. I know that's what my father would call me." She gave a desperate laugh. "Oh, if he could see me now! He'd pick up that bloody family bible and knock me out cold with it."

"Who is he?" Bill wanted to know. "What's his name?"

"You don't know him," said Miriam. "He's not from the factory. He's not from anywhere round here." She looked at him brightly. "You're not jealous, are you? You have got Irene, after all."

Bill said nothing at first. He was furiously jealous, there was no doubt of that, but at the same time relieved, and he couldn't even begin to reconcile the two feelings.

"Are you making this up?" he asked, eventually. "Because if this is just a way of getting me to—"

"He's much younger than you," said Miriam. "About half your age. He's not as good-looking as you, but he's got more . . . stamina, if you know what I mean. And he's not married."

Bill rolled over on to his back, stared at the ceiling.

"Is it serious?" he asked. And: "Where did you meet him?"

Miriam sat up in the bed, climbed astride him, and reached between his legs. She teased him into readiness, and then lowered herself gradually, steadily, with infinite care, infinite attention, until he was deep inside her, his eyes screwed shut with expectation, with helpless pleasure.

"You're the one that I want, Bill. The only one," she said; and there was no more talk that evening.

. . .

The next morning, Miriam's behaviour was even stranger, and his longing for Irene, for the security she represented, became even more acute.

Cutting their losses, they checked out of the hotel before breakfast, and drove out to the Clent Hills. In the tea-shop they ate wedges of fruitcake and drank strong, milky coffee. Then they walked for an hour or more, along the thinly wooded ridges, the bracken wearing the last traces of autumnal gold, the bridle pathways leading them seemingly at random through stretches of dry, bleached-out grassland and ragged clusters of evergreens, the treetops forming makeshift canopies against the keen morning sunlight. After yesterday's rain, they had good weather before them, and the hills almost to themselves. Sometimes a horse might amble by, the rider tipping his hat, or a breathless dog criss-crossing its owner's path, but otherwise, the world left them alone. Half-tamed farmland stretched out beneath them on every side. They could hear, as always, the motorway's distant roar.

Bill asked Miriam to tell him more about her new lover. She dodged his questions nimbly; bounced them back with laughter, changes of subject, evasions. She held his hand, kissed him, walked arm-in-arm, then would turn back, choose a different pathway, stand gazing out over the fields while he walked on ahead. He couldn't make her out.

When they got back into the car, the first thing he said was: "So, are you going to choose, then? Between him and me?"

"What about you?" she answered. "Are *you* going to choose, between me and her?"

But Bill had already chosen. The emergence of this potential rival had only made things easier for him. He no longer felt that he would be abandoning Miriam; he would be relinquishing her, rather, handing her over to someone younger and better qualified. There was something almost noble in the gesture. At the moment he could scarcely bear the thought that he must live without her, that he would never again be allowed to see, or touch, that body he had come to know far better than his wife's. But he was sure it was the right thing to do. He even believed it was what Miriam herself wanted, at heart.

They were driving back towards Northfield, and were only five minutes from Miriam's house, when she became hysterical. She began crying again, and screaming through her sobs that her life meant nothing when she was away from him, that she was going to turn up at his house and confront Irene, that she would kill herself if he didn't leave his wife and come to live with her. Bill pulled over to the side of the road and tried, hopelessly, to calm her down. He began promising things, promises he knew that he could never keep. The noise of her crying and shouting seemed to go on for hours, like radio static at top volume. All he could do was to repeat again and again that he loved her, he loved her, he loved her. They had both lost control of what they were saying.

9

The next morning, Miriam knew she had to get out of the house. Sundays at home were always dreadful: Miriam and Claire lived in permanent fear of their father, Donald, whose forbidding, taciturn presence seemed to have cast a chill over their entire childhoods, and whose demeanour on Sundays was usually even more severe and unapproachable. Although he no longer insisted on the two hours' Bible study that used to be such a dismal feature of their weekends, he still expected the whole family to go to church in the morning. Today, however—perhaps sensing that her sister was in no state to undergo this weekly ordeal—Claire put on a spectacular and unprecedented show of defiance, and refused point blank to accompany him. Donald trembled with rage when she spoke the words; there was a bitter, poisonous exchange, tearful on Claire's side, quietly brutal on her father's; but the result was that both sisters stood firm, and stormed out of the house together at about ten o'clock. They had nothing to do but go for a long walk.

It had been a turbulent year in the relationship between the two of them. Early in December, 1973, a series of Bovril stains on the pages of her private diary had alerted Miriam to the fact that Claire was reading it in her absence. Mayhem had ensued. After an argument of incredible length, violence and intensity, there had been no verbal communication between them for six weeks. Christmas, in these circumstances, had been intolerable;

Claire's birthday was not much better. And yet somehow, through one of those minor miracles that form part of the strange texture of family life, a reconciliation had taken place, and they had emerged better friends than ever before. Her knowledge of Miriam's feelings for Bill Anderton turned Claire, slowly and painfully, from an object of hate into something like a confidante. Miriam had stopped keeping a diary, and she never told Claire the whole story, by any means; but the mere fact that her sister was aware of Bill's existence, knew his name, understood his importance to her, made Miriam eager, not to share secrets with her exactly, but at least to seek out her company, intuitively, whenever the affair was causing her distress. In this way, despite their difference in age, a kind of closeness grew up between them.

That Sunday morning, they rode on the 62 bus as far as it would take them, past the Longbridge factory and all the way to Rednal. They wandered through Cofton Park, dropped into the amusement arcade at the foot of Lickey Road, and wound up back at the bus terminus, sitting in the dingy, fogged-up café opposite the newsagents'. Bill's name had not been mentioned once during this time, although Claire could tell that he was weighing heavily on her sister's mind. On the south side of the park she had stood opposite the Andertons' house for two or three minutes, peering at it from across the road. There had been no car in the drive, and Miriam had moved on without saying anything. She was impossibly quiet this morning.

As they sat in the café, drinking oversweetened Cola and sharing packets of crisps, Claire saw two boys come in. One of them she recognized at once, with a tiny surge of excitement: it was Benjamin Trotter. The other one, presumably, was his younger brother. They seemed to be quarrelling.

"They don't like us being in this sort of place, you know that," Benjamin was saying.

"That, O Well-behaved One, is the whole point of coming here. Blimey, I sat through that bleeding church service with you. The least you can do is stand me a cup of char and a slice."

"A cup of char and a slice? Where do you pick up these stupid expressions? Anyway, I'm not buying you anything."

"That sermon," said Paul, fishing in his pocket for a ten pence piece, "was a masterpiece of intellectual vacuity."

"I don't know why you came anyway. You know I'd rather go on my own."

"Now that my weak-minded brother has fallen into the hands of religious maniacs, I have to keep a protective eye on him." Paul handed Benjamin the money and nodded meaningfully in the direction of Miriam and Claire. "Get me something tasty, and I'll start making headway with those two dishy chicks over there. I bet we can score."

Before Benjamin could stop him, Paul had placed himself at a table next to the sisters, and was already addressing some remark, doubtless of an impertinent nature, at the elder of the two. Benjamin bought two cans of lemonade and hurried over. By now he had spotted Claire and recognized her, but this didn't make the situation any easier, as far as he was concerned. He had no idea what he was going to say, and matters were not helped by the fact that his voice was currently in the process of breaking, and he hadn't the least way of knowing, from minute to minute, at what pitch his words were likely to emerge.

Claire saved him the trouble, in any case, by announcing, "You're Benjamin," in an authoritative way as soon as he appeared, and grabbing one of the cans off him with the words, "Give us a swig."

"I'm sorry about my brother," Benjamin stammered. "He's a pain."

Paul stuck his tongue out, then turned to Miriam and said, "I'll show you mine if you'll show me yours." She stared back at him as if he were pond life.

"You go to King William's, don't you?" Claire continued. "I've seen you on the bus."

"That's right," said Benjamin. It was hardly a brilliant rejoinder. He sucked ferociously on his straw while thinking of something else to say. "Have you both just been to church?" he asked.

"*Church?*" she repeated, incredulous. An abrupt silence fell after that, until Claire, obviously not thinking this topic even worth mentioning again, said to Benjamin challengingly: "I've noticed you with your friends. You always look really snooty and arrogant."

"Oh. Well we're not really. At least, I don't think we are."

"You know Philip Chase, don't you?"

"That's right. He's my best friend."

"And you know Duggie Anderton."

Miriam looked over: a sudden, violent jerk of the head.

"*Duggie?*" said Benjamin. "No one calls him Duggie."

"Oh," said Claire. "I thought that was what people called him." She noticed the livid pallor of her sister's face, and saw at once that it had been a mistake even to mention the family name. She changed the subject quickly. "I wish we did more things together, don't you? The two schools, I mean."

"Yes," said Benjamin. "That would be nice." This suggestion set him on a rapid train of thought, and he asked, casually: "You don't know a girl called Cicely, do you? Cicely Boyd?"

Claire raised her eyes to the ceiling. "God, why do *all* the boys in your school go on about Cicely? Why are they so obsessed with her?" Clearly, Benjamin had touched a nerve. "I mean, what *is* it about her? It's not even as if she's very good-looking."

"Oh, but she is," he countered. "She's beautiful." It was out before he could stop himself.

Claire smiled icily. "I see. Do we have a little schoolboy crush on our hands, by any chance?" She pulled open a new packet of crisps and said, without offering him one: "Well I can tell you one thing: *you're* not going to be at the head of the queue."

"I know," said Benjamin. Her remark had been intended purely to hurt; but he took it for a melancholy truth. "It's Harding that all the girls fancy, isn't it? Just because he's so funny all the time."

"No," Claire scoffed. "Nobody fancies him. He's just good for a laugh. There's only one boy in your year that *everybody's* crazy about."

Benjamin waited for her to elaborate, but apparently it was too obvious to need spelling out. In the end he hazarded a guess. "Is it Culpepper?"

"Culpepper! Give me a break. He's Mister Repulsive."

"OK then: who?"

"Richards, of course."

Benjamin was dumbfounded. "You mean Rastus?"

Claire gasped, and almost choked on a crisp. "You don't call him that, do you?"

"Why not?"

"It's so . . . insulting."

"No it's not. It's a joke."

"You can't call him Rastus just because he's black. How would you like it if nobody ever called you by your real name?"

"Nobody does. Not at school, anyway. They call me Bent."

Claire seemed on the point of giggling at this, or making some caustic reply. But she thought better of it, and now said, without any preamble: "Do you want to come out with me some time?"

"Come out with you?" said Benjamin, as his stomach performed a somersault and a delicious panic took hold of him.

"There's a disco in the church hall this Tuesday. We could go along together and boogie on down."

He had never boogied on down in his life. The prospect was simply terrifying. With some relief he found himself able to say, "I'm already going out on Tuesday. I'm going to a gig at Barbarella's."

Barbarella's was one of Birmingham's trendier night-spots,

and Benjamin's offhand reference to this venue, in combination
with the word "gig," had a marked effect. Claire looked highly
impressed.

"Really?" she said. "Who are you going with?"

"The Hairy Guy."

"Who?"

"Malcolm. My sister's boyfriend. He's taking me along to
see Hatfield and the North."

"Never heard of them. Can I come too?"

"No," said Benjamin decisively. "You wouldn't like the
music. It's very complex and difficult. A bit like Henry Cow."

"Never heard of him either."

"It's just not the kind of thing girls like, I'm afraid."

"Just as I said," said Claire, scrunching up her crisp packet
in a fury. "Snooty and arrogant."

At which point, the sound of a hand making sharp contact
with somebody else's cheek announced that the adjacent conversation had come to a climax. Miriam pushed back her chair
and rose sharply to her feet.

"Your brother," she said to Benjamin, "has got a mind like
the municipal sewer. Come on, you." She grabbed her sister by
the arm and pulled her towards the door, turning only to add:
"And I thought I'd heard everything!"

As they left the café Benjamin managed to snatch just a
moment's eye contact with Claire; and then they were gone,
leaving him bereft; gripped, after all, by an overwhelming sense
of lost opportunity.

"What *did* you say to her?" he was about to ask Paul. But he
saw the smirk on his brother's evil little face, and decided that he
didn't want to know.

In his bedroom that afternoon, Benjamin worked on his latest
composition. It was a piece for two guitars, lasting about a
minute and a half. He had hit upon a primitive overdubbing
technique, having worked out that if you recorded one of the
guitar parts on a cassette machine, you could then play along

with the tape and perform a sort of duet. This piece was in A minor and was provisionally entitled "Cicely's Song." He had toyed, briefly, with the idea of changing it to "Claire's Song": but that would have been fickle. Besides, it was exciting that someone should have asked him out, but really, Claire couldn't hold a candle to Cicely. In looks or personality. There was no comparison to be made between them.

The second guitar part was pretty difficult. An F sharp major seven had popped into the chord sequence from somewhere— it just sounded right—which meant that at this point in the melody, he had to play a C sharp rather than a C natural. It felt peculiar, and he kept getting it wrong. But then, this was what being a musical pioneer was all about. He was going to have to write even weirder things, he told himself, if he wanted to sound like Henry Cow. Malcolm had said that he'd come and listen to Benjamin playing it, the next time he visited the house. He would have to be note perfect by then.

As for Lois, she was being surprisingly relaxed about this unlikely friendship. There didn't seem to be anything that could upset her at the moment. Malcolm had transformed her. She was in her last year at school, and had already applied for a place at Birmingham University so that she wouldn't have to be separated from him when she left. He could do nothing wrong in her eyes, and if he'd decided to take her brother under his wing and lead him through some kind of bizarre musical education, that was fine. Even Colin and Sheila, on being asked whether Benjamin could go to Barbarella's with him on Tuesday night, had given their blessing. That was a measure of how much the family had come to trust him.

"Are you *sure* you don't mind?" Benjamin had asked Lois, the day before. "It's all right if he takes me, and you stay at home?"

"Of course it is," said Lois. "You know I don't like that kind of music. And I'm going to be busy with this dress, anyway." She had just been given a purple velvet maxi dress for her seventeenth birthday, and it needed taking in. It had to be ready by

Thursday, because that was their anniversary: one year on, not from their first date, but from the day that Malcolm had received her letter, forwarded from the offices of *Sounds.* "He's taking me out to dinner," she said, "and he told me to get dressed up. We're doing something special, apparently. He says he's got a surprise for me."

On Tuesday night at Barbarella's, Benjamin found out what this surprise was going to be. Malcolm fished in his jacket pocket, took out a small leather jeweller's box, and held up a diamond engagement ring for his inspection.

"What do you think of that, then, axeman?"

"Wow," said Benjamin, who knew nothing about jewellery. "It's lovely. Is it real?"

This question provoked a loud guffaw from Reg, Malcolm's friend and the third member of their party. Benjamin had not been told that Reg was coming along, and after a few minutes in his company was already intimidated by his tangle of greying, shoulder-length hair, his florid complexion, his three missing teeth and his habit of laughing at everything that Benjamin said. Reg was of indeterminate age—he could have been anything from twenty-five to fifty—and could sink a pint of Brew in about six seconds flat. The other thing Benjamin noticed was that he smoked the most peculiar-smelling cigarettes he had ever encountered. Malcolm referred to him as "Roll-Up Reg," but he couldn't for the life of him see why.

"Of course it's real," said Reg. "What kind of a cunt do you think he is?"

Constant swearing was another of his traits.

"Eighteen-carat gold, that is," said Malcolm. "Nothing but the best for my Lois."

"How do you know she's going to say yes, you cunt?" asked Reg.

"Well I don't, do I?" He turned to Benjamin. "What do you think, axeman?"

"I think she'll say yes, definitely. I think she's dying to marry you."

Reg went off to buy two more pints of Brew, and a Coke for Benjamin, who was not only too young to be drinking, but too young, technically, to be in the club at all. Malcolm seemed to know the guy on the door, though, and a blind eye had been turned.

"What about the age difference?" Malcolm asked. "D'you think it's too big?"

"I don't know," said Benjamin. "How old are you?"

"Twenty-three."

"That's only six years: the same as my parents."

Malcolm nodded solemnly. He seemed reassured. Benjamin had never seen him looking so nervous.

"How old's Reg, by the way?"

"God knows. I met him when I was a student at Aston. He used to hang around the Arts Lab. We got talking one day. He's all right, you don't have to mind him."

"He swears a lot."

"He's got a good heart."

Benjamin looked around at the audience, milling between the tables, swathed in greatcoats and Afghans. The crowd was ninety-five per cent male. The roof of the club was low, and the ochre lighting glinted weakly against the guitars, amps and drum kit lined up on the stage. They had already heard the first two acts, a singer called Kevin Coyne and the piano/saxophone duo of Steve Miller and Lol Coxhill. The music had been strange, in both cases, but often beautiful, with a skewed logic of its own. The audience had listened in respectful silence, their brows furrowed with concentration. Malcolm had told him that the next band, Hatfield and the North, would probably be more accessible, more fun, but Benjamin could still understand, on the whole, why Lois had decided to stay at home.

"When are you going to marry her?" he asked.

"Not till the summer, I suppose," said Malcolm. "When

she's left school. I'm going to stick at this job for a few more months, save up some money, then when we've tied the knot we can head off for a while. Before she goes to college. India, New Zealand. Maybe the Far East."

"Lois would love that," said Benjamin.

"Perhaps we could honeymoon at the Taj Mahal."

"That'd be brilliant."

Roll-Up Reg came back with their drinks.

"Where are you taking her on Thursday night, then?" he asked. "Where are you doing the dirty deed?"

"I thought we'd start with The Grapevine, round about eight. Then we're going to . . ." he searched in his pocket again, and produced a card ". . . this new place. I booked a table for nine o'clock."

"*Papa Luigi's Pasta and Spaghetti di Milano,*" Benjamin read, before handing the card back. "What kind of restaurant's that?"

"Italian," said Malcolm.

"You haven't travelled much, have you?" Roll-Up Reg demolished his pint in a single draught and let out an almighty belch. "God, I'm a filthy cunt," he said, and picked up a copy of the *NME* from a nearby stool. "Here, how much did you pay to get in here, Malc?"

"69p each."

"We could have got in for forty-nine, if we'd brought one of these."

He showed Malcolm a coupon, indicating that this event was part of something called The *NME*/Virgin Crisis Tour. The idea, it seemed, was to bring a little cheer into the lives of Britain's downtrodden young music-lovers, who were continuing to suffer the effects of yet more strikes and fuel shortages. The second general election of the year had been held a few weeks earlier, and another Labour government had been elected—this time with a majority of three—but nobody thought that this would make much difference.

"This cunt Branson—he's all right, isn't he?"

"I reckon he is," said Malcolm.

They explained to Benjamin that Richard Branson was the head of Virgin Records.

"You need men like that, you see," Malcolm told him. "Idealists. People who aren't just in it for the money. Otherwise, what kind of society have you got?"

"Are you a socialist?" Reg asked. "Or a Tory cunt?"

"I don't know," said Benjamin. "A Tory cunt, I suppose."

He roared with laughter again.

"And I bet you think the IRA are a bunch of murdering Micks, don't you? And our boys in Belfast are the salt of the fucking earth?"

"Give him time, Reg. He goes to a posh school. He hasn't had the chance to learn."

"Buy him *The Ragged Trousered Philanthropists* for his birthday. And some George Orwell, while you're at it." Reg leaned almost into Benjamin's face. His breath was a potent mixture of beer and that curious tobacco. "You've got to wake up, sonny, sooner or later. You've got to wake up to what's happening in this country."

"You mean with the unions?"

"No, I don't mean with the unions. The unions are the good guys, you see. I mean the people who are getting together *against* the unions. I'm talking about retired colonels with dodgy ideas who are putting private armies together. With money from the banks and the multi-nationals. And friends in the Tory party." He sat back, winked enigmatically, and concluded, "I'm telling you, there's some far-out shit going on in dear old Blighty at the moment."

Malcolm agreed. "Scary times on the event horizon," he muttered.

"Meanwhile," said Reg, "Malcolm here, the treacherous cunt, is all set to become a paid-up member of the fucking *boorzhwah-zee!*" He slapped him on the back, fondly, but very hard. Malcolm gave a wan smile. "And by the way, I'll give you a bit of advice, for nothing. Don't take her to The Grapevine."

"Why not?"

"Because the beer tastes like piss, and at that time of night it'll be full of cunts in suits."

"So where should I take her?"

"I don't know," said Reg, pulling out another Rizla. "The Tavern in the Town?"

None of this made any sense to Benjamin, however hard he tried. Roll-Up Reg was talking another language. But then, he was no more persuaded by the things his parents told him, or the teachers at school. It was the world, the world itself that was beyond his reach, this whole absurdly vast, complex, random, measureless construct, this never-ending ebb and flow of human relations, political relations, cultures, histories . . . How could anyone hope to master such things? It was not like music. Music always made sense. The music he heard that night was lucid, knowable, full of intelligence and humour, wistfulness and energy and hope. He would never understand the world, but he would always love this music. He listened to this music, with God by his side, and knew that he had found a home.

10

On the night of Thursday, November 21st, 1974, Lois and Malcolm met at a quarter to eight, on the south-east corner of Holloway Circus, outside the Odeon Queensway. They cut through the Smallbrook underpass and walked down Hill Street, a route which gave them a view of the Jacey Cinema, where customers were this week being offered a choice between *Girls Led Astray*, *When Girls Undress* and *Love Play Swedish Style*.

They giggled at these titles.

"I don't need to see films like that," said Malcolm. "You're my girl led astray."

"What about some love play, Birmingham style?" said Lois.

They were both shivering, with cold and anticipation. They were both wearing long overcoats, so Malcolm had not yet had a chance to see Lois's purple velvet maxi dress.

At the junction of Navigation Street and Stephenson Street, in the doorway of Hudson's bookshop, Malcolm put his arms around Lois and said, "I love you, you know."

"I love you too," she said, and they kissed for more than a minute, hungrily at first, then tenderly, Malcolm's hand buried deep in her hair, Lois's hand caressing his neck.

"I thought we'd better do some kissing now," he said. "They'd throw us out if we did this in the pub." Then, noticing something, he pulled away. "What's the matter, love?"

There were tears in Lois's eyes.

"I'm so happy," she said. "You've made me so happy."

They continued up Stephenson Street and turned right into New Street. The city centre felt quiet, friendly, peaceable. There were several other couples their own age, off to the pub or the restaurant. It seemed like a good night for lovers.

The Tavern in the Town was below street level, and after dark, that made it a cosy, welcoming place. You walked down a short flight of stairs and turned into a large, open-plan area, broken up by brickwork columns, the beer-pumps gleaming behind an L-shaped bar, lights flickering on the fruit machines and the juke box, the whole room alive with voices, music, the sound of people enjoying themselves, the sound of fun. Malcolm knew a couple of the customers and nodded greetings. He took Lois by the arm and helped her through the crowd. She was always a little nervous going into pubs, even now. She was still underage, and kept thinking she was going to bump into one of her teachers, although what Mrs. Ridley or Miss Winterton might be doing here she couldn't imagine. It was very busy. Malcolm was worried that they wouldn't be able to find a table, but then he spotted one: there was one still empty, by some stroke of good fortune, the good fortune he knew he was blessed with that night. He sat Lois down, made sure she was comfortable, then went to get the drinks. All she wanted was a tonic water, she wanted to keep a clear head for the restaurant, she wanted to enjoy the food, and the wine they were going to have with it. Malcolm got himself a half. He didn't want to overdo it either.

He marvelled at the dress, told her that she looked fantastic in it. They held hands at the table, and didn't notice the people standing up on either side of them, pressing in close.

"I can't believe it's a year," said Malcolm.

"I know," said Lois. "It's incredible."

"What would have happened if you hadn't seen my advert?"

"What would have happened if you'd chosen one of the others?"

"I only got two answers," he said.

"That's even worse. Suppose you'd gone for her, instead of me."

"It doesn't bear thinking about."

"Our lives would have been totally different."

He kissed her hand and after a while went to get two more drinks. When he got back, it was sixteen minutes past eight, and Lois was humming softly along with the juke box.

"I love this record," she said. "This is my favourite. Don't you love it?"

It was a cover version of "I Get a Kick Out of You," sung by Gary Shearston. It had been in the charts for ages. Lois closed her eyes and joined in with the words.

> I get no kick from champagne
> Mere alcohol doesn't thrill me at all

Malcolm put down his glass and began singing as well.

> So tell me why should it be true,
> That I get a kick out of you?

Lois was surprised to hear him singing. She had never heard him sing before. It made her laugh.

"I didn't think you liked that kind of song," she said.

"The old ones are always the best." He leaned forward eagerly. "Hey—that's what we should have tonight."

"What—cocaine?" said Lois, because the next verse had started.

"No, silly: champagne. Let's splash out on a bottle."

"Can you afford it?"

"Sure. It's a special occasion." And then, taking the long-awaited plunge, he added: "More special than you think."

Lois's heart skipped a beat. "What do you mean?"

Malcolm fingered the leather box in his jacket pocket. He had not meant to ask her so early, but it was no use: he couldn't contain himself.

"Look, love, you know what I think about you, don't you?"

Lois didn't answer. She just looked back at him, her eyes starting to brim over.

"I love you," said Malcolm. "I'm crazy about you." He took a long breath, an enormous breath. "I've got to say something to you. I've got to ask you something." He grasped her hand, and squeezed it tightly. As if he would never let go. "Do you know what it is?"

Of course she knew. And of course, Malcolm knew what her answer would be. They understood each other perfectly, at that moment. They were as close to each other, and as close to happiness, as it is possible for two people to be. So Malcolm never did ask the question.

Then, at 8:20 precisely, the timing device set off the trigger, the battery pack sent power running through the cables, and thirty pounds of gelignite exploded on the far side of the pub.

And that was how it all ended, for the chick and the hairy guy.

The Very Maws of Doom

I

. . . my clearest memory is of the light we saw there, that painters' sky, greyblue like Marie's eyes and like her grandsons' eyes, the colour of a pain that won't go away . . .

Sometimes I feel that I am destined always to be offstage whenever the main action occurs. That God has made me the victim of some cosmic practical joke, by assigning me little more than a walk-on part in my own life. Or sometimes I feel that my rôle is simply to be a spectator to other people's stories, and always to wander away at the most important moment, drifting into the kitchen to make a cup of tea just as the denouement unfolds.

This is by way of apology, I should explain; for I'm about to start telling a story without knowing how it ends. Or at least, I have a version of the ending, but it is only Paul's version: and Paul likes to keep his secrets. But it's a story worth telling, all the same, so I shall give you as much as I know.

It begins in July, 1976, when my father came into the living room one evening while we were all watching television and broke some astonishing news: he told us that we were going to be spending our summer holidays in Denmark this year.

Now, "astonishing" is not a word that I use lightly, and this proposal did indeed mark an audacious and unprecedented break with family tradition. Every summer, for as long as I could remember, we had gone to the same place for our holidays: the Llŷn peninsula in North Wales, where we would pitch our caravan in a windswept field, surrounded by sheep and bracken, and steel ourselves for a three-week battle with the elements, for our arrival there was inevitably followed by a season of ferocious gales and pitiless rain. (It's one more irony, then, in a life which I suspect is destined to be riddled with them, that the very summer we chose not to spend in Wales turned out to be the hottest in memory.) This year, it seemed, everything was to be different. My father had just been speaking on the telephone to his friend from Germany, Gunther Baumann, who had made a generous offer: would we all like to spend two weeks with his family, in a house they had rented for the summer in Skagen, at the very northernmost tip of Denmark?

Five minutes later, my father called Munich to accept this proposal with enthusiasm.

Herr Baumann was my father's German counterpart, you might say. He was a personnel manager at BMW, and over the last two years they had paid several visits to each other's factories, in order to compare working practices and to share thoughts on the difficult subject of industrial relations. It was an informal, mutually beneficial arrangement which in time had led to a friendship. My mother and my brother and I had all met our German "uncle" several times and felt that we knew him well enough now to call him "Gunther."

We did not know the other members of his family, however, and our first sight of them was when we pulled up outside the house in Gammel Skagen one warm August afternoon. We had flown to Copenhagen, connected to Ålborg, and there my father had hired a car in which we drove through a landscape which seemed at once alien and oddly familiar: it had a pale, unassuming loveliness which reminded me of my own country, and yet as we travelled further north there was the hint of something freer and wilder in its low blue sky and sparse, desert-like expanses of grassy sand. Almost at the very tip of Jutland we turned left off the main road (the only road, by now), away from Skagen itself and into Gammel Skagen, no more than a cluster of handsome, yellow-stone summer houses, really, huddled around a tiny inn and then spreading out along the beach. And there the Baumanns were, waiting for us in the doorway. Gunther with his bald pate, glazed nutbrown by the sun, looking with his cherry-wood pipe and lustrous beard every inch the nineteenth-century moral philosopher—an impression somewhat at odds with his stripy blue T-shirt and knee-length shorts; and beside him his wife Lisa, a tiny figure in strawberry-pink summer dress and high heels, with make-up and jewellery more suited to a night out in a restaurant than an afternoon by the beach. And then there were the children, not one of whom seemed to bear the slightest relation to their progenitors; for all three of them were, not to put too fine a point on it, fat; not only their youngest son Rolf but also, I was disappointed to see, his twin sisters Ursula and Ulrike, who were not much older than me and on whose company I had been pinning high hopes; hopes which were swiftly dashed to the ground by their unfortunate complexions, severe steel-rimmed spectacles and sly, giggling demeanours. Though this, in its way, was also a relief. It meant that my loyalty would not be tested. (My loyalty to she who doesn't know that I exist.)

The house itself was glorious. It stood right on the beach and its great, high windows allowed tremendous vistas on to the silver breakers which pounded the length of the seemingly endless strand. It had been built slightly apart from the rest of the village and had only one near neighbour, a more modest dwelling which nonetheless shared the same extraordinary views; shared more than that, in fact, for neither house had a proper back garden, merely stretches of rough turf which touched, blended and then ran together into the rising mass of dunes behind.

Paul and I were so excited by this new habitat that we didn't even baulk at the sleeping arrangements: we were to sleep together in the sitting room, on a pair of camp beds. Normally I had little to say to my brother; but that night, after the thrill of arrival had subsided, I felt my first and only pang of homesickness, listening to the angry roar of the waves and watching the moonlight throw eerie shadows around the room. I whispered to him as we lay wakeful in the dark:

"I'm sorry we couldn't go to Wales this year."

"We go to Wales every year," he answered. "If it was up to you and Mother, this family would never do anything new or interesting at all. I like this place."

"So do I," I admitted, "but I was thinking of Grandma and Grandpa."

My mother's parents always came to Wales with us, staying at a guest house on the road to Porth Ceiriad bay. This year they would be going by themselves, and I knew that they would miss us.

"They'll be fine," Paul said, dismissively. "Now let's get to sleep. I want to swim before breakfast tomorrow."

It was new to me, this enthusiasm for swimming on my brother's part. He is naturally slight of stature, but I realized over the next few days that he must have been taking a lot of exercise recently; his arms had grown strong and muscular, and the solid wall of muscle that had begun to appear on his stomach was explained by the production of a Bullworker from his suitcase: one of those fierce-looking devices which you see advertised in the back pages of magazines and comics, promising the sort of physique which will bring bikini-clad girls running admiringly towards you on the beach. It turned out that he was by far the best swimmer out of our party, ploughing ahead of Rolf through the ocean's choppy depths while Ulrike, Ursula and I would remain floundering in the shallows.

I am not, in any case, one of nature's athletes. Because the countryside around us was completely flat I was happy to make use of the bicycles which we found at the house, but rarely for purposes more energetic than a journey to Skagen itself. Here I found pursuits more to my taste. I spent many hours in the Skagens Museum, which housed a fine collection of paintings by the members of the Skagen school who worked there in the early years of the century, drawn to this Northern outcrop by the special quality of light reflected from the surrounding seas. I enjoyed lingering by the busy harbour, watching the boats arrive with their vast trawls of skate and flounder and herring. I rode out towards Hulsig with my mother and father, to visit the Sand-Filled Church, once the parish church of Skagen but now almost half-buried by the drifting dunes. And it was pleasant simply to walk through Skagen itself, along the tranquil backwater of Østerbyvej, where the yellow and gold houses, with their half-timber work and tarred gables, seemed as trim, courteous and well-meaning as the Danes who inhabited them.

But none of these words, sadly, could be applied to the Danish boys who lived next door to us at Gammel Skagen.

Their names were Jorgen and Stefan, and they shared their small house with an elderly couple whom we took to be their grandparents. I would have guessed that Stefan was about fifteen, Jorgen perhaps two or three years older. From the very beginning, they seemed to take a dislike to us; or at least, if not to all of us, then certainly to the Baumanns; or rather, if not to all of the Baumanns, then certainly to Rolf, whom they teased, taunted and bullied at every opportunity.

Rolf was a strong but clumsy and awkward boy of fourteen. Like all of the Baumanns he spoke excellent English and on this holiday, much to my surprise, he formed a rapid and powerful bond with my brother, who does not make friendships easily. They would engage in swimming contests, run races along the beach, disappear for long cycle rides together and play inexhaustible games of "three and in" with a football on the back lawn. It was in the middle of one of these games, as I watched from my reading chair at the sitting-room window, that Jorgen and Stefan first came to talk to them.

"Hey! Germans!" Jorgen called out. "This is *our* back garden. Who said you could play your stupid games of football on our lawn?"

Rolf said nothing; just looked at the two tall Danes apprehensively.

Paul said: "I'm not German, I'm from England. And this is the back of our house, as well as yours."

"But your friend is German, yes? He looks like a *tyg Tysker*." (Meaning "fat German," I was later told.)

"His name's Rolf," my brother said, "and I'm Paul. And I bet we can beat you six-nil if we play for ten minutes each way."

By this means he managed to defuse the situation, and soon the four of them were involved in a keenly fought contest. Perhaps too keenly fought, to tell the truth: for I could see that every time a goal was scored, it was bitterly disputed by the opposing side, and other loud arguments would erupt every minute or two. The two Danish boys played aggressively, homing in on Rolf whenever he had possession and often scything him to the ground with a vicious tackle. Later that evening I heard him protesting to his mother that he had bruises all over his shins.

"I don't like those boys," he complained again, as we all sat down to dinner that night in the enormous family kitchen. "They're too tough and too rude."

"We still beat them, though," Paul boasted. "A notable victory for the Anglo-German alliance."

"You didn't take part, Benjamin?" Gunther asked, as he passed me a plate of cheese and cold meat.

"My brother doesn't play games," said Paul. "He's an aesthete. He sat by the window all afternoon with a funny look on his face: probably composing a tone poem."

"Really?" said Gunther. "I knew you were hoping to be a writer, Benjamin. You compose music, as well?"

"Not really," I answered, shooting Paul a resentful glance. "I just like to write tunes sometimes, inspired by people, or places."

"Well." Gunther seemed impressed. "Perhaps you would try to compose something inspired by my two beautiful daughters."

I looked across at the Gruesome Twosome, as Paul and I had privately designated the twins, and could not imagine anything more unlikely.

"Perhaps," I demurred.

"How's the car, Gunther?" my father asked, introducing a welcome change of subject.

"Oh, it's not too bad. A little scratch. Nothing that can't be put right easily enough when we get home."

Earlier in the day Lisa had contrived to damage their car—a large BMW estate—while driving to the supermarket in Skagen with her two daughters. She had gone the wrong way down a one-way street, then attempted to perform a three-point turn which went badly awry. The car had actually got jammed sideways in the narrow carriageway and another German holiday-maker had had to rescue her, by completing the turn himself. We were beginning to realize that Lisa was prone to such disasters. The previous night she had broken two plates while doing the washing-up, and I had heard my mother remarking loudly, "You'd think she'd never seen the inside of a kitchen before." I could see that the two women were unlikely to become friends.

There was something untamed and out of control about the Danish boys, it was clear; some kind of instability which made them unpredictable and prone (in Jorgen's case) to sudden acts of aggression. Their grandparents—whom they called Mormor and Morfar—were unfailingly polite and friendly towards us, but every time we tried to play with Jorgen and Stefan, some sort of violence or injury was the outcome, and usually the victim was Rolf. When they weren't attacking him with their fists or their feet, they would attack him with words.

"Hey, German," I heard Jorgen say to him once on the beach. "What did your father do in the War? Was he a Nazi?"

"Don't be stupid," Rolf replied. "My father was only a child during the War."

"If he'd been old enough, I bet he would have been in the Gestapo," said Jorgen, and his brother added, "Yes: just like Bernhard."

None of us had any idea what they might have meant, and I was amazed by the fortitude and resilience with which Rolf bore these insults. It seemed to be almost the case that the more they bullied him, the more eagerly he sought out their company and fought for their approval.

One afternoon, Rolf stayed behind at the house with his mother and sisters, while the rest of us rode our bicycles up to Grenen, at the northern end of the peninsula. We had been told that it was the meeting place of two seas, the Kattegat and the Skagerrak, but I had not appreciated what a strange sight this would be. As we walked the slow distance along the beach towards the very edge of Denmark, the sun was shining brilliantly and the ocean was a breathtaking aquamarine: but I should say oceans, rather, for what we saw, where our path petered out into a sandy nothingness, were two sets of breakers rolling into each other, a beginning and an ending with no distinction between them, just furrows of clear water running together in wave upon wave of foamy, promiscuous couplings. It was such a delightful, eccentric sight that we wanted to laugh out loud. But the guide who drove us back to the car park (in a peculiar, hybrid vehicle consisting of a railway coach towed by a tractor) assured us that the waters at this point were anything but playful. There was no more dangerous place to bathe, he said, in the whole of Jutland, and the attempts of some swimmers to follow a course between the two seas had led to many fatalities.

When we arrived back at the house, you would have thought from the commotion that a fatality had already occurred: for Lisa, Ulrike, Ursula and Rolf were all in tears, although only the latter had any reason, in the form of a rather impressive black eye. We guessed, correctly and at once, that it was Jorgen who had given it to him. After his father had heard the story—a somewhat confused affair, to do with a row of beer bottles, a stone-throwing competition, and an elaborate set of rules which somebody or other had breached—he sat in the kitchen for many minutes, frowning heavily. Then he stood up and announced, "I'm sorry, but this ridiculous business has started to ruin the holiday," and went next door to speak to the boys' grandparents.

There were two immediate consequences. Later in the evening, both Jorgen and Stefan called round, apologized to Rolf, and shook him by the hand: a gesture which for some reason occasioned more crying on the part of the twins, but seemed to satisfy everybody else. More unexpectedly, Rolf, Paul and I received an invitation to go round to our neighbours' house the next afternoon for tea. We were told that Marie (for this, it appeared, was the grandmother's name) particularly wanted to speak to us.

We arrived at the appointed hour, four o'clock.

There is a certain kind of smell you find in old people's houses. I'm not talking about anything unclean, I just mean that there is often a smell of memories, of doors which have been left shut for a long time, a kind of heavy, nostalgic inwardness which can be close and oppressive. Here, there was quite the opposite. Every room was clean, airy and flooded with light from the sparkling ocean. It was so bright in the sitting room, in fact, that the blinds had to be pulled partly shut as we settled ourselves into the sofas and armchairs. The furniture was smart and unfaded but it seemed ancient compared to the low, angular, modernist fittings of our own beach house.

Marie was a tiny yet forceful woman, whose face—once fair, I imagined—seemed to have been scribbled over many times by the Skagen wind and sun until it formed a complex manuscript, a palimpsest of wrinkles and serrations. She served us curious open sandwiches followed by rich, glutinous pastries, and laughed when I asked for milk with my camomile tea, saying that I could have it if I wanted, but it wasn't the custom. Paul smiled and looked superior. Her husband Julius was very tall and very dark and very short of breath; he sat in an upright chair and leaned on his walking stick and never spoke a word all afternoon, just watched his wife's every move with adoring steadiness.

After we had eaten, and made halting conversation about our impressions of Skagen and our homes back in Munich and Birmingham, Marie cleared her throat.

"I wanted to talk to you," she said, "about my grandsons, Jorgen and Stefan. I gather there was an unfortunate happening yesterday afternoon." (Rolf touched his black eye.) "I know they have apologized, so I won't say anything more about it. But I have been watching you playing together over the last week and I must say it has given me great pleasure. I know there have been quarrels but I don't suppose you realize how unusual it is for them to play with other children at all. I want very much, very much indeed, for you all to be friends for the rest of your stay here and perhaps even for longer, and that is why I should like to tell you some things about who they are and why they behave as they sometimes do."

I wondered, briefly, where the two boys were at this moment. Obviously she had sent them away on some errand, in order that she could speak freely to us.

"It is not because you are German that they have been nasty to you," said Marie, looking at Rolf now. "You may think this is the case, when I tell you their story, but I don't believe so. Anyway, it is for you to judge. I must simply warn you that this story is very long and I hope you will be patient with me when I presume to tell you things about my family that happened many years ago, before you were even born.

"To begin, then: we are a Jewish family. My ancestors, who were Sephardic Jews, came to Denmark in the seventeenth century, from Portugal, and we lived here in peace for almost three hundred years. I was born in the very year this century began, and I married Julius in the nineteen-twenties. We had only one daughter. Her name was Inger. In those days we lived in a little town about sixty miles west of Copenhagen. The name of the town is not important. Julius was a lawyer and I looked after the house and some of the time I taught in one of the local schools.

"I don't know what they teach you in your history lessons these days, but every Danish schoolchild knows that the Germans invaded Denmark in April 1940, and from that time until the end of the War, this was an occupied country. I will not say that it was a terrible time to be a Jew—the really terrible time came later—but it was very difficult. There was no real persecution at first, but it was always in the air, as a threat. There were Gestapo men on every street. Many households had German officers billeted on them. Some Jewish families changed their names. Nobody fled, at first, because there was nowhere to flee to. Germany to the south, occupied Norway to the north. You could not get to Britain, because the Germans were patrolling the seas. Only Sweden remained neutral, but it had given no sign that it would open its borders to Danish Jews.

"Inger left school when she was sixteen, in the summer of 1943. She started to earn some money waiting tables in a café in the town square, but had not yet decided what she was going to do with herself. It was impossible to plan for the future anyway. Everything in her life was uncertain: except for one thing. She was in love with a man. A man called Emil. He was the son of one of my husband's friends, a local doctor. Also a Jew. She had known Emil for less than a year but she loved him with the intensity that only a very young girl is capable of. And he was very handsome, actually. Here. Here is a photo."

She took down a small unframed black and white photograph from the mantelpiece and handed it to me. I sensed that it was not usually kept on display; that she had retrieved it today from some long unvisited drawer or album specifically to show to us. We passed it around carefully, handling it as if it were a sacred relic. Two young people, a man and a woman, sat on a wooden bench in the arbour of a rose garden and gazed at the camera. They had their arms around each other, cheek to cheek, and were smiling blissfully. I suppose there must be hundreds, thousands, hundreds of thousands of photographs like this in existence. It was hard to say what was so special about this one, except that there was something about the lovers' smiles that made it more than just the record of one passing moment in time. There was nothing transitory, nothing evanescent about those smiles. There was an agelessness about the picture. I felt that it could have been taken yesterday.

"Here. Here is another."

This time the lovers were sitting at a table in a café—perhaps the one where Inger had used to work—and there was a third person in the frame with them. A tall, burly, fair-haired man in uniform.

"Who's that?" I asked.

"His name was Bernhard. He was a German officer, who was staying with a family just along the street from us."

Emil and Inger were again looking at the camera. Bernhard was looking half at the camera, and half at them. The intimacy between them was violated, this time, partly by the way he looked at them, and partly by his very presence. It was an eloquent photograph. It told its unhappy story concisely, and without ambiguity.

"As you can see from this picture, Bernhard had feelings for Inger. He had met her at the café but also before that when she was still at school. Because she was a Jew and because of what he had been told to believe about Jews it made things worse. He must have hated himself for the way he felt about her, and hated her too, in some sense. It was a very bad situation. And of course he couldn't bear the fact that she was in love with Emil, another Jew. Many times he had made advances to my daughter, and she turned him away. Once . . . Inger never told me the whole story, but he was violent towards her. I don't think he actually raped her, he was not quite an animal in that way, but it was an ugly scene. Humiliating for him, one imagines. But it didn't turn him against her. He kept bringing her flowers, chocolates, stupid things like that. It was Emil that he was determined to punish.

Emil was beaten quite badly in the street one night and I have always thought that Bernhard might have been responsible for that.

"And then, in October 1943, everything changed. An order came from Germany to say that the presence of the Jews in Denmark was no longer to be tolerated. We were to be arrested and shipped to the concentration camps. The Gestapo were planning to raid all Jewish homes throughout Denmark on the nights of October 1st and 2nd.

"The story of the rescue of the Danish Jews is quite famous. It was a proud moment in the history of this country. Word of the German plans was somehow passed to Danish politicians and a clandestine rescue operation began. Jewish congregations were warned of the action that was about to be taken against them and the vast majority went into hiding. The Danish people behaved heroically. They offered sanctuary and hiding places to Jewish people whom they hardly knew. Hospitals and churches were converted into places where large numbers of people could stay undetected. Then the news began to spread that King Gustav of Sweden had made an announcement, declaring himself opposed to the German action and saying that Sweden would give shelter to all Danish Jews who could find their way to his country. This was the first glimmer of hope. The problem was how to get to Sweden.

"Julius and Inger and I had fled to the country, packing as many of our belongings into the car as we could. We took two of Emil's sisters with us, and the rest of his family followed in another car a few hours later. He had three sisters. And then, for many days, we were hiding out in barns and farm buildings in the middle of the countryside. We had no idea what was happening to our homes, whether they had been raided or whether the Germans would come looking for us. They were dreadful days, days of unspeakable terror and anxiety. Except that for Inger and Emil, although they knew the danger they were in, I think there might have been some happiness as well. To sleep under the same roof. To be together in adversity. It sounds a silly thing to say but I think this might have been the case. Things are like that when you are young.

"We waited more than a week for news. Emil's father managed to make telephone contact with some people in Copenhagen who were involved in the resistance and in helping to co-ordinate the rescue of the Jews. At last we were told that if we could make our way to the east coast, north of Copenhagen, there were boats sailing to Sweden from many of the fishing villages there. The details were very vague. It was not clear how big the boats were, or when they were sailing, or whether the fishermen were asking for money to take people across. But we had to take our chance. There was no time to lose. The German High Command was furious that so few of the Jews had been seized, and they were instructing their officers to intensify the search all over the country. And it's true, the Gestapo had been very ineffective, up to this point. They had turned a blind eye to a lot of the people escaping. Bribes were changing hands. They did not really have the stomach for this operation.

"Julius and Emil's father decided that we should attempt to drive to the east coast the next night. We would set out at ten o'clock."

Marie poured some more tea, for herself and for all of us. I noticed that her hand was shaking a little now, as she held the teapot. It had been perfectly steady before.

"The route we chose was a little dangerous," she continued. "It meant passing through the outskirts of our town. That was one of the mistakes we made. The other was that we did not keep our families together. There was no room for Emil, and his mother and father, and his three sisters, and their belongings, all in the same car. His sisters should have travelled with us, as before. That might have been better. But Inger and Emil wanted to be together, and so it was they who travelled with Julius and myself. They sat in the back of our car.

"By ten-thirty we had almost passed through the outskirts of our town and it seemed that the first moment of danger might be over. Then we saw that Emil's father, who was driving the car in front, had been stopped in the middle of the road. There were four German officers and they were making him get out of the car and they were shining torches on to the faces of his family. Julius put on the brakes at once and said that we should turn back. There was still time to turn back and try another route. But I stopped him and said, Look. You see what they are doing. And Julius looked and he could see that Emil's father was handing money over to the German officers. It's all right, I said, all they want is a bribe. We have money, don't we? And Julius said, Yes, we have money, but not that much.

"Now Emil's father was still talking to three of the officers, and giving them money, when the fourth one walked away from the group and came over to our car. It was Bernhard. He recognized us at once and he took out his torch and he shined it on to each of our faces in turn. He shined it on to Emil's face for a long time. He didn't say anything when he did this, but I could see into his eyes and I knew there was a wicked sort of pleasure there and that everything was going to go wrong and something terrible was about to happen.

"Julius said to him, Well, what do you want? Do you want money?, and Bernhard told us all to get out of the car. My heart was pounding as I climbed out but I was also aware that something was happening in the road ahead with Emil's father. The Germans had finished their business with him and they were telling him to be on his way as quickly as possible. I could see that he wanted to wait for our car but they wouldn't let him. Then one of them threatened him with a gun and Emil's father looked back at us and made some movement with his hand, some kind of gesture, and then he got into the car and they drove away. One of the Germans fired a gun into the air as they left and it was a hideous sound, so loud, so shocking, in the middle of the night in that quiet little town. It was starting to rain.

"Now Bernhard had got the four of us, me, Julius, Inger and Emil, all lined up against the car and he said to my husband, How much money have you got? And Julius had to open a suitcase and count all our money and there was just three thousand kroner. So when Bernhard heard that this was all the money we had, he smiled and said, Well, we want four thousand kroner. One thousand for each person. I knew that this was not what they had asked from Emil's father, I knew that he had just made this figure up because he could see that we didn't have enough money. But there was nothing we could do. He took all our money and told us to get back in the car and for a moment I thought this meant that he was going to show mercy. But just as Emil was getting into the car he put his gun against his chest and said, No. Not you.

"By now the other three officers had come over to see what was happening and I heard Bernhard say to them in German, Just this one. And then Inger realized what he was doing and she began screaming and crying. She was saying, No, not my Emil, and . . .

"Well, I think you can imagine what she was saying."

Marie fell silent. We waited for her to tell us the rest of the story. Paul put his plate back on the table. His pastry was only half-eaten.

"I don't think I can talk to you about what happened in the next few hours. I can remember what it was like, but I cannot describe it. The noises that Inger was making, the things—

"Well. To continue. We reached the coast at about two o'clock in the morning. A little port called Humlebaek. Only Emil's father was waiting for us there. His wife and daughters had sailed on a boat about one hour previously. He had stayed behind, to wait for Emil. When he realized that Emil was not with us, he was . . . distraught. There was another boat waiting to take the rest of us away. It was a very black night, there was no moon. We were huddled on the beach, there were about twenty of us. The boat could not wait much longer. I remember Julius took Emil's father aside and they had a long discussion. An argument. They were both shouting. Inger was not saying anything by this time, she was completely silent. After a while Emil's father and my husband came back and then we all climbed into the fishing boat and at last the captain could sail away. It was a long voyage. Very uncomfortable, I remember. We reached Sweden after dawn."

Marie sat back in her chair and took some long breaths. Julius was not looking at her any more. He was still leaning on his stick, but his eyes were closed. There was no noise at all in the room, only the murmur of the waves outside.

"There were eight thousand Jews in Denmark in the summer of 1943," Marie told us. "Nearly all of them escaped to safety, thanks to the courage and the high principles of the Danish people. Just a few hundred were left behind. Emil was one of them.

"The captured Jews were taken back to Germany and then to concentration camps in Czechoslovakia. Some of them committed suicide on the way. I always thought that Emil might have done that. I don't know why, it was just a feeling that I had. Inger never believed it. She always believed that he was alive.

"We lived for two years in Sweden, not very happy years, as you can imagine, and at the end of the War we returned to Denmark. We came back to the same house. It was empty, and waiting for us. Inger was eighteen by now. She waited a few weeks for news of Emil and then she disappeared.

"She was away for many years. She never told us about that time but I know that she went to Czechoslovakia first and then she spent a long time in Germany and other places trying to find out what had happened to Emil. I think she might also have been looking for Bernhard, but again, this is just a suspicion on my part. In any case, she never found either of them. Not a trace of Emil. I knew that she wouldn't. He had died long ago, one way or another. There could be no doubt about that.

"After all she had been through, we knew, Julius and I, that our daughter would never be able to lead a completely normal life. The loss she had suffered was very great. To be so young, and so very deeply in love, and then to have that love . . .

uprooted, in a word, swept away by forces over which you can have no possible control, historical forces . . . You can never recover from something like that, never reconcile yourself to it."

She sipped her tea, which must by now have been quite cold. I was thinking of Lois and Malcolm, and I swallowed hard.

"Anyway, she returned to Denmark at last. This was in the nineteen-fifties. She settled in Copenhagen and married this man, his name is Carl, a businessman, a nice man, not Jewish, as it happens. He was very kind to her, very patient with all her difficulties. They had two sons, Jorgen and Stefan, whom you have met. But . . ." (and now she too closed her eyes for a moment) ". . . there were problems. Continual problems. She was often in hospital. Her behaviour was erratic, her moods were very strange, very changeable. She showed a violent temper, when as a child she had been always gentle and good-natured. It was very hard for the two boys. They had much to endure.

"Julius and I bought this house in 1968, one year after he retired. It had always been a dream of ours to live in Skagen, where we had had so many holidays. Inger and Carl and the boys came to stay with us, just twice, two summers, and they were happy times. Not bad times at all. And then one evening, in the autumn of 1970, Carl telephoned me to say that Inger had died. She had taken the ferry to Malmö, alone, that afternoon, and she had climbed on to the railing, and jumped. She had taken her own life. Just as I had known, in my heart, that she always would."

Having finished her story, Marie rose to her feet and walked to the window. She pulled on the cord of the Venetian blind, and raised the blind to the very top. Instinctively we all turned towards the window, and we looked out at the beach, and when I think of that afternoon now my clearest memory is of the light we saw there, that painters' sky, greyblue like Marie's eyes and like her grandsons' eyes, the colour of a pain that won't go away.

"I'm sorry," she said, smiling graciously at all of us, but especially at Rolf, "I did not intend to burden you with quite so much detail. I know it is very hard to understand these things, when you are only children. But as I said to you, my hope is that you and Jorgen and Stefan might become friends, and have pleasant times together while you are here. I think I have explained enough to make you see that it is not really because you are German that they have sometimes been unkind. Of course, they know the whole history of their mother and Emil and Bernhard—she told it to them many times—but they are not so stupid as that. The truth is simply that they miss their mother very much, and the fact that she is no longer with them makes them angry and sad. I'm sorry if they have turned some of that anger on to you. I think I can promise that it will not happen again."

And then we left, after shaking Julius by his tremulous hand, and after each of us had received a kiss on the cheek from Marie, who then stood in her back porch and waved fondly goodbye to us even though we were only walking ten yards to the house next door.

There is little to say about the next few days.

The second week of our holiday proceeded smoothly, in a flurry of contented activity. Rolf and Paul spent more and more time together, not just swimming and playing energetic games but even holding long, low, earnest conversations on topics which to the rest of us remained thoroughly mysterious. Paul, showing that quick, interdisciplinary aptitude which has always filled me with envy, even seemed to be picking up a smattering of German. The twins and I kept our distance from each other, recognizing that there could be no kinship of spirit between us: they spent most of every day sitting at a card table playing whist and gin rummy, while I read my way steadily through the novels of Henry Fielding in preparation for my first A-level classes in a month's time. Jorgen and Stefan were frequent visitors, and marathon games of rounders and beach cricket brought many of those long cold summer evenings to an enjoyable close. I missed our caravan in Wales, and the company of my grandparents, whatever Paul might have said. But I could not deny that this had been a charmed, magical holiday.

Things only began to go wrong again on the last day but one; and this time it was Lisa and the twins who were responsible.

Ever since her mishap with the family car in the centre of Skagen, Lisa had been reluctant to take it anywhere. Finally, however, perhaps stung into action by the gentle but persistent teasing of her husband, she plucked up courage and drove to Grenen with her daughters. Our description of the oceans' meeting place had pricked her curiosity, it seemed; but once again, catastrophe ensued. Ignoring the prominently displayed warning notices, she had taken the car right out on to the beach, where it promptly collapsed into the yielding sand and could not by any means be extricated. The local rescue service had to be summoned; tractors, policemen and even the fire brigade were involved; and the whole incident provided a most entertaining spectacle for the procession of tourists who had come to visit this beauty spot and now had something even more memorable to record in their photo albums and their postcards home.

The same day, Rolf and Paul had taken a long cycle ride to the eagle sanctuary at Tuen, so that when he returned in the early evening, Rolf had not yet heard the story of his mother's latest ignominy. His first intimation came from the mocking laughter of Jorgen as they walked back through the garden. I was sitting by the window, reading *Joseph Andrews*, and Gunther was on the sofa behind me. We could both hear every word of the conversation.

"What's so funny?" Rolf was asking.

"Did you not hear? Your mother has really done it this time. I thought it was pretty dumb when she blocked the road with that oversized German car of yours in the middle of the town, and managed to cause a traffic jam all the way back to Frederikshavn. But today was even better." He could hardly speak for laughter, so hilarious did he consider the incident. "This time she got it stuck on the Skaw, up at Grenen, when every stupid tourist who comes here knows that you don't take your car on to the sands." Through his forced, throaty chuckling he added: "Tell me, how does it feel to have a mother who can't even get into a car without bringing the whole of the traffic in Jutland to a standstill?"

And now something inside Rolf must have snapped. He had shown that he could put up with almost any amount of abuse when it was directed at him personally, but perhaps it was simply too much to have his mother made the butt of a joke. Whatever the reason, he rounded on Jorgen and said an appalling thing.

"Well, at least my mother isn't a filthy Jew, like yours was."

For once Jorgen and Stefan were lost for words, and before they had had a chance to recover their power of speech, Rolf had run into the house. He ran through the kitchen and down the corridor and was halfway up the stairs when Gunther, who had sprung to his feet as soon as he heard the insult, grabbed hold of his ankle through the banister and said something commanding and peremptory to him in German. Then Gunther followed him up the stairs and they disappeared into one of the bedrooms. I could hear them talking in quiet voices. Rolf was crying a little. It was a long time before they came out.

This was a fortnight of apologies. Last week, it had been the Danes' turn. This time it was Rolf who, under strict instructions from his father, went out to talk to them as they sat morosely in the dunes at the back of the house, and told them that he was sorry for the thoughtless thing he had said. I watched from my usual vantage point as Jorgen and Stefan stood up and shook his hand. They were being remarkably conciliatory about it. "It's all right," Jorgen was saying. "It was just something you said in the heat of the moment. Don't give it another thought. It's quite all right." But something in his manner made me sure that it was far from being all right.

And now I have told you everything that I know. Or almost everything. As I warned you at the beginning, there would come a point in this story when I would simply have to shrug my shoulders and admit that I wasn't around to see what happened next. The moment when I walked offstage, or drifted into the kitchen to make a cup of tea. Well, that moment has come.

Actually I was not making a cup of tea when the climax occurred: I was reading Henry Fielding. For the whole of that last day I stayed in my chair by the window, finishing *Joseph Andrews* and then making serious inroads into *Tom Jones*. Early in the afternoon, Jorgen, Stefan, Rolf and Paul had gone cycling: I didn't know where. At about four o'clock, just as Tom was rescuing Mrs. Waters from the dastardly Ensign Northerton, the Danes came back together and went straight into their house. Half an hour later, as I was deeply immersed in the story of The Man of the Hill, that curious, lengthy digression which seems to have nothing to do with the main narrative but is in fact its cornerstone, Rolf and Paul returned. I could hear that there was some sort of commotion, but I didn't go to investigate. Gunther came into the sitting room, I remember, and fetched a bottle of brandy from the drinks cabinet. I realized afterwards that this must have been for Rolf, who was subsequently taken up to bed. When he joined us for our final dinner that evening, he seemed subdued but otherwise normal. Nobody talked about what had happened during the afternoon.

What little I learned, I learned that night, as I lay awake in my camp bed next to Paul. The lights in the house had only been off for about five minutes when I heard footsteps coming softly down the staircase. Then Rolf appeared in the doorway. He went over to Paul's bed and knelt down beside it. I heard him whisper a few words in German—Paul's name being one of them—and heard my brother answer in the same language. And then Rolf said, quite distinctly, in English:

"You saved my life today. I will always remember that." He kissed my brother tenderly on the forehead. "I will be for ever in your debt."

When Rolf had padded out of the room, I said to Paul:

"What on earth was all *that* about?"

He did not answer for a long time. I began to assume (since

it would have been in character) that he was not going to answer at all. But at last he replied, yawningly:

"Just as he said: I saved his life today."

Exasperated by his continuing silences, I asked, "Well, do you mind telling me how?"

"The Danish boys tried to drown him," said Paul, in a quite calm and unemphatic way. "They hate him because of what he said to them yesterday and they tried to kill him this afternoon."

"Paul . . ." I sat up in bed. "What *are* you talking about?"

"I don't mean they held him under the water or anything like that," he explained. "But we all went up to the Skaw, up to where the seas come together, and they teased him again, saying that he was too weak to go swimming there. He didn't know how dangerous it was. I tried to warn him but he thought I was exaggerating. So he went in. I could see he'd only gone about ten yards before he was in trouble. Stefan tried to hold me down but I was stronger than him so I threw him off and went in after Rolf. I got there just as the current was taking him away and he knew that he wasn't going to make it, so I grabbed him around the neck and managed to bring him back. Jorgen and Stefan ran away. So technically speaking, yes—" (he gave another yawn) "—I did save his life. Now look: we have to pack up early tomorrow. D'you mind if we get some sleep?"

And that was all he would say to me on the subject.

I think about this story, sometimes. It's one of the things I try to make sense of. I thought of it as we drove away from Skagen to return our hire car to the airport at Ålborg the next morning. I thought of it today as I walked home from the bus stop to my parents' house. But slowly, irresistibly, I can feel it beginning to dissolve into the hazy falsehood of memory. That is why I have written it down, although in doing so I know that all I have achieved is to falsify it differently, more artfully. Does narrative serve any purpose? I wonder about that. I wonder if all experience can really be distilled to a few extraordinary moments, perhaps six or seven of them vouchsafed to us in a lifetime, and any attempt to trace a connection between them is futile. And I wonder if there are some moments in life not only "worth pur-chasing with worlds," but so replete with emotion that they become stretched, timeless, like the moment when Inger and Emil sat on that bench in the rose garden and smiled at the cam-era, or when Inger's mother raised the Venetian blind to the very top of her high sitting-room window, or when Malcolm opened up his jeweller's box and asked my sister to marry him. If he ever did.

> *. . . my clearest memory is of the light we saw there, that painters' sky, greyblue like Marie's eyes and like her grandsons' eyes, the colour of a pain that won't go away . . .*

(Unpublished story, found among Benjamin Trotter's papers by his niece, Sophie, in 2002. A very much shorter version won the 1976 Marshall Prize for creative writing at King William's School. Judges: Mr. Nuttall, Mr. Serkis, the Chief Master)

2

At the end of the art history lesson, Mr. Plumb took Philip to one side.

"All set for Saturday?" he said, laying a hand as if unconsciously on his arm. Saturday was the day for a proposed excursion to London, where Mr. Plumb's O- and A-level classes were to visit the George Stubbs exhibition currently showing at the Tate Gallery.

"Sure," said Philip.

"Good. It will I'm sure be the most revelatory experience for you. Epiphanic, if I may be so bold."

"Yeah," said Philip. "I'm looking forward to it." He could not quite see where this was leading, and was anxious to be getting on to his next lesson.

"Your mother," said Mr. Plumb, suddenly, and with a kind of nervous tenderness to his voice. "She's well, I hope?"

"Yes, yes. Very well."

"Good. That's very good. In which case, I wonder . . ." He appeared to hesitate for a moment, fished for something in his briefcase, hesitated again before pulling it out, and finally presented Philip with a plain white envelope, on which his mother's name was inscribed in Mr. Plumb's baroque, spidery handwriting. "I wonder if you might object—or might *not* object, I should say—to passing on this small—em—communiqué.

A notelet, nothing more, entirely innocent in manner and import."

"This is for my mother?" said Philip.

"You have it in a nutshell."

Philip looked at the envelope. Nothing could be deduced from it, beyond the simple fact that Mr. Plumb wanted to send his mother a private message. He put the envelope in his pocket.

"OK," he said, and walked on. He could feel Mr. Plumb's eyes upon him until he reached the end of the corridor and turned a corner.

Eric Clapton was standing on stage at the Odeon New Street, his eyes screwed tight, his left hand caressing the neck of his guitar, high up the fretboard. He was in the middle of some extended solo, bending a note on the second string. "Motherless Children," maybe? "Let It Rain?" Impossible to say. He seemed to be enjoying himself, at any rate, and to be happily oblivious of the fact that he was standing in front of an enormous swastika. Beneath his platformed feet the word "RACIST" had been printed in eighteen-point bold type.

Philip examined the image critically.

"Well," he said, "it's not exactly subtle, is it?"

Doug chewed on his pencil for a moment or two before replying.

"Subtlety," he pronounced, with studied contempt, "is the English disease."

There was no answer to this; at least, Philip couldn't think of one, offhand. Sitting opposite him, on the far side of the wide editorial table, Claire Newman began to write something down. She made a proper show of it, muttering the words beneath her breath and placing great emphasis on *"English disease."*

"What are you doing?" Doug asked.

"I've decided that your *bon mots* have to be preserved for posterity," she said, in the tone of cutting facetiousness she seemed to reserve for Doug alone. "I'm going to be Boswell to your Johnson. Your amanuensis."

The others smiled; even those who didn't understand the word.

"I'm glad to hear it," said Doug, briskly. "So what do you think about the cover?"

"It's all right."

Philip, meanwhile, had thought of a new objection. "It might be libellous," he said.

"You think Eric Clapton's going to sue a school magazine?" When this was merely greeted with a shrug, he added: "If he does, so much the better. We'll get into the newspapers."

Mr. Serkis, the young English master who oversaw these meetings, pulled thoughtfully on his long, soon-to-be-unfashionable hair.

"I might have to show this to the Chief, you know. We should really run it by him before we go to press."

"Come on, that's censorship, pure and simple," Doug protested. "We're living in Callaghan's Britain, not Ceauşescu's Romania."

Claire picked up her biro again. "Are you spelling Romania with an 'o' or a 'u?' " she asked.

"Any halfway decent amanuensis would know that already," said Doug. This time, there was a flirtatiousness in his smile which she registered but refused to return. Rebuffed, and conscious that the others had seen it, he spread his hands and turned to rhetoric. "I thought we were agreed," he said, "I thought we were agreed that if this paper was going to be anything more than a sixth-form gossip sheet, we were going to have to give it some edge. And that means politics. I mean, there's always been politics in this paper before. We've got to keep that going. Sharpen it." He looked again at Claire, sensing that she was, in this at least, his closest ally. "I thought we were agreed on that."

"Well yes," said Claire, doodling on her notepad now. Upside down, it was hard to see what she was drawing. A tree, perhaps. "That's true. But I'm not sure this is . . . I don't know, the right approach . . ."

Silence descended. Mr. Serkis glanced at the clock on the wall, which showed 3:20. The meeting would overrun if they didn't reach a decision quickly.

"Well," he said, "we've got to make up our minds about this. The Chief'll be going home in half an hour, so if there's anything he needs to see . . ."

Benjamin, sitting on the windowsill which afforded a sweeping view of the school rooftops, had taken no part in the discussion so far. He stared into the encroaching dusk, watched as the neon lights flared up, one by one, in the language laboratories across the courtyard. There was a remoteness about him, nowadays; something more than abstraction. It was possible, Mr. Serkis thought, that the distance opening up between Benjamin and his friends might soon become unbridgeable. He wanted to do everything in his power to prevent that from happening.

"What do you think, Ben?" A slight turn of the head; eyelids heavy with indifference. His thoughts might have been anywhere. (As it happened they were on a chord change: D minor 6th to C seven.) "You're a fan of his, aren't you?"

"Used to be," said Benjamin. He rose stiffly from the windowsill and crossed over to the table, the better to inspect Doug's illustration. All eyes were upon him, awaiting his verdict (none more intently than Claire's). But he merely picked the collage up between finger and thumb, glaced at it for a listless moment, and blew out his cheeks. "Oh, I don't know . . ."

"What did he actually *say*?" Philip wanted to know. "What did Clapton actually say?"

Doug wasn't sure. "I haven't got the exact quote," he said. "I haven't been able to find it. Something about Britain becoming one of its own colonies. He mentioned Enoch Powell, anyway. I'm sure of that. Said that Powell was right and we should all be listening to him. It's in my article."

"He was drunk, wasn't he?"

"So? What difference does that make?"

Mr. Serkis watched as Benjamin drifted away from the table and picked up a bag from the corner of the room. It was a plastic carrier bag, twelve inches square, and bore the name and address of a shop called Cyclops Records, much patronized by the sixth-formers of King William's. Benjamin's books and exercise pads had been crammed into it with some difficulty. A briefcase would have been more practical but would not, he suspected, have radiated the same aura of would-be cool. Then Benjamin hovered in the doorway, intending to say goodbye to his colleagues, it seemed, and waiting for a suitable hiatus in their conversation. By now Doug and Philip had given up on the specifics of Eric Clapton's recent *faux pas* and moved on to the subject of racism generally. Birmingham, Doug maintained, had produced two notable racist thinkers in the last few decades: Enoch Powell, and J. R. R. Tolkien. Philip was outraged by this statement. Tolkien was unquestionably his favourite author and in what way, he wanted to know, could he be described as racist? Doug suggested that he reread *The Lord of the Rings*. Philip assured him that he did, at six-monthly intervals. In that case, Doug replied, surely he must have noticed that Tolkien's villainous Orcs were made to appear unmistakably negroid. And did it not strike him as significant that the reinforcements who came to the aid of Sauron, the *Dark* Lord, are themselves dark-skinned, hail from unspecified tropical lands to the south, and are often mounted upon elephants?

"This racism thing is beginning to obsess you," Philip retorted. "It's about time you changed the record."

"It's about time *you* changed your reading habits," said Doug.

Benjamin had gone.

He still nursed a residual fondness for Tolkien, even though it was years since he had read *The Lord of the Rings*. He had moved on to Conrad and Fielding, and was beginning to struggle with *Ulysses*. In any case, it was *The Hobbit* that held a special place in his affections; and although it had never struck him before that it was written by a local author, now that Doug had mentioned it, he could see that it made a kind of sense. Why else, after all, had Benjamin remained so partial to Tolkien's own illustration of Bag End and Hobbiton-across-the-Water, the limpid colours of which still, after so many years and changes of taste, glowed soothingly down upon him from his bedroom wall? Surely it was because somewhere in that painting, in the diffident contours of its landscape, in its artless evocation of one morning "long ago in the quiet of the world, when there was less noise and more green," he found sentimental echoes of the area where he himself had grown up. More particularly, it reminded him of a place just a mile or two south of Longbridge: the Lickey Hills, where his grandparents lived, and where he was heading that same afternoon. It wasn't just the slow inclines and occasional muted, autumnal glades of this semi-pastoral backwater that made him think of the Shire; the inhabitants themselves were hobbit-like, in their breezy indifference towards the wider world, their unchallenged certainty that they were living the best of all possible lives in the best of all possible locations. These were attitudes, Benjamin knew, that Paul was already beginning to despise; and no doubt with some justice. But for his own part he had grown up with them, inherited them, and he could not shed them. Not completely. He loved his grandparents precisely for, and not in spite of, their preposterous, unspoken belief that God had somehow chosen them, marking them out for special favour, by placing them where all of life's blessings seemed to be gathered together in one unassumingly hallowed spot. It was a belief from which he at once recoiled and drew strength.

When he rang the doorbell it was his grandmother who answered and said, "Hello, love," giving him a soft and camphored kiss on the cheek. She seemed to have been expecting him, even though he had given no forewarning. "Come for tea?"

Good manners demanded that he sit on the sofa for a while, dunking digestive biscuits into his mug of pallid tea and telling her about his week at King William's. It was no hardship, really. Benjamin's grandmother took an amused, unforced interest in his life at school, her mind was sharp, she even had a better memory for the names of his friends than his parents had. He liked talking to her, almost as much as he liked talking to his grandfather, who could be glimpsed in the garden raking the first of the fallen leaves into a bonfire and who even now was probably dreaming up some silly joke or terrible pun to make him groan over the tea-table.

Nevertheless, Benjamin had not come here to see his grandparents, however much he liked them. He had come to use their piano; and at the earliest opportunity, while his grandfather remained busy with the gardening and his grandmother went next door to the kitchen to begin work on a shepherd's pie, he hurried up to the spare bedroom, retrieved a small suitcase containing his two tape recorders, and ran downstairs again to begin setting up his makeshift studio.

His latest musical project, slotted in between occasional work on his novel and short stories, was a series of chamber pieces for piano and guitar called *Seascape Nos. 1–7*. They were inspired both by his memories of Skagen and, inevitably, by his continuing, unrequited longing for Cicely. The first three had already been recorded and, listening back to them over the last few days, Benjamin thought that he could hear a new maturity, a measured, reflective lyricism beginning to emerge in his writing. He was aiming for something simple but resonant; austere but heartfelt; a suitable antidote, he hoped, to the different excesses against which he imagined himself rebelling, namely the ridiculous symphonic pretensions of Philip's progressive heroes, on the one hand, and on the other, the neo-neanderthal dynamism of punk, which Doug was just beginning to discover and enthuse about to his horrified friends. To map out another creative path altogether, not so much between these two courses as on some lonely, blasted heath of his own choosing, appeared to Benjamin a fine thing, noble and romantic. He was sure that Cicely herself, if she ever heard any of the music (which seemed highly unlikely), would have been moved and intrigued by it.

The practicalities of recording at his grandparents' house were a little on the mundane side, all the same. First of all he had to stop their cuckoo clock by detaching the pendulum, since it was ticking far too loudly and was liable to sound the hour at the most inappropriate moment. Not something that Richard Branson's roster of musicians ever had to worry about when recording at the Manor, he imagined. And then there was the whole problem of extraneous noise generally, not just the traffic noise from the Old Birmingham Road but the everyday sounds of his grandparents going about their business, for he had never been able to impress on them the need for absolute silence while he was making these secret bids for musical immortality. There had been many times, three-quarters of the way through a take, when everything had been ruined by the ringing of the telephone or the careless slamming of a door.

But tonight's recording proceeded smoothly, for the most part. *Seascape No. 4* was a bittersweet composition lasting about four minutes, song-like in form, with the guitar playing an erratic, plangent melody over a gentle backwash of minor chords ebbing and flowing on the piano. After the verse-chorus structure had run its course, everything dissolved into a wash of lazy, wistful improvisation. Benjamin always regretted that these pieces never turned out to be quite as avant-garde as he would have liked; but he still believed that they were, in their way, original. Behind them lay a strange compound of influences absorbed from modern classical composers and the English experimental pop groups into whose busy, eccentric soundworld Malcolm had once fatefully guided him; but out of these influences Benjamin was starting to fashion something entirely his own. So much his own, in fact, that he knew he would never share these recordings with anyone—not even Philip, his closest friend—which meant that it scarcely mattered if, as this evening, he played a handful of bum notes, lost time on three separate occasions, and was interrupted towards the end of his chosen take by the sound of Acorn, his grandparents' cat, miaowing outside the French window. The miaow was clearly audible when he played the tape back, but Benjamin didn't mind. The composition was fixed, now, sculpted in time, in a version which at least approximated to his first intentions. He would listen to it, grow tired of it, and move on. These pieces, he already realized, were merely stepping stones at the start of a journey towards something—some grand artefact, either musical, or literary, or filmic, or perhaps a combination of all three—towards which he knew he was advancing, slowly but with a steady, inexorable tread. Something which would enshrine his feelings for Cicely, and which she would perhaps hear, or read, or see in ten or twenty years' time, and suddenly realize, on her pulse, that it was created for her, intended for her, an that of all the boys who had swarmed around her like so many drones at school, Benjamin had been, without her having the wit to notice it, by far the purest in heart, by far the most gifted and giving. On that day the awareness of all she had missed, all she had lost, would finally break upon her in an instant, and she would weep; weep for her foolishness, and for the love that might have been between them.

Of course, Benjamin could always just have spoken to her, gone up to her in the bus queue and asked her for a date. But this seemed to him, on the whole, the more satisfactory approach.

His grandparents knew nothing of the fierce, undisclosed passion that was burning in Benjamin's young heart as the three of them tucked into their shepherd's pie that evening. As usual, his grandfather was in a facetious mood and every request for the salt cellar or the bread and butter was accompanied by atrocious wordplay, which Benjamin parried and returned as best he could. He relished the atmosphere of these simple, animated meals. His parents' house seemed so cold by comparison. At home Benjamin hated the fact that he would have to sit opposite Paul and watch him sneering at the food, picking fastidiously over his mother's latest well-intentioned offering. He hated the fact that his father would still be preoccupied, hours after the event, with the memory of some humiliating encounter at work. And he hated the fact that Lois wasn't there any more. That was the worst of it. He hated that more than anything at all.

3

"Large feline." Five letters, beginning with T, ending with R.

Now come on, Philip's father said to himself, you must know the answer to this one. A feline was a cat, he knew that for sure. A kind of cat, five letters, beginning with T? What about tabby?

He would just double-check on the meaning of "feline."

"Pass me the dictionary, will you, love?"

Barbara handed him their *Reader's Digest* dictionary, without looking up, and went on reading her magazine. Or rather, she went on reading the letter she had concealed within the pages of her magazine.

The night wind rattled against the windowpanes Sam had failed, for the third year running, to have fitted with double glazing. The television muttered its way through a regional documentary, unwatched, unnoticed, the volume turned down almost to nothing.

"The first time I saw you, at the parent—teachers meeting, I felt as Giornado must have done, when he first glimpsed the Meninas *of Velázquez. I experienced the electric thrill of which Herbert Howells writes so movingly, describing his first encounter with the* Tallis Fantasia *of Vaughan Williams. I knew that I was in the presence of greatness; not merely the presence of a perfect human being (perfect physically and, I venture to imagine, perfect in spirit, flawless in quintessence), but of what might also be described, without too much*

*recourse to fancy, as a perfect work of art: for you, Barbara, are the
masterpiece for which I have been looking all my life, my very own
opus magnus . . ."*

feline—*adj.* **1** of the cat family. **2** catlike.—*n.* animal of the
cat family. **felinity** *n.* [Latin *feles* cat]

He knew all along that this was what it meant. So it had to
be tabby, didn't it? Were tabbies large? Well, Mrs. Freeman's
tabby next door was bloody enormous. Two weeks ago it had
seen off a fox. So the "R" must be wrong.

The "R" came from "Rotten." What was the clue? "Putrid."
Six letters, fifth one "E." He was about to look up "putrid" again
when Barbara held out her hand absently and said, "Pass me the
dictionary, will you, love?"

He sighed and handed it over.

Barbara thumbed through the pages, rapidly but with a
furtive air that Sam, absorbed in his crossword puzzle, failed to
notice.

quintessence *n.* **1** (usu. foll. by *of*) purest and most perfect
form, manifestation or embodiment of a quality etc. **2** highly
refined extract.

Highly refined!

quintessential *adj.* **quintessentially** *adv.* [Latin *quinta
essentia* fifth substance (underlying the four elements)]

He thought that she was "highly refined." That settled
it, then. Mr. Plumb—Miles, as she must learn to call him—
was, in the old-fashioned sense, making love to her. She was
being pursued. She had—the word came to her suddenly,
unheralded, with a bewitching sense of rightness—an admirer.
Her cheeks began to tingle. They burned, and she knew that
she was blushing deep scarlet. Ashamed, deeply, delightfully
ashamed, she slipped the letter away between the pages of
Woman and forced herself to concentrate on the magazine. She
mustn't read any more. It was all wrong, horribly wrong, the
whole business.

*"PRESSURE COOKERS—Some of you love them, some of you
hate them."*

"YOUR STARS CAN HELP YOU SLIM. Are you Pisces—The Indulger? Aries—The Gourmet? Gemini—The Nibbler?"

"Cancer—The Solace Seeker: Food makes you feel good and that's half your trouble. When the bluebird of happiness eludes you, you shrink into your shell and eat yourself better."

Barbara reached for another chocolate biscuit as Sam said:

"Pass me the dictionary, will you, love?"

Putrid *adj.* **1** decomposed, rotten. **2** foul, noxious. **3** corrupt. **4** *slang* of poor quality; contemptible; very unpleasant. **putridity** *n.* [Latin *putreo* rot (v.)]

Well, there it was: *rotten*. Just as he had thought. But if the large feline was a tabby, as it obviously was, then this word had to begin with a "Y" and *rotten* would have to go. So he was looking for a six-letter word beginning with "Y," fifth letter "E" meaning *putrid*.

Got it! "YUCKEY."

"O Barbara, my Barbara, my paragon, callipygic enchantress, apogee of all that is pulchritudinous in this misbegotten, maculate world, will the truculent forces of peripeteia ever vouchsafe us the sweet euphoria of sybaritic congress?"

"Pass me the dictionary, will you, love?"

Sam gave a more irritable sigh, this time, as he handed it over. "I don't know why you need a bloody dictionary to read that magazine," he said. "It's not exactly *Doctor Chicago*, is it?"

Barbara stuck out her tongue. "Shut up and do your crossword."

He wrote "Yuckey" carefully over the letters of "Rotten," then paused to see what difference this had made. It meant that 11 across now began with "C" rather than "T." The clue was: "electrically powered passenger road vehicle running on rails." It had four letters and ended with "M."

Damn and blast it, Sam thought to himself. I could have sworn that was *tram*. Now that "C" has gone and spoiled everything.

Barbara had given up on trying to understand Miles's last sentence and was reading the letters page of *Woman* instead.

"The very aptly named leader of a local hiking club is a Mr. A. Mountain!" Joanna Prior from Clitheroe had written.

"If a cassette tape breaks, don't throw it away," wrote Amelia Fairney, from South Shields. *"The spools can be pulled out and the tape used as party streamers or for tying up presents."*

Sarah Day from Newbury advised: *"Don't waste electricity drying smalls in the tumble dryer. Pop them in a salad spinner and twirl it until they're dry."*

"In order to go to night class recently," another correspondent wrote, *"I had to let my husband cook dinner for my two kids, 6 and 4. The next morning I asked them if they had enjoyed themselves, and their only complaint was that they didn't like the ice lollies Dad had given them for pudding. When I checked in the freezer, I wasn't surprised. They were frozen carrots!"*

After this letter, the editor had written: *"Has YOUR husband ever done anything really daft? Write in and tell us about it!"*

I wouldn't know where to begin, Barbara thought, as she looked across at Sam, frowning over the crossword, happily unaware that he was sucking on the inky end of his felt-tip pen.

He admitted defeat on the electrically powered passenger road vehicle and turned his attention to the bottom left-hand corner.

"Round open vessel, for washing hands and face."

Five letters, beginning with "B." That was easy. "B-O-W-E-L."

Twenty-three across had seven letters and ended with "A."

"Condition of perfect bliss," he read.

"I must see you again," Miles Plumb had written. *"It is my belief, Barbara, my homeostatic credo, that we are destined to be one. Only when we are together, coalescent, infibulate, will I attain that fugitive condition of nirvana which has been the sole desideratum of my infructuous, miscarried existence."*

"Pass me the dictionary, will you, love?" Barbara asked.

She looked up "nirvana."

nirvana *n.* (in Buddhism) condition of perfect bliss.

Sam tossed the newspaper aside in frustration.

"Giving up again?" Barbara asked, with just the hint of a taunt in her voice.

" 'Quick and easy,' it says," Sam grumbled, his lips and tongue now blackened with ink. " 'Quick and easy crossword.' I ask you! I mean, what's a 'condition of perfect bliss,' when it's at home?"

"I'm sure I wouldn't know," said Barbara regretfully, and once again struggled to bury herself in the magazine.

When they arrived on the top deck of the bus, Claire already had the front two seats to herself. Benjamin was the first to get there. He knew that Claire would like it if he sat next to her, but instead, he took the other seat, next to the window. Doug was the second. He knew that Claire would prefer it if he didn't sit next to her, but he did it anyway. Philip was the last, and he sat next to Benjamin. He was looking upset, but Claire was the only one to notice. The others had seen nothing unusual in his recent behaviour. And so, after sitting in near-silence for ten minutes or more, she finally stirred herself to nudge Doug and remark:

"He's been awfully quiet, the last few days."

Doug replied: "He's always quiet."

"No, but he's been *especially* quiet."

Presumably to disprove his own theory about subtlety being the English disease, Doug leaned across the aisle and said: "Hey, Philip! Come on, what's up? Claire thinks you're pining for something."

"I didn't say that," Claire insisted. Then, to Philip: "You just seem a bit low, that's all. I wondered if there was anything the matter."

It swiftly occurred to Benjamin, staring out of the side window and as always slightly disconnected from the conversation, not only that Claire was right, but that he alone knew the cause of Philip's recent dejection. He was worried about the band. And, indeed, with good reason. Who wouldn't be worried about the band? Two years in the assembling, many months in the naming (and even now Benjamin thought that they had chosen the wrong name), the band was supposed to have had its first rehearsal last week, but it had been cancelled: due to lack of material, of all things. Benjamin himself, although he was supposed to be the keyboard player, had decided not to provide any songs, claiming that his own writing wasn't suited to the five-piece format; and all that anybody knew about Philip's contribution was that he had been engaged for some time on an improbably ambitious piece—either an epic song, or a series of songs, no one could be quite sure—which he was constantly withholding from the scrutiny of his fellow-musicians (Benjamin, Gidney, Stubbs and Procter). Last Friday was when it had been hoped, finally, that the great work might be unveiled. But Philip had bottled out at the last minute, saying that it still needed some fine-tuning. And of course this, Benjamin thought, must be why his friend had lately been so subdued: he would be feeling both embarrassment at letting down his colleagues, and the natural anxiety of the artist as his creation nears fulfilment.

Benjamin was wrong. Philip was worried because his parents were not speaking to each other and his father had moved into the spare bedroom.

There were many distressing aspects to this situation. His mother had received a love letter. That was distressing. His father had found it, concealed between the problem pages of the latest issue of *Woman*. That was distressing, on several counts. Why had his father been reading the problem pages of *Woman* in the first place? Clearly because, with their increasingly frank discussion of orgasms, erogenous zones and other recondite facets of female sexuality, they were the most titillating literature to be found anywhere in the Chase household. That, at any rate, was why Philip himself read them; but it was upsetting to find that his father, twenty-seven years his senior and supposedly much better versed in the ways of the world, still shared the same prurient curiosities, and could find no better outlet for them. Philip didn't know what the letter had said. He had asked both of his parents, but his mother wouldn't tell him, and his father, conversely, couldn't tell him, because he had been unable to understand a word of it, despite enlisting the help of the *Reader's Digest* dictionary. The gist of it, anyway, he told Philip, is that this bloke is after your mother. He wants her in bed with him. He might wrap it up in a lot of fancy words, but that's what it boils down to. He wants to give her one.

That, too, was distressing, but there was worse to come when Philip found out who the letter was from. It was from Miles Plumb.

Mr. Plumb! Sugar Plum Fairy, the creepy art teacher! Philip was studying A-level art and he had to have lessons with Mr. Plumb four days a week. How could he look him in the eye, when he knew that he was mounting an assault on his parents' marriage? Suddenly Harding's legendary taunt at the Girls' School Revue—*"Homebreaker!"*—didn't seem so funny. Philip's first instinct had been to go straight to the Chief Master and tell him exactly what his head of art was playing at. But his father, surprisingly, had warned him not to do this on any account. It's between me and him, he had said. Neither you nor the school nor your mother is going to have anything to do with it. I'm going to sort out this little creep, and I'm going to do it my way. I don't know how, but that's what I'm going to do. I'm going to hit him where it hurts.

And those were the last ominous words that had been spoken on the subject. Philip had no idea what his father might have meant.

Needless to say, he could not mention any of this to his friends.

"Nothing's wrong," he answered, in a tone of abject despair. And when they looked unconvinced, he was forced to improvise: "I'm just . . . worried about this Closed Circle article, that's all. I'm not sure we're going down the right road."

Doug shook his head in disbelief. "We went over all that at the last meeting."

"I know we did. I'm still not convinced."

The Closed Circle was a select debating society, composed

of no more than sixteen members at any one time, drawn mostly from the upper sixth and very occasionally from the year below. Nobody outside the society knew how often it met, or where, or what exactly went on at the meetings. Everything about it was cloaked in impenetrable (and somehow infantile) secrecy.

"The Closed Circle is a nasty, divisive bit of elitist bollocks," said Doug. "It's like a bunch of schoolkids pretending to be the fucking masons. It's high time somebody did a proper exposé of the whole thing and showed these guys up for the self-important wankers they are."

"Have *you* been asked to join?" a voice asked.

Doug wheeled around to find that Paul, Benjamin's unsavoury little brother, was sitting directly behind him.

"What are *you* doing here?" Benjamin asked. Even after three-and-a-half terms, he had still not adjusted to the horror of realizing that Paul now attended the same school, and travelled home on the same bus. There was no end to the nightmare of his continued presence.

"It's a free country, isn't it?" said Paul. "Besides, there aren't any other seats."

This, unfortunately, was true.

"Well, look, we don't want you talking to us."

"It's a free country, like I said. Anyway," (he was addressing Doug now) "I asked you a question."

Doug could not believe the boy's presumption. He gazed at him with the cold disdain of a pedigree bloodhound whose tail has just been tweaked by a mongrel pup.

"Have *you* been asked to join?" Paul repeated.

"Of course not."

"Well, there you are then. You're only jealous."

"*Jealous?*"

"You don't fool me with all that guff about elites. If you're not an elitist, what are you doing at this school? You had to take an entrance exam, didn't you?"

"Yes, but—"

"Elitism's a good thing. Everyone but a handful of blinkered ideologues knows that. Elitism leads to competition and competition leads to excellence. And as for The Closed Circle, *I'm* going to ask if I can join."

Benjamin howled with incredulity. *"You?* You're about five years too young, for one thing. And you don't *ask* to join. *They* have to ask *you."*

Before Paul could enrage him any further the bus reached Northfield, and it was time for Claire and Philip to get off. As they said goodbye Benjamin looked out of the window again, not meaning to be rude, but wanting to avoid Claire's eyes; he knew that when she said goodbye he would find a challenge there, that she would try to force some kind of response, just as she had been trying to do ever since he had first taken notice of her, at this same bus stop, three long years ago. Since then he had probably been the last person, out of all his friends, to recognize the obvious fact that she nursed a passion for him, an inexplicable crush which he had done nothing to encourage. It had become a source of monstrous embarrassment between them. Even Claire, at some level, seemed to hate herself for it; but there it was. Apparently these things couldn't be reasoned away. And it was hard on Doug, as well, who had his own feelings for Claire, but had never met with the slightest encouragement. So there was always a little tension in the air, between Benjamin and Doug, whenever Claire was around, or in their thoughts. Which was why, perhaps, they said nothing to each other for a while (Doug having moved on to Benjamin's seat) after she had gone.

"So," Doug asked finally, "are you coming to London with me at the weekend?"

This, too, was ground they had covered before.

"I don't think I should," said Benjamin. "I haven't been invited."

"I'm not the only one who's been invited. They'd like to meet anyone from the magazine."

Benjamin squirmed in his seat.

"I think you'd better go by yourself."

Doug looked at his friend for a moment, then laughed—a
short, sad laugh—and said: "You just won't do it, will you?"

"Do what?"

"You won't get out there. You won't take life by the throat
and give it a good old shaking. You'll never do that, will you,
Benjamin? You'll never take your chances. Someone gives you a
way to get *out* of this shitty place for a day or two, and go and see
something *happening*, something really happening, but no, you
won't do it. You'd rather stay home with your mum and dad
and . . . I don't know, put your stupid record collection in alpha-
betical order, or something. Make sure your Soft Machine
comes before your Stackridge."

Benjamin could feel the sharp justice of these words. They
were like a rain of blows, each landing on their target with perfect aim. He cowered beneath them. It was true, he would never
have gone down to London with Doug, whatever the circumstances. He could never walk brazenly into an unfamiliar office
and introduce himself to a roomful of strangers, all older than
him, all more experienced and knowing and bristly with metro-
politan cool. The very idea terrified him. But he also had an
excuse, a real excuse, and he felt entitled to use it.

"It's not that," he said. "I just have to be back here on Saturday. There's something I always do on Saturdays."

And he told Doug that on Saturdays, he always visited the
asylum. Which was true. And so Doug said that he was sorry
and then fell silent. There could be no arguing with that.

4

Every time he drove past the end of her street, Bill felt peculiar. This, after all, was not just where she had lived, but where he had last seen her. It was here that she had broken down in his car and begun screaming, threatening to kill herself if he did not leave Irene. He had pulled over to the side of the road and attempted to comfort her. For five or ten minutes they had raged at each other and later that day he could barely remember a word they had said. And even now, so long after the event, this otherwise anonymous junction where her street intersected with the Bristol Road preserved the terrible, savage energy of that encounter somewhere in its memory; Bill had to pass through it, like a forcefield, every time he drove this way into central Birmingham.

She had not turned up at his house, as he had feared. She had attempted to contact him only once, phoning him at home and requesting that they have an urgent conversation. He had agreed to see her at their regular meeting-point, one of the shower blocks at the plant, the scene of some of their most frantic clandestine lovemaking. But Bill didn't go. His nerve had failed him.

For most of the next two evenings he had surreptitiously left his phone off the hook, wedging the receiver away from its cradle with a pellet of india rubber, but it soon occurred to him that he couldn't do this forever. At 9:30 on the night after he had broken his appointment, he returned the telephone to its normal state, and within five minutes it was ringing. He picked up the phone and found himself speaking to Donald Newman, Miriam's father. He seemed to be on the verge of hysteria and the first thing he did was to threaten Bill with murder, but Bill was not scared of violence, and he knew that he had to allow this man to confront him. They arranged to meet in The Black Horse in Northfield, half an hour later, and that was where Donald had told him the extraordinary news: Miriam had disappeared.

He *was* a violent man, Bill could see that. Potentially, at any rate. But that night he confined himself to abusing Bill verbally, calling him every filthy name in the dictionary, accusing him of having seduced his daughter and corrupted her and defiled her and probably getting her pregnant and forcing her to have any number of abortions and anything else that was thrown up by an imagination Bill might have characterized as raving if so many of the accusations had not been, in point of fact, uncomfortably close to the truth. Anyway, he barely heard or understood most of what he was being told: his mind was reeling from the impact of so much new and horrific information. Miriam had kept a diary, apparently. She had never told him that. Not for the whole of their time together, thank God, but certainly at the beginning, and now her father had read all of it. Humiliation and exposure stared him in the face that night—the end of his marriage, the loss of his job—and he found himself pleading with Donald, begging him for the sake of Irene and Doug to keep the affair secret. But Donald wasn't interested in any of this. All he wanted to know was where Miriam was. Where is she, he kept repeating, where is my daughter, and all that Bill could answer was, I don't know. I really, really don't know.

The only thing he could think to tell Donald was about the other man. He remembered the teasing way—except that it was too reckless to be called teasing, too desperate—Miriam had led him to believe that there was someone else, another lover, some unnamed rival who was "not from the factory, not from anywhere round here." She had even threatened to run off with

him, and perhaps that was what she had done. Donald pressed
him for the man's name but he didn't know it. And then Donald
asked: Do you think she could have killed herself?, and once
again Bill shook his head and this time behind his wire-rimmed
glasses his haggard grey eyes were pooled with tears as he said: I
don't know.

Donald had gone.

Eight anxious days later there had been a curious, inconclusive postscript. Bill had contacted some of his friends in the
Anti-Nazi movement and made some further inquiries about
the Association of British People, the group to which Roy Slater
belonged. It turned out to be just the sort of rabble he had
expected, on the lunatic fringe of the lunatic fringe, too minor
to be considered dangerous although it had a record of involvement with small-scale racial violence. Bill had called for a meeting with Roy Slater and accused him of disseminating racist
propaganda in the workplace. Slater asked him what he was
going to do about it; Bill said that he would report it to the
union, with the recommendation that Slater was stripped of his
position as shop steward and, quite possibly, his job.

"Do it if you like," Slater had answered, unexpectedly. "But
if you do—I'll tell Irene about you and Miriam Newman."

The blackmail had worked. Bill said nothing to his union
colleagues, and Slater had been more than true to his word.
The last thing he had told Bill at that meeting was: "No one will
hear about it, Brother Anderton. Ever. You have my personal
guarantee."

Bill didn't know what he had meant by that, exactly, any
more than he knew how Slater had found out about the affair in
the first place. He decided, in the end, that he had probably
heard about it from Victor Gibbs, and he continued to suspect
that there was some murky, unfathomable conspiracy between
the two of them. But he had no evidence more concrete than the
words in which they had both, independently, described Doug's
school—"that toffs' academy"—and later on, when he was able
to reflect upon the whole business more calmly, he even won-

dered whether Gibbs *had* known so very much about Miriam and him. Had it not been all bluster, and Bill's own paranoid imagination? Speculation was pointless by now. Gibbs's embezzlement and forgery were exposed and he had been dismissed. Bill never heard from him again. And one year later, Slater got married, moved to Oxford, and managed to get himself a job at Leyland's Cowley plant, with the help of a laudatory reference provided, in what he was determined should be his final act of dishonesty, by Bill himself.

As for Miriam, he did his best to forget. It had been impossible at first. Night after night he found himself on the point of phoning Donald Newman and asking if there had been any news. Each time, he stopped himself; he couldn't face the man's rage and contempt a second time. There was no story in the newspapers, and no word in the factory except a fragment of conversation, half-overheard one day in the canteen, about Miriam having run away with another man. Bill could never know how well-informed this gossip had been, but he was forced to accept, in the end, that the other, mysterious lover must have existed, and that she had fled to him. For months relief and jealousy fought for supremacy in his heart and in the end they called an exhausted truce. Nothing took their place. He struggled to kick the habit, the draining, corrosive habit of thinking about Miriam day in day out, and tried to reconcile himself, instead, to the virtues of routine, of self-control; of marriage. He had stayed faithful to Irene from then on, in deed if not in thought. But even now, almost two years on, all it took was a journey like this, a quick glance out of the car window, to bring all the grimness of that final weekend back to him. To have come so close to the brink, without even knowing it, without having the faintest idea, really, what he had been dealing with! A long shudder rippled through him whenever he thought of it.

He found that he had driven almost as far as King William's, and could remember nothing about the last four miles, not even the Selly Oak stretch where there must have been heavy traffic.

It was a miracle that he never had an accident. Doug was waiting for him outside the school gates. He had changed out of his uniform, which he had scrunched up and rolled under his arm. After years of wearing flares, he had suddenly converted to black drainpipe jeans which made his legs look impossibly thin and reedy. He was wearing no jacket, just a white T-shirt.

"Get in, for God's sake," said Bill. "You must be freezing out there. What's happened to your jacket?"

Doug threw his uniform and his black sports holdall into the back of the car, then climbed into the passenger seat next to his father.

"I don't need one, Dad."

"You're not going down to London without a jacket."

"I left it at home."

"Then put your blazer on."

"Are you kidding?"

"Take it down with you in your bag. You'll need it."

Doug snorted and buckled up his seat belt. "Thanks for the lift," he muttered.

"No problem." Bill eased the car back into the line of traffic streaming into Birmingham. It was only two o'clock, but the rush hour seemed to have started early. As usual, the gear change from third to fourth proved difficult, prompting a violent lurch forward and a groan of complaint from the engine.

"Bloody gear box," said Bill.

"Why don't you buy a decent car for once? A foreign one."

"Less of that," his father snapped. "This car was made by craftsmen. British craftsmen. And I should know." He slipped through a set of lights as they changed back to amber. "Anyway, how can I? What would people say?"

It was Friday, 29th October, 1976, and Doug was about to embark upon a great adventure: a trip to London, his first without parental supervision. He would be travelling entirely alone, in fact, although it hadn't exactly been planned this way. Without really knowing why—except that he had somehow wanted to impress his heroes—he had sent a copy of *The Bill Board*'s

Eric Clapton cover and article to the offices of the *NME*, and two weeks later the magazine's assistant editor, Neil Spencer, had sent him a brief, generous reply. The issue had been passed around the *NME* staff, apparently, and much admired. Doug and the magazine's other contributors were invited to submit ideas for features, if they had any, and to send in reviews of any noteworthy gigs in Birmingham. A scribbled postscript added that if they ever found themselves passing through London and wanted to drop by, they should feel free. Doug had read this letter aloud at the last editorial meeting and was astonished that his colleagues not only showed little interest, but actually refused to believe that the invitation was meant seriously. For no other reason than to prove them wrong, he had phoned the *NME* offices a few days later and spoken to a staff member. True, this person had seemed to know nothing about the letter, but he was very friendly, and when he heard that Doug was planning to come to London that weekend (something he had made up on the spot), he had said, Yes, sure, pop in whenever you want. Friday afternoon would be a good time. Doug had mentioned that he didn't, at the moment, have anywhere to stay in London and the voice at the other end of the line had said that was no problem, he was sure something could be fixed up. It was all turning out to be fantastically easy.

"Have you not even got a phone number?" his father was now asking. "Just somewhere we can contact you in an emergency."

"They didn't say exactly who would be putting me up," said Doug. "The editor, probably. I'll give you a call when I get there."

Bill's next question was the inevitable, "They don't take drugs, do they, these people? You're not getting into that kind of scene?"

"Of course not, Dad. It's not that sort of paper. They're respectable journalists." Doug was hoping and assuming, even as he said it, that this was anything but true. The procurement of mind-altering substances was the second of his reasons for going down to London. It was a little habit he'd got into in the last few months. "Anyway, I can look after myself. I know how to say no."

If you do, Bill said to himself, you didn't learn it from me. He dropped his only son off at New Street Station, waved goodbye to the disappearing figure who failed to wave back and still looked, to his eyes, absurdly frail and vulnerable, then glanced at his watch and realized that he had about three hours to kill before tea-time. The latest strike was well into its second week and he had cleared his backlog of paperwork days ago. A free afternoon in Birmingham stretched before him. What could he do with all that spare time, given that the pubs were firmly shut? Go to Samuel's in Broad Street, maybe, and buy Irene a surprise present. There was no money coming in at the moment and they had no savings to speak of, but the nice earrings he had noticed in the window last time were only fifteen pounds the pair, and she would appreciate it. It would be a gesture.

There could be no end to the gestures he owed her.

London was brown and grey. That late October afternoon, almost every other colour seemed to have been bleached out of the city's palette, so that the peeling red and white railings of Blackfriars Bridge appeared shockingly festive; frivolous, even. Beneath Doug's feet, the waters of the Thames churned queasily, sewagebrown, with just a hint of Joyce's snotgreen. It was coming on to rain, as it had been threatening to do ever since the train had disgorged him at Euston Station half an hour earlier. Doug had struggled to Blackfriars on the unfamiliar tube system, confounded first of all by the branching of the Northern Line at Euston, and then by the thoroughly ambiguous relationship between Bank and Monument, where there both did and didn't appear to be a real interchange. Now he stood on the bridge, somewhat rattled and hugging himself with goosebumped arms, for although the wind coming off the water was fierce, nothing on earth would have persuaded him to wear his King William's blazer this crucial afternoon.

It was approaching 4:30, and night was falling fast. The shadowy, looming bulks of countless brutalist tower blocks, their office windows dotted with squares and oblongs of strident neon light, made the city seem even stranger, even less hospitable; a concrete encyclopedia of hidden stories, unguessable shards of secret life. Doug supposed that the tallest of the buildings on the South Bank, a monstrous symphony of variegated browns jutting rudely over the others like a sculpted turd, must be King's Reach Tower, the final object of his journey. Jostled by early commuters, flayed by the lashing rain and the wind rising in random, vindictive gusts off the filthy water, he made heavy progress towards the end of the bridge. Apprehension slowed him down with every footstep.

King's Reach Tower seemed to be home to any number of magazines. Blown-up covers of *Woman and Home*, *Amateur Photographer*, *TV Times* and *Woman's Weekly* graced the smoke-tinted windows. There was no sign of the *NME*, but when Doug approached the uniformed doorman sitting behind his mean little desk, looking very much like a junior porter in a two-star hotel, his inquiry met with a cursory nod. "Twenty-third floor," the doorman said, and pointed him towards the bank of lifts.

He waited there self-consciously for a minute or two, until a blonde, slightly stocky woman in her twenties entered the building and swapped a cheerful greeting with the doorman, with whom she was clearly a favourite. Then she joined Doug beside the lifts and pushed one of the buttons, making him realize that he had failed to do this himself. Not a great start.

"Where to?" she asked him, when they got inside.

"Twenty-three, please."

"Same as me," she said, smiling and allowing her eyes to settle on him for a moment.

"*NME*?" Doug asked, hopefully.

"Gosh, no. *Horse and Hound.* Not nearly so glamorous." She had a piercing Home Counties accent. "Do you write for them, or something?"

"Well, I . . . I'm a sort of out-of-town contributor, I suppose."

"What a hoot. I say—do you like punk rock?"

"Some of it," said Doug, stifling a grin at her enunciation of this phrase. "I haven't heard that much. It hasn't really hit Birmingham yet."

"Birmingham! Gosh, how priceless! Down on the King's Road you see them all the time. Punk rockers, and so on. It's frightfully exciting."

"Yes, it must be."

The conversation ground to a halt. When they left the lift at the twenty-third floor, they turned separate ways.

Doug found the door to the *NME* offices open. When he entered the large, open-plan space the first thing he registered, apart from an impression of general disarray, was a heavy and uncompromising silence. He had expected bustling activity: smoking hacks crouched over their typewriters, banging out album reviews; harassed-looking secretaries shuttling press releases and promo copies from one desk to another. Instead, at first, he could see no one at all. A section of overhead strip lighting flickered erratically and a few pieces of paper flapped in the breeze generated by an ancient wall-mounted fan. It felt as though this place had not been inhabited for weeks. Then, at last, a distracted young man with long hair and horn-rimmed glasses wandered into view, his eyes fixed on a sheet of typewritten paper. Doug coughed as he went by and the man looked up, his eyes glazed with boredom.

"Hello," Doug said, nervously.

"Hi." And then, after an epoch: "Did you want something?"

"I'm Doug. Doug Anderton." When this name failed to produce the slightest flare of recognition, he added: "I phoned up earlier in the week and said I'd be coming down. From Birmingham."

"Right. Right."

"Is . . ." (Doug craned his neck around hopefully) ". . . is Nick here?"

"Nick? Nick who?"

"Nick Logan? The editor?"

"Oh, *Nick*. No, Nick's not in today."

"What about Neil?"

The man looked around the office; or at least, looked a few degrees to the left, and then a few to the right, in a perfunctory way, before saying: "Haven't seen Neil today. Don't know where he's got to."

Doug could feel all of his hopes slipping away. As if he was trapped in that elevator and plummeting down all the way from the twenty-third floor.

"Was it you I spoke to on the phone?"

If the man was trying to remember, he wasn't trying very hard. "Where did you say you were from again?"

"Birmingham. The name's Doug."

"Maybe Richard spoke to you." He called across the office. "Rich!"

From behind a filing cabinet came a disembodied voice: "Yeah?"

"Did you speak to Doug from Birmingham on the phone?"

"No."

"He's here now."

A short silence. "What does he want?"

The man turned to Doug, asked, "What do you want?" and Doug was unable to think of a reply. He wanted a warm welcome, a slap on the back and a trip down to the pub for a celebratory round of drinks. It was increasingly obvious that he wasn't going to get it.

"Hang on," said the disembodied voice, "is he the bloke from the school magazine?"

Clutching at this lifeline, Doug almost shouted: "Yeah— that's right."

"Hi." A gangly, straw-haired man in his mid- to late-twenties, sporting a lopsided smile and what would come to be known a few years later as designer stubble, emerged from behind the cabinets and held out his hand.

"Hello. I'm Doug. We spoke on the phone."

Richard shook his head. "Don't think so. Maybe you spoke to Charles. Anyway, what can we do for you?"

"Well, I was just . . . Just passing through, and . . ." Doug's voice faded away, not because he couldn't think of an answer (although he couldn't), but because his attention had suddenly been drawn to a surreal detail. The office space was divided up into cubicles, and on top of one of the partitions someone had laid out a tangle of barbed wire and broken glass. Inside the cubicle itself, between the two desks, a noose was hanging from the ceiling and swaying very slightly from side to side in the moving currents of air.

Richard followed his gaze and said: "Yeah, that's Tony and Julie's bunker."

"Tony *Parsons*?" said Doug, awestruck, and beginning to feel that he was finally getting close to the fountainhead.

"They just put up that stuff to scare us. They're like naughty kids. Take a seat, Doug."

They sat down, and Richard offered him a cigarette. Doug took what he hoped was a practised drag, wincing slightly at the acrid burn which still never failed to give him a jolt.

"Great piece on Clapton," Richard now ventured. "We really dug it."

"Thanks," said Doug. "I just felt that he really deserved it, you know? Coming out in support of Powell, after all the things he's lifted from black music himself . . . It was so out of order."

"Is that why you came down?"

Doug looked blank, not understanding at first.

"There's a gig tonight," Richard explained. "The Rock Against Racism people. Kind of a launch event, over in Forest Gate. Carol Grimes is playing."

"Oh, right. Yeah, I was . . . hoping I could get to that." He assumed this was what Richard wanted to hear; it was hard to tell. Boldly, he added: "Maybe I could write about it."

"Maybe." Richard didn't sound too keen. "Trouble is, people here see it as kind of a *Melody Maker* thing. They got on to it first."

"Oh."

"Maybe you could do another gig for us. How long are you in town?"

"Just tonight."

"Well . . ." He rummaged around on his desk, produced a list from somewhere and scanned it without enthusiasm. "I dunno . . . We've got Steeleye Span at The Marquee."

Doug shook his head. "Not really my thing."

"National Health at University College. Have you heard of them?"

Doug hadn't.

"New band: sort of hippy, intellectual stuff. Most of them used to be in an outfit called Hatfield and the North."

"Oh, yeah." Doug did remember this name, vaguely. Benjamin had been to see them once, at Barbarella's, with Lois's then boyfriend Malcolm. He had enthused about it at tiresome length for the next couple of days (until other things had driven it out of his mind). Doug hadn't liked the sound of them at all. He craned over to get a look at the list himself, and something immediately caught his eye. "Wow—The Clash are playing tonight. Can I go to that?"

Richard drew in his breath sharply. "Well . . . it doesn't say anything here, but I'm sure Tony'll be doing that one. You know, it's kind of on his turf." He thought for a few more moments. "Look—let's give this Rock Against Racism thing a go. It might be worth five hundred words or something."

Doug broke into a smile which he quickly tried to check, not wishing his gratitude to show quite so nakedly. It was his first commission. His first venture into national journalism, at the age of sixteen. In his excitement, he never even noticed that no one had offered him anywhere to sleep for the night.

Doug had left the *NME* offices with mixed feelings. True, he hadn't got to meet Tony Parsons, or Julie Burchill, or Nick Logan, or Charles Shaar Murray; but he had left with a stack of free records under his arm. True, he would have liked these records to have been white label copies of "New Rose," "Anarchy in the UK" and the first Eddie and the Hot Rods album; instead, Richard had given him "Money Money Money" by Abba, "Ring Out Solstice Bells" by Jethro Tull and "Morning Glory" by The Wurzels. And it was flattering, of course, to have been given a commission to cover something as important as the first Rock Against Racism gig; but it would have been even better if Doug had been able to find the venue.

Apparently it was taking place in a pub called The Princess Alice in Forest Gate. Doug didn't possess anything as practical as a London *A–Z*, so he was reduced to approaching strangers at Blackfriars tube and asking them how to get there. The first three people he asked ignored him completely. The fourth one denied that there was any such place as Forest Gate. Doug told him that it was somewhere in East London. The stranger shook his head and said that he must be talking about Forest Hill, which was in South London. Doug assured him that it was Forest Gate, but agreed it was sensible to assume that Forest Hill and Forest Gate might be next to each other. So the stranger told him how to get to Forest Hill. It was extremely complicated. This part of London wasn't covered by the tube network: you had to go by bus, or British Rail, or both. The connections were difficult, and Doug spent more than forty minutes waiting at a stop in Camberwell while successive buses coasted by, crammed to the full with exhausted commuters going home for the weekend. When he did get on a bus, finally, it took him to the wrong place.

It was eight o'clock when he reached Forest Hill. The first person he asked told him there was no such pub as The Princess Alice. Doug told him that it was in Forest Gate, which he had been assured was near by. The man told him that Forest Gate was in East London, across the river towards Romford, about ten miles away. Doug's eyes widened in horror, and once again he felt that he was standing in the lift at King's Reach Tower, plummeting down from the twenty-third floor. The man apologized—

not that it was his fault, strictly speaking, that Forest Gate was in East London—and Doug consoled himself by going to the nearest pub, which was called The Man in the Moon, not The Princess Alice, and drinking two pints of lager. In a rare stroke of good fortune, the barman didn't ask how old he was.

So it was official, anyway: his trip to London was a fiasco. What could he salvage from it, in order to avoid humiliation when he got back to school on Monday morning and had to face the questioning of his friends?

There was no chance of battling all the way over to Forest Gate at this time of night. He would have to phone the office in a few days and apologize to Richard, who hadn't sounded too bothered about the review anyway. No doubt, from their perspective, it would be no great loss. Yes, there was still time to get back to Euston and catch a train to Birmingham, but that was too dreadful to contemplate. This was his weekend of escape, his great adventure. In an uncomfortable corner at the back of his mind lingered the thought that he still had nowhere to stay, but he dismissed it for now. There were bound to be youth hostels in London, or cheap hotels. He could find something. Meanwhile he took out his copy of the *NME* and looked again at the gig guide. The Clash were playing at Fulham Old Town Hall, wherever that was, with The Vibrators and Roogalator. He had ten pounds in his pocket. Surely it would cost less than that to get there by taxi?

It was a fantastic night. You could lose yourself in this noise. Little problems like the fact that you had no money and nowhere to stay dissolved in the sea of chords and sweat and beer and feedback and pounding bodies throwing themselves manically up and down in a distant approximation to the rhythm of the music. Doug had never heard any of these songs before but in the months and years to come they would become his closest friends: "Deny," "London's Burning," "Janie Jones." He was transfixed by the sight and sound of Joe Strummer shouting, screaming, singing, howling into the microphone: the hair lank with sweat, the veins on his neck tautened and pulsing with blood. Doug surrendered to the noise and for an hour he pogoed like a madman in the dense, heaving heart of a crowd two hundred or more strong. The heat and the energy were overwhelming. When it was over he stumbled to the bar and jostled for place as the fans clamoured to slake their thirst. He was pushed and shoved and he pushed and shoved back with the best of them and he felt, for the first time that day, wonderfully and unexpectedly at home.

Then, suddenly, there was a tap on his shoulder and he was staring at a face which should have been familiar, although he didn't at first know why.

"Hello! It's you again!" said a voice which might have belonged to a BBC continuity announcer. "Gosh, isn't this a *hoot!*"

Then he remembered. It was the woman from the lift at King's Reach Tower. He hadn't recognized her in her leathers and T-shirt. Her blonde hair was slicked back and the sweat was causing her make-up to run and she no longer looked stocky or comical but achingly sexy.

"Oh, hi!" he said.

"Can I get you a drink?" She was nearer to the bar than him.

"Thanks. Lager, please."

When they had forced their way out of the throng, she led him to a spare corner where two men of about her own age, neither of them dressed for the occasion, were leaning against a wall glancing warily around them, as if expecting (with some reason) to be attacked at any moment.

"This is Jacko, and Fudge," the woman said. "Boys, this is—"

"Douglas," he prompted, not quite knowing why he was using the full name.

"And I'm Ffion." She held out her hand. "Ffion ffoulkes. With four 'f's."

"Four?" said Doug.

"Two in each name."

He didn't understand a word of this, but let it pass.

"Douglas is a journalist for the *NME*," she explained, proudly. "Are you going to write about this concert?"

"No, not tonight. I'm just here as a punter."

"Well I thought the last lot were *awfully* good," Ffion said. "My goodness, they gave it what for! My ears are ringing like nobody's business."

Fudge said nothing and Jacko yawned.

"Look, Fee, are we going to slope off soon? This racket's brought on a stinking headache and all these proles are giving me the willies."

"We might catch something unspeakable," Fudge added.

"I'm a 'prole' myself, actually," said Doug, his hackles rising.

"Douglas is from Birmingham," Ffion told her friends.

"Oh, hard cheese," said Jacko. "What rotten luck, old boy."

"I must say you've picked up our lingo frightfully well," said Fudge, beaming. "I can understand you almost perfectly."

Doug, on the other hand, was having great difficulty understanding this peculiar pair, whose accents were even more alien than Ffion's to his unpractised ear. It didn't help that when he could decipher what they were saying, he had some trouble believing it.

"I can't see the point of a place like Birmingham, myself," said Jacko. "Full of Pakis, isn't it?"

"Pakis and proles," Fudge confirmed.

Doug turned away from them wordlessly and said to Ffion, "Could we go and talk somewhere else? I think your friends are the stupidest pair of stuck-up wankers I've ever met."

Jacko seized him by the neck of his T-shirt and said, "Look here, pipsqueak. How would you like a bunch of fives smack in the middle of your oiky little face?"

"Try it," Doug answered. "But I think you should know I've got a flick-knife in my pocket."

Jacko released his grip slowly. His face was drained of what little colour it had once possessed when he turned to Ffion. "Come on, Fee. I said we'd meet McSquirter and the rest of the gang down at Parson's."

"I'm staying here."

They stared at each other for a few angry seconds, then Jacko stamped his foot in fury and walked off.

"You silly little tart," said Fudge, following him.

Ffion and Doug sipped their lager in silence for a while. She was smiling at him again.

"Have you really got a knife?" she asked.

"No, of course not."

She leaned over suddenly and gave him a fierce, open-mouthed kiss. It tasted of lager and lipstick.

"You're a sweetie," she said. "What about some cocoa and rumpy-pumpy back at my place?"

"OK," said Doug, ninety per cent certain that he had interpreted this invitation correctly. "Can I stay the night?"

"Of course you can."

Doug lost something important that night. Not his virginity, which had already been surrendered to a co-operative fifth-former from the girls' school at the age of fourteen, in a tiny Left Bank hotel on one of Mr. Plumb's invaluable weekend outings to Paris. What he yielded, instead, to the preposterously named Ffion ffoulkes was less easy to define, but in its way just as impossible to recover. It had to do with his sense of self, his sense of belonging, his loyalty to the place and the family he came from. In the space of a few hours, a lifelong allegiance was severed, and a newer, more tenuous one formed. That night, in short, he became enamoured of the upper classes.

He became enamoured of where they lived. As he walked with Ffion through the icy rain of that October night, heading back towards the studio on the King's Road her father had impulsively bought for her one weekend, he fell in love with Chelsea's solemn Georgian terraces and reposeful, well-fed squares. Here, Doug could see, life was lived on a grand scale. Rednal seemed mean and wizened by comparison.

He became enamoured of how they lived, too. He admired the cluttered Bohemianism of her flat, the careless way that beanbags and Afghan rugs jostled for attention with a full-length portrait, thick with oilpaint, of a bright-eyed woman in tweeds who Ffion later identified as her mother. She told Doug the name of the artist and could hardly believe that he'd never heard of him. He could hardly believe that she had paintings by famous artists on the wall of her flat. Everything that night seemed new and surprising, and Doug also became enamoured of the upper-class ways of eating, drinking, waking the neighbours up with deafening music, taking drugs and, of course, having sex, which he had never realized could be so boisterous, cheery, polymorphous or strenuous an experience.

"You mean you've never tried it this way before?" Ffion would ask, with bright incredulity, having arranged herself into some implausible position which like as not required her to address him through the crook of her elbow or from beneath the arch of her left knee. "You're not a virgin, are you, Duggie?"

Some hours later, as she clung to him by a tuft of his hair and locked his head firmly between her legs, his tongue working at her clitoris with steady, unflagging enthusiasm, she suddenly let out a high whinny like a thoroughbred pony and said, with a delighted sigh: "Oh Duggie, isn't this topping? I think I could keep going all weekend."

"Me too," said Doug, truthfully but indistinctly.

"What a . . . bother," Ffion added, forming the words as best she could through the ripples of sensation that his labours were continuing to stir up inside her, "that I'm expected for lunch tomorrow . . . in Gerrards Cross."

"Cancel it," came Doug's muffled voice.

"But it's with my—oooh!—fiancé's parents."

He stopped abruptly, and looked up. His face wore an expression of profound astonishment that would have been comic even if his hair hadn't been pulled wildly out of shape, and his mouth smeared with pubic hair and vaginal juices.

"You're engaged?" he asked.

"Yes," Ffion answered glumly. "And to the most frightful bore."

"When will you be back?"

"Not till Sunday night. I think we're going riding."

Doug raised himself on to one arm and wiped his mouth with the back of his hand. In a flash, he realized that he would never see Ffion again. In another flash, it occurred to him that he didn't really mind.

"That's all right," he said, and kissed each of her nipples in turn before beginning to trace a line with his mouth back across her stomach and her belly-button and towards the wiry haven beyond. "I've got masses of homework this weekend anyway."

Ffion grabbed him by the hair again and yanked him back up into her line of vision. Now it was her turn to look astonished.

"Homework?" she said. "You mean—you're still at school?"

"That's right."

Their eyes met, and all at once it seemed to both of them that they were sharing the most exquisite hash- and music- and sex- and alcohol-fuelled joke. They burst into laughter, and laughed and laughed until the breath had left them and their entangled naked bodies were helpless and heaving. Doug was the first to recover his speech, but all he managed to say, in a high-pitched mockery of her own perfect vowels, was "What a *hoot!*," and that set her off again, shrieking like a nervy adolescent, so that anyone passing in the corridor outside might have thought that Doug had started to tickle her, instead of returning one more time to the succulent exertions that waited for him between Ffion's sheened and glistening legs.

5

"So—are you ready to go out?

"I'm just going to put this record here, for now. I wanted to talk to you about it, but we'll do that later.

"I think you'll need a coat. It's really been getting wintry out there, the last few days.

"All set? You'd better lead on. I keep getting lost in this place. All those corridors.

"Hang on, hang on, we don't have to go quite that fast. We've got all afternoon, you know.

"That's better.

"I suppose you can't wait to get out.

"There—I told you it was going to be nippy, didn't I? Come on, let me tuck that scarf in. Give your neck a bit of protection. That's it. This coat's lasted you a little while, hasn't it? I remember you wearing that in the fifth form. This one's new. Mum got it for me last month. Said she was sick of me wearing Uncle Len's old greatcoat. It went off to the jumble sale, in the end.

"I thought we'd go up to the Beacon again. Would that be all right? Or the duck ponds, maybe?

"OK, the Beacon it is.

"I thought you might get tired of doing the same thing every week.

"You're looking better, you know. Much better. Mum said

that, after she'd been to see you on Wednesday, and it's true. Much fuller in the face. You must be eating more.

"I bet the food in that place is pretty grim, though, isn't it?

"Look out for the cars, now. They tear down this road at about fifty miles an hour, some of them. The police are never there when you want them. There, it's safe to cross.

"Funnily enough, we came to these woods on Wednesday ourselves. Me and Harding and some of the others. I don't know if I told you, but Mr. Tillotson persuaded the Chief to set up this new option on Wednesday afternoons. It's called the Walking Option and . . . well, that's what it is, really, it means that people like us who tend to get beaten to a pulp when we go on to the rugby field, and are hopeless at running and all the other things, well, we don't have to do any proper sport any more, we can just change out of uniform and we pile into the minibus and we come out somewhere like this and we just wander around for a couple of hours. So we get some fresh air and a bit of exercise and at the same time we can improve our minds with a bit of fine conversation, that sort of thing.

"The only problem is, I don't seem to have much to say to Harding any more. I don't know why. He thinks I'm boring, probably, and I think he's . . . Well, he's strange. There's no getting away from it. He's becoming strange. So we don't really know what to talk about. Those scripts we were going to write together . . . Nothing seemed to come of that, anyway.

"God, Lois, you're shivering. You really do feel the cold these days, don't you? It's because you're just sitting around all the time, I reckon, and they keep that room of yours too warm. I know it's better than being too cold, but it means that when you come out on a day like this—you feel it, don't you? Look, I've got this terrible bobble hat in my pocket. Grandma knitted it for me, and I have to carry it around in case she asks me what I did with it. Here you are, put it on. Get those ears covered. They've gone all pink. Just feel your cheek! There, that's better.

"On the subject of rugby—which isn't a subject that preoccupies me as a rule, I know—it's all about suppressed homosexuality, if you ask me, and not so suppressed either, some of the time, if you see what goes on in the showers after some of those games—anyway, sorry, I'm wittering, it's nerves, don't worry, only sometimes I don't even know if you can hear me, but of course you can, they've told me that, so I should just carry on, that's what they said, just carry on as if I was having a normal conversation, except that with most normal conversations the other person says something back occasionally, but anyway, that's not the point . . . What was I saying? Oh yes, rugby, on the subject of rugby, well, there was a bit of a scandal this week, because Astell House were playing Ransome House, and Richards was playing scrum-half for Astell and Culpepper was playing for Ransome, on the inside right or silly mid-off or whatever those stupid positions are called—and nobody really knows what happened but there was some sort of tackle, and the next thing you know, Culpepper's down on the ground screaming in agony—and I mean literally screaming—and it turns out he's broken his arm. Well, Richards is very contrite, as you might expect, and very upset about it, actually, because he's a gentle sort of bloke and doesn't like to hurt anybody, but now Culpepper's going around telling people that he did it on purpose. Which is rubbish, anyone'll tell you that. The fact is that he just hates Richards and he'll do anything he can to make life hard for him. He's hated him ever since he first came to the school, some people say it's because he's black but I don't think that's the reason, I think he just hates him because he's a better athlete than he is, a better sportsman, better at everything really. But it just seems to get worse and worse. He seems to hate him more and more every day and nobody can see where it's going to end.

"Anyway, Richards is going to add another string to his bow soon. We just heard about it yesterday. He's joined the drama society. Or not joined it, exactly, but . . .

"Sorry, I thought we'd take a bit of a detour, there. That was

Mum's friend Mrs. Oakeshott, from the W.I., and the last thing we want is her talking to us for half an hour. I don't think she saw us. Anyway, this way's probably quicker, now I come to think of it. Nearly at the top, now.

"Oh, yes, Richards and the drama society. The thing is, he's never acted before in his life, but he's just landed the lead in the Christmas production. Which is *Othello*, naturally. Well, they don't have a very extensive pool of black actors to choose from, do they, at our school? Harding offered to do a Laurence Olivier and get to work with the boot polish again, but that suggestion didn't go down too well this time, for some reason. As for Desdemona . . . well, I don't have to tell you who *that's* going to be. Cicely, of course. Now all they need to do is cast Culpepper as Iago and we've really got a production on our hands.

"And yes, I'm still mad about her. I know, I know, it's been going on for years now and I haven't even said a word to her yet. It's getting ridiculous. I've practically written four symphonies and half a dozen verse cycles about the woman and still she wouldn't know me from Adam if we were to meet in the street tomorrow. But . . . Nothing ever seems to *happen*, at school, that would make our paths cross. It's almost as if the gods were against me, on this one. I mean, the main reason I started working for the magazine was because I assumed she was going to be one of the editors, too. But then she never showed up to the first meeting. Then they decided to set up joint English lessons with the Girls' School, and she and I were put in different classes. I can't act, so I can't get to know her that way, and I'm no good at public speaking, so I can't join the debating society . . . I don't know what I should do. The only way I could get to know her is through Claire, because Claire sees her all the time, but Claire . . . well, she's the last person I could ask to do something like that. The last person on earth. For obvious reasons.

"Philip told me a funny thing about Claire, actually, just the other day. He and Claire see quite a lot of each other, these days, what with the magazine, and her just living a couple of streets away. But apparently—and I don't know if you knew this, perhaps you did, but . . . no, maybe not, because it happened just after . . . Anyway, apparently, Claire's sister—who I met once, incidentally, down at the café by the bus terminus, as did Paul, who was *particularly* rude to her, I seem to remember—Claire's sister—Miriam, her name was—she's . . . Well, she's disappeared. Vanished, completely. I don't know all the details—don't know *any* of the details, to be honest—but there was something about a lover, some affair she was having, and then she left Claire a note, or left her parents a note, and went to join this man, somewhere in the North, and that was it. They never heard from her again. Not a word.

"I think Claire feels awful about it. In fact I'm sure she does. Anybody would, wouldn't they?

"By the way—still no sign of the holiday photos from Denmark, I'm afraid. Dad's furious with himself for putting them in the post when he could have got them done at the chemist down the road. It's been two months since he sent them off now but the people at the processing factory are still on strike, apparently. He almost has a fit every time you mention it to him. Says that strikes are going to destroy this country, like cancer destroys the body. I'm sure we'll get them in a week or two. I hope they came out well. It was an amazing place, Lois. It was such a shame you couldn't have gone there with us.

"Well, here we are. I love this view, don't you? I know that places like Skagen have more beautiful views, but . . . I shall always love this one. There's the Longbridge factory, see? Where Dad works. And Doug's father, too. And there's the university tower. School's just behind that, do you remember? And this tower here, just the other side of Rubery, the one with the green tip, that's where we've just come from. That's where you live at the moment. But not for much longer. You'll be out of there very soon, now. Everybody says so.

"Oh Lois, I wish you'd say something, just something, I know you're listening to me and I know you understand everything I say and I know you like it when I give you all this stupid news about school but if only you could just *say* something again, be like you were a few months ago when we all thought you were over the worst and it seemed like . . . I don't know, it seemed like you were going to be all right again.

"You *are* going to be all right again. You have to be.

"I pray for you, you know. Every night. And that *works*. I know it does. I'd never tell anyone else about it because no one would believe me, but it's true. I've told you that story, haven't I? So you know what I mean. And it happened. It really happened. *You* believe me, don't you, Lois? And that means it can happen again. I just have to work harder at it this time, because what I'm asking for is so much bigger. But He listens to me, Lois. I know He does. He listens to me and I know He's going to put things right. It's going to happen soon.

"OK, we'd better get back.

"Of course, the other big news at the moment is that the band's going to have its first rehearsal in a few days. Finally, after all these years of talking about it. It was supposed to be last week but now we've put it off till next Thursday. The day before bonfire night. And I have to say, I'm *really* curious to see what Philip has up his sleeve, because he's been very cagey about—

"Shit! No! No, Lois, it's all right.

"Really, it's all right, it's just a dog. Just a dog barking.

"It's just a—

"Come on, hold me, hold me tight.

"Really, it's OK, calm down, calm *down* now.

"It's just a—

"Will you *please* keep your *fucking* dog under control!

"I don't care about that. Can't you see he's scaring her to death?

"Come on. Come on, now. It's OK.

"Come on. Still. Be still. Deep breaths.

"Hold on to me. Hold *on to* me, Lois. The dog's gone. The noise has gone. It's all right. Everything's going to be all right.

"Home now.

"Back to your room.

"I have to go now, Lois. It's been a lovely walk. Really lovely. And you're looking so much better.

"I wish I could stay longer. I really do. I wish I could stay with you here all the time.

"It'll be your dinner time soon, won't it?

"Now look: I wanted to give you this, before I go. This is the record I was telling you about.

"Dr. Saunders was telling me they've got a record-player in the patients' room, and sometimes you listen to music there. Yes? He says you've been listening to Bach, and Mozart, and stuff like that. Relaxing music. Good for the nerves.

"Well, I just thought you might want to listen to this. I mean, I thought you might be . . . ready for it.

"I don't know if you remember, but just before . . . just before Malcolm died, he took me to see a concert in town. We went to Barbarella's, and we heard all these weird bands. You remember the kind of music he used to like? Well, the people who made this record were playing that night, and they were his favourite. He liked them more than anyone. And I thought that if you heard it, it might remind you . . . might help you to think a bit about the kind of person he was.

"And there's another reason, too. You see the title of the record? It's called *The Rotters' Club.*

"*The Rotters' Club:* that's us, Lois, isn't it? Do you see? That's what they used to call us, at school. Bent Rotter, and Lowest Rotter. *We're* The Rotters' Club. You and me. Not Paul. Just you and me.

"I think this record was *meant* for us, you see. Malcolm never got to hear it, but I think he . . . knows about it, if that doesn't sound too silly. And now it's his gift, to you and me. From—wherever he is.

"I don't know if that makes any sense.

"Anyway.

"I'll just leave it on the table here.

"Have a listen, if you feel like it.

"I've got to go now.

"I've got to go, Lois.

"I've got to go."

6

(On Monday, 13th December, 1999, Douglas Anderton, along with five other figures from public life, took part in an event called "Goodbye To All That" at the Queen Elizabeth Hall in London. To mark the end of the second Christian Millennium, the speakers were asked to write a short piece on a valedictory theme, explaining "what they most regret leaving behind or what they are happiest to see the back of." This is an unedited version of the text he read on that occasion.)

BONFIRE NIGHT

There was a boy at school called Harding. I suppose there's a boy like him at every school. He was the class jester, the school clown. I wouldn't say that he had a lightning wit: there are no *bon mots* that I can recall, and he didn't crack jokes or anything like that. All I can remember is that he made us laugh, and that nobody could consider themselves safe when he was around.

To choose one instance from among many, there was the case of Mr. Silverman, the maths teacher. Sweaty Silverman, we used to call him, although come to think of it he never used to sweat much until Harding got hold of him. I don't know why this inoffensive specimen should have been singled out for persecution, except that he was young and inexperienced, fresh out of teacher-training college. Harding could always sense nervousness in someone and would home in on it ruthlessly. His campaign began, I remember, after just a couple of weeks, when Silverman was pacing up and down the classroom during a maths test and suddenly jumped about three feet in the air when he noticed there was a pickled rat from the biology labs sitting perkily up in the inkwell on Harding's desk. A couple of days later, further humiliation was visited upon him when he was standing over some other boy's work, helping him out with a quadratic equation, whereupon Harding and two accomplices began shifting their desks towards him, inch by inch, until the poor man was imprisoned, corralled in on all four sides, and in the end he nearly broke his leg climbing over the desks to get out. That was the first time we saw an outbreak of the uncontrollable perspiration that was soon to give him his nickname. It got worse and worse after that, and the chaos of his lessons quickly became legendary (another time, Harding persuaded us *all* to turn our desks through 180 degrees before Mr. Silverman arrived, so that he turned up to find the entire class facing in the wrong direction) until in the end the Chief Master decided to attend one himself, to see if the reality was even half as bad as the rumours suggested. All went well at first until Silverman, sweating profusely as he scribbled a sequence of logarithms on to the blackboard with shaking hand, reached into his pocket for a handkerchief, and pulled out Harding's very own underpants, a magnificent pair of off-white aerated Y-fronts which he must have placed there a few minutes earlier. Sweaty Silverman mopped his brow with them for about five seconds before he realized what was going on, and in the ensuing furore, as the rest of us screamed with laughter, Harding, I recall, just sat back in his chair with a tiny, self-satisfied grin on his face: the smile of the skilled craftsman, the great orchestrator of mayhem, checking that he hasn't lost his touch. The lord of misrule, surveying his kingdom and noting that all is well.

What happens to people like Harding, I wonder? Do they sign away their senses of humour with their first mortgage payment and turn into quantity surveyors? I lost touch with him as soon as we left school—we all did—so probably I'll never know. I never worked out why he was like that, either: what motivated him. I was going to say that his only pleasure in life was to make people laugh, but maybe that wasn't the point. Perhaps he was really doing it for himself. He liked to shock people, to find out how far he could go, and the kick was probably in seeing how other people reacted. The delirious outrage he used to provoke. Political correctness hadn't been invented then, and increasingly, as we all got older, his comedy observed no boundaries, no standards of taste. It began to seem that the whole idea was simply to offend as many people as possible: boys, teachers, it didn't matter.

There's one time in particular that sticks in my mind. About eighteen months before that other story. It was November, 1976, to be precise, two days before bonfire night. It would have been a Wednesday afternoon because that was when the Senior Debating Society used to meet. This was the time they were going to stage a mock version of the next day's by-election, and Harding had volunteered to speak for the National Front.

People forget about the 1970s. They think it was all about wide collars and glam rock, and they get nostalgic about *Fawlty Towers* and kids' TV programmes, and they forget the ungodly strangeness of it, the weird things that were happening all the time. They remember that the unions had real power in those days but they forget how people reacted: all those cranks and military types who talked about forming private armies to restore order and protect property when the rule of law broke down. They forget about the Ugandan Asian refugees who arrived at Heathrow in 1972, and how it made people say that Enoch had been right in the late sixties when he warned about rivers of blood, how his rhetoric echoed down the years, right down to a drunken comment Eric Clapton made on stage at the Birmingham Odeon in 1976. They forget that in those days, the National Front sometimes looked like a force to be reckoned with.

This particular by-election was a local affair, being held a few miles away in Walsall, and it had been prompted by the antics of another of the 1970s' more colourful figures: John Stonehouse, the former Labour MP who had disappeared in Florida in November, 1974, was apprehended by the police in Melbourne a month later, and finally, after lengthy legal proceedings, received a prison sentence of seven years on twenty-one charges of fraud, conspiracy, theft and forgery totalling £170,000. (They did things properly back then.) His sentence was handed down during that fateful hot summer of 1976, when Britain had to appoint a minister for drought and Eric made his unfortunate remark at the Birmingham Odeon and we were all busy gearing ourselves up for life in the sixth form. The by-election was held on November 4th and it was the day before that that the Debating Society staged its own version.

My memories of the occasion are blurred, obviously. I know that the music school concert-hall was packed out, and I was standing at the back with my friends Benjamin and Philip. Nice enough kids, despite having hippie-ish tendencies. At this stage in their lives it was an uphill struggle to get them to talk about anything except the band they were endlessly on the point of forming. A couple of years before, along with Harding, we had made up an inseparable foursome. Those loyalties were now beginning to fracture, slowly; but we were all still intrigued by him, and curious to know what kind of performance he was planning to lay on for us today.

When he got up to speak, after the other three candidates had collectively bored us to tears, the first thing we noticed was that Harding had managed, somehow, to transform his physical appearance. He shambled on to the stage, crook-backed, bow-legged, his eyes glaring sullenly around him with a mixture of venom and settled disappointment at the world's stupidity. He appeared to have aged about sixty years. I think the idea was to produce a parody of A. K. Chesterton, an unfamiliar figure to most of us, although the fact that he had been the NF's leader for a few years was just the sort of thing Harding would make it his business to know. The rules of the debate stipulated that the candidates write their own speeches, but Harding ignored this, and reaching awkwardly into his blazer pocket with those palsied, old man's hands, he produced what was clearly one of the Front's own printed leaflets. All he did, from that point on, was to read it aloud.

The reaction he got was probably the last that he—or indeed I—would have expected. The heckling died down and soon an astonished hush fell upon the audience. If nothing else, we learned that day that there is, in the language of pure racism, a kind of malign talismanic potency. Some of those phrases lodged in my memory and are still there, a quarter of a century later, like burn marks on the unconscious. He talked about "droves of dark-skinned sub-racials," "race-degeneration," "the lie of racial equality" and the threat to our "Nordic birthright of freedom." After less than half a minute of this stuff Steve Richards, the only black kid in the school (nicknamed "Rastus," in case you were wondering), walked out of the concert-hall, hot with pent-up fury. Harding noticed but it didn't stop him. He started talking about "the maws of doom." If the government didn't abandon its policies of racial tolerance, he was saying, that's where we would find ourselves. "The maws of doom!" he kept repeating. "The very maws of doom!" It became so absurd that a few people did start laughing, nervously. It became just about possible to regard the whole thing as an elaborate piss-take. But some of us were beginning to feel that Harding's humour, if that's what it was, was taking us to some pretty strange places lately.

He got six votes, by the way: more than five per cent of the total. Not bad, but the NF candidate in the actual by-election did much better. We were a friendly lot, in the West Midlands, back in 1976.

The following day I was privileged, if that's the word, to attend the first and, as it turned out, only rehearsal of Philip and Benjamin's band.

I should reiterate, at this point: the 1970s was a very strange era. Music is another example. You wouldn't believe the stuff that people—clever people, too, for the most part—used to listen to with a straight face on their dads' music centres or in their student bedsits back then. There was a band called Focus—Dutch, I think they were—whose keyboard player used to break off from hammering away at his Moog synthesizer to start yodelling into the microphone. There was a band called Gryphon who used to call a sudden halt in the middle of some rock'n'roll riff, whip out their recorders and crumhorns, and launch into a spot of medieval riddle-me-ree. And the grand-daddy of them all, of course, was Rick Wakeman, with his monstrous concept albums about Henry VIII and King Arthur—one of which, I seem to remember, he presented as a live ice-skating spectacular at Wembley Stadium. Peculiar times.

If this sort of music was your thing, there was one book that was bound to be weighing down the Army and Navy Stores rucksack you carried into school with you every morning. My reference, of course, is to J. R. R. Tolkien's *The Lord of the Rings*. Needless to say, this was Philip's favourite reading matter and this fact was reflected in the series of names which he'd attempted to inflict, over the last few weeks, on his unfortunate musical colleagues. Lothlorien was one of them. There was also Mithril, Minas Tirith and Isildur's Bane. In the end, though, they managed to surpass themselves and settled for the silly name to end all silly names. They called themselves "Gandalf's Pikestaff."

Philip and Benjamin had somehow managed to dredge up a trio of would-be collaborators for that first rehearsal, and I've never seen anxiety written so eloquently on three faces as when Philip started handing out the chord sheets to the first song, which must have extended to at least fourteen pages. They were covered with dwarfish runes, Gothic calligraphy and Roger Dean-style illustrations of dragons and busty elfin maidens in various stages of provocative undress.

"What's this?" said the drummer, apprehensively.

Philip explained that his first composition was to be a rock

symphony in five movements, totalling some thirty-two minutes in length (i.e. even longer than "Supper's Ready" from the
Genesis album *Foxtrot*), and narrating the entire history of the
universe from the moment of creation up until roughly, as far as
I could make out, the resignation of Harold Wilson in 1976. The
title of this catchy little number, destined to be a surefire hit in
the soul clubs of Wigan, was "Apotheosis of the Necromancer."

Well, they gave it their best shot, I'll allow them that. For
about five minutes, anyway. But Philip had chosen the wrong
moment, historically, to make his personal bid for progressive
rock superstardom. This was late in 1976, remember? Word was
beginning to filter through, even in a cultural no-man's-land
like Birmingham, of a new kind of music that was springing up
in places like London and Manchester. Names like The Damned
and The Clash and, of course, The Sex Pistols were beginning
to be whispered around. It was the glorious rebirth of the two-
minute single. No more guitar solos. Concept albums were out.
Mellotrons were *verboten*. It was the dawn of punk or, as Tony
Parsons more accurately called it, dole-queue rock. And even my
upper-middle-class schoolchums were beginning to catch on.

It was the drummer who sounded the first note of rebellion.
After tinkling away on his ride cymbal for what must have
seemed an eternity, as part of an extended instrumental passage
that was meant to evoke the idea of zillions of far-off galaxies
springing into life, he suddenly announced, "Fuck this for a
game of soldiers," and started to lay down a ferocious backbeat
in 4/4. Recognizing his cue, the guitarist whacked up his volume
and embarked upon a riotous three-chord thrash over which the
lead vocalist, an aggressive little character called Stubbs, began
to improvise what the charitable might describe as a melody.
Now here's an interesting thing. He was singing the first words
that came into his head, probably, but what do you suppose they
were? Bizarrely, it was that stupid phrase from Harding's fascist
speech the day before. "The maws!" he was screaming. "The
maws! The very maws of doom!" Over and over, like an incanta-
tion, as the music got more and more frantic and Philip ran to

the front, waving them to stop this hideous racket, and then, when they just ignored him, standing and watching with his arms folded, until Benjamin joined him, and put his arm around his shoulders, and they both just stood there on the sidelines, watching it crumble, this project which had taken them years to put together. There was a fire in Stubbs's eyes, at that moment: a kind of demonic exhilaration, fuelled by sheer, unpolluted delight in trashing something, kicking something over. That was how our school's first punk band was born, and that was their name, from then on, The Maws of Doom, and although it was funny watching it happen like that, I felt sad as well, sad for Philip, sad for the dream that had so quickly fallen to pieces around him.

It wasn't really until the next evening, though, that I knew exactly how he must have felt.

It was Guy Fawkes' night, and there was a massive bonfire being lit in Cofton Park. A thin crowd of people gathered, rockets were sent flying into the Longbridge sky, and sparklers were passed around. I spotted Benjamin and his family soon enough, but was wary of making contact. There was a problem between his dad and mine. Mine was a shop steward, Benjamin's was management. Both worked at the Leyland factory. They said hello to each other, eventually, and there was some kind of edgy conversation. Benjamin's dad was in a good mood because of the by-election result. The Tories had won, with a massive swing. The biggest swing since the War, we were being told. The signs had been stacking up all year and now there was no escaping it: the Callaghan government was finished, even if they could last out their current term. The Labour majority was wiped out, Denis Healey was going to the IMF begging for money and you could just feel public confidence ebbing away. This result proved it. Meanwhile, waiting in the wings was a new breed of Tory and these people meant business. Their rhetoric was fierce: it was anti-welfare, anti-community, anti-consensus. In a couple of years, maybe less, they were going to be in power and they were going to be there for a long time.

Benjamin had a little brother whose name was . . . well, perhaps I shouldn't tell you that. He might not thank me for it, these days. He was a few years below us at school, but we all knew him. You couldn't miss him, actually. There was something strange, something freakish about this boy. He was wise— or at least intelligent—way beyond his years. He was a Midwich Cuckoo, and he scared the shit out of us. When it came to politics, I didn't know what his views were, but he was bound to have them. He had views about everything. Anyway, that night, I found out.

"Hey—Duggie! Duggie! Duggie!" He came running up to me, sparkler in hand. I felt like sticking one on him, the cheeky bastard. Nobody called me Duggie.

He held the sparkler up in front of my face and said, "Wait. Wait."

I was already waiting. What else was there to do?

"Here you are," he said. "Look! What's this?"

At that precise moment, his sparkler fizzled out. I didn't say anything, so he supplied the answer himself. "The death of the socialist dream," he said.

He giggled like a little maniac, and stared at me for a second or two before running off, and in that time I saw exactly the same thing I'd seen in Stubbs's eyes the day before. The same triumphalism, the same excitement, not because something new was being created, but because something was being destroyed. I thought about Philip and his stupid rock symphony and I swear that my eyes pricked with tears. This ludicrous attempt to squeeze the history of countless millennia into half an hour's worth of crappy riffs and chord changes suddenly seemed no more Quixotic than all the things my dad and his colleagues had been working towards for so long. A national health service, free to everyone who needed it. Redistribution of wealth through taxation. Equality of opportunity. Beautiful ideas, Dad, noble aspirations, just as there was the kernel of something beautiful in Philip's musical hodge-podge. But it was never going to happen. If there had ever been a time when it might have happened, that time was slipping away. The moment had passed. Goodbye to all that.

Easy to be clever with hindsight, I know, but I was right, wasn't I? Look back on that night from the perspective of now, the closing weeks of the closing century of our second millennium—if the calendar of some esoteric and fast-disappearing religious sect counts for anything any more—and you have to admit that I was right. And so was Benjamin's brother, the little bastard, with his sparkler and his horrible grin and that nasty gleam of incipient victory in his twelve-year-old eyes. Goodbye to all that, he was saying. He'd worked it out already. He knew what the future held in store.

After that, anyway, I didn't hang around at the bonfire for much longer. It was nearly eight o'clock, which meant *The New Avengers* on ATV. Joanna Lumley would soon be running around the countryside in some skimpy outfit, and I wasn't going to miss it just for the sake of a few Catherine Wheels. You had to take your pleasures where you could, in those days.

THE **BILL BOARD**

Thursday, 9 December, 1976

THEATRE SPECIAL

As the Senior Drama Soc goes into dress rehearsals for its Christmas production of "Othello," we bring you exclusive interviews with the two leading players.

Steve Richards as OTHELLO

Interview by Doug Anderton

"I see him as a noble man, a man of courage and action, but he has this fatal weakness which is that he has a bit of an ego on him. And that's where Iago is able to move in and do his bit of mischief."

This down-to-earth but insightful reading of one of Shakespeare's greatest tragic heroes is typical of the fresh perspective being brought to the role by Steve Richards of the lower science sixth.

Already well known as the undisputed star of both the rugby First XV and the cricket First XI, Steve is a newcomer to the world of back-stage tantrums and first-night nerves. But is he enjoying the experience so far?

"It's been fantastic," he grins. "The rest of the cast are a great gang, and despite the heaviness of the drama, we've been having a real laugh most of the time. You know, at first I was daunted by the challenge of this part. I'd read 'Othello' when I was doing O-levels and I knew there was a real mountain to climb there, for any actor. But I like to drive myself. I like to push myself. That's how you get the best out of yourself and that's what I reckon this school is all about, isn't it?"

Steve's parents, Lloyd and Connie, came to this country from Kingston, Jamaica, in the mid-1950s. They settled in Handsworth but, like many of their fellow Jamaicans, did not find it easy to assimilate at first. Lloyd was a cabinet-maker by trade but the only work he could find at the time was unskilled. He started as a panel-beater in the Hay Mills plant of what was then the Wilmot Breedon company, and has since worked his way up to become a British Leyland foreman. Steve's mother Connie works in medical catering. They have another son, Steve's younger brother Aldwyn, named after Aldwyn "Lord Kitchener" Roberts, one of the most famous exponents of calypso in the Caribbean.

"Yeah, we're a close family," Steve agrees. "It was tough for my mum and dad because they left a lot of relatives behind in Jamaica. So as far as family was concerned, they had to start again from scratch. They're going to be there to see me on the first night, that's for sure. And the second, and the last!"

A few people were surprised, I told him, when it was announced that he had been catapulted straight to this starring role. In a school not exactly overflowing with members of the ethnic minorities, was he not worried that he had landed this plum part simply—to put it bluntly—because of the colour of his skin?

"Sure, it was the drama committee's idea that I should read for it," he answers. "But the bottom line is that I auditioned for this part like everyone else. We're not talking about tokenism here."

Finally, rumours have been flying around the school corridors for the last few weeks about the on-stage (and off-stage) chemistry between Steve and his leading lady, Cicely Boyd. Bad news for the gossip-mongers, though: Steve insists that there's nothing in it. And when he tells me why, it turns out there's further bad news for his legions of admirers on the other side of the Founder's Drive.

"Sure, Ciss and I have got a very intense rapport going on stage," he says, "but that's as far as it goes. I've got a girlfriend called Valerie and we've been going steady now for about six months. We've known each other for years, actually, because we met at Sunday School, which makes it sound really boring, but she's a great girl and she's going to be sitting right there in the front row, making sure I don't cross the line in any of those love scenes!"

A smart handclap from the show's director, Tim Newsome (whose "Endgame" proved a bit too austere for some tastes last term) signals that my time is up and Steve is wanted for another run-through of the demanding finale. On my way downstairs I drop in at the Porter's Lodge and am told that ticket sales so far have been extremely brisk. So one thing at least seems certain: both schools are convinced that this is going to be an "Othello" to remember.

• • •

Cicely Boyd as DESDEMONA
Interview by Claire Newman

There's a certain kind of hair which is just made for tossing, and without a doubt, Cicely Boyd has it in spades. The legendary flaxen locks which cascade over her perfectly formed shoulders have probably inspired more fourth-form poetry, over the years, than the Dark Lady ever managed to get out of the Bard—and they also give her the most expressive repertoire of tosses I've ever encountered.

This girl can toss with disdain, toss in agreement, toss with impatience, and of course (how many English masters have found this out, since joint lessons were introduced?) she can toss flirtatiously, too. No wonder that you often hear her awestruck schoolmates remarking "What a tosser!" whenever they pass her in the corridor.

Today, though, she is tossing with passion and sincerity, as she discusses the draining experience of immersing herself in the part of Desdemona for Tim Newsome's upcoming and eagerly awaited production of "Othello."

"You have to do a lot of what I call 'emotional eurhythmics,' " she gushes. "On the night of the performance, you have to be at your absolute peak, physically and spiritually. The karma has to be just right. I find that meditation helps enormously. I've taught Steve quite a lot about this, and before rehearsals what we'll often do is just sit cross-legged on the floor, staring into each other's eyes for half an hour or so."

Straight out of the RADA textbook, I'm sure. "Steve," by the way, is Steve Richards, he of the pulsing thigh muscles and gleaming pecs, who will be making his theatrical debut opposite <u>la</u> Boyd as the insanely jealous Moor. Was she finding it hard, so far, working with a relative novice?

"Steve was my own choice to play Othello," she pouts. "And I think I've been proved right. For a long time I've thought he was just the most intriguing person. He has this very ordinary facade, very upfront and straightforward, but I was sure that when I peeled all of that away, there'd be something enormous and fascinating underneath, which I really wanted to explore." (She means his talent, I think.) "I just know he's going to be fantastic in the part. He has a real feeling for the verse."

Somewhat nervously, now, I take my life in my hands and suggest that there are critics, in some quarters, who maintain that she has come to wield too much power on the Drama Committee, and that her style of management has been described—again, only in some quarters—as dictatorial. How does she respond to these comments?

At first she doesn't respond at all—at least, not in words, but simply with a majestic toss of the hair that could stun a rhino at fifty yards. Then she purrs:

"I can't help it if people become jealous. That's simply not my problem. We're enjoying a wonderful year and we've already put on some wonderful shows. All I can say is that that gives me enormous satisfaction."

And this jealousy, I venture, might have something to do with her looks?

"It's true, you know, Claire—there is this prejudice that makes people think a woman can't be beautiful and intelligent at the same time. But the truth of the matter is, I don't consider myself to be beautiful anyway." (She looks to me for confirmation, or perhaps disagreement, but I am preserving, at this point, the studied neutrality of the professional reporter.) Now she leans forward, confiding. "Actually, Claire, I'm going to let you into a little secret." I point out to her that, as I'm inter-viewing her for the school newspaper, it will hardly remain a little secret for very long, but she tells me anyway. "I have a serious problem with my body-image," she whispers. "I actually have a kind of loathing of my own body, and the only way I can fight it is by confronting that image daily, hour by hour, minute by minute. Which is why my bed-room wall at home is simply plastered with polaroids of me. Stark naked."

At which revelation my cub reporter's pencil, upon which I have been sucking abstractedly, breaks off between my teeth and I decide it's time to bring this interview to a hasty conclusion. I thank Ms. Boyd and she heads back to rehearsals with a lovely valedictory toss. Truly, I reflect, she is a magnificent creature sent down to us as a gift from the gods, and no self-respecting pupil of King William's, male or female, will want to miss next week's performance. Meanwhile, boys, don't let the thought of all those polaroids distract you too much from your Greek irregular verbs . . .

• • •

("Othello" will be reviewed in the first issue of next term by our new drama critic, Benjamin Trotter.)

• • •

LEISURE NEWS
The Walking Option
For the third week in a row, the members of Mr. Tillotson's walking option got hopelessly lost last Wednesday, this time in the grounds of Waseley Country Park. Next term the Option will also be opened to girls. Let's hope one of them brings an Ordnance Survey Map.

The Wanking Option
The first meeting of this group was cancelled owing to mass non-attendance. It's believed that members were unable to read the rele-vant noticeboard.

8

the BILL BOARD

Thursday, 13 January, 1977

"OTHELLO, THE MOOR OF VENICE"

(Big School, 13, 14, 15 December)

Reviewed by BENJAMIN TROTTER

Ah, the mystique of the theatrical life! Here I was, stepping into the shoes of Harold Hobson, Kenneth Tynan and . . . erm, other famous drama critics. My first foray into the glamorous world of the jobbing reviewer. The stretch limo waiting at the door . . . the coy flirtation with the hat-check girl as I hand over my gloves and topcoat . . . the gentle embrace of the plush velvet as I ease myself into the front-row seat. The audience's hushed expectancy . . .

OK, so it was like this. There I was, still waiting at my Lickey Road bus stop at a quarter to seven for a 62 bus which should have turned up half an hour ago. Then, when I reach Big School with 90 seconds to spare, I find I have lost my "press pass"—a crumpled sheet of paper, as it happens, on to which Tim Newsome has scrawled "WE HAVE TO LET THIS PILLOCK IN FOR FREE, APPARENTLY." Fighting my way past the bouncers on the door, I squat down on one of those wooden benches which seem to have been bought at a job lot from some pensioned-off Dickensian workhouse, and am just in time to catch the end of Scene One.

First, flustered impressions, then: Julian Stubbs as Iago. Great casting. He has the right diabolical sparkle, and he really chews on the verse, audibly relishes the sibilant venom of his lines. Three hours later, he will be on stage again, down the road at The Bournbrook, fronting for King William's very own punk prodigies The Maws of Doom (in whose birth your reviewer himself had a small part to play), and you can see that he brings the same spiteful energy to both roles. This scene would be fair cracking along, if it weren't for lacklustre support from Graham Temple, whose Roderigo is wooden by comparison.

Othello enters, and you can feel a shiver of admiration run through the audience. Steve Richards looks the part. He is massy, imposing; the man has a presence. Emily Sandys' simple but effective costume enhances his bearing, his easy militaristic swagger. This is a figure to be reckoned with. When he begins to speak, the voice, initially, is a disappointment. He falters, stiffens, seems to mishear the rhythms. He is in fear of the verse, not in command of it. One's heart sinks: this isn't going to do. It has been too much to ask, throwing the whole weight of the play on to a first-time actor.

But this is a false start. A few more speeches, and Richards has gained immeasurably in confidence. He can sense the audience's respect, and is buoyed up by it. Soon he is into his stride:

> Rude am I in my speech
> And little blessed with the soft phrase of peace,
> For since these arms of mine had seven years' pith
> Till now some nine moons wasted, they have used
> Their dearest action in the tented field.

Richards missed none of the tonal ambiguity of this passage: his delivery was courteous, but he caught the undertow of boastfulness, of thinly veiled scorn for the men of peace, which lies beneath these honeyed words. This, you could tell, was going to be a rich, pregnant, multi-layered performance. And so it proved right up until the end.

Then comes the fatal moment. Act I, Scene iii, line 169. A simple stage direction, "Enter Desdemona." And suddenly the whole production starts collapsing like a house of cards.

Later in the play, Cicely Boyd's Desdemona will ask Iago, "What wouldst thou write of me, if thou should praise me?," and the wily manipulator replies, "O, gentle lady, do not put me to it, For I am nothing if not critical." Well, Cicely—sorry and all that, but I'm with Iago on this one.

The point about Desdemona, surely, is that she has to have some kind of spirit, some kind of pluck and resilience, if she is not just to come across like some annoying little wallflower that the men happen to be fighting over. The grounds for this can be found in Shakespeare's verse: all any actress has to do is remain faithful to its supple, muscular movements, and the rest will follow. But Miss Boyd, either wilfully or through sheer incompetence, betrayed the verse at every point. One's heart sank as soon as she opened her mouth and pronounced her first line—"I do perceive here a divided duty"—with two quite meaningless and inappropriate stresses on "<u>do</u>" and "<u>duty</u>." What could she be thinking of? Sadly, this set the tenor for the rest of her performance. Desdemona can be seen either as a loyal and virtuous wife, or as a saucy temptress who is responsible, in part, for precipitating the play's tragic denouement. Better still, an actress can try to negotiate a path between these readings, and portray a character of real complexity and contradiction. Instead, all we got from Cicely Boyd's Desdemona was sing-song delivery and a range of responses to her husband which never stretched much further than moonstruck adoration. This was a performance which let down her fellow-actors, the play itself and, worst of all, Cicely Boyd's own reputation as one of King Willliam's most gifted thespians.

An even worse disappointment was in store with Jennifer Hawkins' Bianca. This supposedly tough-as-nails strumpet managed to radiate, in Ms. Hawkins' version, all the erotic allure and raw sexual energy of a comatose mullet.

Tim Newsome got what he could out of these players and the rest of his sterling crew, but we were left at the end of the evening with an "Othello" which carried absolutely no tragic weight. Given the success the senior Drama Soc enjoyed with "Kiss Me Kate" a couple of years ago, I was left wondering whether an upbeat musical version mightn't have better suited the lightweight talents involved. I'll even suggest the

title myself, free of charge: "OTHELLO, or 'The Moor the Merrier.' "
How about it, Mr. Newsome?

• • •

LETTERS TO THE EDITOR
From Arthur Pusey-Hamilton, MBE

Dear Sir,

I much enjoyed the school's recent production of "Othello." I was
not previously familiar with the work, but it seemed to me aptly chosen
in the present political climate. I found that the climax illustrated, most
powerfully, Mr. Powell's chilling vision of "rivers of blood," and provided an ample demonstration of the perils of unrestricted immigration,
as experienced in 16th-century Venice. Bravo Mr. Newsome!

I am writing, however, to complain about the shocking display of
moral degeneracy which met my astonished eyes at the so-called "cast
party" following the final performance.

My young nipper Arthur Pusey-Hamilton Jnr is a healthy enough
lad in his third year at K.W. He was employed on this production in the
capacity of scene-shifter and it was a source of some pleasure, both to
myself and to Gladys, my good lady wife, to reflect that he was
involved in some robust extra-curricular activity which might "bring
him out of his shell" (to use the vernacular phrase employed by his child
psychologist). Although neither I myself, nor Gladys, my good lady
wife, could see that there was much awry with his regular leisure activities (Pusey-Hamilton Jnr likes to sit on his bed, sometimes for hours at a
time, rocking backwards and forwards while gazing fixedly at the
walls of his bedroom, which he has painted matt black), it was deemed
desirable, both by the aforementioned psychologist and by the team of
social workers from the City Council who have recently been, to use
their own lingo, "looking into his case," that he should perhaps social-
ize a little more with his young schoolchums.

In the light of this, it was with some enthusiasm that we agreed to
his attending the small and—we fondly imagined—civilized celebra-

tion which was to take place at the home of one of the cast members after the final performance. Of course, this meant that Pusey-Hamilton Jnr would be staying up long past his usual bedtime (5:30 p.m., unless a particularly instructive edition of "Horizon" or "Panorama" happens to be showing), but neither I myself, nor Gladys, my good lady wife, have ever seen any reason to be "stick-in-the-muds," and we firmly believe that there are some rules which are meant to be broken! (Though not, of course, the rule which dictates that his hands must be firmly cuffed behind his back whenever he is in bed or taking a shower. Oh no.)

Accordingly, it was well after 10 p.m. and the party had been in full swing for at least fifteen minutes when I arrived at No. 43, Pickworth Road, B31, on the night in question. I had no difficulty in finding the house, because the primeval, incessant beat of so-called "reggae" music was thumping down the street, for all the world as if Satan's own timpani were pounding a tattoo at the jaws of Hades. I was immediately concerned about the effect that this infernal cacophony might have on the delicate sensibilities of Pusey-Hamilton Jnr, who of course is not allowed to listen to so-called "pop" music at home, it being the belief both of myself and Gladys, my good lady wife, that a regular diet of such fine old English classics as Delius' "First Cuckoo in Spring" makes far more wholesome listening for a lad his age; although we are not averse, occasionally, to his "letting his hair down" with something lighter along the lines of Elgar's Pomp and Circumstance Marches.

When I rang the doorbell of No. 43, therefore, I was already expecting the worst. And yet the reality was far more appalling than anything my wildest imagination could have conjured up.

I shall not dwell, in any detail, on the scenes of decadence which I found awaiting me behind the innocent-looking door of No. 43, Pickworth Road. Suffice it to say that I witnessed acts of depravity which would have brought a blush to the libertines of Caligula's Rome. So this, I thought, is how aspiring members of the theatrical profession "celebrate" their dramatic triumphs! My heart pounding, my palms sweating, my eyes darting this way and, quite frankly, that, I stepped my way gingerly through a sea of writhing bodies in search of poor Pusey-Hamilton Jnr, whose vulnerable temperament would, I knew, already have been done irreparable damage by his exposure to this degenerate behaviour. Finally I found him, sitting halfway up the staircase, sipping on a can of ginger beer (how quickly corruption sets in!—for at home he is allowed to drink nothing but natural spring water and the occasional tumbler of unsweetened prune juice), while behind him on the stairs, not three feet away, two members of the supporting cast were engaged in an act which I had not seen performed since one regrettable occasion during the last war, when, as a doughty foot-soldier in the campaign against Rommel, I awoke one evening, bound, gagged, naked and indubitably drugged (as I explained to my senior officer during the subsequent court-martial) in the precincts of an Egyptian bordello insalubrious even by the standards of that fetid country.

Nor, I might add, were these lewdnesses confined to the minor players in that night's drama. While watching the play I had already been struck by what I believe is called the "chemistry" between the two leading performers, naively believing that this was the product of skilful acting on their part. Not so, I was soon to discover! For, on accompanying Pusey-Hamilton Jnr upstairs to the improvised "cloakroom" in search of his cagoule and ear-warmers, we came upon none other than the two principals—Othello and Desdemona themselves, to conceal their identities no longer—occupied on one of the beds in a procedure which could hardly fail, were it to proceed to its seemingly inevitable conclusion, to result in miscegenation.

This, to be sure, was more than could be borne by man, beast or indeed Pusey-Hamilton Jnr, whose feelings on being caught up in these scenes were now clearly discernible from his whines of distress, his pitiful tugging at my hand, and his repeated cries (obviously directed at the other partygoers) of "Go home, go home, I hate you, you're ruining my life." There was no time to be lost in extricating him from that sink of iniquity, and sure enough, within thirty minutes he was safely at home, had been (firmly) tucked up in bed by Gladys, my good lady wife, and was enjoying the kind of sleep for which the only prerequisites are youthful innocence, an untroubled conscience and, of course, a powerful dose of barbiturates.

How soon my son will recover from this dreadful ordeal remains to be seen.

Through your columns, I address myself to the Chief Master of King William's School. And I demand of you, Sir: are you to allow this kind of carry-on from your pupils? Is the name of this once-great institution to be dragged through the mud, thrown in the gutter and flushed down the toilet? This is no hysterical over-reaction from someone "out of touch" with our modern, "swinging" era. I am no fogey, "square" or fuddy-duddy. Good grief, Sir, I can tolerate a little friendly buggery between schoolpals, now and again: but congress—physical congress— with the opposite sex? At so tender and impressionable an age? And between the races, for pity's sake? This will not do. It will not do at all. I call upon you to act now, to stamp out all trace of this rancorous canker, to purge the surge of this verminous scourge, which threatens, in my view (and that of Gladys, my good lady wife), the very honour and lifeblood of this school.

Be decisive on this issue, I beg of you! As we used to say in my army days, "Come on, Sir—play the white man!"

Yours faithfully,
Arthur Pusey-Hamilton, MBE.

SEALED with the ancient and noble Seal of the Pusey-Hamiltons.

"HIC HAEC HOC"

9

Mr. Serkis came back to school in the second week of term. He had recovered from his appendicitis, but he wasn't a happy man.

"I'm very, very disappointed," he told the editorial committee.

It was another grey, rainswept Friday afternoon, and the radiator in the meeting room was not working. This was perhaps the coldest room in the entire school, at the very end of the Carlton corridor, which was reached by a narrow and somehow mysterious flight of stairs beside the entrance to the prefects' locker room. Only sixth-formers were allowed to penetrate this remote spot, and even then there were severe restrictions. Membership of the Club itself, which gave access to its desirable, oak-panelled clubroom, was by election only, and every year more than half of the applicants were turned away, weeded out by some time-honoured vetting procedure whose intractable criteria were never explained. Benjamin himself would not be eligible for membership until next year. Meanwhile, even to be allowed to sit once a week in this icy and inaccessible garret, with its cracked plaster and antique plumbing, had seemed, a few months ago, an unimaginable privilege. But the editorial meetings had never quite lived up to his filmy, undefined expectations. An air of anticlimax always seemed to settle in, even after the first few minutes.

"You were left to produce two issues by yourselves, and look what happens." Mr. Serkis indicated a wad of paper on the table in front of him. "Seventeen letters of complaint. Including one from the Chief." He skimmed through them, while Doug, Claire and Philip looked on, abashed. "Most of them," he said, "were about the letter." He looked up. "Does anybody know who wrote it?"

"Harding," everybody (except Benjamin) chanted in unison.

Mr. Serkis sighed. "That figures." He contemplated the authentic waxen seal at the bottom of the offending typescript. "It bears his mark of perfectionism."

"He did that with his own signet ring," Philip said. "He picked one up somewhere—an antiques market, or something—and now it's never off his finger."

"You should never, ever have published this," said Mr. Serkis, glancing through the letter again and tutting over its worst excesses. "At the very least, you should have edited it. You should never print somebody's home address. And this bit about Steve and Cicely—it practically suggests they were having sex in public. That line about 'miscegenation' is horrible. Horrible. You'll have to print an apology."

"OK," said Doug, resigned, scribbling a memo. "Apology."

"Now, I don't know who wrote that gag about the wanking option, but the Chief went ballistic. It wasn't just the word, it was . . . Well, as he says here—" (picking up the Chief Master's lengthy, ornately handwritten note) "—'I would have hoped that, in the spirit of editors past, the present team might occasionally be able to rise above the level of cheap undergraduate humour.' "

"We're still at school, aren't we?" Philip pointed out. "So I would have thought undergraduate humour was pretty good going."

"Print an apology," said Mr. Serkis, unmoved by this argument, and Doug scribbled another memo. "Now—" he turned to Claire "—your profile of Cicely's come in for a lot of stick. And I have to admit, it's one of the bitchiest things I ever read in my life."

"She deserved it," Claire answered; but the defensive edge to her voice was very noticeable. "She's a prima donna of the first order. Everybody knows that."

"You didn't give her a fair hearing. And the stuff about her flirting in class was completely out of order."

"But it's *true.*"

There was a short silence; the sound of deadlock.

"This is going to be some bloody apology," said Doug, scribbling. "There'll be no room left for anything else, at this rate. Who's going to write it?"

When it was obvious that there would be no volunteers, Mr. Serkis chose Benjamin.

"Why me?"

"Because you're the best writer on the magazine." Assuming (correctly) from Benjamin's dumbstruck response that this compliment was both unexpected and overwhelming, he qualified it by adding: "Also, you're the only one whose stuff doesn't seem to bring in a deluge of complaints these days."

Unwittingly, here, Mr. Serkis had touched a nerve.

"Well why doesn't it?" Benjamin wanted to know. "I was incredibly rude about that play. Why haven't *I* caused a bit of controversy?"

Nobody seemed to know the answer to that one, and Benjamin was promptly despatched to the adjacent office to compose a fulsome yet subtly unrepentant apology.

He sat at the typewriter and looked out at the rooftops, glistening silver with rainwater. Above them, the two tall oak trees which flanked the South Drive swung feverishly in the wind. He stared at the trees for a few moments, then allowed his eyes to glaze over until the objects before him lunged out of focus. A blur of slate grey and chocolate brown and pastel green. His fingers rested on the keys of the typewriter, passive, stupefied. The question that had been nagging at him—*Why was it? Why was it that nothing he did seemed to . . . bother anybody, get under their skin?*—withdrew to some inaccessible corner, was absorbed, swallowed up. A kind of numbness took its place. Dimly, Benjamin remained aware that the life of the school was proceeding, winding down, in the many rooms and corridors that lay beneath his feet. The Friday afternoon Options would be coming to an end: the chess players packing away their pieces, the War Games fetishists abandoning their maps and charts, the artists washing their brushes under Mr. Plumb's distracted supervision, the Combined Cadet Force swapping their prickly green uniforms for civvies, the musicians and radio hams and bridge players and fives enthusiasts all preparing to go home. How the world strained to keep itself busy! Already Benjamin felt so distant from all of that, so far removed. He continued merely to sit at the typewriter, in a swoon of heaviness and incuriosity. Claire entered the room, at one point, retrieved a couple of box files filled with back issues of the magazine; she may have spoken to him. Philip, certainly, looked in on his way downstairs, a raincoat slung over his shoulder, and said, "How's it going, maestro?," or "Don't be too long," or "See you Monday, then," or something along those lines. And one by one, Benjamin supposed, the others must have left as well. He would have to go too, in a minute. Couldn't very well sit here all weekend. And yet there was something strangely comfortable about this listlessness, this solitude. The silence of the corridor outside agreed with him.

Sometimes, when he was alone like this, Benjamin would wait for God to speak to him. He was reminded of the silence in the locker room, and then the door of the nearby locker swinging open and shut, and then his own footfalls as he went to retrieve the gift that had been left for him that momentous day. But God had not spoken to him since then. He would, of course; some time, some time soon, He would speak to him again. But there was nothing Benjamin could do, for now, except wait. Patience was everything.

He heard footsteps in the corridor. A light, feminine tread, heading past his own half-closed doorway, in the direction of the editorial meeting room. He took no notice.

Benjamin wondered if he should begin work on the apology.

But the effort suddenly seemed tremendous, the physical effort of lifting his finger and striking one of the typewriter keys, striking it firmly enough for a letter to be imprinted on the page, to say nothing of the mental effort, deciding which key he should strike, and therefore, by extension, which word should bear the awful responsibility of coming first. He would write it at home, tomorrow or on Sunday. There was plenty of time. Far preferable now just to savour this aloofness, to close himself off, settle further still into a luscious insensibility that no sound, no image would ever be able to pierce.

And indeed, it wasn't a sound or an image that roused Benjamin from his inertia at all. It was a smell. The smell of a cigarette.

This was very odd. Smoking in school was forbidden, so strictly forbidden that even Doug had never been known to try it. As soon as the unmistakable stagnant odour reached his nose, Benjamin was intrigued. He rose immediately from the chair in which he had come to assume an almost supine position, and walked carefully—even stealthily—along the corridor towards the meeting room. On reaching the doorway he paused, and then for some moments feasted his startled eyes on the seated figure of Cicely Boyd.

She was sitting, or rather crouching, at the editorial table, with her back to the door, and with one bare foot (the shoe seemed to have come off) tucked beneath her bottom. Her posture radiated tension and nervous expectancy. She was wearing fawn trousers and a loose, chunky, navy blue Argyll sweater, with the famous golden hair swept into a long ponytail which reached almost to the small of her back. Ash from her unfiltered cigarette fluttered down on to the table, unnoticed, as she stared intently towards the window, favouring Benjamin with a view of her left profile. Her nose was thin and aquiline, her eyes were the palest blue imaginable, there was a galaxy of tiny freckles above her cheekbones, and one even tinier mole on her left cheek. All of these details were new to Benjamin, who realized now that he had never really seen Cicely before, except at a distance, or in snatched glimpses. Here, close up, in the flesh, she was fifty, a hundred, a million times more beautiful than he could have thought possible. For many seconds, it seemed, his heart stopped beating completely.

Then she turned; and he knew at once, before their eyes had even had a chance to meet, that she had come here for no other purpose than to see him.

He took a faltering, involuntary step forward.

"You're Benjamin," she stated, baldly.

"Yes." And for some reason, the next thing he said was: "You're not allowed to smoke in here, you know."

"Ah." She let her cigarette fall, picked up her shoe and carefully ground the glowing stub into the floor. "We must stick to the rules, mustn't we?"

She looked at him for a while, until he felt compelled to say something else:

"Everybody's gone home."

"Not quite everybody," she answered. "It was you I wanted to meet." She took a breath. "You wrote—"

"—a review of your play, yes, I know. I'm . . ." (and suddenly the word seemed useless, although it was the only one he had) ". . . sorry."

She took stock of this comment; absorbed and pondered it.

"Why did you write it?" she asked, after what seemed like a long pause.

Benjamin had been dreading this question. It was the same question he had been pointedly refusing to ask himself, and now that it confronted him, there was no plausible answer that he could see. Quite simply, some sort of madness must have seized him when he sat down at the typewriter that evening. Here, after all, was the opportunity he had been dreaming of for years: the chance to compose, not just a love letter to Cicely, but something infinitely more potent—a public statement of his admiration for her, a panegyric to her beauty and her talent which couldn't fail to put her endlessly in his debt. And yet for some crazy, unfathomable reason he had done nothing of the kind. He had sacrificed this glorious opening on the altar of some half-baked notion of critical objectivity. Yes, her performance had been bad; of course he had realized that, of course he had believed it; but to have said so, in such uncompromising terms, when every motion of his heart was telling him to do the opposite—well, this was idiotic. This was perverseness of the first order. The whole episode, in fact, raised a much larger question, just as unanswerable, and one which was pressing itself upon him a good deal these days: what was the *matter* with him, exactly?

Cicely, in any case, did not wait for his response. She had her own, ready to hand.

"I'll tell you why you wrote it," she said, and then her voice cracked and broke. "Because it was true. Every word."

As soon as she said this, Benjamin had, for the first time in his life, what might be called an out-of-body experience. He could see himself, quite clearly, rushing towards her, kneeling down beside her chair and putting a comforting arm around her shoulder. He could hear himself, quite distinctly, saying, "No, Cicely, no. It wasn't true. None of it was true. I was stupid to write it." He could see at once that this was the right and natural thing to do. But he didn't do it. He said nothing, and remained by the doorway.

"The last few weeks have been dreadful. Unimaginable." She took another cigarette out of the packet and began to twirl it between agitated fingers. "First of all that interview. That . . . thing Claire wrote." She screwed up her eyes at the recollection. "So hurtful."

"I think Claire has a problem," Benjamin volunteered, tentatively. "Where you're concerned. I think she may be a bit jealous."

"She used to be my friend," said Cicely. She was speaking to herself, and gave no indication of having heard his remark. "I must have done something awful to her."

"I don't think so," said Benjamin, but again she ignored him.

"I hate myself. I really do." She looked at Benjamin directly now. "Do you know what that's like? Do *you* hate yourself?"

"Perhaps I should, after what I did to you," said Benjamin; or would have done, if he wasn't having another out-of-body experience. Instead he mumbled: "I don't know, really."

"But in a way," Cicely continued, "what she wrote . . . What she wrote is easier to cope with. Because she didn't mean any of it. She was just being a bitch. And none of it was true. Whereas *you* did mean it, didn't you? You hated my performance. Everything about it."

"No, I . . . I was being very harsh. I don't know why."

"Did I really get all those stresses wrong?"

"So did everybody else, actually," Benjamin said, in a vain attempt to make things better. "If anything it was Tim's fault. He was directing you, after all."

Cicely stood up, and drifted towards the window. She was taller than he had thought, and so slender, and lovely, and so full of grace. Benjamin cowered at the thought that he might have vandalized such beauty, done violence to it in any way.

"What about . . . Harding's letter?" he found himself compelled to ask, rather to his amazement. "That wasn't true either, was it?"

Cicely turned sharply. "About me and Steve?"

He nodded.

"It was wicked of them to print that. Steve's girlfriend saw it. She dumped him." And now her whole body shook, with a visible sob. "It happens so easily. You're working with someone, things get very intense. It was only a little fling, I never meant it to do any harm. Oh, I'm a terrible, terrible person."

Benjamin had run out of reassuring words, and besides, the knowledge that Richards had indeed enjoyed this good fortune, however briefly, filled him with an irrational and paralyzing jealousy. Once again some better-natured but inaccessible part of him suggested that he should be offering physical comfort to Cicely. Once again, he remained frozen to the spot.

Even without his assistance, she managed to compose herself after a moment or two. She stood by the window with her back towards him, and wiped her cheeks with a scrap of tissue. Then she turned. Her eyes, though still red-rimmed, now carried within them the hint of a different, steelier light.

"You could be good for me," she said, unexpectedly.

"Pardon?"

"I think you have an interesting mind."

"Thank you," said Benjamin, after a stunned pause.

"Sometimes I can be vain but that doesn't mean I take no notice of criticism. Because most of my friends are a bit scared of me, they only say what they think I want to hear. Whereas you . . ." (and the smile she suddenly turned on him was at once combative and bewitching) ". . . you'd give it to me straight, wouldn't you? Every time."

"Well . . . I'm not sure I know what you mean, but—yes, I'd try to."

"When I said that I hate myself," Cicely continued, sitting on the table, now, so that she was almost at Benjamin's level and there were only three or four feet between them, "I wasn't being flippant. Everything about me is going to change. It has to."

"I don't think . . ." Benjamin began.

"Yes?"

But he had already forgotten what he was going to say.

"You know, they told me you didn't talk much," she said, once he had tailed off, "but I didn't expect you to be *quite* so silent. You're practically a Trappist."

"Who's they?" Benjamin asked. "Who told you that I didn't say much?"

"Everybody," said Cicely. "I've been asking around about you, of course. Who wouldn't, after reading that piece?"

"So what . . ." (Benjamin swallowed hard) ". . . what did they say, exactly?"

Cicely looked at him gravely. "You know, Benjamin, it's not always a blessing to know what other people think of you." She let this advice hang in the air, could see that it was wasted, and went on: "Anyway, you've got nothing to worry about. Most people just said that they couldn't make you out. 'Inscrutable' was the word that seemed to keep coming up. People seem to think you're probably some kind of genius, but not necessarily someone they'd want to be stuck on a train with."

"I don't know about that," said Benjamin, laughing uneasily. "The genius bit, I mean."

Cicely assured him, with quiet emphasis: "The world expects great things of you, Benjamin."

He stared mutely at the floor, then looked up and met her gaze for the first time: "I don't think you should change, you know."

"That's sweet of you," said Cicely. "But you're wrong. What do you think of my hair?"

Benjamin's little moment of forthrightness had already passed, and instead of saying, as he would have liked to, "It's amazing" or "You've got the most beautiful hair I've ever seen," he mumbled: "I like it. It's very nice."

Cicely laughed acidly, and shook her head. Then, noticing a pair of paper-scissors at the other end of the table, she reached across, picked them up, and passed them over to Benjamin. "I want you to cut it off," she said.

"What?"

She sat on the chair again, turned her back on Benjamin, and repeated: "I want you to cut it off. All of it."

"All of it?"

"All—" she tugged the bottom of her ponytail, as if it were a bell-rope "—all of this stuff."

"I can't do that," said Benjamin, shocked.

"Why not?"

"I've never cut anyone's hair off. I'll make a mess of it."

"For God's sake, I'm not asking for a perm. One big snip ought to be enough."

Benjamin stepped forward and reached out a terrified hand. It would be the first time he had touched her. It would be the first time he had touched any girl, apart from his sister, since reaching puberty.

He drew back and said: "Are you sure about this?"

Cicely sighed. "Of course I am. Just do it."

Benjamin took the ribbon of hair into his shaking hand. The fineness and softness of it were hardly to be believed. It glimmered between his fingers. The act that he was about to perform seemed frightful in its wanton finality.

Gathering together Cicely's hair to put it between the jaws of the scissors, he could not help brushing against her skin. At once he felt her whole body stiffen, either anticipating the cut, or in response to the careless touch of his fingers against the fine down at the back of her neck.

"Sorry," he murmured. And then: "Here we go, then."

Cicely tautened again.

"Ready . . . Steady . . .

"*GO.*"

The action of the scissors was sudden and entirely effective. The hair came away in his hand, and he clutched it tightly, not letting a single strand fall to the floor. Cicely stood up.

"Here."

She handed him the Cyclops Records bag he had thrown earlier on to a side-table, and with loving deliberation he folded the hair three times over, so that it fitted neatly inside. Meanwhile Cicely had whipped a compact out of her pocket and was inspecting her new bob with an appalled, curious gaze.

"Makes you look a bit like Joanna Lumley," Benjamin suggested. "In *The New Avengers.*"

This was not true at all. It made her look like one of the inmates of a Nazi concentration camp he had seen recently on a TV documentary. But anyway, she didn't seem to hear him; turning the mirror this way and that she merely whispered to herself, "Oh my God . . ."

"What, erm . . ." Benjamin gestured with the bag of hair. ". . . What shall I do with this, then?"

"Do whatever you want with it," said Cicely, still preoccupied.

"OK." He put it down on the table for now. "Right."

After a few more seconds' contemplation, Cicely snapped the compact shut and put it away. "Good," she said. "That's a start." She found a sheet of paper on the table, scribbled some figures on it and handed it to Benjamin.

"What's this?" he asked.

"My telephone number."

He looked at the seven digits inscribed in blotchy, pale green biro. A few hours ago he would have traded anything, anything in the world, for the courage even to speak to Cicely, let alone to be offered this priceless information. Suddenly his life was transformed. It was more than he could comprehend.

"Thanks," he said.

"You're welcome. Thanks for the haircut."

She turned, and was about to leave. She had to be stopped.

"About that review—" Benjamin began.

"I dare say we'll be seeing more of each other," said Cicely, in a tone so neutral, so parched of feeling that he knew their conversation was at an end. "We can talk about it then."

"Fine," said Benjamin; and then she was gone.

He carried the plastic bag full of hair all the way home and up to his bedroom. Then he dropped it on to the bed and lay down himself with an exhausted sigh.

What on earth was he going to do with it?

10

Five days later Philip asked him the key question and Benjamin had to admit that he didn't know the answer.

"So—is Cicely your girlfriend now?"

"I don't *think* so," Benjamin replied, and then held up his finger to test the direction of the breeze, in a futile attempt to ward off further interrogation.

"You don't *think* so?" said Philip, incredulous. "What does that mean? I mean, someone's either your girlfriend or she isn't."

"Well then, she isn't." He hadn't a clue which direction the breeze was coming from. He had an idea that you were supposed to lick your finger before holding it up, but had never been able to understand why. Besides, now that he thought about it, there wasn't much of a breeze anyway. "I think this must be east," he added, hazarding a wild guess and pointing further up the mud-spattered lane.

"So what did she mean?" Philip persisted. "What did she mean when she said 'We'll be seeing more of each other?' "

"I suppose she just meant—well, that we were bound to bump into each other, in the normal course of events." The truth was that he didn't know what Cicely had meant, and it annoyed him that Philip seemed to suspect this. "Look, don't you think it would be more helpful—rather than standing here discussing my love-life, or lack of it—if we tried to work out where the hell we are?"

It was a Wednesday afternoon, the day of the Walking Option's weekly expedition, and already a typical scenario was unfolding. Not only had they managed to get lost after walking about five hundred yards, but in the course of trying out alternative directions and rounding up the dawdlers who had almost immediately begun to loiter out of sight, the group had managed to disperse. Now Philip and Benjamin were alone in a country lane somewhere in the vicinity of the Upper Bittell reservoir, and had not seen the hapless Mr. Tillotson and his frayed, famously inadequate road atlas for about half an hour.

"This is too much like hard work," said Philip, after they had staggered on for another twenty yards or so. "Let's have a break for refreshment."

A nearby stile presented itself obligingly for this very purpose. They sat down, one on either side, Benjamin facing the lane and Philip overlooking a long stretch of pastureland, green-yellow in the sunshine, dotted here and there with contentedly masticating Friesians. He opened his Army and Navy Stores rucksack, took out a thick stack of cheese sandwiches wrapped in tin foil and passed one of them to Benjamin. They split open a can of Guinness and took it in turns to wince over its heavy, bittersweet oiliness.

"Nothing like a good bit of exercise, is there?" said Philip, after they had eaten and drunk in silence for a few minutes. "Tones the muscles up. Makes you feel on top of things."

Benjamin had mellowed under the influence of the sunshine, the food and the alcohol. He was prepared to be philosophical about Cicely's ambiguous declaration now. The important thing was that she had spoken to him at last. They were in a relationship, of sorts.

"We can't be *that* lost," Philip was saying, as he scanned the horizon in a half-hearted way. "You only live a couple of miles from here, don't you?"

"I suppose so," said Benjamin. He looked around vaguely. "It does look a bit familiar. I think Mum drives this way sometimes."

Two girls wandered past, and stopped to talk to Philip. "Any sign of Mr. Tillotson?" he wanted to know.

They shook their heads, and the shorter of the two, who had frizzy, pale blonde hair, a big bust and a permanent, rather earnest and unsettling smile, said: "I think he went down to the canal. We told him some of the boys had sneaked off there for a smoke."

"Ah well," said Philip, leaning back comfortably against the slats of the stile, "I dare say he'll catch up with us soon enough."

"So this is what you call walking, is it?" the girl asked, her smile ever so slightly broadening.

"Join us if you want."

"No thanks. We think we can get to Barnt Green this way. We can get a bus from there, and be home early."

"Suit yourselves."

As the girls walked on, Benjamin said: "Who were they?"

"I don't know who the dark one was. Pretty, though, wasn't she? The other one's called Emily. Emily Sandys."

"I've heard of her. She designed the costumes for *Othello*."

"Quite possibly. Doug was telling me she might be joining the paper, too. Doing lay-out and stuff." He gazed after the receding female figures, a familiar look of wistful but unconcealed lust setting his face into momentary slack-jawed immobility. "I should have said something to the dark one. I fancy her something rotten."

Emily and her friend disappeared from view, and the boys fell silent. Their thoughts became, for a while, impenetrable. The scene of rural idyll laid out before them might have given rise to any number of reflections. Although they were only a mile or two from Longbridge and Birmingham's outer suburbs, the gently undulating countryside, with its indolent, nodding herds and tidy hedgerows, might have inspired a Betjeman to verse or a Butterworth to composition. The pastoral stillness remained undisturbed for several minutes, until Philip asked:

"How often do you think about girls with no clothes on?"

Benjamin gave this question the serious thought it deserved. "Quite often," he said. "All the time, in fact."

"Do you undress girls with your eyes? Try to, I mean."

"Sometimes. You know, you try not to stare at them that way, but then again, you can't help it. It's only natural."

Looking into the middle distance, as his mind took an unexpectedly abstract turn, Philip said: "The female body is a beautiful thing." He glanced at Benjamin then and said, urgently: "Have you ever—you know—*seen* one? Got a really good look?"

Benjamin shook his head. "Not really. Only on the telly."

Now they could hear the whirr and the click of an approaching bicycle, and the voice presumably of its rider, who was singing to himself at top volume. The rustic mood of that afternoon might have led them to expect some cheery cowhand, wending his way either to or from a milking session while giving lusty voice to some fine old English folksong. But the words reached them in an excruciatingly tuneless boy soprano, and they were quite distinct:

> *I am an anti-CHRIST*
> *I am an anar-CHIST*

The singer seemed not to know any more than that, because after a second's pause he began again, even louder and even more wildly off-key:

> *I am an anti-CHRIST*
> *I am an anar-CHIST*

Then he came into view and skidded to a halt beside them. It was Paul.

"Well *well!*" he said, grinning delightedly at the spectacle of these two shirkers, caught *in flagrante*. "And what do we have here? Hilary and Tensing, defeated at first base while mounting a new challenge on Everest? Captain Scott and Captain Oates, heading off for the South Pole and calling it a day just outside Watford?"

"Fuck *off*, Paul," said Benjamin, outraged to find that he wasn't safe from his brother even here. "Why aren't you at home, anyway?"

"I can ride my bike wherever I want, can't I? I like to nurture the fantasy that this is a free country, despite the last-gasp efforts of our socialist leaders."

"The reason you didn't go to school today," Benjamin reminded him, "is that you told Mum you had a terrible cold and were going to have to stay in bed with a hot-water bottle."

"A little white lie," Paul confided, laying a finger to his lips in a gesture of mock-conspiracy. "Of course I realize that *you*, the man who never swerves from the path of duty and righteousness, would never—"

"Come on, Phil." Benjamin jumped to his feet in an impatient movement. "I'm sure you don't want to listen to his gibberish any more than I do." He began to march forward with athletic strides, trying to outpace his brother who was pedalling languidly behind him at a couple of yards' distance. "What were we talking about?" he called over his shoulder.

Phil hurried to catch up, wriggling the rucksack on to his back. "We were talking about naked women," he said.

"Ha!" Paul laughed contemptuously. "Now there's something *you* two won't be seeing in the near future."

"Would you just go *away*?" Benjamin demanded, rounding on him.

But Philip had noticed a peculiar, pregnant undertone in Paul's latest taunt; the hint of some tacky piece of information he was anxious to share with them, perhaps.

"Why—have *you*?" he asked.

"Have I what?"

"Seen a girl without any clothes on."

"Yup," said Paul, pedalling faster and easing ahead of them.

"Oh yes, of course you have," said Benjamin, his voice leaden with sarcasm. "Loads of times, I suppose."

"No," said Paul. "Just the once."

Benjamin grabbed him by the shoulder and forced him to a halt, almost pulling him off the bicycle.

"Go on then," he said. "Who was it?"

Paul took a moment to size up the situation.

"What's it worth?" he asked.

"What it's worth," said Benjamin, "is that if you tell me, I won't chop your legs off."

His grip on Paul's shoulder tightened and he enjoyed watching him screw up his eyes in pain.

"Let go," said Paul, and when Benjamin did, he told him: "It was your friend's sister."

"Who? What friend?"

"You know—those two girls we met down at the café by the bus stop, ages ago."

Benjamin's mind raced back to that humiliating encounter: the Sunday morning when Claire had asked him for a date, and Paul had been so rude to Miriam that she'd slapped him in the face.

"Claire's sister, you mean?"

"That's right. I saw her down by the reservoir. Not this one, the one by Cofton Park. She was starkers. I saw her bush and everything."

In his surprise, Benjamin made the mistake of loosening his hold, and Paul seized the opportunity to leap back on to the bicycle and begin his escape.

"Paul," his brother called after him, "what *are* you talking about?" There was no reply, and he shouted louder still as the bicycle sped off. "That was *pathetic*, you know. Couldn't you have thought of something a *little* bit more likely?"

But all he heard in return, floating back to him through the mild winter air, was:

I am an anti-CHRIST
I am an anar-CHIST

And the words looped and repeated themselves, over and over, as Paul vanished round a corner, pedalling furiously, his little legs fuelled as always by some limitless, manic, mysterious energy.

II

"You've been a good friend to me," said Barbara Chase to Sheila Trotter.

Sheila stared into her coffee, embarrassed. It was a nice thing to be told, but she didn't know how to respond.

"You probably think I'm very weak and foolish," Barbara added.

"No, not at all. Anyway, it's not for me to say, is it?"

Barbara smiled sadly and squeezed her hand.

It was a cheerless, blustery morning, and they were the only customers in the Baker's Dozen, a café which fronted on to the Bristol Road in the centre of Northfield. Coffee rings were stamped on to the formica tables and crumbs of doughnut and chocolate éclair filled up the cracks between the plastic cushions. As a venue for two women to share their deepest marital confidences, it didn't have much going for it. But then there wasn't a lot to choose from, in Northfield, in 1977.

"You have to stop seeing him, Barbara. You have to."

"I know." She stirred her coffee thoughtfully, as if trying to find meaning in its swirling depths. "But the thing is, when I'm with him, he makes me feel so *special.* He makes me feel so *alive.* He makes me feel so *appreciated.*" She stared out at the traffic, the queue at the bus stop, the dogged housewives walking by with their shopping trolleys, faces clamped against the wind. "I need your advice, Sheila. What should I do?"

"I just told you. You have to stop seeing him."

Barbara didn't make any answer to this. She merely said: "I told you how it started, didn't I?"

"You told me, yes: how he kept chatting you up at parent—teachers meetings. I was there, remember?"

"And then how he got Philip to give me a note."

"You told me."

"He wanted me to come on a day trip down to the Tate Gallery. Help him to look after his school group."

"You told me that, yes."

"One thing led to another. We got separated from the boys. He started showing me all these paintings, telling me about art, about sculpture, things I'd never thought about before. I could listen to him all day talking about art. I could go round galleries with him forever. And now that was months ago, and the ridiculous thing is, we still haven't . . . gone to bed together or anything. Did I tell you that?"

"Yes, you did."

"All we do is talk."

"I know. You told me."

"But he talks so beautifully. That's what I like about him. He has such a—"

"—way with words. I know. You told me that."

Two more customers came in. They sat at the far end of the café. Even so, Barbara lowered her voice.

"I love Sam. Of course I do. He's been wonderful to me. He's done nothing to deserve this at all. And I know you don't need to be a brainbox to be a coach driver but I just wish . . . I just wish he had a bit more to *say* for himself, sometimes."

"Does Sam know you've been seeing him again?"

"Yes."

"What did he say?"

"He told me I had to make a choice. Him or me, he said."

"And what did you say to that?"

"I told him that he'd been a good husband and I'd stay with him."

Sheila sighed with relief. "Good. That was the right thing to say. So now you've broken it off?"

"Not yet."

"Then you've got to. Write him a letter, and tell him you can't carry on like this."

"I've tried that, lots of times. He just writes back, using all these words. These beautiful long words that I can't understand. Oh, Sheila, what am I going to *do*?"

"I've told you what you should do. Three or four times now."

But Barbara wasn't listening. Her head was filled with words—not Sheila's words, of course, but *his* words: a torrent of phonemes, a polysyllabic whirlpool in which she could even now feel herself drowning: *sublimity concupiscence veneration Aphrodite inamorata dalliance coquetry blandishment chastity billet-doux purity adulation betrothal epithalamium*—swirling faster, more dizzyingly even than the coffee which she had unconsciously been stirring with more and more violence for the last few seconds, until Sheila stilled her hand and said once again:

"Barbara, you must stop seeing him."

Mrs. Chase raised her eyes and seemed to have noticed her for the first time.

"You've been such a good friend to me," she said, dreamily. "But the thing I need to know is—what's your *advice*?"

Colin Trotter and Sam Chase met at The Black Horse one rainy evening. They sat at a corner table and drank pints of Brew XI. "These are on me," said Sam. "My way of saying thank you. For being such a good friend."

Colin was very touched. They clinked glasses, and drank deeply.

"I think it's probably safe to say," Sam continued, "that the crisis is now over. Thanks to you, the moment of danger has passed."

"Thanks to me?"

"I took your advice, and it seems to have worked."

"What happened?"

"Well, as you know, I was all for confronting him. But you suggested a more subtle approach."

"It's been my experience at work," said Colin, "that you can't go at these things like a bull at a gate."

"Exactly. But you do have to take the bull by the horns."

"So you spoke to Barbara?"

"I did. I said, Barbara, we've reached a crossroads. This is the end of the road. It's him or me, I said. You have to choose between the devil and the deep blue sea. I told her straight out: you can't have your cake and eat it."

"And what did she say to that?"

"She told me to stop talking in clichés." He put down his beer glass and leaned forward confidingly. "The thing is, Colin, I've got a lot to make up, education-wise. My parents never thought it was that important, you see. So I'm having to start all over again, from square one. I've started reading some of these fancy books that Philip brings back with him from school. I take them away with me on the long drives and try to improve myself a little bit. It's hard work, but I'll get there. Every dog has his day."

"Well, I think that's great, Sam. I really do."

"I can win her back, Colin. I know I can."

"I think so, too."

"We're over the worst now, I'm sure of that. The clouds are parting and I can see the light at the end of the tunnel. This is the calm after the storm."

"The calm comes before the storm," Colin pointed out.

"Yes, but every cloud has a silver lining."

"That's true," said Colin, and they clinked glasses again.

"I'm not one for making predictions," said Sam, and Colin smiled to himself, for even he had noticed by now that this was his friend's invariable prelude to making predictions, "but I think I can safely say that those two won't be seeing each other again."

12

Claire watched in fascination as Mr. Plumb scooped out a large chunk of coffee and walnut gâteau, then offered it to Barbara on his fork. Her mouth opened and slowly, awkwardly, he eased the cake past her teeth and on to her waiting tongue. Her eyes were closed, languorously. In performing this action they did not make actual physical contact, but there was a striking intimacy about it. They might as well have been making love on the table.

It was Saturday afternoon and Claire was sitting in the café of the Ikon Gallery in John Bright Street. There was a pillar next to her table and it was from behind this that she took her occasional surreptitious glances at the amorous couple, either one of whom might have spotted her if they were not so deeply absorbed in their conversation (which seemed, Claire thought, rather one-sided), not to mention their leisurely, inescapably sensual consumption of the gâteau. She was not worried about Mr. Plumb, so much: she had never been taught by him, and the only reason he might identify her as a pupil of King William's was that she had a pile of back issues of *The Bill Board* on the table with her, dating from 1974 and 1975. With Mrs. Chase, though, there was a more serious danger of being recognized. They had often passed each other in the Northfield streets, and had been introduced to each other by Philip, once, after a chance encounter in the Grosvenor Shopping Centre. It would be best to keep out of sight.

They seemed—or rather, Mr. Plumb seemed—to be talking about art, while Barbara looked on in hypnotized admiration, her mouth half-open, her lips sticky with coffee cream and crumbs. Claire could only make out the occasional word, which was frustrating. But what words they were! She heard *triptych*, *aquarelle*, *gerotint* and *gouache*, whispered as if they were terms of the most guileful seduction, plucked straight out of Casanova's pocket-book. She heard him talk of *chiaroscuro, ceroplastics, petroglyphs* and *grisaille* as if he were a wandering troubadour serenading her at the foot of some Veronese balcony. Clearly, this monologue could only be a prelude—or perhaps the sequel—to a visit to the gallery itself. Had they been, or were they about to go? Were they billing and cooing pre- or post-coitally? Claire willed the other patrons into silence as she strained to listen for clues.

And then, suddenly, Mr. Plumb and Mrs. Chase pushed the remains of their gâteau aside, left the debris of their meal scattered on the table like two lovers abandoning an unmade bed in a cheap motel, and headed for the door to the gallery.

Claire rose to her feet, intending pursuit, but then checked herself swiftly. Really, she had no business to be doing this. She was here to do some work, and it was no concern of hers if Mrs. Chase had decided to have an affair, or if Mr. Plumb had succeeded in adding another name to his long list of conquests. She was kidding herself if she thought that she'd be helping Philip by finding out more about this sorry liaison; and besides, that wasn't even her real motivation, if she were to be honest. Her immediate, unthinking impulse to rise from the chair could be explained away in one word: sex. She had caught a whiff of something to do with the subject that always commanded her most eager, most morbid attention.

Her parents were to blame. They were to blame for everything, she had come to feel; everything that had gone wrong in the last few years. By refusing to talk to their daughters about sex, refusing to mention it, refusing even to acknowledge its existence, they had achieved nothing but to inspire in them both an obsessional curiosity, and in Miriam's case, the results had already been disastrous. It seemed to Claire more than probable that none of them would ever see her sister again, and the thought of it tore her apart. Even today, when she had work to distract her or at least, failing that, the passing sideshow of Miles' and Barbara's antics, the sense of Miriam's absence gnawed at her, filled her with a wintry void she knew she would never grow used to. She missed her every waking minute of every day. And the not knowing, the awful infinity of speculation about what might have become of her, that was even worse.

The facts were these. There was one weekend, in November 1974, when Miriam had begun to seem especially distraught. She had not spoken about anything in particular, but Claire knew that she had been away with Bill for the night, and for some reason it hadn't worked out. On the Sunday morning they had gone for a walk together, and wound up at the café next to the number 62 bus terminus in Rednal, where they had shared a table with the Trotter brothers, Paul and Benjamin. The next day, Miriam had gone back to work, and the worst of the trouble seemed to be over. And then eight days later, on Tuesday 26th November, she had disappeared. She had gone into work as normal, and not come back. Her parents had sat up for most of the night, weak with anxiety, and in the morning Mr. Newman was on the point of going to see the police when Claire felt it necessary, much against her will, to tell them the secret: Miriam had a lover, and in all probability she had spent the night with him. The Friday before last, when they had both thought she was staying over with her friend Judith, she had been with her lover, at a hotel in Stourbridge, and she was probably with him last night as well. Her father had wanted to know his name; she had refused to tell him, but that evening, when she returned from school, he had forced it out of her. She closed her eyes and shuddered, now, to think of the way he had treated her that night; it had been her first and—so far, anyway—only glimpse of the capacity for violence which she had always believed lay not far beneath his pious, preternaturally self-controlled veneer. Anyway, she had told him: it was Bill Anderton, Doug's father, one of the most important shop stewards at the Longbridge plant where Miriam worked as a typist.

She had thought then that her father really was murderous. The things he had threatened to do to Mr. Anderton were frightful. Not even her mother had been able to restrain him, at first. But eventually he was persuaded that he should call him on the telephone, rather than just turning up on the man's doorstep.

For two hours the Andertons' phone had been engaged, but just as Donald was on the point of giving up and going round to the house after all, his next call was answered. After a brief, hostile conversation he got straight into his car and drove away.

Claire learned, subsequently, that her father had met Mr. Anderton at a Northfield pub, but she never learned the details of this encounter. All she knew was that it had been inconclusive. The next morning Donald went to the police and reported Miriam as a missing person. The police seemed profoundly unconcerned, especially when they heard that there was a man involved. They gave him to understand that this sort of thing happened all the time, and that Miriam would almost certainly turn up or contact them in the next few days. And, to give them credit, they were right. Twelve days later a letter arrived.

The letter. Two years on, it still lay in Donald's writing desk, unanswered and indeed unanswerable. Its single sheet of A5 paper folded crisply, the envelope with its typewritten address (curtly directed to "Mr. and Mrs. Newman") cut open along the fold with a single, clean swipe of the letter-knife. Neither Donald, nor Claire, nor her mother Pamela had looked at it for at least eighteen months. They didn't need to. They had all read it so often during those first few weeks that it was stamped on their memory, every clue, every drop of possible meaning squeezed out of it so that it now seemed a useless thing, sterile, desiccated.

The letter, too, had been mostly typewritten. It had said:

```
Dear Mum and Dad,          ⸱
   This letter is to tell you that I have left
home and will not be coming back. I have
found a man and I have gone to live with him
and I am very happy. I am expecting his baby
and will probably have it.
   Please do not try to look for me.
   Your loving daughter,
```

Miriam had signed the letter herself, and had added a postscript, also in her own handwriting:

"*P.S. The postmark on this letter is not the town where I am living.*"

The envelope was postmarked Leicester, and the date on the stamp said 9th December, 1974. It had arrived on the next day, a Tuesday. There was no date on the letter itself.

Claire had become fixated on this last detail, although she had never been able to make her parents see the significance of it. What it proves, she had told them—or what it *suggests*, at least—is that Miriam could have written this letter at any time. Even *before* she disappeared. So what? said her father. Well, Claire had said, and took a deep breath: Supposing somebody had . . . done away with her. Killed her. And supposing they had found that she was carrying this letter, in her handbag. What a perfect opportunity. All they had to do was to wait a week or two, take a train to another town—Leicester, let's say—and post the letter from there. And then nobody would think that she was dead. They would just think that she had run away to be with her lover.

Donald had two objections to this theory, one of them rational and the other not. His rational objection was that it was too much of a coincidence. It was quite simply implausible to suppose that any putative murderer—they had to use words like this, it was hideous, but they had to do it—might have been handed this perfect smokescreen, this oh-so-convenient means of covering his tracks. And in any case there still had to *be* a lover, for Miriam to have written the letter in the first place. At which point his irrational objection would arise, and take everything over. As soon as he had learned about Miriam's affair with Bill, he had ransacked her bedroom in search of her diaries, understanding their significance now, realizing why their discovery had caused such a terrible rift between Claire and her sister. And when he read them, when he became aware of the intimate, the physical detail in which Miriam had at first fantasized about the relationship and then recorded it, his feelings towards his eldest daughter were changed, irrevocably. He began to feel revulsion for her, mingled with a kind of severe, contemptuous pity, and any suggestion of Claire's that there might be more to her sister's disappearance than the letter implied was rudely dismissed.

"We don't know how many men that slut of a sister of yours might have been sleeping with," he had said. "She might have been servicing the whole factory, for all that we know."

Claire had wept when he threw these words at her, and tears sprang to her eyes now, when she remembered them again. She hated her father: a terrible thing to admit, but it was true, and she had lived with the dull knowledge of it for so long now that it didn't surprise or appall her any more. She hated his smoothness, his hypocrisy, his subtle but complete domination of her mother and above all she hated the atmosphere of rank, overheated religiosity that pervaded their house at all times; the same atmosphere that had driven Miriam away, first of all, and was now driving Claire herself out of doors most weekends, to the forlorn refuge of public spaces like this café.

Claire wanted to stop thinking about all this and to concentrate instead on her pile of back issues, which she was intending to scour for sparks of editorial inspiration. But there was something else she had to decide first. Something about Doug.

Doug fancied her; she was in no doubt about that. And under normal circumstances, she might have been flattered and interested: he was good-looking, and funny, if a little too sure of himself. But the circumstances were not normal. She knew that she was unfriendly towards him, sometimes unforgivably so, and she knew that Doug had no idea why she behaved in this way: he was ignorant, she believed, quite ignorant of the story of Miriam and his father. This would have made her relationship with him difficult in any case, but the thing that made it worse, much worse, was that she could never quite stop herself from wondering whether Bill Anderton might, in some way or another, have been implicated in Miriam's disappearance.

To put it more bluntly: how could you possibly go out with a boy, when you suspected that his father may have murdered your sister?

It wasn't quite as nasty or as simple as that. But she was beginning to think that there were two measures she must take: first, that she should stop being so unpleasant to Doug, and making him suffer for her family problems, with which he had no direct connection; and second, that she should attempt to meet his father. She knew, actually, that she would have no peace of mind until she *had* met him, and she had asked him, straight out, to give his own account of the end of his affair with Miriam.

Today it occurred to her, for the first time, that these two resolutions might be connected.

Claire sighed and drank the last bitter dregs of her cold coffee. These reflections had plunged her into a terrible depression, and the thought of snooping after Mr. Plumb and Mrs. Chase suddenly seemed to have lost all its air of fun. Effortfully she began to sift through her pile of old copies of *The Bill Board* and soon turned, with weary inevitability, to the issue of Thursday, 28th November, 1974: the week of Miriam's disappearance.

It did not make for cheery reading.

KING WILLIAM'S PUPIL A VICTIM OF PUB BOMBING

ran the main headline, and underneath it was a picture of Lois Trotter, Ben's older sister. Claire scanned the article quickly, since she knew most of the story already. It was amazing that

Lois had emerged almost unscathed, physically, given that her boyfriend Malcolm had been sitting right next to her and had been killed in the blast. There was no explanation here of how that might have happened. Claire laughed bleakly when the article ended, "Lois is currently in the Queen Elizabeth Hospital, being treated for severe shock." So severe, she thought, that she still hasn't recovered more than two years later. She had given up asking Benjamin about her; the subject was too painful. Although somebody had mentioned to her that Lois was back at home now, living with the family again.

The next issue, for 5th December, 1974, was particularly dull. It must have been a quiet news week, because the leading story concerned a persistent leak in the Girls' School swimming pool. But in the corner of page 5 there was something that caught her eye: a short column headed "LONGBRIDGE NEWS."

Questions are again being raised [it said] about safety at Longbridge after a fatal accident on the shop floor. Jim Corrigan, an Irish maintenance worker aged only twenty-three years, was attempting to shift machinery weighing 2000 lb from one shop to another, using a purpose-built wheeled trolley. One of the trolley wheels became stuck in a joint on the concrete floor, and it is believed that Corrigan then used a trolley jack to raise the load, which overbalanced and crushed him to death. There was an almost identical incident in the same workplace less than three months ago, which resulted (thankfully) in only minor injuries for another worker. A Longbridge health and safety spokesman said that the coincidence was "freakish," but admitted that the offending joint in the floor had not been repaired following the earlier accident. Mr. Corrigan leaves behind a wife and one small daughter.

This story, upsetting enough in itself, also reminded Claire of something: that the paper had had a tradition, not so long ago, of running regular stories about the Longbridge plant, on the basis that pupils should be encouraged to take an interest in the affairs of a factory which gave so much employment to the surrounding area. The series had been dropped, presumably, because it was so unpopular—she could remember giving scant attention to these items herself—but why shouldn't it now be revived? Not because it was such a great idea, of course, but because it might give her the perfect excuse for having a long and private conversation with Bill Anderton: a full-length interview, a profile of one of the key figures in so many of the factory's recent labour disputes.

Yes, that might work . . .

Poor Jim Corrigan, she thought, pushing the stacks of paper aside and rubbing a tired knuckle into her eyes. Twenty-three years old; picked cruelly at random, the life crushed out of him one Tuesday afternoon, an ordinary working day. Poor Malcolm. Blown to oblivion, one ordinary Thursday evening; sentenced to death for wanting to take his girlfriend out for a drink in a city-centre pub. And poor Miriam, wherever she was . . .

Three deaths?

Please God (the invocation came unbidden, before she could stop it), let that not be the truth of it. Let Miriam not be dead.

Three curtailed narratives, then. Three stories, with no connection between them except that they had been truncated, savagely, when their opening chapters had barely been written. All in the same few days. The same fatal few days. What days those had been, for unfinished stories.

13

THE **BILL BOARD**

Thursday, 17 March, 1977

LETTERS TO THE EDITOR
From R. J. Culpepper, lower science sixth

Dear Sir,

I write in response to the article by S. Richards which you published in your last number, entitled—with stunning originality—"end of an era." It is some time since you favoured your readers with quite such an outpouring of sentimental claptrap.

Mr. Richards appoints himself spokesman for all that he considers decent and honourable in British sporting life, and laments the fact that this year's Oxford v. Cambridge Boat Race is being funded, for the first time in its history, by a commercial sponsor, viz. Ladbrokes the bookmaker. He points out that the victors' trophy has even been re-named—horror of horrors!—the "Ladbroke Cup."

If Mr. Richards could just raise his head for a few moments from the sandy depths in which he has buried it, he might pause to reflect on the advantages of this arrangement.

There are few more inspiring events in the sporting calendar than the Oxford and Cambridge Boat Race. The spectacle of two crack racing eights speeding along the Thames, once seen, can never be forgotten. (I write as someone who has witnessed the race at first-hand, which Mr. Richards hasn't, to the best of my knowledge.) Furthermore, this splendid entertainment is enjoyed every year by thousands of Londoners and millions of television viewers—all, I might add, without paying a penny for the privilege.

Does Mr. Richards believe that crews can undergo months of rigorous training without incurring any expenses, or even that racing boats themselves grow on trees? It might interest him to learn, on the contrary, that they cost £3000 each: a sum which can now be met out of private sponsorship, so that the survival of this great British institution remains assured for the forseeable future.

The sixteen members of The Closed Circle, a "think-tank" composed of the finest minds in King William's (to which Mr. Richards has not, I believe, been elected) last week held a fascinating discussion on the subject of "continuity and change." A most telling point was made, on this occasion, by the newest of our members, P. D. Trotter, who has recently secured election at the unprecedentedly young age of thirteen. Trotter made the observation that only people with a deep love and knowledge of tradition understand it well enough to realize that radical, sometimes brutal measures can be needed to keep it alive. Modernize—modernize or die, was his rallying-call: a slogan that should be pondered long and hard by Mr. Richards and all those like him—including the members of the present government—whose complacent, backward-looking attitude has led this country into its present state of social and economic inertia.

In conclusion, I would suggest to Mr. Richards that the safeguarding of British traditions is best left to those whose familiarity with them goes back more than one generation.

Yours faithfully,
R. J. Culpepper.

14

There were many different theories concerning Culpepper's hatred of Richards. Some people put it down to racism; others observed, rightly enough, that Richards had matured into the finer athlete, and his rival was chewed up with envy.

Doug had another explanation. "I reckon it's all because he never managed to have it off with Cicely, and Steve did."

Benjamin, who still hated to think about what had happened at the cast party, went suddenly very quiet. But Claire was intrigued. She had never heard the whole story of Cicely and Culpepper's failed romance.

"It was all because of Sean, of course," Doug began, and for a moment Benjamin was sidetracked into thinking how strange it sounded, even now, to hear Harding being called by his first name. It was one of the great moments of transition at King William's, that crossing of the Rubicon from surname to first name, and with Harding, no doubt because of the wariness or even fear with which he was regarded by some of his classmates, it had happened later than most. Benjamin himself still called him "Harding," nine times out of ten. Not that they spoke to each other much any more.

"Culpepper fancied Cicely," Doug explained. "He was obsessed with her."

Claire said: "Of course he was. Like all of you." She glanced at Benjamin, who said nothing.

"And last summer, he thought he'd cracked it. He was play-ing tennis one day, and then she turns up with a friend to play on the next court, and before you know it they've hooked up and they're playing mixed doubles. Now she's crap at tennis, unfor-tunately, but he doesn't tell her this. He gets her thinking that she's just playing with the wrong sort of racket. So he says to her, If you like, next time you're playing, you can borrow my racket. Of course, he's got the most expensive bloody racket in the world, the sort that Björn Borg and Ilie Nastase play with, or something. So she says, Thanks very much, you're my hero and what have you, flutters the old eyelashes, the usual Cicely sort of thing.

"OK, so next week, she's ready to borrow his racket. It's in his locker, and the locker's got a combination padlock on it. So—big show of generosity towards Cicely, he tells her the combination. Just go and help yourself, he says. The trouble is—Sean knows the combination too. Don't ask me how. It's just the kind of thing he knows. And he gets there half an hour before Cicely, and does his business."

"What did he do?" asked Claire.

"Well, if there's one thing Culpepper's famous for, apart from being a prize dickhead, it's his porn collection. He's addicted to the stuff. Can't get enough of it. Not that he keeps it in his locker, of course. That'd be asking for trouble. But that must have been what gave Harding the idea. Because Cicely gets to the locker, opens it up, and this is what she sees. Every square inch of that locker is *covered*, covered from top to bottom, with pictures from wank mags. And not just your regular porn, but the weirdest, sickest kind of things. Women doing it with dogs, and guys sticking vacuum cleaners up each other's bums, and all kinds of incredible stuff. And standing there in the middle of it is Culpepper's lovely new tennis racket, but I don't suppose she took much notice of that."

Claire laughed delightedly, and even Benjamin had to join in, although he'd heard the story many times before. It was one of Harding's finer moments, he had to admit.

"What did she say to him?" Claire wanted to know.

"I don't think she said anything." Doug stood up and collected their empty glasses. "Anyway, here she is now—you can ask her yourself."

He went to the bar for another round of drinks just as Cicely entered the pub and made her way towards their table. Spearheading the fashion for *Annie Hall*–inspired clothing, she was wearing a man's tweed jacket, green baggy corduroys, a collarless shirt and a wide-brimmed hat. Benjamin thought that she looked extraordinarily elegant and heart-stoppingly beautiful. Claire thought that she looked ludicrous.

"Hi, Ciss," she said, rising to her feet. "Fabulous clothes."

The rift created by Claire's interview had been healed some time ago; on the surface, at least. But there was still something brittle and mannered about the way they now kissed each other on the cheek. As for Benjamin, she didn't kiss him at all; simply said: "Shall we go and sit by ourselves for a while?"

"Did that seem terribly rude?" she asked, as they found themselves a seat by the window. (The nice thing about The Grapevine was that it had big picture windows. The not so nice thing was that they overlooked a busy underpass known, inappropriately, as Paradise Circus.)

"I don't think so," said Benjamin, who couldn't have cared less. He would have ditched any pretence of good manners for the sake of this thrilling intimacy. "I think there's something going on between those two tonight, anyway."

"I just find it so hard to talk to Claire after what she wrote about me. I feel she betrayed me. Can you make her out, at all?"

Benjamin shrugged. As usual, in Cicely's presence, he was afraid of appearing inarticulate, and as usual, this fear robbed him of his power of speech.

"People are so . . . opaque, so *enigmatic*," she mused. "That's fascinating, though, isn't it? That must fascinate you, as a writer."

"Yes, it does," said Benjamin. He had rashly told Cicely that he was working on a novel, and now she had him marked down as a keen observer of human nature. It was a pretence he felt obliged to sustain, for her benefit. "The complexities of social behaviour, the . . . subtle nuances of character are all . . ." (what the *fuck* was he talking about?) ". . . well, I'm really into all that."

"I find it rather terrifying," said Cicely, with a smile, "to think how closely you must be watching everything I say and do. Do you write it all down afterwards?"

"I don't need to," said Benjamin, solemnly and truthfully. "I can always remember it."

"I hope you aren't going to put me in your book. I'm sure your portrait would be very unflattering. I'd emerge as some ridiculous egotist, totally obsessed with myself and not at all interested in the world around me."

It pained Benjamin that every time he saw her (and this was the fourth of their meetings at The Grapevine), she would fall into this way of talking: this endless, punishing self-denigration.

"Is that really how you see yourself?" he asked.

"It's how you've *made* me see myself," Cicely answered, and there was nothing but gratitude in her voice and eyes as she said it.

"I'll get you a drink," muttered Benjamin, and as he waited at the bar he bit his lip and told himself, yet again, that the time had come to confess the truth: to tell Cicely once and for all that it was absurd, this rôle she had found for him, casting him as her severest critic, her conscience, almost, when the fact of the matter was that he worshipped everything about her with unquestioning fervour. Only one thought was holding him back—the awful suspicion that once she knew what his real feelings were, she would lose interest in him, and not want to see him again. He was in a grotesque situation, in other words, being permitted to spend as much time as he wanted in the company of the person he idolized more than anyone in the world, but only on condition that he never said anything affectionate to her, never paid her a compliment, never mentioned that he loved or valued or was even attracted to her. The price he must pay for seeing Cicely was to live a permanent lie.

In any case, shortly after returning to their table with a half pint of Guinness and a Bloody Mary, Benjamin learned that this particular ordeal would soon be coming to an end.

"You're very special to me, you know," Cicely said. A tiny piece of snot was peeping out from her left nostril, and he watched, enraptured, as she absently removed it with a delicate stroke of her finger, and wiped it on a handkerchief. My God, he even adored the way she picked her nose. If it had come to a choice, at that moment, between watching Cicely pick her nose, or being slowly fellated in turn by Brigitte Bardot and Julie Christie, he knew which he would have preferred.

"We'll always be friends, from now on," she continued. "And not just ordinary friends. There's something different about our friendship. A kind of . . . precious quality to it. The way it started! God!"

She threw back her head and laughed, but for some reason Benjamin couldn't share in her hilarity. He had a nasty, hollow intimation that something dreadful was about to happen. He smiled weakly.

"I'll always be grateful, you know, for what you did for me. The way you revealed me to myself. No one could ask for anything more than that. And I've loved these meetings we've had. Coming to this pub, and talking to each other, so frankly, so honestly."

"You've . . . *loved* these meetings?" Benjamin said. She looked at him inquiringly, so he explained: "You said 'loved.' You used the past tense."

"I know." She stared into her drink, unable to meet his eye. "I can't come here and see you any more, Ben. I'm sorry."

A fuse was suddenly blown, in some far distant galaxy, and the universe went black.

"Why not?" Benjamin heard himself saying, light years away.

"My boyfriend says he doesn't like it."

"Your . . . ?"

"I've started going out with Julian. Julian Stubbs." She was almost weeping into her drink, now. "It'll be a disaster, I know. Oh, I'm a terrible, terrible person."

The evening turned out more successfully for Claire. Her reward for being friendly to Doug all evening was that he invited her home for coffee. They were both slightly drunk, and on the back seat of the number 62 bus as it rattled its way up Lickey Road, past the Longbridge factory gates, she allowed him to slip his arm around her shoulder. She drew the line when he made fumbling but unmistakable overtures towards her left breast; but it was pleasant, on the whole, to sit back on that warm spring night, not saying much, not attempting to make conversation, just watching the play of amber light on the seats in front as the streetlamps passed overhead and the bus made its slow progress towards the terminus, taking Claire closer and closer to the next stage of her quest; or perhaps even its end.

When they arrived at Doug's house, his mother was watching television and his father was still working, his papers arranged in careful stacks on the dining-room table, his cigarette burning out almost untouched in the ashtray. They both rose to their feet when they saw that their son had company. For a terrible moment she thought that Doug was going to tell them her full name, so that Bill would realize she was Miriam's little sister and would become hostile and suspicious and reluctant to talk to her. But all he said was, "Mum, Dad—this is Claire," and then Bill went back to work, and she talked in the kitchen for about half an hour with Doug and Irene, and then just as she was leaving she went back into the dining room and asked Bill if she could interview him for the school magazine, and he looked amazed but clearly very pleased by the idea, and Doug also looked amazed and slightly less pleased, but then Claire kissed him on the mouth when they said goodnight in the front door-way and that seemed to make things better.

15

THE **BILL BOARD**

Thursday, 28 April, 1977

<u>LETTERS TO THE EDITOR</u>
From Arthur Pusey-Hamilton, MBE

Dear Sirs,

A recent article by your correspondent, Douglas Anderton, high-lighted instances of what he describes as "anti-Irish sentiment" among the good people of Birmingham. Since 1974, the year of the pub bombings, he alleges a catalogue of firebomb attacks, lynchings and unprovoked assaults on Irish citizens, and describes these incidents as a "disgrace."

For once, I fully agree with Mr. Anderton. These incidents are indeed disgraceful. There have been far too few of them, for one thing, and they have not been nearly serious enough.

Does Mr. Anderton not realize that we are fighting a war in Ireland—a war designed to protect legitimate British interests? In these circumstances, it is surely incumbent on every right-thinking British citizen to do everything in his (or her) power to support the government in its campaign against those forces of sedition that are massed against it on the other side of the Irish sea.

There are a number of simple but effective measures which all of us can take in this respect. Take, for instance, the controversial (to some minds) British policy of "internment." It was in fact Gladys, my good lady wife, who first found a way of putting this into practice at home. We had long nursed a suspicion that our next-door neighbour, Mr. O'Reilly, was—not to put too fine a point on it—Irish. Although we had no concrete proof, there were certain factors—his name, his choice of colour (emerald green) for the family car, his habit of whistling "Danny Boy" while mowing the lawn—which convinced us pretty firmly that he had Irish blood in him. It was the work of just a few hours for Gladys to set up a primitive booby trap across his front drive, and then, when he was dangling helplessly by his left ankle from the nearest lamp-post, to bind him securely and carry him kicking and screaming upstairs to the airing cupboard, where he is confined to this day. One less Paddy to contaminate the streets of this fair city, say I!

My own approach, I might add, has been somewhat more radical. It has for some time been rumoured—although why there should be any secrecy about this, I can't imagine—that the British army operates a "shoot to kill" policy in Northern Ireland. Despite having written numerous letters to No 10 Downing Street, I have been unable to obtain official confirmation of this fact, and yet I thought there was no particular reason why, as a patriotic Englishman, I should not attempt to instigate something similar in our own pleasant, tree-lined avenue. Accordingly I obtained a modest bank loan in order to purchase some ammunition and convert our loft into a small gun turret, and began to keep watch on the street outside. It wasn't long before I noticed that the name on the local butcher's van, which drove past our house every Tuesday and Thursday morning at 10 o'clock, was none other than "Murphy's—Suppliers of Fine Meat and Poultry." Could anything have been more blatant? The driver might just as well have spray-painted the words "Troops Out" on to his van in six-foot lettering. Right, I thought. Right, you little Provo bastard—I know what your game is. Accordingly, the very next time that he passed by, I let rip with a couple of rounds from my trusty Kalashnikov. Sadly, my aim is not quite what it was (my eyesight has been dicky ever since a trivial argument with Gladys, my good lady wife, over the correct position to adopt while singing the third verse of the National Anthem; tempers got a little frayed and our ornamental Burmese corkscrew was rather too close to hand) and the only target I managed to hit, on this occasion, was a dog belonging to an elderly passer-by—it was an Irish wolfhound, I'm pleased to say—while the cowardly blighter Murphy swerved as soon as he heard my fire and crashed into a nearby tree, sustaining what tragically turned out to be only minor external injuries. He then had the effrontery to report this incident to the police, and they, showing a lack of judgement and an absence of patriotic decency that can scarcely be credited, thereupon arrested both myself and Gladys, my good lady wife. Even now we find ourselves detained at Her Majesty's Pleasure, but we remain confident that our names will be cleared at the forthcoming trial, which takes place on Wednesday next. The presence and support of all of your good readers on this historic occasion would be much appreciated.

I remain, Sir, yours indefatigably,
Arthur Pusey-Hamilton, MBE.

SEALED with the ancient and noble Seal of the Pusey-Hamiltons.

"FLOREAT VAGINA!"

16

CN: . . . this tape recorder, if that's OK?

BA: Certainly, certainly. Whatever suits you best.

CN: I mean, obviously, I won't use everything we say. I'll edit it all down.

BA: I'm in your hands, Claire. This new-fangled technology's beyond me.

CN: (laughs) Not that new-fangled, really . . . Anyway, here we go. Ready?

BA: (laughs) Ready as I'll ever be. Fire away then. Do your worst.

CN: OK . . . Well . . . I'm not quite sure where to start. I'm talking to Bill Anderton, Convenor of the Works Committee at the British Leyland Longbridge plant, and a senior—senior shop steward?—

BA: Senior, yes, that's fair to say.

CN: —in the Transport and General Workers' Union. Perhaps you could begin by telling me why you think that the readers of this magazine should be interested in what happens at Longbridge.

BA: Well, Claire, that's a very interesting question, and I can think of two ways of answering it. One is simply to say that everyone who lives in Birmingham is affected by Longbridge. You can't get away from that. The life of a factory this size has an impact on every part of the local community. From the dealers who sell the cars, the engineering firms who help supply the parts, the supermarkets where the men's wives spend their money at the end of the week . . . The list goes on and on. I think everybody can agree about that. But the second thing I'm going to say is more contentious, if you like. There's a struggle going on at Longbridge—a war, you might say. The struggle between labour and capital. This struggle is as old as history or at least as old as capitalism, but you don't read about it much in the history books. I've looked at the books my son brings home from school and they're the same as the books I used to read when I was a kid—the history of kings and princes and prime ministers. The history of the ruling class, in other words. But the ruling class is only a tiny part of history and over the centuries it's been sustained and supported by the labour of the rest of the population, and those people have a history as well. So what I'm saying is that the kids at King William's ought to be interested in Longbridge because it provides a—a microcosm, if you will, of society as a whole. The ruling class versus the labouring class. Management versus workers. That's what history is all about and that's what society is all about and that's what life is all about, to be honest. I'm not sure . . . I don't know whether I've put that very well.

CN: You see the relationship between these two classes as a struggle, a war.

BA: Essentially, yes.

CN: Isn't it just this attitude which has won you a reputation as a militant?

BA: I reject that word. That word is an invention of the ruling class. It's just a word they've invented to put down someone who is standing up for his Brothers' interests. The ruling class owns the language, you see, as well as everything else. Words become corrupted that way.

CN: Are you a Marxist?

BA: Well, that's a pretty . . . loaded question, Claire. Do you know what a Marxist is?

CN: (laughs) Not really. Only Doug said that he thought you were one.

BA: I've read Marx, obviously. I studied him at night school, and I agree with his interpretation of history. That doesn't make me a Communist, of course.

CN: But some of the shop stewards at Longbridge are Communists. Some of your colleagues.

BA: Who told you that?

CN: It's been in the papers.

BA: It's not true. Think about it, Claire. The papers aren't owned by the workers: they're owned by the bosses. That's why every story they print is favourable to the management, told from the management's point of view. Who owns your magazine?

CN: Well, I don't know if anybody <u>owns</u> it . . . The school, I suppose.

BA: Exactly. And does the headmaster allow you to print anything you want?

CN: Not anything, no.

BA: It's in the press barons' interests to run damaging stories about the workers. Calling their elected representatives Communists is just one of the things they can do. I'm not a Communist, never have been. I'm a socialist. What they have in Russia isn't real socialism anyway.

CN: You say that as an elected representative, you're just standing up for your members' interests. But there's a general perception that many of the strikes at Longbridge aren't in anybody's interest. That they're bad for productivity and bad for the company's image.

BA: Well, I don't know what you mean by a "general perception."

CN: I was thinking that we had a Debating Society meeting, where the motion was "This House believes that the unions have too much power," and it was carried by about ten to one.

BA: That tells you everything you need to know about your school, and very little about the feelings of the country as a whole.

CN: What do you feel are the qualities needed to become a successful shop steward? Why, for instance, have people like you and Derek Robinson achieved such a high public profile, out of all the union figures at British Leyland?

BA: Well, I'm glad you mentioned Derek, because that means I can talk about him, and it doesn't sound like I'm blowing my own trumpet. (laughs) Obviously you need to be a good speaker, you need the gift of the gab. It takes guts to get up in front of 10,000 people in the middle of Cofton Park and make the kind of speech that's going to carry them along with you. Derek's fantastic at that. He's a natural born orator. A lot of it comes back to language, you see—if you've got control of language, then you've got power. A sort of power. Then you need tenacity as well, you need the courage to stick with your beliefs and to carry on fighting even when things aren't going your way. But there's something else, too, which is what I'd call a sense of the . . . broader picture.

CN: What do you mean by that, exactly?

BA: Well, as I've been trying to explain—not very well, I dare say—the struggle at Longbridge isn't an isolated thing. It's been going on throughout history for centuries and it's going on all the time in all the different parts of the world. The socialist movement is an international movement. It cuts across national borders and it cuts through the different races, as well. This is a very important point and it's also one of the most difficult to get across to the workforce as a whole.

CN: Why's that, do you think?

BA: Because racism is endemic. In this day and age a worker's job is very vulnerable and his livelihood is very vulnerable and it's very easy for someone to play on that and to sow discord among people who would otherwise be standing together in a common cause.

CN: Are you thinking of anyone in particular?

BA: There are lots of cases. A couple of years ago we had a shop steward—I won't mention his name, he's left the factory now—who was putting Nazi pamphlets around the shop floor. Disciplinary measures had to be taken. More recently, you've got that bastard—I'm sorry about the language, but this is just what I feel—you've got that bastard Enoch Powell making a speech to his Tory friends at the Monday Club suggesting that Africans and Asians should be given a thousand pounds each to go home. What he calls their home, anyway. I just find that sort of thing contemptible. That's why the strike at Grunwick is so important.

CN: Grunwick?

BA: You do study . . . current affairs and so on, don't you? I mean, there are special classes for that, at school?

CN: It comes under General Studies, yes.

BA: But no one's told you about the Grunwick strike? Have you not seen it on the news?

CN: Sorry, I . . .

BA: All right then, in a nutshell, Grunwick is a film processing plant in Willesden, in West London. Maybe your dad's sent some holiday snaps off in the post to be developed and they haven't come back yet. Well, this is the reason. There's a white collar union called APEX: the Association of Professional, Executive, Clerical and Computer Staffs. Grunwick employs a lot of Indian staff in its mail room and last summer they went on strike over working conditions, and then when they tried to join this union they were sacked. All hundred and forty of them. They've been picketing the plant ever since—risking life and limb half of the time, because the management cars drive right through the picket line and so do the buses they use to bring in the blacklegs—and one of the things I've been doing is trying to organize the members of my union to get down there and show support. Stand on the picket line with them. Now most of them show willing but when there's a grumble it's usually along the lines of "Why should we be helping out a lot of Pakis?"

CN: And how do you try to counter that kind of prejudice?

BA: Well, where do you begin? I've been in close contact with the shop steward down there—Jayaben Desai, her name is . . . (pause) Here, I'll write it down for you—a wonderful woman, really tough, really inspiring. I'm trying to get her to come up to Longbridge, talk to my members, so they can see that . . . Well, when you actually meet someone like that, hear them speak and so on, you realize that you're all on the same side. A lot of it's to do with ignorance. Fear of the unfamiliar. Of course it's not

always the blacks or the Asians. After the pub bombings there
was a lot of anti-Irish feeling on the shop floor. Some nasty
things were being said, threats being made, that sort of thing.
Oh, yes, nationalism's a terrible scourge, in my view. That's the
real enemy. Get rid of nationalism and you've solved ninety per
cent of the problems in the world. Anyone who tries to play the
nationalist card and make political capital out of it is just
beneath contempt. They're just the scum of the earth, those
bastards, if you'll pardon my French.

CN: To sum up, what sort of role do you see yourself having in the
next few years? Do you think that despite all its recent problems,
the future of British Leyland is safe?

BA: The future of the company is safe because ultimately Longbridge
is a good factory with a good workforce and a good product,
so ultimately the bosses will find a way to make money out of it,
by hook or by crook. How ruthless they are allowed to be in this
pursuit is dependent on the skills and the fighting spirit of the
union men, so if I have a small part to play in defending the jobs
and the pay packets of the average car worker then I shall feel
quite satisfied. I will have done my bit.

CN: Mr. Anderton—thank you very much.

BA: (laughs) Oh, I see, we're being formal now, are we? Well, thank
you very much, Miss, er . . .

CN: Newman.

BA: Newman?

CN: Claire Newman.

(An edited version of the preceding transcript appeared in The Bill
Board, *dated 5th May, 1977. The following section was never
published.)*

CN: (continued) Are you all right, Mr. Anderton? Is something the
matter?

BA: No, I'm fine. Fine.

CN: Didn't you know my name before?

BA: No, I don't think Doug mentioned it.

CN: I'm Miriam's sister. (<u>long silence</u>) You do know who I mean by Miriam, don't you? Miriam Newman?

BA: No. No, I don't. I don't think I heard that name before.

CN: I think you did. I think you must be mistaken. Miriam Newman?

BA: No. Nothing.

CN: You had an affair with her, three years ago. It started three years ago. She was a typist, in the Design Room. (<u>long silence</u>)

BA: And?

CN: And what?

BA: What about it? What do you want?

CN: I thought we might . . . talk about her.

BA: (<u>pause</u>) Where is she?

CN: I don't know. We don't know.

BA: Did she come back?

CN: No. I was wondering . . . I was wondering if you might be able to shed some light on what happened to her.

BA: Did your father send you to come and talk to me?

CN: No. He doesn't know I'm here. Anyway, I don't think he . . . I don't believe he thinks about it much any more.

BA: I spoke to him, when she first went missing.

CN: I know.

BA: I told him everything I knew. After that, I was going to phone, ask if there'd been any news, but I couldn't. Couldn't bring myself to . . . (<u>silence</u>)

CN: There was a note.

BA: A note?

CN: She sent us a letter.

BA: When was this? What did it say?

CN: A couple of weeks later. It said she'd gone away with another man.

BA: That's what I'd heard. I overheard someone in the canteen say something about that.

CN: Did she ever talk to you about another man?

BA: Yes. The last time I saw her . . . We went and stayed at a hotel in

Stourbridge . . . A dreadful weekend . . . She was talking about him then. Said he wasn't from around here.

CN: The letter was postmarked Leicester. She also said—she said she was pregnant. (long silence) Is that possible, do you think?

BA: Of course it's possible.

CN: Do you think it could have been your baby?

BA: (pause) Yes, I suppose so. It could just as well have been his. The other guy's.

CN: I don't believe there was another man.

BA: Why not? Isn't that what she said, in the letter?

CN: I just don't believe it. Miriam wasn't that sort of girl. She never spoke to me about anybody else. Never once. The only person she spoke about was you. She was obsessed by you. She loved you.

BA: (long silence; unidentified noise, perhaps creaking of chair, BA sitting up, changing position) I think you're right. I know you are. (silence) Yes, she was obsessed by me. I allowed that. I allowed it to happen. It was very flattering to me, and . . . I didn't see where it was leading. I should have seen. Anyone with any sense would have seen. I suppose the reason . . . The reason I allowed . . . I loved her too, you see. I did. It wasn't love to start with but that's what it became, in the end. Oh, I never stopped loving Irene but that made no difference, that was what made it worse, in fact, worse for everyone. And she knew. I'm sure Irene knew. Of course she did. Women aren't stupid. We lived like that for months. Don't know how. I don't know how we got through those months. I know what it was like for us, I don't know what it was like for Miriam. We saw each other every day, at the factory. Most days. We used to meet in one of the shower blocks. That last day, the last day anyone saw her, we'd arranged to meet. But I never went. I don't know how long she must have waited for me. It was always like that. We didn't have any nights together. Just that once. That terrible time. I always had Irene to go home to, she didn't have anything like that, I don't think she was getting on with your mother and father, she said things were difficult at home, but she talked about <u>you</u> sometimes. Her sister. Said nice things about you. She was so unhappy, everybody was so unhappy, the whole bloody stupid thing was causing so much misery and I don't know how long I would have let it carry on. For ever. But even so that was no way for it to end, just for Miriam to go away like that. That wasn't the right way for it to end. I don't think it was her way, either. I don't think she chose to end it like that. Something funny must have happened. Something . . .

<u>(Silence. Traffic noise. Rustle of tissue paper: BA? CN?)</u>

BA: Your sister's dead. That's what I think.

CN: I'm going to turn this off now.

17

Whenever Benjamin went to church, which he did every week, and whenever he prayed, which he did every night, he would always ask God for the same thing: to end his exile from Cicely. But his prayers went unanswered. He was now condemned to a banishment every bit as complete, it seemed, as the one he had suffered before, in the days when he had never even spoken to her.

When religion failed him, he turned to the consolations of art. He began by writing a verse sequence, entitled "In Your Absence," but it was abandoned after nine lines of a sonnet and half a haiku. Then he resumed work on his novel, attempting to recast his recent history with Cicely as a digressive and brutally ironic chapter, so that his continuing pain and sense of rejection might be transmuted into high comedy. It was abandoned after two paragraphs. A proposed string quartet got no further than a title and a dedication at the top of a sheet of manuscript paper. He heard, at second- or third-hand, that her affair with Stubbs had only lasted a few weeks; but still she made no effort to contact him. He also knew that she had resigned as secretary of the Drama Society; but he didn't know why. She would always greet him, affectionately enough, whenever they passed in the school corridors. They waved to each other at their respective bus stops. But there was to be no return, it was clear, to the closeness they had fleetingly enjoyed during the first few weeks of the

Easter term. Benjamin's only souvenir of that ecstatic but dreamlike episode was a secret drawer at the bottom of his bedroom cupboard, containing a plastic carrier bag full of blonde hair.

Meanwhile, the rivalry between Richards and Culpepper intensified. By the time of the annual Sports Day, in early July, 1977, it had become so public, and was the object of so much interest throughout the school, that the editors of *The Bill Board* decided to overcome their collective prejudice against sports coverage and assign someone to follow the two competitors as they prepared to battle it out on the athletics track. Philip agreed to undertake this task, and duly turned up in the sports pavilion changing rooms fifteen minutes before the first race (the 400 metres) was about to be run.

He found Culpepper energetically performing sit-ups on the tiled floor, while Steve Richards hunted through the contents of his kit bag with an increasingly panic-stricken air.

"What's the matter, Steve?" Philip asked.

"He's lost his lucky charm," Culpepper explained, between ostentatious bouts of huffing and puffing. "You know what these natives are like. Superstitious as hell. It's some heathen icon he has to kiss three times before each race, or something."

"It's a St. Christopher's medal, you wanker," said Steve. "Which is about as Christian as they come. And I had it here a minute ago."

"You'll be accusing me of stealing it next, I suppose."

"Nothing would surprise me, where you're concerned," Steve muttered.

Philip began to scribble frantically in his notebook. "*. . . in an atmosphere heavy with sweat and bad temper . . . accusations being slung backwards and forwards even before the races had started . . . Richards already at a psychological disadvantage . . .*"

A tiny, curly-haired first-former called Ives put his head round the door and said: "Mr. Warren wants everybody outside in five minutes."

Steve was still talking about his lost medal as the runners assembled at the starting line.

"It's not superstition," he said. "That medal's got sentimental value. It was a present from Valerie."

"I thought you'd split up with her," said Philip.

"That's why it's so important. It's the only thing she ever gave me."

"It'll turn up."

Steve did not seem convinced, and he continued to glare suspiciously at Culpepper as they took their places side by side on the track. Steve was running for Astell House, and Culpepper was running for Ransome; but the House competition was not really the important thing, as everybody knew. Every year, at the end of Sports Day, a silver trophy was presented to the individual who had proved himself the most outstanding sportsman in the school over the last three terms. He would then be crowned with the title *Victor Ludorum*, and it was this honour that both Steve and Culpepper craved so fiercely. They were the only serious contenders.

Before the race began, Philip retreated to a bank above the athletics track, where he could get a good view of the runners over the heads of the crowd. He settled himself and turned to a new page in his notebook. When he saw what was at the top of the page he smiled, regretfully. This book consisted of unruled sheets and also doubled as his sketchpad. Here, more than eight months ago, he had begun to compile what he had hoped would be a complex "Rock Family Tree" in the manner of Pete Frame, telling the story of his long and successful collaboration with Benjamin. Instead, he had ended up with this:

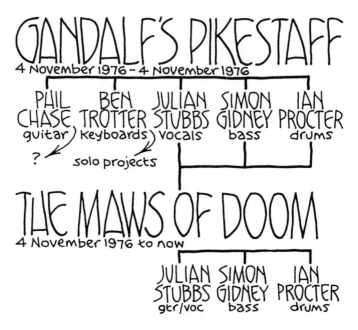

GANDALF'S PIKESTAFF
4 November 1976 – 4 November 1976

PHIL CHASE (guitar) BEN TROTTER (keyboards) JULIAN STUBBS (vocals) SIMON GIDNEY (bass) IAN PROCTER (drums)

? solo projects

THE MAWS OF DOOM
4 November 1976 to now

JULIAN STUBBS (gtr/voc) SIMON GIDNEY (bass) IAN PROCTER (drums)

And the Maws were still going strong, it seemed, pulling in respectable crowds every Friday night down at The Bournbrook in Selly Oak. Any old rubbish could get an audience these days, Philip thought, as long as it was riding on the punk bandwagon. These were desperate times for someone like him, whose heroes—specialists, to a man, in fifteen-minute instrumentals, usually with a bit of cod classical mythology and an electric violin solo thrown in—had until recently commanded two-page features in the music press but could nowadays barely get themselves a recording contract. There were bands he could have discussed avidly with his friends a year ago, whose very names would now provoke howls of derision if he so much as mentioned them in the sixth-form common room. What was so funny about Camel and Curved Air and Gentle Giant anyway? Oh, but it was a cruel world . . .

A sudden outburst of cheering disrupted these thoughts and made him realize that he had not been paying attention to the race, which now seemed to be over. He scrambled down from the bank and grabbed hold of Ives as he rushed past.

"Who won? Who won?"

"Culpepper. Didn't you see it?"

"No, I didn't. What happened? Was it a close thing?"

"You'll have to go and ask someone else. I'm in a hurry."

"Oh, come on, Ives. Just tell me how it—"

"No time! Can't stop! He'll kill me if I'm not there by three o'clock!"

And with that mysterious exclamation, Ives was on his way.

It seemed that everyone had gone to watch the sports. Everyone, that is, except Benjamin. Once again he sat alone in the little office next to the editorial meeting room, high up in the Carlton corridor, and relished the atmosphere of a school entirely abandoned by its staff and pupils. It was in just these circumstances, after all, that Cicely had first come to find him. This same unbroken silence. This same heaviness and apathy. Except that then, he hadn't been able to identify its source, whereas now, he knew precisely what he was suffering from: a paralyzing nostalgia, an almost unbearable longing for the chance to return to that day and to will his relationship with Cicely along a different course. How could he, how could he *possibly* have let that opportunity slip through his fingers? What had happened between the two of them, exactly? (Or failed to happen?) Whatever the explanation, there was one bitter certainty which he had been trying to ward off, but which he might just as well accept: it would take more than a few Spenserian stanzas or piano études to bring her back to him now.

Benjamin sat immobile at his desk, looked out over the rooftops and drifted into a reverie. He stared into the paleness of the blue summer sky and remembered something: a scene from his early childhood. Perhaps the earliest of all his memories. He was with his mother, at some sort of garden fête or summer fair. How old would he be: three, maybe? Four? He had an image of traction engines and vintage cars, bedecked with coloured ribbons. Tombola stalls and Aunt Sallies and games of pin-the-tail-on-the-donkey. On one side he could feel the tight clasp of his mother's hand, while his other hand was clutching a balloon, a yellow balloon, on a long piece of string. They were leaving the fair and making for their car, a green Hillman Imp. And then something happened. A moment's inattention. The string slipped from his grasp and suddenly this balloon, the most precious thing he had ever possessed, was gone. It broke free and rose into the sky. Did he wail with distress, call out his mother's name, burst into tears? He had no memory, no memory at all of the sound of that day. In fact, whenever he thought of this scene (and yes, he often thought of it, felt compelled to revisit it again and again) the only sound that he heard was the sound of music; as if the memory was a film clip, complete with orchestral soundtrack. It was always the same music, as well. In his head Benjamin felt that he could hear, quite distinctly, the rising chords, the sweet modal harmonies of Vaughan Williams' "The Lark Ascending." As the balloon drifted implacably away, as his three- or four-year-old face tilted to watch it disappear, crumpled into a mask of childish desolation, the violin entered, and it too gathered momentum, took flight, spiralling into the hot Sunday sky, with innumerable loops and turns, until, like the balloon, it dwindled and faded, melted slowly into the infinite distance, leaving nothing behind but a yellow dot burned on to the retina and an aching, insupportable sense of loss. A sense of loss that Benjamin had always felt could never be surpassed. Until now, that is . . .

But then he realized something. For once the music wasn't inside his head at all. He really *could* hear it. Unless he was going quite mad. Somewhere, from another room, in a distant corner of the school, he could hear someone playing the opening section of "The Lark Ascending." A record-player, turned up extremely loud. Where could it be coming from?

Benjamin stuck his head through the open window and craned his neck to the left, looking towards the music school.

This had to be the source. It was the only place he knew there was a record-player, in the big upstairs room called the Gerald Hill Studio, where the school's library of miniature scores and classical records was housed. But who would be there, this afternoon? Someone as bored by the prospect of Sports Day as he was, obviously. Benjamin hurried down the corridor to investigate, made his way down the main staircase and past the Porter's Lodge, then paused when he reached the quadrangle outside. He had a good view of the music school from here, and could see a solitary figure leaning against the huge picture window of the Gerald Hill Studio, his face relaxed in blissful attentiveness as the Vaughan Williams tone poem swelled to the first of its climaxes. Benjamin blinked in surprise when he saw who it was. It was Harding.

Steve had won the 200 metres, and Culpepper had won the 800. Culpepper was one of the few contenders left in the high jump (with the bar now standing at 1.9 metres), while Steve had already broken the school records in the long jump and javelin. Mr. Warren, who had devised the elaborate points system used on these occasions, and who alone seemed to understand it, was keeping quiet about the positions of the two rivals: but evidently there was little to choose between them. The tension continued to rise, fuelled even more by the mystery surrounding Steve's St. Christopher's medal, which he now openly accused Culpepper of stealing. Whatever the outcome of today's contest, there would be sourness and bad feeling at the end of it.

Philip had made a few more notes—*"an astonishing succession of neck-and-neck finishes . . . faces taut with effort and exertion . . . where does competition end and antagonism begin?"*—but the contest did not grip him in the way it seemed to grip most of the spectators. He wanted Steve to win because he liked him more, but that was about as far as his involvement went. To tell the truth he was beginning to feel slightly bored.

He resumed his position on the bank above the race track, turned to a blank page in his notebook and began to sketch the elaborate, fussy outline of the school chapel, which commanded the skyline in the middle distance. Under Mr. Plumb's tutelage, he was turning into a good draughtsman. After a few minutes a small group of younger boys had gathered around him and his efforts were the subject of admiring comments.

"Of course, you know the history of the chapel, don't you?" said Philip, as he began to sketch in the terracotta brickwork. "The school's only been on this site for about forty years. It used to be next to New Street Station, but they decided to move it here just before the War. And the chapel isn't really a chapel at all. It's just part of the old upper corridor. They took it down brick by brick and then numbered all the pieces so it could be put up again on the new site. The bricks just sat in a heap here all through the War, for about five years."

Well, Philip thought it was interesting, even if his audience didn't. He had recently begun to pick up pieces of arcane information like this, partly from books in the local library, partly from the long walks he had begun to take at weekends, looking for interesting places to sketch. He had become fascinated, in particular, by Birmingham's huge network of disused and neglected canals, and was lobbying Mr. Tillotson to organize a Walking Option expedition around these forgotten backwaters. Many of their most intriguing corners were too remote to explore by himself.

Soon there was another noisy eruption from the crowd below. A throng of boys had descended on the finishing line, and through them Philip could glimpse Culpepper crouched on the grass, head in hands, his shoulders heaving.

"Shit!" said Philip, jumping to his feet. "I've missed another one!"

This time it was the 1500 metres, which Steve appeared to have won, again by the narrowest of margins. There were only two more races to be run, now. It was still impossible to say who would emerge victorious.

.   .   .

With the wistful strains of the "Five Variants on Dives and Lazarus" murmuring behind them, Benjamin and Harding continued to discuss their love of Vaughan Williams. They had both agreed that the third and fifth symphonies were masterpieces, and that the eighth was severely underrated. They talked about the London symphony and wondered whether it would be possible for anybody to write a "Birmingham symphony" of the same grandeur and resonance. Benjamin thought not. He recommended that Sean (he was calling him Sean, now, without hesitation or embarrassment) should check out the oboe concerto: a minor work, but very beautiful. Sean said that his personal favourite was the "Serenade to Music," a choral and orchestral setting of lines from *The Merchant of Venice*. It had been his introduction to this composer; he had heard his mother sing one of the solo parts when he was only eight years old, at a performance given by the local choral society.

"I didn't know your mother was musical," said Benjamin; reflecting, as he said it, that he actually knew nothing about Sean's parents at all.

"Mum and Dad have both got good voices," he said. "They were always singing together. It was one of the things they used to have in common."

"Used to?"

"They're living apart at the moment," he confided. It was amazing how this music was loosening his tongue, like wine. "Dad moved out a few weeks ago."

"Oh. I'm sorry."

He crossed over to the other side of the room, picked up a record sleeve, pretended to read it. It must have been difficult for him to reveal so much. "It's been building up for some time," he said. "Dad comes from a big Irish family, Mum's English through and through. And she can be . . . well, she can be a difficult person to be around. She's pretty strict."

Benjamin thought for a moment about the bizarre fantasy world Sean had created around the Pusey-Hamiltons—the shy, stunted boy subjected to a punishing parental régime, the insane lampoon of anti-Irish prejudice—and found himself wondering for the first time whether there was more to his humour than simple anarchic clowning.

"When you say strict . . ." he prompted.

And then Sean said, very quickly and emphatically: "I love my mother." Benjamin had not meant to suggest otherwise, but it seemed of paramount importance that this fact should be stressed. "She's an incredible woman. One in a million, actually."

After that he abruptly clammed up, and for a while there was only music to fill the silence. Luckily, before very long, they heard a gentle knock on the door.

Sean shouted, "Come in!"

It was Ives. It was five to three, he was out of breath, and he had beneath his arm a carrier bag from Vincent's, a classical record shop in central Birmingham.

"Well? Did you get it?"

"Yes. It was 20p more than you said it was going to be."

"Never mind that."

He opened the bag and inspected its contents with a cry of satisfaction. It was another record of Vaughan Williams orchestral pieces. This one included the tone poems "In the Fen Country" and "Norfolk Rhapsody No. 1."

"You've got to hear this, Ben," he said, cutting "Dives and Lazarus" off in mid-stream and slipping the record on to the turntable. "I couldn't believe they didn't have this one in the library. It'll blow you away." Ives was still loitering in the doorway. "Run away, little boy," Sean chanted, waving him off impatiently. "Don't worry about the money. I'll pay you later."

"Norfolk Rhapsody No. 1" began with a thin, misty shimmer of strings, over which a solo clarinet scattered plaintive fragments of melody. Then, as the other instruments started to add their voices, a theme slowly emerged: a long, wandering tune, impossibly noble, impossibly sad. It felt like a melody Benjamin had known all his life, even though it had until now been kept secret, locked in some hidden, innermost chamber of the heart.

"Oh," he sighed, and found only these insufficient words: "That's nice."

"It's a folk tune," said Sean. "He found it in King's Lynn." As the music continued, he sat down opposite Benjamin and began to explain, animatedly: "Picture it. It's 1905. He's spending day after day cycling round these Norfolk villages. Whenever he can he goes into a pub and he gets talking to people, and after a while he asks them to sing for him. Old people, especially. This guy in King's Lynn was seventy. A seventy-year-old fisherman! Just imagine. Vaughan Williams buys him pint after pint. Maybe he slips him a shilling or two as well. And then after a couple of hours—just before closing time, say—he starts to sing. And this, *this* is what he comes out with! Did you ever hear a tune like it?"

"Does it have a name?"

" 'The Captain's Apprentice.' Vaughan Williams loved this tune. He used it again and again. And do you know what the words are about? It's about a bloke who's lying in prison. He's lying in prison on a charge of murder. He was a sea-captain and this fatherless boy was bound apprentice to him, and one day the boy annoys him somehow—the captain doesn't say how, he disobeys him or something, I suppose—so do you know what the captain does? He ties him up to the mast, and he gags him, and he beats him to death with a piece of rope. He spends the whole day on it. The whole bloody day beating this poor little kid to a pulp. And now he's lying in prison saying how sorry he is about the whole thing."

Benjamin listened to the song's dying fall, and felt a shiver run through him. "Wow. But it's so beautiful, and so . . . English."

"Have you ever been to Norfolk?" Sean asked.

"No."

"You should. It's an incredible place. Parts of it are like the end of the earth." Reverently, he allowed the music to fade away into absolute silence, then he raised the stylus. "The English are a very violent people," he said as he did this, talking half to himself. "People don't realize it, but we are. We repent afterwards, which is why we're so melancholy. But first of all we do . . . whatever has to be done."

Benjamin pondered these words as he walked slowly down to the bus stop a few minutes later. Violence and melancholy . . . They were both in the air that day. Philip telephoned in the evening to let him know the Sports Day results, and Benjamin shuddered to think of the anger that must have burned in Culpepper's breast when Steve was crowned *Victor Ludorum*. As for Steve himself—what had he felt when he accepted the trophy? Only triumph, or was it tinged, as well, with sadness, and the wish that it was Valerie's lost love-token that he was kissing and raising high above the cheering crowds?

18

Benjamin's conversation with Harding may have revealed that they shared some musical enthusiasms, but otherwise, the consequences were disappointing. It didn't lead to any significant renewal of their friendship. The summer holidays intervened too quickly. By the time of the new term, with rumours circulating that his father had left home and returned to Ireland, Harding seemed to have become even more solitary and difficult. His jokes continued; or at least, whenever any particularly outlandish incident disturbed the regular flow of school life, Harding was given credit for it. Culpepper, for instance, passed his driving test and began driving into school, and one afternoon in October he unlocked his car only to find that there was a heavily sedated goat stretched out on the back seat. But Harding never admitted to any involvement in the event, and no one could ever explain where he might have obtained the goat.

Philip gave up on his musical ambitions, sold his guitar through the school notice board and used the money to add to his growing library of volumes about "hidden" Birmingham, its history and architecture. Benjamin saw little of Cicely. The police sent a letter to Claire's father saying that the file was still open on his daughter's disappearance, but no further progress had been made. Claire and Doug went on three or four dates but then called it a day. Life, in other words, continued.

This had been a stagnant summer. Issues were left unresolved, narratives failed to reach their conclusion. The Grun-wick workers' strike and the affair between Mrs. Chase and Miles Plumb had started almost at the same time, in the late summer of 1976. Now, more than a year later, neither was showing any sign of coming to an end. In both cases, there had been long periods of deadlock and sudden flurries of activity; there had been negotiation, followed by breakdowns in commu-nication; the judgement of external advisers had been sought. But even after all this time, the Grunwick employers still refused to acknowledge their workers' right to join a union, and Miles Plumb could not recognize or accept the integrity of Bar-bara's marriage to Sam. The difficulties remained intractable.

On November 7th, 1977, the Grunwick strikers called for a new mass picket of the factory, and among those being bussed in to offer support from around the country was a British Leyland delegation led by Bill Anderton. They hired a coach from a local firm, and the driver turned out to be Sam Chase. He spent most of the three-hour journey to London thinking vengeful thoughts about Miles Plumb and nearly drove the coach right off the hard shoulder on the M1 just past Northampton.

They stopped for breakfast at Watford services. Sam settled into his driver's seat and told them not to be more than twenty minutes.

"Are you not coming with us, then?" Bill asked.

"No, thanks. I'd rather just sit here with a good book. Bring us a cup of tea, if you can."

As it happened, he had two good books with him: *Twenty-five Magic Steps to Word Power*, by Dr. Wilfred Funk, and a bat-tered American paperback called *Change Your Life with the Power of Words*, picked up last July at a local jumble sale. He had read these books again and again over the last few weeks. He had learned passages by heart and made whole exercise-books'-full of notes. But still he felt that his life had not been fully trans-formed by them. Still he was convinced they must have further mysteries to yield.

He opened one of the books at a well-thumbed page and began by reciting what had recently become his personal mantra:

"My words are **daily dynamite**."
"My words are **easy energizers**."
"My words are **helpful friends**."
"My words are **confidence-builders**."
"My words are the **new me**."

Then he turned to the contents page.

> *You Can Choose The Way You Speak.*
> *Learn To Correct Your Verbal Responses and You'll Be Calm In Any Situation.*
> *Energize Yourself With Verbal Vitamins.*
> *Power-Packed Speech Means Power-Packed Experiences.*
> *Command Your Speech and You'll Hear Your "Enemies" Surrender.*
> *Positive Words Are Elevators. Are You Going Up?*

Bill Anderton arrived with his cup of tea.

"Here you are, Sam, get it down you."

Sam looked at the grey concoction being handed to him in a plastic cup. A mottled, particularly unappetizing film of some sort had already formed on the surface.

"Thanks, Bill," he said; then added, by way of experiment, "The fervour of my gratitude is well-nigh inexpressible."

Bill gave him a worried look and went back inside.

The coach arrived in Willesden, north-west London, at about half-past seven. As Sam drove carefully down Dudden Hill Lane, he found that he couldn't turn into Chapter Road, where the main gates to the Grunwick factory were located. His way was blocked not by pickets but by police. There seemed to be many hundreds of them.

"I'm going to have to leave you here," he told Bill. "There's no way that lot are going to let me through."

The seventy-odd Leyland workers filed off the bus, and Sam watched as Bill Anderton negotiated with one of the policemen for access to the Chapter Road entrance. Beyond the heavy cordon of police, standing five or six deep, Sam could see an even bigger but more ragged crowd of pickets awaiting the arrival of the bus which had been chartered to bring in those Grunwick workers who had chosen to break the strike. He watched as the police drew back, very slightly and with obvious reluctance, to allow Bill and his men to pass through and join the picket. Then he drove the coach another hundred yards up Dudden Hill Lane and parked it by the kerb.

"It's time you became a word-collector!" he read. *"As some people collect stamps or match-boxes of all nations, you should systematically add to your store of words.*

"The word-collector must train himself to be a careful observer, able to ignore the common specimens, but to be instantly alert for new and unusual words. And as the butterfly-collector mounts his captures on card and knows them all, the word-collector must write his new specimens in a small notebook and memorize them."

He turned to today's exercise.

"V is for VARIETY. Try your hand at the meanings of these twenty words, all beginning with the letter 'V.' Then look at the answers on page 108 for the measure of your success."

Viscous	*Vortex*
Vicarious	*Volition*
Vainglorious	*Versatile*
Venerate	*Vigil*
Venal	*Viand*
Venial	*Vernal*
Veracious	*Vernacular*
Voracious	*Verify*
Vixen	*Verbatim*
Votive	*Vacuity*

Sam did the test and found that he scored four out of twenty. Yesterday, on *"U is for UNUSUAL"* he had scored six, and the day before, on *"T is for TABLE-TALK,"* a confidence-boosting eleven. And now four! It was incredible! He was getting worse!

When he saw the ranks of pickets gathered outside the factory gates and spread throughout the surrounding roads, Bill felt intensely proud. The object was not to prevent the strike-breakers' bus from getting into the factory—it would probably make for the back entrance, anyway—but to provide a show of support for Grunwick's beleaguered strikers, who had not wavered in their resolve for fifteen months now, despite many setbacks in the Appeal Court and at best equivocal encouragement from the TUC. Bill was to learn on the news that evening that eight thousand pickets had travelled from all over the country to be at the factory. It was an extraordinary display of faith and goodwill and solidarity: just what the British labour movement needed at the moment. His own men, a week earlier, had voted against his wishes to accept a new centralized bargaining arrangement from the managers. He had been disheartened by this, and he didn't trust the plans of British Leyland's new Chairman, Michael Edwardes, whose appointment had been announced on November 1st. These were bad times to be a socialist, he thought. He could feel the old certainties slipping away. But this morning seemed to contradict all that. This morning was going to be remembered as a great day in the history of the workers' struggle.

Word got around from the other end of the factory that a bus had indeed managed to squeeze through the picket lines, and the company's handful of loyal workers were safely inside. Then a scattered cheer warmed the frosty air as Jayaben Desai climbed on to a makeshift wooden platform and prepared to make a brief speech to her supporters. She had run into Bill in the crowd a few minutes earlier and they had exchanged friendly greetings. Looking at her now, Bill again felt ashamed of the way he had automatically responded to so many women in recent years, that tired reflex, that deadening habit of seeing nothing but a quick sexual possibility. It was impossible to watch Jayaben without feeling . . . well, more than impressed. His admiration for her bordered on awe. She seemed tiny, on that platform—she was less than five feet tall—but somehow she could make of herself an amazingly charismatic focus of attention. Perhaps it was the brightly coloured sari, in a black sea of overalls and donkey jackets. But Bill thought it was more than that. It was her hurried eloquence and still determination and restless, inquisitive, laughing eyes. It was the mantle of authority the long months of this dispute had draped on her.

The speeches were over, and it was time to leave. Police cordons were blocking both exits from the road, making it impossible, at the moment, either to enter the tube station at Dollis Hill or to reach Dudden Hill Lane where the coaches were parked. The pickets were confused, but patient. Soon enough the police would draw back and let them through. The men stood in groups, laughing, swapping jokes and cigarettes, waiting for movement. The police ignored them, keeping rank and staring fixedly ahead, unreadable, impassive.

Where did the order come from? How was it passed along so quickly? Bill was never able to work it out. All he knew was that suddenly, there was a mighty rush of feet and a surge forward and the pickets were under attack. The police charged into them and set to work with fists and truncheons.

He had no coherent memory of the assault but some images lodged in his mind.

A teenager being lifted by two policemen and smashed head first into the bonnet of a car.

A press photographer having his camera seized and stamped to pieces.

An elderly West Indian being rammed up against a low garden wall and then levered over it, his legs contorting as he landed in a twisted heap.

Jayaben Desai being dragged by her hair through the flinching and bewildered crowd.

A middle-aged white woman seized by the neck and forced to the ground.

A black worker in his thirties, one of Bill's coach party, pinned to the road and repeatedly kicked in the neck and face by two young officers.

Screaming and shouting and swearing all around him, cries of distress, eyes flaring to life with fear and hostility, faces caked with blood, blood on the pavement and driveways too, torn clothing, the crashing of glass, shop windows, car windows, windscreens, all splintering into chaos, and then the last thing of all, a young policeman, no more than a boy, nineteen or twenty maybe, young enough to be his son, his lips curled in a meaningless parody of hatred, something spilling out of his mouth that was halfway between a swearword and a primal scream, his truncheon upraised. Bill could remember lifting up a feeble arm and feeling it jolted aside with a horrible crack and then the truncheon must have come down and he was well and truly out of it.

Later that afternoon, the coach was parked at Watford services again. Bill stayed on board with Sam this time. His head was bandaged up and his arm was in a sling but he felt OK. Other people had suffered worse. There'd been about two hundred and fifty pickets treated for injuries that day. MPs were already pressing for an inquiry that would never materialize and a crowd had been demonstrating outside Willesden Green police station for most of the afternoon. It had turned out to be a historic day, all right, but not quite in the way he'd envisaged.

"What are you reading?" he asked.

Sam had been absorbed in a book for the last five minutes. Now he held it up for Bill's inspection.

"*Twenty-five Magic Steps to Word Power,*" Bill read, and chuckled. "Trying to improve yourself, are you?"

"Language is very important," said Sam.

"That's true."

"It says here—" (Sam flicked back through the pages to the author's introduction) "—Listen to this, it says: *The leaders of the world through the ages have recognized the miracle of words.*"

"Also true."

"*The English statesman, John Selden, said three centuries ago that 'Syllables govern the world.' *"

"I'd go along with that."

"*When a Hitler, a Mussolini or a Peron takes over, his first act is to commandeer words—the press, the radio, and books.*"

"Very well put."

"*Even in a democracy words are magic instruments. He who governs, or wants to govern, must be skilled in the science of employing words. Man is more influenced by language than the facts of surrounding reality.*"

"That guy knows what he's talking about."

"*In truth,*" Sam concluded, "*a word can cut deeper than a sword.*"

Bill laid an exploratory hand on his bandaged head, and winced. "Still," he said, "a crack on the skull with a truncheon can get your message across, too. D'you know what I'm saying?"

Sam smiled, and put the book aside thoughtfully.

19

THE **BILL BOARD**

Thursday, 15 December, 1977

EDITORIAL: Disband the Praetorian Guard

Here's a question for all KW's go-getting Oxbridge candidates, the much-vaunted <u>crème de la crème</u> of Birmingham's intelligentsia: what links the mass picket at the Grunwick processing factory, as shown on our television screens last month, with something you see in Big School every day at morning assembly?

Stumped? Well, think of that scary image from the Grunwick protest: row upon row of hatchet-faced policemen, truncheons at the ready, all lined up to protect the interests of the managers. And now think of the row of prefects standing in front of the stage in Big School every morning, forming a protective barrier between us lot (the mob) and our esteemed Chief Master as he stands there dispensing his nuggets of homely wisdom.

OK, so the prefects don't carry truncheons. (Yet.) And there isn't much in the faces of Lambert, C. J. or Pinnick, W. H. C., as they stand there swaying from side to side and looking justifiably embarrassed, to strike fear into the soul of the prospective school revolutionary. But the principle is the same. What is a school prefect, after all, for all the ludicrous "prestige" that is supposed to attach to the job, but a glorified henchman for the Chief Master? A hired thug, in other words: except that the thugs the Chief Master hires usually look as though they would have difficulty roughing up a mischievous cub scout, and all they receive for their pains is a nice new tie and a pretty little badge for their Mummies to sew on to their blazers over the Christmas holidays.

In classical times, the Praetorian Prefect was the commander of the imperial bodyguard, an elite squad formed by the Emperor Augustus to prevent any recap of that nasty business with Julius Caesar. Unfortunately they did not prove the most trustworthy of helpers and the institution was abolished by Septimius Severus who concluded that they were just as likely to kill him as protect him. Would that today's prefects showed as much spirit!

The Bill Board has not run many campaigns in the last few terms: our editorial policy has usually been to present our readers with the facts, and allow them to make up their own minds. But this is an issue about which we all, collectively, have very strong feelings. Quite simply, we believe that this enfeebled hangover from the days of imperial skulduggery has no place in a distinguished and forward-looking school in the 1970s.

We urge our readers to petition the Chief Master and Mr. Nuttall on this subject. And, since another batch of prefects will have been "elected" (how, or by whom, we mere commoners are never permitted to know) by the time this edition comes out, we also make this plea to the new appointments. Resist! Say no to those establishment perks! It is no kind of privilege to become the oppressor of your former comrade-in-arms!

SIGNED,
Doug Anderton . . .

". . . Signed, Doug Anderton, et cetera."

Doug finished reading from his typescript and looked around for support. He found it at once.

"Good stuff," said Claire, emphatically. "Very good indeed. I don't mind signing that."

She scribbled her signature beneath Doug's and passed the

sheet of paper on to Philip. He shook his head worriedly. "This'll put the cat among the pigeons," he muttered. But he agreed with everything that Doug had written, and added his signature to Claire's.

"Benjamin?" said Doug.

Benjamin hesitated for longer than Philip. As always, he was impressed by the power of Doug's rhetoric and the clarity of his thinking. He envied him his ability to choose his position and defend it fiercely when, for his own part, he was cursed with the compulsion always to see both sides of every argument. He was friendly with several prefects and tended to think that they were decent people trying to do a difficult job. It was all very complicated.

"Well . . . OK," he said, and signed the editorial too. He was an artist, after all, and artists had to do something politically controversial every so often.

That left only Emily Sandys, the newest recruit to the editorial team, who seemed more reluctant than anyone to commit herself to this act of subversion. Doug stared at her, almost accusingly, as if this was exactly what he had been expecting. He disliked Emily for the very same reason that Benjamin was secretly drawn to her: she was one of the leading lights behind the joint Boys' and Girls' School Christian Society. Benjamin had never actually aligned himself with this unfashionable organization, of course. By temperament he was not a joiner of groups, and in any case, he could never have lived with the social stigma. The Christians were held to be at the very bottom of the King William's evolutionary scale, even lower than the Combined Cadet Force or a miserable-looking trio of bus-spotters who called themselves the Public Service Vehicle Group. The very thought of them conjured up grisly images of woollen sweaters and table-tennis evenings and Bible-study meetings heavy with the scents of furtive adolescent sexual attraction and lingering body odour. These people were simply too awful to contemplate. But Emily, in Benjamin's eyes, was different. She was clever and she could take a joke and her design ideas had transformed the paper in the last few months and neither he nor Philip nor even Doug had failed to notice that she also had a thoroughly distracting body, in a plump, curvy sort of way.

"What will happen if I don't sign it?" she wanted to know.

Doug looked around the table, and let out a long breath to signify the gravity of the situation.

"Well, to be honest, Emily, I think you would have to resign. Because the rest of the board is completely united on this one, and we're planning to throw the whole weight of the paper behind the campaign."

"Oh." She looked very disappointed. "But I love coming to these meetings. They've been such good fun."

Doug shrugged his shoulders. The choice was hers.

"All right," said Emily, and the fifth and final signature was added to the typescript. Doug took the sheet of paper back and looked at it with a smile of satisfaction.

"Excellent," he said. "A significant moment in the history of *The Bill Board.*"

Significant but, as it turned out, short-lived. Ten minutes later, Benjamin was forced to resign from the editorial team. A messenger from the Chief Master had put his head round the door of the meeting room to tell him that he had just been made a prefect.

"You couldn't have turned it down," said Philip, consolingly, at the bus stop later that day. "You don't get *asked* to be a prefect, you get *told* to be a prefect."

"Exactly," said Benjamin.

"I mean, if you turned it down, there are all sorts of ways the school could take it out on you."

"Quite."

"They might never give you a reference. Or they might write to Oxford or Cambridge and tell them you were a trouble-maker and weren't to be trusted."

"Absolutely. That's what I've been telling everyone."

"You had no choice in the matter, really. It's just your rotten luck that they decided to pick on you."

Benjamin smiled his gratitude and wondered, not for the first time, why everybody couldn't be as reasonable as Philip. It was all the more magnanimous of him given that he and Doug and Harding had not even, inexplicably, been elected to the Carlton Club. Why had Benjamin been singled out for such high distinction, then? It seemed to make no sense. Almost all of his friends had been scathing when they heard of the appointment. Doug had treated him to a ten-minute lecture on "selling out to the establishment." Claire had simply stopped talking to him. Emily had been quite kind, it was true, but a more reliable foretaste of the delights to come was provided at this very moment by two of Paul's little contemporaries, running up to him at the bus stop.

"Excuse me, Mr. Prefect," they said, crowding around his legs. "May we stand in the bus queue please?"

"May I put this chocolate wrapper in the litter bin, please, Mr. Prefect?"

"Do you mind if my friend and I talk to each other, Mr. Prefect? You won't put us in detention?"

"Just piss off, the pair of you," said Benjamin, and they ran away laughing delightedly.

He tried to tell himself that the furore would soon die down. It was the same at the end of every term when the new prefects were announced. And at least this time there was another, genuine scandal to keep everybody talking: the snubbing of Culpepper. Most people had assumed that he would become School Captain, or Vice-Captain at the very least. But it turned out that he had not even been made a prefect. Accounts varied, but the most colourful said that he had been weeping openly by the notice board when the names were posted up. He had used expressions to describe the Chief Master and the Deputy Chief, Mr. Nuttall, which had shocked the few members of the sixth form who were worldly enough to understand them. And—but again, versions of this story differed, and few people could believe that it was really true—some witnesses said that he had spat at Steve Richards, another of the newly appointed prefects, when they passed in the corridor.

The bus was a long time coming, today, and before it arrived Benjamin glimpsed Cicely approaching him from the other side of the Bristol Road. It was 4:30 on a wintry December evening. Dusk was already falling, and she was protected against the cold by a full-length cashmere overcoat and enormous cloche hat; as usual, she drew the attention of everyone waiting at the bus stop; the crowd even pulled back a little to let her pass, and it was a source of unspeakable pride to Benjamin when she walked straight up to him and planted a kiss on his cheek. The coldness of her face was delicious, and they held each other in a lingering hug: the sort of hug you might expect between an affectionate brother and sister.

"Oh Benjamin, I'm so proud of you," she said. "You'll make a wonderful prefect, I know you will."

"Do you think so?" (It was the first time anybody had said anything like this to him all day.) "Everybody else has been so . . . funny about it, so censorious. Do you think I'm doing the right thing?"

"Everything you do is right, as far as I'm concerned. I have absolute faith in your judgement."

He felt on the point of exploding with happiness when he heard these words. He had barely spoken to Cicely this term and had almost forgotten (no, that could never be true; had forbidden himself to remember) what wonders she was capable of doing for his self-esteem. Suddenly he knew that he had to see her again.

"This is your bus," she said, kissing him goodbye. "Don't let me keep you."

"Cicely—do you think we could go for a drink again soon? Some time over the Christmas holidays? It seems ages since we talked."

"Gosh, that would be lovely, wouldn't it? Absolute heaven. I'll call you."

Something in the way she said it made Benjamin know that it would never happen. And Philip, who had overheard most of their conversation, broke it to him on the bus home that these days, so the rumour went, Cicely was having an affair with Mr. Ridley, the husband of her Latin teacher, and he would never let her go out for a drink by herself with someone from the Boys' School. Benjamin sighed and watched the first flakes of snow start to settle against the window of the bus. He always seemed to be the last person to find out.

Bewildered by the events of the closing days of term, he sought to anchor himself, over the Christmas holidays, in the relative certainties of family life.

Lois had come back from hospital again, and was living in her old room. The intervals between her severest, most paralyzing bouts of depression were getting longer and longer, to everyone's relief. Loud noises still scared her, and she could not tolerate violent films on the television. They had to be careful not to present her with anything that might remind her of the events of November, 1974. But she was able to hold down a job, for the time being, even if it was nothing more arduous than a few hours each day behind the counter of the local off-licence, and there were other encouraging omens. When her Aunt Evelyn gave her a postal order for Christmas, she spent the money on a five-year desk diary, and began writing in it on New Year's Day. Everyone interpreted this as a sign that she had begun to think more hopefully about the future.

Paul kept himself to himself. He sat in his room most of the day, either working on his school holiday assignments, or poring over the pages of *Time*, *Newsweek*, *The Spectator*, *The Listener* and the other political weeklies that had lately become his favourite reading matter. On Christmas night, when the rest of the family gathered round the television to watch *The Morecambe and Wise Show*, he stayed upstairs, reading a collection of essays by the economist Milton Friedman.

Colin and Sheila were delighted at Benjamin's success.

When she sewed the new prefect's badge on to his school blazer, Sheila's eyes were so cloudy that she could barely see to thread the needle.

Even though they only lived a few miles up the road, it was a family tradition (in a family which regarded tradition as inviolable) that Benjamin's grandparents should come to stay for three days at Christmas. The subsequent seventy-two-hour orgy of over-eating and television-watching had always seemed to Benjamin to be one of the highlights of the year, but this time, perhaps because he was weighed down by thoughts of his new responsibilities, perhaps because he was simply so unhappy with the recent progress of his relationship with Cicely, he could not raise any real enthusiasm for it. He went through the motions, but that was all.

There was only one moment which, whenever he thought about it, days or months or even years later, seemed to have a different texture to it, almost an aura of the numinous or sublime. It happened on Christmas night, while Paul was upstairs absorbing the rudiments of monetarism and the rest of them were watching Morecambe and Wise, and it concerned Benjamin's grandfather.

Benjamin had been feeling a new kinship with his grandfather over the last few months. It dated from a time in mid-August, when the family had been holidaying in North Wales and his grandparents (because this—of course—was the tradition) had come to stay in a nearby guest house for a week. One uncharacteristically sunny afternoon, Benjamin and his grandfather had gone for a walk along Cilan Head, and had stopped, as was often their custom, to rest for a while on the twin mounds of Castell Pared Mawr. From here they had an incomparable view of the immense, azure ocean as it slapped restlessly against vertiginous cliffs; despite the dense afternoon haze they could see right across Porth Ceiriad bay and towards the islands of St. Tudwal's. They contemplated this awesome scene in silence for many minutes, until Benjamin's grandfather, without any kind of preface, said an extraordinary thing:

"Who could possibly look at this view," he asked, "without believing in the existence of God?"

It was a question that required no answer, which was a good thing because Benjamin, as usual, would not have been able to think of one. He had never suspected that his grandfather held religious convictions, and had never mentioned to him (or to any of his family, besides Lois) his own strange moment of revelation in the locker room at King William's more than three years ago. Benjamin had come to feel that religious belief, at its most sincere, was an essentially private thing, a wordless conspiracy between oneself and God. It was overwhelming to discover, almost tangentially, through an offhand remark, that his grandfather might be a fellow-conspirator. Benjamin glanced at him curiously, but he was staring out to sea, his eyes almost closed, his silver hair rippling in the breeze. Nothing more was said on the subject. A few minutes later they moved on and continued their walk.

Benjamin's experience on Christmas night was very different. Harder to think about, harder to pin down. It happened in the middle of *The Morecambe and Wise Show*. Benjamin was sitting on the sofa, with Acorn—now an old, fat cat—stretched out on his lap. His grandfather was sitting in an armchair, to his left. Morecambe and Wise were doing a sketch with Elton John. Ernie was trying to put together a musical number, in which Eric sang the main tune and then Ernie added a counter-melody, while Elton John accompanied them on the piano. Every time they tried to rehearse it, it went wrong. Eric would sing the first few bars, but then as soon as Ernie entered with the counter-melody, Eric would stop singing the main tune and join in with his partner. It was a corny routine, but the consummate timing of the performers, the electrical rapport and empathy between these two middle-aged men who by now were the most loved entertainers in Britain, turned it into a miracle of spiralling hilarity. Suddenly, sitting entranced before the television, Acorn's purrs sending slow vibrations of contentment through his body, Benjamin had a fleeting vision: it came to him that he was only one person, and his family was only one family, out of millions of people and millions of families throughout the country, all sitting in front of their television sets, all watching these two comedians, in Birmingham and Manchester and Liverpool and Bristol and Durham and Portsmouth and Newcastle and Glasgow and Brighton and Sheffield and Cardiff and Stirling and Oxford and Carlisle and everywhere else, all of them laughing, all of them laughing at the same joke, and he felt an incredible sense of . . . oneness, that was the only word he could think of, a sense that the entire nation was being briefly, fugitively drawn together in the divine act of laughter, and looking across at his grandfather's face, convulsed with joy, a picture of gurgling ecstasy, he was reminded of the face of Francis Piper, when he had come to King William's to read his poetry, and how it had seemed to resemble the face of God, and at that very instant Benjamin found himself thinking that perhaps his ambitions were all wrong—his desire to be a writer, his wish to become a composer—and that to be a bringer of laughter was in fact the holiest, most sacred of callings, and he wondered if he should set his sights on being a great comedian or a great scriptwriter, but then the feeling passed, the sketch ended, some boring singer came on instead, and Benjamin knew that he was really just an ordinary teenager, an ordinary teenager in an ordinary family; even his grandfather's face looked ordinary, after all, and Benjamin noticed for the first time that Lois hadn't been laughing with them, and the sense of blinding clarity was gone, and once again everything in his life seemed fraught, complex and uncertain.

20

Benjamin awoke, opened his eyes, and noticed some peculiar things.

Firstly, opening his eyes had made no difference. He still couldn't see anything. Secondly, he was in excruciating pain. His back ached and he had cramp in both legs but this was small fry compared to the pulsing, shuddering pain in his temples, which periodically spread out in waves of unmitigated agony, making him feel that his entire skull was enclosed in a slowly contracting vice. Thirdly, he could not move. His freedom of movement was restricted on all sides, apparently by four walls made of some sort of wood.

Finally, there was the most peculiar thing of all. He was holding something strange in his hand. An unidentified object. It was soft and fleshy and smooth, except at the nub where he could feel something harder and coarser, though still yielding. For the first few seconds of wakefulness he had no idea at all what it was. Then, when he had managed to free his hand and some of the sensation had started to return to his fingers, he began to explore the object further and discovered that it was attached to other objects which seemed more familiar and recognizable. A human collarbone, for instance, and a shoulder and an arm. Then he realised what the first object must be. It was a breast. A female breast!

Now a female voice let out a low groan in the dark next to him.

"Ohhh, *shit* . . ."

There was the sound of a hand groping along the surface of the wood, and then the creaking of a door being pushed open, and then a rectangle of faint orange light appeared. Benjamin could now see out into a bedroom, lit dimly by the glow of a streetlamp, containing a double bed on which three half-naked bodies lay entangled beneath a pile of coats. It was not yet dawn. Benjamin began to remember where he was. This was Bill and Irene Anderton's bedroom. They had gone away to Málaga for a winter break and Doug, left in charge of their house for the first time in his life, had taken the opportunity to have a party. It had got ever so slightly out of hand. The drinks cabinet had been opened and its contents devoured. Benjamin himself had drunk at least three-quarters of a bottle of vintage port. That much he could remember. And he could remember talking to this friendly girl with short red hair and a pale, freckly face. He had been talking to her about National Health and explaining how really it was the same band as Hatfield and the North only with a different bass player. She had seemed very interested. Remarkably interested, in fact. All the same, he was surprised to find that he had been sleeping with one of her breasts in his hand for the whole night. And what were they doing in Bill and Irene's wardrobe?

Having opened the wardrobe door, the red-haired girl struggled to her knees and crawled out. She was wearing a full-length navy blue Laura Ashley party dress which was rolled down to her waist. Once she was standing up in the bedroom she realized that she had lost her bra and began to look around for it. Benjamin found it on the floor of the wardrobe—it was white and lacy—and handed it out to her, feeling gallant and embarrassed at the same time. She took it from him matter-of-factly and slipped it on. Then she pulled her dress over her shoulders, and Benjamin crawled out of the wardrobe and helped her to zip it up.

"Thanks," she said, her voice husky with tobacco and alcohol. She pointed down at Benjamin's flies, which were undone. He did them up. "Come on, let's get out of here."

He followed her downstairs to the kitchen, stepping over more bodies in the landing and the hallway. When she switched the kitchen light on, it revealed a predictable scene of devastation. Broken glasses, empty bottles and spilled food were everywhere. Irene's fondue bowl had been used as an ashtray and was overflowing with cigarette ends and the butts of several dozen joints.

The girl examined her reflection in the kitchen window and grimaced.

"I've got to get home," she said. Then she looked down at the front of her dress and said: "Ugh."

"Oh," said Benjamin, noticing the patchwork of very obvious white stains. "What's that?"

"Well, I don't think it's Horlicks."

Benjamin was shocked.

"Did I do that?"

The girl smiled for the first time. "With a little bit of help from me." She stood close to Benjamin and touched his chest lightly, sliding a finger between the buttons of his cheesecloth shirt. "Don't you remember?"

The memory was fuzzy at the moment, but getting clearer all the time.

"Yes," he said, and he kissed the girl on the mouth, feeling her tongue slide between his lips and entwine itself gently around his own.

"So what's your verdict?" she said, detaching herself and smoothing down her hair. "Not bad—for a comatose mullet?"

Benjamin stared at her blankly. This seemed a very odd thing to say, even though the phrase was, now that he came to think of it, distantly familiar.

"Pardon?"

"Do you have a comb?" she asked, examining her reflection again.

"What did you just say?"

She turned and faced him, with a look of quiet triumph on her face. "This time last year," she explained, "when I was in *Othello*, you said that I radiated 'all the erotic allure and raw sexual energy of a comatose mullet.' Now—where did I leave my coat?"

She went to look for it in the living room. Benjamin followed her, in a sudden panic.

"You mean—you're Jennifer? Jennifer Hawkins?"

"Didn't you recognize me?"

"I've only ever seen you on the stage before."

She had found her coat, a knee-length fake fur affair which at least concealed the worst of the stains.

"I've really got to go," she said. "My folks'll be going crazy. What about yours?"

Benjamin hadn't given this the slightest thought. "I . . . told them I'd be staying over," he said, dimly remembering telling his mother some such story. A far more serious problem had occurred to him. Tomorrow was the first day of the term, and tonight he was supposed to be having dinner at the Chief Master's house with the other prefects. At the moment all he felt capable of doing was having a long and much-needed vomit and then crawling into bed to die.

"My car's outside," said Jennifer. "D'you want a lift?"

"Erm, no. No thanks. I can walk from here."

"Suit yourself." She kissed him on the cheek, briskly but not without a certain sharp fondness. "Oh well, so long, Tiger. I never did it in a wardrobe before."

"Did we actually . . . *do it*?" said Benjamin, aghast.

"Don't worry, you didn't get to know me, in the biblical sense," Jennifer told him, kindly. "It was just a bit of fun. You're quite a performer, though. Thirty or forty seconds, I reckon. Fastest shot in the West."

With this backhanded compliment she left him, easing the front door open and trotting down to the road in the blue light of the pre-dawn. A few birds were beginning to sing, tentatively, in Cofton Park. The noise of her car engine was deafening. Benjamin clutched both sides of his head and knew that he would never drink port again as long as he lived.

The Chief Master's house stood in the school grounds, between the science labs and the new sports hall. Benjamin approached it from the Bristol Road South and saw Steve Richards arriving from the other direction. It was seven o'clock, and it felt strange to be at school at all, after dark and out of term. School uniform had always suited Steve well, and tonight he seemed smarter than ever, if a little nervous. For his own part, Benjamin knew that he looked terrible, but Steve was too well-mannered to say anything. He had spent most of the day in bed, and at four o'clock had been convinced that he wasn't going to make it this evening, and perhaps would never even regain the use of his legs. But his mother, silent and mortified, had pumped him full of black coffee and now he reckoned that he might just about survive if he didn't touch any alcohol for the rest of the week.

"Sherry, Trotter?" said the Chief Master, handing him a glass almost as soon as he had entered the hall.

"Oh—erm . . . Thank you."

"Rather pale, I'm afraid."

"Yes, sir, I know. I didn't sleep very well last night. All the excitement, I expect."

"I was referring to this somewhat anaemic Fino. However, now that you mention it, your pallor is a mite spectral, even by your usual standards. Would you like to go upstairs and lie down for a while?"

"No thank you, sir. I shall be fine."

"As you wish, as you wish. Ah, Richards! No one could accuse you of looking pale, eh, what?"

With these and other such pleasantries, the Chief Master kept his guests entertained before dinner.

At the long dining table, Benjamin sat between Richards and Mr. Nuttall, the amiable Deputy Chief Master who had also been his form master in the first year, and with whom he had always been on good terms. Besides Mr. Nuttall, there were eight prefects on one side of the table, and seven on the other. The Chief Master sat at the head of the table, and his wife, a quietly formidable woman with severely permed brown hair and an unfortunate twitch in her right eye, sat opposite him at the other end.

"Well, Trotter," said Mr. Nuttall, breaking open a bread roll, "it's good to have you on the team, I must say."

"Thank you, Sir."

"Sinclair and I were just discussing the firemen's strike. What's your view on the matter?"

"Well . . ." Benjamin had no views, needless to say. He was aware that there had been a national firemen's strike for the last two months, but that was about it. "I think it's a terrible shame if people's houses are on fire, and there's nobody there to put them out."

"That's true, Trotter. But you must also remember that the only way that some people can make their voices heard, under the existing political system, is by withholding their labour. This may come as some surprise to you, I know, but I'm a Labour man. Always have been. This country has a tradition of standing up for the little fellow, and the Labour Party best embodies that tradition, in my view. We who teach and study at King William's are the privileged few, Trotter. We have to stand up and do our bit for those less fortunate than ourselves."

Benjamin nodded earnestly, although even standing up to say grace, which was the next task required of him, proved a debilitating effort. He sank down into his chair afterwards and groaned softly as he contemplated the prawn cocktail which a uniformed maid had placed in front of him. The Chief Master's wife heard the groan and looked at him with some interest. Benjamin noticed that she was staring at him. Her eye twitched three times. He was the only person not to have realized that the Chief Master's wife had an unfortunate twitch. He thought that she was winking at him. Not knowing what you were supposed to do, etiquette-wise, when your host's wife started winking at you across the dinner table, he winked back. The Chief Master's wife jolted up in her chair as if she had been bitten. Benjamin looked across at the Chief Master, who was staring at him in amazement. He returned to his prawn cocktail, feeling the waves of nausea rise in him more violently than ever.

During the main course he spoke mainly to Steve Richards. They had never had much to say to each other before, but Benjamin now found himself warming to this polite, modest and witty young man. He began to realize what Cicely might have seen in him.

"Cicely and I—we never did any of that stuff, you know," Steve said. "All that stuff that was mentioned in the magazine. We just got a little too friendly at the party, that's all. It happens all the time."

"Of course it does," said Benjamin, feelingly.

"I lost my girlfriend because of that letter they published. That's what really hurts. We were only together six months but I thought we might have had . . . you know, some kind of future."

"What about your parents? Did they see it?"

"Yeah, they were pretty upset for a while. Thought I'd let them down. We got over it. This—" (he pointed at the prefect's badge) "—has cheered them up a lot."

"Mine too. Funny, isn't it, what makes your parents proud?"

They had been given glasses of French red wine with their silverside of beef and roast potatoes. Steve took a long sip. Benjamin left his well alone.

"What are you going to do after A-levels, Ben? Stay on for Oxbridge?"

"I think so."

"Me too. I want to do physics at Trinity. That's where Isaac Newton went, you know. Mr. Nagle thinks that I can make it. I'll need to get straight As, basically, but he reckons if I really push myself over the next few months . . ."

"I hope all this prefect stuff isn't going to be too much of a distraction."

"No. We'll be fine. Don't worry. A kid could do it."

Their conversation grew more fitful. Benjamin started to enthuse about the Morecambe and Wise sketch, but he could tell that Steve didn't really understand. His family didn't watch television on Christmas night, he said, and besides, "I've never quite seen it, with those two."

After dessert (fruit cocktail, of which Benjamin managed to eat about half) the school captain, Roger Stewart, got up to make a speech.

"Gentlemen," he said, "you have been chosen for the highest honour that King William's has to offer to its senior pupils. You have been chosen for one reason only: because, in the eyes of the Chief Master, Mr. Nuttall, and other members of the Senior Common Room, you have all achieved excellence in your chosen field, whether in your schoolwork, athletics, sport, the Combined Cadet Force or even—" (looking at Benjamin) "—even literature. Remember this: you have been chosen on your merits. King William's is a meritocracy, not a bastion of privilege. At the same time, the school has its traditions, and these must be protected. There has been talk in some quarters of abolishing the position of prefect altogether. This talk is being put about by failures, raddled with envy, and it must be discouraged. The office of prefect is not a perk. It creates a solemn bond of duty between you and the school. You must reflect on that. Tonight is an occasion for celebration but it is also a time for us all to ponder our new responsibilities.

"Now, Mr. Nuttall is going to pass around a bottle of the Founder's Port. In keeping with a tradition going back to the eighteenth century, we shall all declare our loyalty to King William's, and drink our glasses down in one draught."

By the time Benjamin returned from the bathroom, he was feeling slightly better. The others had left the dining table by now, and were grouped informally in the Chief Master's sitting room, drinking coffee and laughing among themselves. He did his rather desperate best to join in. On the coffee table in front of him he found what looked like a life-size plastic model of a hand, which for some reason he took to be a prop from the Drama Society's store room. He entertained the others for a while by picking it up, shaking hands with it, scratching his head with it and using it to relieve an itch under his armpit. Only when he pretended to pick his nose with it did the Chief Master's wife lean across, take it from him without a word, and strap it with skilful, practised movements on to the smooth and rounded stump at the end of her arm. He was the last person to have noticed that she only had one hand.

Alone at the number 62 bus stop thirty minutes later, Benjamin was already trying to block this incident from his mind. Whichever way you looked at it, the beginning of his career as a prefect had not been a striking success, but right now he had something else to think about, something far more important, in its way. Upstairs in the Chief Master's bathroom, after throwing up for the third time, he had been struck by a momentous revelation. He had realized that he was in love with Jennifer Hawkins.

At 10:30 that evening, Benjamin telephoned Doug, who sounded even worse than he did. (He did not come to school the next day, or even for the rest of the week.) He asked for Jennifer's number and Doug told him without raising any awkward questions, which was a relief. Benjamin called her there and then.

"Hello?" said her frail and throaty voice, after he had exchanged a few words with her father.

"Hi, Jennifer? It's me."

There was a long pause at the other end of the line. "I'm sorry—who is this?"

"It's me. Benjamin."

"Oh." It took another few seconds for it to sink in. She sounded very, very surprised, although not entirely displeased. "Hello, Tiger. To what do I owe *this* pleasure?"

"Well . . . I don't know . . ." Once again, this master of the written word seemed to be having trouble with its spoken counterpart. He wished he had thought a little harder before making the call. "It just occurred to me that maybe—maybe we started something last night, and it would be good to . . . see where it went?"

There was a long silence. "What does that mean, exactly?"

Benjamin didn't know.

"Are you asking me out, Benjamin?"

"Well—yes."

"Do you think that's such a good idea?"

Here was a question he had never anticipated. "Well, yes. Of course. Isn't it?"

"Look, all that happened last night is we both got blind drunk and had a bit of a grope. You don't have to take me for candlelit dinners."

"No, Jennifer." He couldn't bear this offhand way of describing it. She mightn't realize it yet, but something bigger had happened. Something more meaningful. "I really think . . . I really think it's important that we see each other again."

Jennifer sighed. "Well, OK. If you say so. What did you have in mind?"

At least he was prepared for this one. "There's a season of early French surrealist shorts at the cinema in Cannon Hill Park at the moment. They're showing some rarely seen works by René Clair and Man Ray."

"How about a drink down at The Grapevine?"

So a drink down at The Grapevine it was.

21

THE BILL BOARD

Thursday, 19 January, 1978

LETTERS NOT TO THE EDITOR

The following missive—intended, apparently, only for the eyes of R. J. Culpepper—has made its way by circuitous means to the offices of The Bill Board. We publish it unedited and without comment, as a fascinating insight into the thought processes of some of KW's better-known pupils. Many thanks to the anonymous mole who passed it on.

10 January, 1978

Dear Ronald,

I hope you have recovered by now from the shock of learning that you have not been made a prefect. It is indeed an appalling condemnation of the buffoons who make these decisions, and to tell the truth it confirms my worst suspicions about them. To promote a mediocrity like Richards, simply as a liberal gesture because of the colour of his skin, is little short of pathetic. You could even argue that to be snubbed by such cretins is really a compliment, but I know it must be hard for you to see it that way. Your overwhelming feeling must be that you have suffered a terrible insult.

In one respect, however, Anderton and his fellow-Trotskyist scribblers have got it right: the office of prefect is quite worthless, from most points of view. A prefect is really nothing more than the Chief Master's lackey. You must remember that you hold a far more important position as Secretary of The Closed Circle.

I know from our previous conversations on the subject that we are in agreement about the future of this society. Instead of remaining a sterile forum for debating esoteric academic issues, it can be built into something far more exciting: an alternative power-base for carefully chosen, like-minded individuals. The sort of people who care far more deeply about the future of King William's, and understand far better how to safeguard it, than those who nominally stand at its head.

To give you an example: I have it on the personal authority of my brother that Mr. Nuttall is a supporter of the Callaghan government. Just think of it! Was ever an administration more mired in the past, more hopelessly adrift, more feebly in thrall to the whims and demands of a selfish, militant faction? (I mean the unions, of course.) And yet this is our Deputy Chief Master's notion of good leadership! No wonder King William's itself has slipped into smugness and inertia over the last few years.

The tasks facing the school, it now seems to me, are as follows:

1. MODERNIZE. We need better science labs, better sports facilities, a better music school. (All of this costs money and money, of course, means FEES from parents—not more handouts from the govt.)

2. RATIONALIZE. There are simply too many pupils at the moment, and some of them are frankly not up to scratch. The entrance requirements must become more rigorous.

3. AGGRANDIZE. The national perception of King William's is of a school in decline. This must be reversed. Oxbridge must be made to sit up and take notice of us again. It is a disadvantage being located in Birmingham, which the rest of the country loathes, and with good reason. More effort must therefore be devoted to not just maintaining but PUBLICIZING our sporting and academic excellence.

Let me spell out, in addition, why I think that The Closed Circle, out of all the school's institutions, is the best placed to make a difference in these crucial areas.

1. SECRECY. The Circle is accountable to no one but itself. Consequently it can develop its views with absolute freedom, under the influence of no lobby or pressure group. (An analogy might be drawn with the National Association For Freedom, in my view the most important of the many unofficial right-wing alliances now coming into being, drawing together a range of intellectuals who alone seem to understand how grave the situation is in this country—John Braine, Peregrine Worsthorne, Winston Churchill Jnr, etc.)

2. PATRONAGE. The Circle's other great trump card is that it can choose its members not only from the sixth form but also FROM THE MASTERS' COMMON ROOM AS WELL. Thus the flabby thinkers (Nuttall, Serkis etc.) can be excluded and the kindred spirits (Pyle, Daintry, Spraggon) co-opted into our cause.

3. ELITISM. The Circle does not have to listen to the voice of the rabble. It is not a bearpit like the Senior or Junior Debating Societies. There is no time wasted listening to peabrains or crackpots. In essence it is anti-democratic, and that is its strength. Ideas and policies can germinate much more quickly and efficiently in this atmosphere.

In conclusion, it has been an honour to be chosen as the Circle's youngest-ever member and a privilege to watch the society begin to transform itself under your guidance. My plea to you is this: do not lose momentum, merely as a result of this temporary and insignificant setback. The Closed Circle, and by implication the whole of King William's, still looks to you for leadership.

With sincere good wishes,
Paul.

• • •

Fascinating words, there, from Trotter Jnr. Seems we were right to warn our readers, more than a year ago (see BB, 18 November, 1976) about the loopy philosophy behind this secretive outfit. After that, it's almost a relief to welcome back one of the Board's most regular and lucid correspondents.

THOUGHTS ON THE PREFECT QUESTION
From Arthur Pusey-Hamilton, MBE.

Sirs,

I was very struck by your recent editorial, entitled "Disband the Praetorian Guard"; struck not so much by its argument (which I whole-heartedly deplore) but by your reference to the fact that the prefects at King William's do not carry truncheons about their person; or at least—as you yourselves put it in a suggestive parenthesis—"not yet."

Well, Sirs, let me ask the question straight out, in the plainest possible terms: why the devil not? If, as you say, the prefects are the school's equivalent of a police force, then they should surely be equipped accordingly. Good God, have not these brave men got a dangerous and difficult job to do? You would send these men out on Litter Duty, to confront a vicious and unruly mob of eleven-year-olds, many of them armed with catapults and conkers, and yet you would not allow them this most basic means of protecting themselves? For shame, Sirs! For shame!

To take the argument further, it seems to me that not only should the prefects be allowed to carry weapons, but they should be encouraged to imitate our Great British Police Force in other respects as well.

Take prefects' detention, for instance. It's all very well getting miscreants to come into school on a Saturday morning, but wouldn't the punishment carry slightly more force if a certain amount of discreet "roughing up" took place beforehand? This tactic has worked wonders, I believe, for the West Midlands Police. Surely it would act as a powerful deterrent to any potential criminal if he knew that, on his way to detention in the company of two burly prefects, there was every chance he might meet with a small "accident" while being escorted down the stairs?

And what of those inevitable unsolved mysteries that militate so strongly against the smooth running of school life? The mystery of Richards's medal, for example, or Culpepper's goat? Again, the prefects could take a leaf out of our local police force's book. Why appoint someone of Miller's imposing bulk, if not to beat the odd confession out of unco-operative suspects? Why appoint someone with the literary gifts of Trotter Snr, if not to forge those confessions in the most convincing manner? These methods have worked for the Birmingham pub bombers (or so I am told), so they can work for the school's own smaller-scale but no less recalcitrant offenders.

In short, Sirs, let us not stop at truncheons. Riot shields! Helmets! Cattle-prods! Fully equipped interrogation chambers! If we are going to have a school police force, let us have one that we can be proud of!

These sentiments are fully endorsed, I need hardly add, by Gladys, my good lady wife, and it only remains for me to assure you that I am, until you receive full and unequivocal notice in writing to the contrary, your most loyal and obedient servant,

Arthur Pusey-Hamilton, MBE.

SEALED with the
ancient and noble Seal of the
Pusey-Hamiltons.

"PILAE AD MUNDUM"

22

One Monday evening, the last Monday of that bitterly cold January, Philip left school a few minutes later than usual, after dealing with some business up in the editors' room. Using the south doorway, for a change, he noticed a distant figure in the frozen dusk, picking up litter on the square of asphalt which at most schools would have been called the playground, although here it was known as "the Parade Ground," in keeping with King William's pretensions to military grandeur. Philip came a little closer and realized that the lonely figure was Benjamin.

"Hello," he said. "What on earth are *you* doing?"

"Litter duty," answered Benjamin shortly. "Can you give me a hand?"

Philip started helping him to retrieve the chocolate wrappers and discarded bus tickets.

"This may sound silly," he said, "but I thought the whole point of litter duty was that one of the younger forms came out here with you, and you supervised them picking up litter for ten minutes?"

"That's right," said Benjamin.

"So why are you doing it all yourself?"

"Well . . ." Benjamin stood up straight, and wiped his brow. Despite the cold weather, he was hot and out of breath from his exertions. "This was my first litter duty, and I was supposed to be doing it with form 1B—you know, the eleven-year-olds—so I got them out here, and I lined them up, and I told them I wanted them to split up into groups of five, and spread out in a sort of big pentagon, and comb the Parade Ground anti-clockwise for five minutes, and clockwise for another five."

"What happened?"

"They ran off down the Founders' Drive and went to the bus stop. All twenty-six of them." He sighed despairingly. "I have no natural authority, Phil. None at all."

"Come on, Kojak. Let's go home."

"Don't *you* start calling me Kojak," said Benjamin, as they set off together. This was the new nickname Doug had coined for him. Doug had also developed an annoying habit, whenever he was talking to Benjamin and saw some younger boys misbe-having in the vicinity, of saying, "Book 'em, Danno," in homage to another American cop show. So far Benjamin had not fol-lowed this advice and after three weeks as a prefect he congratu-lated himself, privately, on having set no impositions and put no one in detention. It was his own form of passive resistance; an attempt to soothe his conscience for having slipped into a rôle which he knew, at heart, he should never have accepted.

"You're not the only one with problems, you know," said Philip, as they walked past the empty but brightly lit classrooms. "Things are terrible at home at the moment."

"Why's that?"

"Oh, because of stupid old Sugar Plum Fairy."

Benjamin was horrified. "That's not *still* going on, is it? Him and your mother? I thought that was over years ago."

"My mother keeps breaking it off, and then seeing him again, and then breaking it off again . . ."

"You should say something about it. How can you bear to go to his classes when you know what he's up to?"

"I don't think he knows that I know. Anyway, Dad says he's finally going to put a stop to it. He's really furious this time."

"I'm sorry, Phil," said Benjamin. "I didn't know." Now that he was no longer on the board of the magazine, and now that he used the prefects' locker room, and now that he spent every lunch hour in the oak-panelled retreat of the Carlton Club, Benjamin felt that he was starting to lose touch with his friend. They hadn't really spoken to each other all term. "Hey—did you know that I've got a girlfriend now?"

"Yeah, I know. Jennifer Hawkins. Doug told me."

"Oh?" Benjamin waited for something—congratulations, maybe, some sort of stamp of approval—but all Philip said was:

"He said he was going to talk to you about it."

This sounded ominous, and Benjamin was left to ponder its possible significance until lunchtime the next day, when Doug greeted him as he was leaving the dining hall.

"Philip said you wanted to talk to me about something."

"Just a few words from the wise, that's all. What are you doing after school?"

Benjamin grimaced. "It's my week for litter duty. I'll be finished by four-thirty or so."

"I'll come and find you."

"You wouldn't . . ." (this was grotesquely embarrassing, but he asked it anyway) ". . . You wouldn't like to come and help, would you? Only it's with one of the fifth forms tonight, and some of them . . . well, some of them are bigger than me."

Doug burst into laughter when he heard that, but he could see that Benjamin was genuinely nervous, and didn't milk the joke for as long as he might have done. "Don't worry, Kojak. The sight of a prefect's badge can be a terrifying thing. They'll be like putty in your hands."

It took him a few minutes to locate Benjamin after school. Doug found him, eventually, with his bottom wedged into one of the litter bins, his legs akimbo and his hands tied behind his back with his prefect's tie.

"How did it go?" he asked.

Once he had pulled Benjamin out, undone the elaborate series of reef-knots and dusted him down, he said: "So, what's it like, then, being a member of the ruling classes?"

"I can't do this, Doug," said Benjamin. "I'm going to have to resign."

"You can't resign, old son. It's a job for life." He chuckled. "You really are a prize prannet, Ben. Anyone could see you weren't cut out to be a member of the Special Branch."

"Yes, well I'm beginning to realize that, aren't I?"

"How's Steve coping?"

"Better than me," said Benjamin, as they began to walk together down towards the Bristol Road. They could see the buses rumbling past in the distance, crammed full of schoolkids. In the foreground, the rugby fields stretched vast and ghostly in the dying light. "They seem to respect him a bit more. We had a nice long chat the other night, actually. Some parents came to look round the school and the two of us had to make seventy cups of coffee for them and then wash them all up. Gave us a chance to talk for a couple of hours."

"So in between doing stints as a tea lady for the Chief Master, and having it off with Jennifer Hawkins, I don't suppose you're getting much work done, are you?"

"I'm not having it off with her."

Doug snorted in disbelief. "Come off it, Ben. We all know what happened at the party. I'll never feel the same way about my parents' wardrobe again. Every time Dad goes to get himself a new pair of socks I get these incredible mental images."

"Yes, well that was just a one-off. We haven't done anything since."

"But you've been seeing her, haven't you?"

"Yes." Irritated by Doug's tone of continued puzzlement, Benjamin said: "What happened in that wardrobe—yes, I know, I know, so it's funny—but what happened that night was important to me. To both of us. The circumstances may have been weird, but it wasn't meaningless. It was the beginning of something very special."

"Oh, grow *up*, Ben, for fuck's sake. Just because you get drunk at a party with a girl and she pulls you off, it doesn't mean you're . . . betrothed to her, or anything. This isn't some Jane Austen novel we're talking about here."

Benjamin looked at him crossly. "You must have been reading some different Jane Austen novels to me. I don't remember any scenes like that."

"You know what I mean. You and Jennifer don't belong together." He stopped walking and turned to Benjamin, with a new urgency in his voice. "Listen. I'm going to tell you two things. You remember that time I went down to London to see the *NME* people? The time I wanted you to come with me, and you wouldn't do it? I met this girl down there. She was a typist or something, worked for *Horse and Hound*. We went and saw The Clash playing in Fulham and afterwards we went back to her place, and for the rest of that night, I'm telling you, Ben . . ." (he dropped to a whisper) ". . . We fucked each other's brains out. We did it so many different ways, we did things you wouldn't believe were possible. What we did makes your thirty seconds with Jennifer seem like *nothing*."

"It was forty seconds, actually."

"Whatever it was—the point is that I never saw this girl again. We didn't bother to swap phone numbers or anything. It was just one night of fantastic sex and then goodbye."

Benjamin thought about this for a second or two, and then walked on. "Well, that's a beautiful story, Doug, that's a very touching little anecdote. Real Romeo and Juliet stuff. A Troilus and Cressida for the nineteen-seventies. But some of us just have a different approach to these things."

"All right, then," said Doug, running to catch up, "I'll tell you something else. And this really *is* important. You're seventeen years old and you're going to meet hundreds more women in the next few years. If you're going to go all soppy over someone from this craphole of a city you might as well choose the right person: and there are only two girls round here who are worth anything at all."

"Oh yes? And who might they be?"

"Claire and Cicely, of course."

Benjamin slowed down, then came to a halt. They were near the gates to the main road, now, outside the entrance to the sports hall. The upper-sixth common room was on the top floor (home to the fifty or so boys who had not been elected to the Carlton Club), and light from its windows spilled out on to the tarmac around them, throwing long distorted shadows. It suddenly seemed to Benjamin that this was another of those fateful moments he had recently learned to recognize: supernatural, charged. A moment when crucial choices were being offered to him.

"Claire and Cicely?"

"I know you've never had any time for Claire. I don't know why, I think she's fabulous. Always have done. But we tried going out and it didn't work, so . . . there you are. It's just not meant to happen. As for Cicely: she isn't my type, to be honest, but . . ."

"Yes?"

"Well she's *your* type, isn't she? She's perfect for you. You're perfect for each other. God, Benjamin, you're the only person who's ever been able to talk any sense into that woman. She worships you, actually. She hangs on your every word. If there were ever two people who were made to be with each other it's you and Cicely, and to see one of you being fucked over by a married man and the other one trying to pretend he's in the middle of something deep and meaningful with Jennifer Hawkins . . . Well, it's heartbreaking."

Benjamin didn't speak for a long time. He looked at the ground, tracing shadowy patterns with his foot, his Cyclops Records bag swinging gently in the air.

"It's Jennifer's birthday tomorrow," he said at last. "I can't break up with her on her birthday."

"You can break up with her any time," said Doug. But he knew, then, what he had always known: that Benjamin was a lost cause, and he had been wasting his breath. "What did you get her?"

"A record," said Benjamin.

"She'll hate it," said Doug, moving on. "Don't tell me what it is, I don't need to know. I just know that she'll hate it."

"Mmn, lovely," said Jennifer, pulling off the wrapping paper. "What an unusual present."

Benjamin had bought her *Voices and Instruments*, one of the new releases on Brian Eno's Obscure Records label. One side consisted of some e. e. cummings poems set to music by John Cage, sung by Robert Wyatt and Carla Bley. On the other, a Birmingham musician, Jan Steele, had composed some minimalist settings of texts by James Joyce.

"I know you said you wanted the *Evita* record," said Benjamin, "but you weren't serious, were you?"

"This is much nicer," said Jennifer.

For her birthday treat, they went to see *Star Wars*, which had just opened at the Odeon New Street. It was Jennifer's choice. They sat in the back row but one and waited patiently through the first ten minutes of trailers and local adverts, then gave up and started French kissing instead.

"King William's Prefect In Public Snogging Scandal," said a voice behind them.

Benjamin turned and saw that he was sitting in front of Ives, the annoying little curly-haired second-former he had met with Harding in the Gerald Hill Studio last year.

"What are you doing here?" he said. "Haven't you got homework to do?"

"Keep quiet, or I'll tell Chiefy," said Ives.

Afterwards, they went to the fish and chip shop in Hill Street and talked about the film. Benjamin thought it was all "sound and fury, signifying nothing." Jennifer said it was the best film she had ever seen. They agreed to differ.

They said goodbye at the Navigation Street bus stops with an ambiguous kiss: too long to be formal, too brief to be passionate. Jennifer was a good kisser but Doug's words had already taken on a haunting quality, and Benjamin found himself wondering, on the journey home, whether he would ever get another glimpse of the breasts he had clasped unknowingly for those dark sleepy hours three weeks ago.

She didn't call him "Tiger" any more, either. That wasn't a good sign.

23

you are the very personification of narcissistic obliquity

*your effrontery and culpability are beyond the terminus of
legitimate forbearance*

I abhor and depreciate your supercilious carnality

*your contrivance was simply to mesmerize her with your
meticulosity and dilettantism*

*you are a syphilitic, leucodermatous, febrile, pyretic and fistular
marasmus*

Bill clutched tightly at his coffee cup and looked around him.
The décor was austere, imposing, designed to intimidate. The
hotel's oak-panelled walls reminded him of a club room; they
might even have called to mind the Carlton Club room at King
William's School, had he ever seen it. The message they sent out
to visitors was the same: don't mess with us; we have been here
for a long time; decisions have been made here; the conversations of the influential and the elect have echoed around these
walls. You may stand here awhile, but soon you will go. You do
not belong.

peccable
scrofulous
obscurantist
charlatanism
unctuosity
pinguescence
persiflage
spavined
suppurate
improbity
fustigate
compurgation
scorbutic
malignancy

There were about twenty-five people drinking coffee in the back room. Outside, in the conference hall, there were another seven hundred waiting to be addressed by British Leyland's new Chairman, Michael Edwardes. The audience contained many national union officials as well as Leyland shop stewards. The twenty-five in the back room were considered among the most influential. Michael Edwardes himself was there, looking nervous but resolute.

Bill should have been talking to his colleagues, gearing himself up for the speech ahead, which was sure to be important. Edwardes would be talking to the workforce about the state of the company as he saw it, explaining the decisions which he and his advisory board had been making, in private, over the last few weeks. There were bound to be redundancies. Bill should have been focusing on these issues but instead a weariness was lying over him this morning. He was already seeing his own defeat, and Edwardes's victory, as inevitable. And he was thinking about a conversation he had had the day before. A Pakistani worker, Zulfiqar Rashid, had come to ask him about the television interview Margaret Thatcher had given two nights previously (the night of Benjamin's first, abortive litter duty). What had she meant, Zulfiqar wanted to know, when she said that the British people were beginning to feel "rather swamped" by different cultures? Was immigration really going to be halted under a Tory government? His wife and three children were still in Lahore. They were planning to come and join him in Birmingham in two or three years' time. Was this no longer going to be possible if Mrs. Thatcher became Prime Minister? Were his wife and children—were his skills, for that matter—wanted in Britain or not?

"You've got nothing to worry about," Bill had said. "The Labour Party will be re-elected anyway." But he had known that he was lying.

Sam picked up the telephone. Barbara was out shopping, and he was alone in the house. It was ten to eleven. He knew that this was the time for morning break at King William's. He knew that for the next twenty minutes, the teachers would be relaxing and drinking coffee in their common room.

He looked down at the list of phrases he had been composing for the last three nights.

your contemptibly inelastic fealty to the twin malpractices of sensualism and dissipation stimulates only my profoundest, most hypogeal and bathyphilous inculpation

He dialled the number of the school and listened to the ringing tone. The Chief Master's secretary answered the telephone and he asked to be put straight through to Mr. Miles Plumb.

market share
contingency
lack of production output
over-manning
efficient management
product strategy

corporate plan
executive meetings
over-capacity
reduced scale of operations
dinosaur
de-manning

Sam could hear the hum of conversation in the Common Room, the clinking of cups, the creaking of chairs. The voice had said "I'll just go and find him," without giving any indication of how long it was likely to take. The seconds were ticking by. He had been waiting a minute and a half at least.

your insouciant ruttishness is tantamount to nymphomania
you are a temerarious poltroon, a rebarbative mooncalf, a
pixilated dunderhead and a milksop of unmitigated flagitiousness

The words were beginning to lurch and blur in front of his eyes. The phrases which had sounded so impressive when he had mouthed them to himself in the half-light of the living room at two o'clock in the morning now seemed forced and inadequate. He had no idea what some of them meant. And yet he had to meet this man on his own terms. He had to employ the same tools that Miles himself had used to draw Barbara away from him.

He could hear footsteps approaching at the other end of the line.

the time has come when we simply have to face up
to the situation

The atmosphere in the hall was sombre, attentive; almost funereal.

difficult, and no doubt unpopular choices will have to be made

Bill was one of the few people in the audience who knew how much was at stake this morning. What they were listening to was not a simple statement of beliefs. Just a few minutes before taking the floor, Michael Edwardes had announced to the delegates in the back room that he would be calling for a vote of confidence at the end of his speech. He was going to present his case, cloaked in these terms of agonized reasonableness, and then call for it to be endorsed after allowing only a few minutes for the shop stewards, unrehearsed and unprepared, to present their counter-arguments. They were being shrewdly out-manoeuvred.

a painful but necessary process of de-manning

Painful for whom?

something in the region of twelve and a half thousand jobs

Bill tensed in his chair, expecting uproar. He heard one or two rapid intakes of breath, but that was all. His Brothers were silent. Two rows behind him, Colin Trotter was nodding in melancholy agreement. He could see the logic behind all this. Bill could see the logic too, but he hated it, hated it with a passionate vengeance that had driven him onwards in the past but today just seemed to flatten and exhaust him. He caught Derek Robinson's eye and they exchanged a long, dispirited glance.

"Yes?" said the voice on the telephone.

So this was it, then; the long-awaited moment of confrontation.

agapistic libertine
nefarious subterfuge
abominable philanderer
invidious entanglement
nyctalopic cuckold

317

"Is that Mr. Plumb?"

"It is."

"This is Sam Chase here. Barbara's husband."

sanctimonious
attitudinizer
deviationist
tergiversator
prophylactic
febrifugal
incandescence
cruciation
legerdemain
apoplexy
shenanigans

There was a long silence. Neither man seemed to have anything to say to the other. Sam tried to form the words, but they wouldn't come. More than a year's worth of frustration and resentment boiled up inside him, but he had no means of expressing it. It was more than he could bear.

"Do you have something to say to me?" Mr. Plumb asked. "Is it your intention that we should be the participants in some sort of colloquy?"

Furious at his opponent but even more at himself, Sam crumpled up the sheets of paper, screwed his eyes tight shut, and instinctively, without thinking about it, blew the longest and loudest raspberry he had ever blown in his life.

He had to admit, on later, more sober reflection, that it had not been his finest hour. It was hardly the action of a mature and articulate man. But it seemed to have done the trick. There had been a shocked pause, the line had gone suddenly dead and neither he nor Barbara ever heard from Sugar Plum Fairy again.

The delegates spilled out of the conference hall, into the hotel's grounds and the February sunshine. A crowd of journalists was standing by and they surrounded Michael Edwardes eagerly. He was exhausted, but beaming. His speech had been a triumph. His words had won the day. The meeting had voted by 715 to five in favour of his proposals. A few "extreme militants" had tried to oppose them, but nobody had listened. The restructuring of British Leyland was under way.

Bill sat on a warm patch of low wall and gazed out over the ornamental garden. He heard footsteps approaching across the loose gravel and looked up to see his friend and fellow-steward Derek Robinson standing over him.

"We fight this, Bill," said the man soon—very soon—to be demonized in the newspapers as "Red Robbo," and to be sacked by Michael Edwardes for trying to orchestrate protests against his programme of redundancies. "We fight this every inch of the way."

"Of course we do," said Bill.

Derek looked at him with searching, worried eyes, and said, "Don't lose the faith, Bill," before walking away.

A coach was waiting to take the men back to Longbridge. Bill checked to see whether Sam Chase was the driver. He would have liked to chat with Sam. But it was somebody else.

"You might as well head off," he said to the driver. "I think I'm going to stay here for a while."

The crowd was breaking up. Michael Edwardes had been whisked away in a chauffeured car, and the journalists had followed. Bill wandered back into the hotel's gloomy interior and stared around, not knowing what to do next. Colin Trotter and a group of other junior managers were drinking pints of bitter and gin and tonics at a table in a corner of the bar. Once again, the dark wood panelling and the air of conspiratorial good humour between these men made Bill think of a club, a gentleman's club. The sort of club to which you had to be elected but nobody ever told you the rules, nobody ever explained why some people were in and others were out. So what would this one be called? The Bosses' Club? The Scoundrels' Club? The Liars' Club?

Twelve and a half thousand redundancies. A painful but necessary process. He pitied the management their twinges of conscience, those long, distressing meetings, the salaried anguish of executive decision-making, and thought too about the weeks and months and maybe lifetimes of hardship and hopelessness that so many thousands of his men were going to face in the bitter, market-driven era to come. Was there anything he could do about it, now that everyone had swallowed the pill like trusting children and voted themselves out of a livelihood? Oh, yes, there had been plenty of days, good days, and not so long ago, when he truly believed that the struggle could be won; but the decade was old now and he was growing old with it, and he knew that those days would never come back, any more than those days of hot, secret pleasure with Miriam Newman would ever come back, any more than Miriam herself would ever come back from the dead.

24

Dear Chiara (as I must learn to call you now),

*A grey and miserable day here. Howling wind coming in off
the sea. Amazing how it can reach even as far as campus
and make the air wet and salty. I am sitting in the
library—the only person here, as far as I can make out—
watching fat drops of moisture race, or rather stagger, down
the window-panes. An anthology of worthy critical writings
on eighteenth-century poetry open on my desk, along with a
few volumes of Pope and Gray, all of them unread. Where is
everybody? Is there a vital lecture I'm missing, or
something? Anyway, I'd much rather be writing to you than
thinking about boring old rhyming couplets.*

*And how is autumn in Mantova? Exquisite, I'm sure. I
have a vivid image of you in your new life. You are sitting
at a café in some piazza, sitting beneath a colonnade,
drinking cappuccino. The autumn leaves are flapping across
the flagstones. An old woman dressed in black is pushing her
bicycle across the square, her basket full of bread and
tomatoes and cheese and milk. And there's a crowd of darkly
handsome Italian boys clustered around their motorbikes in
the corner, and they're looking at this beautiful enigmatic*

student who's just arrived from England and they're talking about her and they're arguing about who's going to ask her out first. And there's a bell sounding from the <u>campanile</u>, and . . . OK, so it's nothing like that at all, I'm just piling cliché on to cliché, but I can be allowed my little fantasies, can't I, on this dismal Devon morning?

Incidentally, are you planning to revert to being plain Claire when you come back to England? But no, you could never be plain.

Well, so <u>Philip</u> is going to come and see you in a few weeks' time. It seems we have both managed to surprise each other with news of impending visitors. You and <u>Philip</u>, though? Wonders will never cease. Yes, of course, I know there is nothing in it, he's a friend, he's coming to stay with you in Italy for a few days: what's the big deal? There was just something about the way you mentioned it in your letter. Anyway, you will have a very good time, I'm sure. He's very sweet, good company, etc. I've always thought that. Of all of us who worked on the magazine in those days he was probably the nicest and least complicated—wouldn't you agree?

Which is more than can be said for Benjamin.

Yes, <u>I'm</u> surprised that he's coming to see me, as well, even for a long weekend. I think I just wore him down with two years' worth of endless, persistent invitations. Now that it's finally happening I find I'm terribly nervous about it. I mean—<u>Benjamin</u>? For two and a half days? What are we going to talk about? What would you talk about to Benjamin for two and a half hours or even minutes? Can I stand a whole weekend of those long mysterious silences, those aeons of depressive staring out of the window while he slowly ransacks his brain for the <u>mot juste</u> with which to answer your latest question, which was probably something along the lines of "Would you like a cup of tea?"

Oh, I know, I'm being unfair, dreadfully unfair. We were all fond of Benjamin. I know you were, especially. And perhaps Oxford has opened him up no end. (Ha! OK, so that rates low on the scale of probability.) And, to stop being facetious for a moment, there were reasons why he always looked so sad and thoughtful, I think. In fact I know there were. Benjamin had hidden depths, if you must know. I glimpsed them once.

Actually I have never told anybody this story, but hey, it's ten-thirty in the morning, all my friends have disappeared somewhere without me, the library is deserted and I've got a whole pad of blank A4 just waiting to be filled up. If I'm ever going to tell it to anybody, I might as well tell it to you, now.

It's rather horrible, to be honest. And it's more about his sister, Lois, than about Benjamin himself. That's the part I'll come to at the end, though.

It happened . . . goodness, three and a half years ago. How time has started to slip away from us, already! February, 1978, if my memory is correct. Just after he had started that appallingly unsuitable affair with Jennifer Hawkins. The less said about that the better.

Do you remember Mr. Tillotson, and the Walking Option? I don't think you were ever a member. It started as a Boys' School thing, a sort of remedial home for the terminally unathletic, but then some girls were allowed to join too and it became much more popular, as you can imagine. All sorts of naughtiness used to go on but that's another story altogether. The standing joke about it was that we all used to get lost every week and like all good jokes this one was completely true: Mr. Tillotson was a sweetie but he couldn't read a map to save his life. After a while we all became quite curious about how soon we would get lost and how long for, and some people would even be taking bets on it. It all added to the fun.

I think there are lots of nice bits of countryside around Birmingham, whatever people say, but after a few months we managed to exhaust even those and then one week Mr. T *had a brainwave and decided he was going to take us on a walk around all the disused canals. Most of us didn't even know that there <u>was</u> a canal system in the city, but we were wrong—there are miles and miles of canals in fact, none of them in use any more, all superseded by the motorways now, of course. It was very atmospheric, I must say: a view of the city you don't normally get, just the backs of dozens of empty factories and warehouses, all cracked window-panes and creepy abandoned spaces. Apart from anything else, it was an ideal place to get lost.*

Benjamin and I managed to become separated from the others and after a while it began to grow dark and frankly we were starting to get a little scared. We hadn't a clue where everyone had got to but we reckoned the safest thing would be to stay exactly where we were, at least for a while, and wait for someone to come by rather than running around in a different direction and getting hopelessly confused.

So then we sat down and we started talking.

Benjamin made some remark about the canals and I can remember that was what got us going. He said that apparently—or at least this was what Mr. T had told him—Birmingham had more miles of canal than Venice. Sounds incredibly unlikely, doesn't it: perhaps you could nip across there one day and do some measuring and tell me what you think. And I said something like, That's all very well, but at least when you go round the canals in Venice you've got all those palazzos to look at, and those beautiful churches. And then Benjamin said a funny thing: he said it annoyed him when people made comparisons like that, and the important thing about a church wasn't what it looked like, it was the kind of worship that went on in it, the <u>sincerity</u> (or something) of the religious feeling, and he said that in that respect the churches in Birmingham were just as impressive as the churches in Venice or anywhere else.

He said it with amazing passion, I thought, and it came

quite out of the blue, so I said to him, "Benjamin, you're not religious, are you?," and he said, "Yes I am, actually," and when I asked him why he'd never mentioned it before he said that he'd been wanting to talk to me about it for some time but the right moment had never come up, and he'd never joined the Christian Society because he thought that belief was a very private thing and not something he felt comfortable sharing with other people.

Now, I bet <u>that's</u> surprised you, hasn't it? And I dare say you're none too pleased to hear it. I know you've always hated any kind of religion and I've never said anything about it before, but I can say it to you now, in a letter: I can say that you're <u>wrong</u>, Claire, and I know why you feel the way that you do, but the kind of religion your parents go in for has got nothing to do with real Christianity, it's just a perversion of the Faith as far as I'm concerned. Real Christianity is about love and forgiveness and understanding people and being tolerant and not condemning people when they make mistakes and there is nothing <u>sinister</u> about it, nothing to be suspicious about. But no, I'm not going to get evangelical on you now, I just wanted you to see why it is that there's some kind of sympathy, some kind of connection between Benjamin and me, however different we might be on the surface.

I asked him then when he had found God and he told me but he didn't go into details. He said that when he was younger, about thirteen or fourteen, he had got himself into some sort of fix and he had started praying, and then incredibly his prayers had been answered. There and then! He said it was some sort of miracle but he never told me what had happened, exactly. He said it was a secret between him and God and that he had never told anybody, not even Philip. Then he said, Oh, I did tell one person once, but that was Lois. I told her when she was really ill because I thought it might make her feel better.

So that got us talking about Lois. He began to tell me

what really happened to her that night, and I have never forgotten a word.

All I knew were the same things that you probably knew and everybody else knew. She had been out at the pub with her boyfriend when the bomb went off, and he was killed and she wasn't. She was very badly injured in the leg, though, and had to walk on callipers for months afterwards. And there were burns, too. Really she was terribly lucky, from that point of view, but the main effects were psychological and nobody really knows how deep those kinds of wounds go, how long they are likely to last. Sometimes they never heal at all. There was a very long period when she was in total shock and after that she seemed to be OK for a while, but then she would relapse and gradually these relapses got worse and worse, until she succumbed to complete depression and had to be hospitalized for a long time. This was about two years after it happened, I think. As far as I know that lasted for a few months and then she came home again, but the family always had to be very careful not to do anything to upset her. Philip told me something about this once, I remember: a little detail that Benjamin had let slip to him one day. He said that at the moment the bomb went off the juke box was playing "I Get a Kick Out of You"—you know, the Cole Porter song?—and always after that they had to make sure that she never heard that song, because it would just set her off, crying uncontrollably. They were living on a knife-edge with her all the time.

Anyway, it was while she was in the hospital that Lois and Benjamin got really close. He used to go and see her at weekends and take her for long walks up on the hills. I don't know how often her parents went to see her, or Paul, for that matter—probably never, in his case, nothing would surprise me as far as that little weirdo is concerned—but it was Benjamin that she started to bond with. They started to call themselves The Rotters' Club after a record that they both liked (you remember at school how people used to call them

The Rotters?) and Benjamin would tell her about everything that had happened at school that week because he couldn't think of anything else to talk to her about, and he always used to wonder whether she was taking any of it in, because a lot of the time she would never answer him, never say a word to anyone, but he told me, that afternoon on the canal, that in fact she could remember everything about it, every tiny detail, she had perfect recall of all his stories and ended up knowing more about his schooldays than he even did himself. Ironic. So that was when he told her about the mysterious miracle. And slowly she began to say things to him as well, started talking again, and that was how he learned the story of the bomb and what happened to her boyfriend.

I suppose it's another kind of miracle that Lois could have been through an experience like that and one of the consequences was that it brought her closer to her brother. God makes sure that some good comes out of everything, you see. But I'm not going to start preaching at you.

Lois's boyfriend was called Malcolm, and she was totally, deeply in love with him, and when they went out to the pub that night it wasn't for just an ordinary date. Benjamin knew what was going to happen, because Malcolm had told him, but Lois didn't know. It was going to be a surprise. Malcolm had bought her a ring and he was planning to propose to her.

It's funny as I write this that I have two pictures in my mind. One is of Malcolm and Lois sitting in the pub together but the other, the one that stays with me more, is of Benjamin and me as we sat by that freezing canal in the dark, with a few lights beginning to come on in some of the factories, sending reflections over the ripples in the water. Only a few, as I said, because it was very quiet, and ghostly, in that forgotten part of Birmingham where nobody came any more. Just us, today. And that was more or less by mistake.

"And did he ever propose?" I asked, egging him on to finish the story, because Benjamin was becoming very silent. His words were coming very slowly and he was starting to shiver.

"No," he said. "No, he never got the chance. He was going to, but . . ."

His voice tailed away, and I put my arm on his. It was a brave thing to do, really, only I wasn't thinking about it. He's the kind of person you don't touch, the kind who doesn't like it when you get physical with him.

"You see," he went on, after what seemed like ages. "That was when it happened."

Then he said: "Lois doesn't remember anything about the next few minutes. She doesn't remember feeling any pain. It went completely dark and there must have been screaming everywhere and it would have been a while before she could see anything at all. After that, all she remembers . . . is looking down . . . and seeing Malcolm."

"Where was he?" I asked, and Benjamin said:

"She was holding his head in her hands."

I can guess what you're thinking when you read those words; it's the same thing I was thinking when I heard them. I thought—and it was a stupid thought, but it came to me anyway—I thought, Well, that's a romantic image. The two lovers. He's lying in her lap. She's cradling him as he dies. Maybe they whisper something to each other. Benjamin said that was what he'd thought, as well, the first time Lois told him. But no.

*"Not **him**," he said to me. "She wasn't holding him. Not Malcolm. Not the whole of him. She was holding his head.*

"Just his head."

And while I was trying to take this in he managed to say a few more words, he said, "A bomb . . . A bomb can do terrible things to a human body . . . You've no idea . . . There were people there . . ."

And that was all he said. Then he started crying. And I

put my arms around him properly and he cried into me for I
don't know how long, these huge sobs, just the two of us, in
this weird, empty place, this weird, empty place where we
had found ourselves (or I should say, lost ourselves) that
frosty afternoon I'll never forget.

I'll never forget it as long as I live.

What some people have to survive . . .

So now I've told you the story of Benjamin and Lois and
Malcolm. And I wonder where you're sitting when you read
it. Out at that table, I hope, in the piazza, under the
colonnade. Perhaps your cappuccino has gone cold.

I think I shall go and get myself a coffee, now.

I shall write to you in a few days and let you know what it
was like having Benjamin to stay for the weekend. And you
can do the same when Philip has been to see you. We must
never lose touch, you and me, never stop sharing things with
each other. My memories of schooldays are very precious and
I can already feel them fading away. What fun we had,
putting that paper together! I loved that time and you were
one of the very best things about it.

Oh well, I'm getting maudlin. Time to put a stop to all
this. Life beckons. Or what passes for it, at the moment.

Work hard and enjoy this wonderful opportunity you have
made for yourself and don't trust those Italian boys with
their motorbikes and their surly Latin good looks.

Ciao Chiara, bella amica,
With very much love,
Emily xxx.

25

Months passed, and Cicely fell ill. Just before her exams began, in the summer of 1978, she was struck down by glandular fever. Her friends said that she had been overworking, that she was having a nervous breakdown because of her complicated emotional life, and that they should have seen it coming. Her detractors said that she was an incorrigible self-dramatist and the whole illness was psychosomatic. Whatever the truth of the matter, she was laid up in bed for three weeks and then sent away to her uncle's house in Wales to recuperate. She had missed her exams. She would have to come back to school next year and study for them all over again.

On the very last day of term, 20th July, 1978, Emily found Benjamin tidying out his locker and handed him a card to sign. It was a get-well card for Cicely, with about thirty signatures on it. Benjamin looked at the envelope, which had already been addressed, and the first thing he said was: "But that's where my family go on holiday every year."

"Really? Well her uncle lives there, too."

The name of the house was Plas Cadlan, and it was in a village called Rhîw, through which Benjamin had passed many times with his family, on their drives to Aberdaron and Bardsey Island. The caravan site where they stayed every year was only about five miles away. He could scarcely believe that Cicely herself might have some connection with this place, which he considered sanctified, holy, not because of its history of religious settlement dating back to the fifth or sixth century, but because it had come to be a repository of some of his own most treasured childhood memories. Paul, Lois and his parents would be going there again, in about two weeks' time. Benjamin had resolved to stay at home, this year, and to spend some time with his grandparents instead, since his grandfather had now been diagnosed with prostate cancer and was too ill to travel. He had been looking forward, as well, to a fortnight of relative solitude and freedom. But still, if Cicely was going to be there . . .

"How long will she be staying with her uncle?" he asked.

Emily had no idea. Perhaps she would be in Wales all summer, perhaps she would be back in Birmingham next week. Everything depended on her health.

This information merely added to the strangeness of what was already a thoroughly strange day. Ever since exams had finished a few weeks ago, school had had an unreal, carnival atmosphere. There were no more lessons. For the thirty or so boys who, like Benjamin, would be coming back in the autumn term to sit the Oxford and Cambridge entrance exams, there were informal meetings called "Syndicates" to discuss possible reading programmes for the summer. The House sporting championships were still in progress. Otherwise, there was no incentive for any of the upper sixth to come to school at all, and most of them didn't. Benjamin spent much of the time hanging around at home, listening to records, making trips into Birmingham to buy more records, taking Jennifer out for occasional drinks and telling himself that he really must think of a way of ending the relationship before she ended it first. As House tennis captain (being too hopeless to make the cricket XI), he led his team to an ignominious nine defeats in a row, each match being lost 6–0, 6–0, 6–0. And now, on the last day of all, everybody he knew was roaming the corridors, signing each other's leaving books, making protestations of eternal friendship or, just as often (and with rather more feeling), telling old enemies in no uncertain terms how happy they were at the thought of never seeing them again. It was all a bit overwhelming.

By mid-afternoon, word got around that a party was developing up in the Carlton Club. Benjamin went to investigate and found that the place had been taken over by non-members. A marathon game of pontoon was in session around the main table and the air was thick with cigarette smoke. Culpepper was acting as banker and doing very nicely out of it. His laughter and cries of triumph could be heard halfway down the corridor. Meanwhile someone had filched a crate of the Founder's Port from the kitchens and most of it was already gone. A boy called Foote had thrown up into the quadrangle outside, leaving a long trail of buff-coloured vomit down the window of the Chief Master's study, which stood directly underneath. He had been expelled. Apparently it was quite common to get expelled on your last day at school. As a punishment, it was somehow lacking in sting.

Only one person failed to join in the revelry. He sat in one of the leather-covered armchairs and drank his way steadily through some port, the scowl of depression on his face gradually, with every drained glass, transmuting into anger and outright hostility. It was Steve Richards.

Steve had been behaving very oddly for these last few weeks. He was convinced that he had done badly in his exams; or, to be specific, that he had failed one crucial physics paper: failed it so decisively that it had killed his momentum and made him under-perform on the other papers as well. At Speech Day, the previous weekend, he had taken Benjamin aside during a break in their official duties and confided further in him. Messing up that paper, he said, had not been his own fault. He had fallen asleep in the exam hall.

"You fell asleep?" Benjamin repeated.

"I must have done. I'm telling you, I looked at the clock and it was 2:15 and the next time I looked it was 3:50 and I hadn't written a bloody *thing*, Ben. I hadn't written a thing."

This seemed to make no sense. Benjamin said: "Were you tired?"

"Of course I wasn't tired. I was on peak form, for God's sake. I'd been working up to it for weeks."

"There's this disease where people fall asleep," said Benjamin, pensively. He had just been reading *The Third Policeman*, in which Flann O'Brien (another of his new passions) had wrung some comic mileage out of the narcoleptic episodes suffered by one of the main characters, a mad scientist called De Selby. "Maybe you should see a doctor about it."

"I don't have any *disease*," Steve insisted. "Somebody did something to me that day."

"Did something to you?"

"They messed with my brain."

Benjamin had found some excuse for cutting the conversation short soon after that. He was beginning to think that Steve, like Cicely, had perhaps been working too hard and was losing his grip. But Steve didn't drop the accusation. He started spreading it around his other friends and linking it with Culpepper's name, implying that his old rival had found a way of taking some twisted sort of revenge for all the defeats and embarrassments he had suffered over the last two years. Nobody wanted to listen. The general perception, in any case, was that Steve and Culpepper had buried their differences in the run-up to exams. By coincidence they had even applied to go to the same Cambridge college, and this seemed to have made them accept, ruefully, that their paths were destined to run together. Culpepper himself had even discovered the famous St. Christopher's medal, at last, while rooting around in Mr. Nuttall's lost property box, and he had given it back to Steve personally. They had shaken hands on it. So nobody could see what Steve was getting at, when he started dropping these sinister hints. Nobody took him seriously.

Not, at any rate, until this very last day of term.

Now, after Culpepper had pulled in a particularly large haul from the luckless card players, followed by a jubilant yodel, a loud tattoo on the table with his fists, an enormous draught of port and a belch which set the silver sporting trophies rattling in their glass-fronted case, Steve jumped to his feet and stood directly behind him. He tapped him on the shoulder and said, in a tone of quiet fury:

"Look, Culpepper—are you actually a member of this club?"

Culpepper turned around slowly. When he saw who was addressing him, his face relaxed into a contemptuous smile.

"Oh, come on, Richards, don't be such an arsehole. It's the last day of term."

"I'm not being an arsehole. This is a members' club and I'm asking you if you're a member."

"Of course I'm not. Nor are any of these people."

"Then get out."

"Don't be stupid."

"I'm telling you, as a prefect, to get out of this room *now*."

Culpepper laughed spitefully. "And what are you going to do if I don't? Put me in detention?"

"Yes," said Steve, all too aware that the whole room had gone silent and that this conversation was being closely followed by everyone present. "You can go in the first detention of next term."

"There's one flaw in that proposal," said Culpepper, after a measured pause. "Next term is the Oxbridge term, and *I* will be here, because I'll be taking the entrance exam, but *you* won't, because your grades aren't going to be good enough." And still he saved the worst insult until last: because that was when he used the name, the one name that no one in the sixth form had used for as long as anyone could remember. "Now, do you mind if we get back to our game—*Rastus*?"

With that he returned to his pack of cards, and began to shuffle them placidly: until all at once, Steve seized hold of his collar, and there was a sudden, unthinkable thud and a crack as he slammed Culpepper's head down against the table with murderous force.

"Jesus Christ, Steve!"

And now there was blood everywhere. It oozed in thick rivulets down the card table and ran over the edge in little cascades. Culpepper was motionless for a second or two—with shock, presumably—then stumbled into an upright position, like a punchdrunk bull, and stared around him. When he got Steve into focus he lunged at him wildly, but there were already three people to hold him back. A couple of the card players had grabbed Steve too, by now, and for a few hideous moments the two adversaries stared at each other, one of them breathless with rage, the other scarcely able to stand, his face and his blazer and shirt and hair all clotted with crimson blood. Bayley ran off to get help, and when Mr. Warren arrived with his first-aid kit, it was quickly decided that an ambulance had to be called. Meanwhile Steve, unresisting, was frogmarched down to the Chief Master's study.

He was the second person to be expelled from the school that day.

Doug, Philip and Benjamin came to see him as he stood waiting to be called in for his interview. It was fairly clear that he had been crying, but now he seemed unnervingly calm and softly spoken.

"*You* know what happened," he said accusingly, to Doug and Philip. "You were there in the room with us that day. I'm not making it up. Think about it."

Then a voice from behind the door called "Richards!," and he was gone.

"So what was *that* about?" Benjamin asked. "What did he mean?"

The three of them were lying on the grassy bank leading down to the rugby fields. It was after four o'clock on this blazing, humid afternoon, and the school was almost deserted. His friends had brought a four-pack of Carling Black Label, but Benjamin, conscious of his status as always, felt obliged to abstain. It was all right for the others: they wouldn't be coming back next term.

"Steve's got this idea into his head," Doug answered slowly, his eyes closed against the burning sun, "that Culpepper did something to him, the day of his big exam. Gave him something."

"Like what?"

"A drug."

Benjamin laughed; the very idea made him nervous. "How could he possibly have done that?"

"What do you think, Phil?"

"If it happened," Philip said, "it happened when we were all in the room together."

"All right then." Doug sat up. "Let's think about it."

"I don't even know what you're talking about," Benjamin protested. "Which room do you mean?"

And so Doug and Philip explained. It all hinged on the fact that King William's expected its pupils to study for an additional O-level in the sixth form, at the same time as their A-levels. Sometimes this could lead to problems with the examination timetable, and on this particular Tuesday morning, Doug, Philip, Harding, Richards, Culpepper, Gidney and Procter all had to take O-level papers which clashed with their A-levels. Their A-level papers, as a result, had to be rescheduled for the afternoon, and between the hours of 11:30 a.m. and 2 p.m., they had to be closeted somewhere away from the rest of the school, so that no cheating could take place. For two and a half hours, then, they were locked up together in Mr. Nuttall's room, with nothing more exciting to look forward to than the arrival of Mr. Tillotson at 1:15 with a plate of sandwiches and seven cups of tea. (If he could find his way.)

"Now hang on," said Doug. "Did we all know beforehand that we were getting tea?"

"Yes, I think so," said Philip. "I certainly did."

"OK. So we knew the tea was coming. Fine. Now—" (he closed his eyes again) "—I'm trying to remember. Did anything happen in those two and a half hours, apart from the sandwiches and the tea and Culpepper finding the medal?"

"Of course it did. There was Harding's joke."

"Oh, yes," said Doug, drily. "Sean's joke. How could I forget?"

"Sean's joke?" said Benjamin, for whom old habits died hard, and who remained perennially curious about his erstwhile friend's antics.

"We'll come to that in a bit," Doug promised. "You'll split your sides. Now then: when exactly did Culpepper find the medal?"

"Just after the tea arrived."

"Are you sure of that?"

"Positive."

"Well, that's a giveaway, isn't it?"

"Why's it a giveaway?" said Benjamin. "You're not explaining this very well."

"OK, listen." Doug sat up, put his lager can down on the grass and applied himself to the task of laying out the facts. "We all get a plate of Mrs. Craddock's delicious crab paste sandwiches, or whatever. Yum yum, munch munch, thank you very much. Then the tea arrives. One big pot, seven cups and saucers. But just for the moment, Culpepper seems to have lost interest in his din-dins, and he's decided to start rummaging around in the lost property box beneath Nuttall's bookcase: no doubt hoping to root out some hardcore pornography, for which he has a notorious predilection. Anyway, he hasn't been talking to the rest of us all morning. You know what he's like. Ever since we published that letter your brother wrote to him, me and Philip have been *persona non grata*. So we just let him get on with it and do his own thing.

"Now, the upshot is that he doesn't find any blow jobs or split beavers, unfortunately, but he *does* come across something interesting: Steve's St. Christopher's medal, which went missing about a year ago, and caused an almighty rumpus as we all remember. So he turns round, and he hides it in his hand, and he says . . . Let me get this right . . . He says, 'Richards, I think you should come and see this.' And *then*—*then* he says, 'Actually, I think that everyone should.' "

"That's right," said Philip. "He did say that."

"So we *all* go over, like good little boys, and he puts the medal down on Nuttall's desk, and says to Richards, 'There you are—*now* do you believe that I never took it?' And Steve looks pretty surprised, and doesn't know what to do, and Culpepper says to him, 'I think that a gentleman might consider an apology in order, at this point,' or some such bollocks. So Steve does the decent thing, he apologizes, and what's more he does it really nicely, you can see that he means it, and *then* . . ."

"I know, I know," Philip interrupted, excited. "Then *we* all stand by the desk, and look at the medal while Steve puts it round his neck again, and Culpepper wanders off back to the tea tray. *All by himself.*"

"Exactly," said Doug, and explained to Benjamin: "You see, Steve has this theory. He's been thinking a lot about that day, and about the seven of us alone in that room, and how tired he felt afterwards. He said his tea tasted funny, as well. So he reckons that somebody spiked it with something, to screw up his chances in the exam that afternoon. Which happened to be physics, the most important one of all, from his point of view."

"But where does the medal come in?"

"Culpepper could still have taken it, last Sports Day," Philip said. "Then he hangs on to it for a year, not really knowing what to do with it. And then—bingo—he comes up with this plan, and he's got the perfect diversionary tactic. He knows we're going to be in Mr. Nuttall's room. He knows the lost property box is there. He can keep the medal in his pocket and then fish it out when the time comes, so everyone goes over to have a look and he can do his dirty work with the tea cups. Simple."

However plausible they tried to make it sound, Benjamin still didn't want to believe them. "What would he have put in the tea?"

"Don't ask me," said Doug, shrugging. "I don't do chemistry. Unlike Culpepper."

They all three fell silent for a while.

"It doesn't make sense to me," said Benjamin, "that anyone could think of anything so . . . wicked."

"You've got a lot to learn, if those books of yours are going to be any good," said Doug scornfully. "Not everybody goes through life like you do, auditioning for the part of Little Lord Fauntleroy. Of course he could do it. For God's sake, they both want to go to the same college, doing the same subject. For two years, Richards has beaten him at everything they've done. And he's black, don't forget. Don't think that doesn't count. D'you think Culpepper could stand turning up at Cambridge and finding it was going to be the same thing all over again?"

Benjamin was chastened. It all seemed to make sense, now. "I suppose not," he said.

The sun was beginning to draw back and melt into the haze. Traffic fumes from the Bristol Road were drifting their way, clogging the hot and heavy air.

"Do you think we should do anything?" Philip asked. "Tell someone?"

"Tell them what?" Doug shook his head, resigned. "We can't prove anything."

"Yes, I know, but . . ." Benjamin felt a sense of the world's unjustness welling up inside him. But his anger was formless, ungraspable, and all he managed to say was, "Poor Steve . . ."

Philip echoed these words, and added: "And now look what's happened to him. Now he's really blown it." He threw his empty lager can across the playing fields in a slow, angry curve. Then he said: "We haven't told him about Harding's joke."

Doug laughed shortly, mirthlessly. "You tell him."

Philip glanced at Benjamin and asked, "Do you want to hear it?"

"Mm?" He had already forgotten there was another part to the story, and was thinking about Cicely instead; Cicely and her illness, and how she, like Steve, had been defeated by these exams. It had been a disastrous time for both of them. "Yes," he said, eventually. "Why not?"

"OK." Philip sighed, and leaned forward, clasping his knees. It was hardly the prelude to a sparkling anecdote. "Well, just after all this had happened—a couple of minutes after—there's another strange thing. We're all sitting there—Steve and Culpepper have got their books, me and Doug and Gidney and Procter are playing cards, Harding's sipping his tea—when suddenly there's this noise at the window. A little bump. And then it happens again. Someone's throwing something against the window, right? So Culpepper goes over to investigate, and he sees that little pipsqueak Ives standing on the drive outside. He's got a crumpled-up ball of paper in his hand, and that's what he's been throwing at the window. So he throws it up again and says to Culpepper, 'That's for you!,' and Culpepper catches it and Ives runs off.

"Well, he comes back into the middle of the room and opens up the paper. Everyone's looking at him by now. And what do you suppose it is?"

Benjamin couldn't guess.

"It's only the exam paper, isn't it? The physics exam paper. The very thing that Steve and Culpepper aren't supposed to see. The whole reason they've been locked up in this room for half the day."

"Wow. So how did Ives get hold of it?"

"Nobody thinks about that, at the time. About twenty people have taken that exam this morning. Any one of them can have chucked the paper away into a waste bin, or passed it over to him . . . There are any number of ways. The important thing now is the moral dilemma it poses. Or doesn't pose, to be precise. There's no moral dilemma for Steve—you throw the thing away, and don't take another look at it—and there's none for Culpepper either—you read it through from start to finish and spend the next thirty minutes going through your text books for the answers. The question is, which of these particular philosophies is going to win the day?

"So, Culpepper and Steve start having the most incredible argument. Then the rest of us join in. It's five against one. Me and Doug and Procter and Gidney and Steve are all for grabbing the paper and throwing it back out of the window. But Culpepper won't let go. We start chasing him around the room with it. Steve does a rugby tackle on him and brings him to the floor. They're on the floor, fighting each other for this bloody stupid bit of paper. The only one who doesn't join in is Harding. He's still sitting there, sipping his tea like he couldn't give a toss. And then he says something. He looks down at these two clowns rolling around on the floor and he says, 'What's the date?' And Culpepper can't believe what he's hearing. He says, *'What?,'* as if this is the daftest question in the world. Which it does seem to be, I must say, to the rest of us. But then Harding says, 'What's the date on the exam paper?,' and they look at it, and . . ."

"And?" said Benjamin, although he thought he could anticipate the answer.

"1972. June the 20th, 1972."

Benjamin threw back his head, and began to laugh, but it was the laughter of admiration rather than genuine amusement. "Yes, of course. He'd just got an old one out of the library. And he's always getting Ives to run errands for him."

Doug was gazing into the distance, his eyes narrowed. "God, I can still see the look on his face, too. He's sitting there, and he's just tapping away on the edge of his teacup with that bloody signet ring of his. Clink, clink, clink, he's going, and you've never seen any one look so smug or inscrutable. That crazy pleasure he gets from winding people up. He'd reduced the whole room to chaos. Mayhem. Just for the hell of it." Drinking down what was left of his warm beer, he added, "Hell's the right word, too, where he's concerned. That man—" (Doug chose the phrase carefully) "—is the spawn of Satan. Reluctantly, that's the conclusion I've come to." He flopped back on to the grass and groaned, rubbing his eyes. "Shit, what a day it's been. What a bloody school this is. I don't wonder that Steve cracked in the end. Nobody sane could survive a place like this.

It's nothing but a breeding ground for freaks and weirdos." He glanced at Benjamin and smiled, half-teasingly. "Look at you, with your prefect's badge and your desk drawer full of unfinished masterpieces. What's the matter with you?"

He struggled to his feet, and the other two followed. It was time to go home.

"I can't wait to get out of here," Doug said, as they headed for the gates, for their last-ever journey together on the number 62 bus. "I tell you, London's the only place for me."

26

(N.B. Lois's diary from this period is sometimes hard to decipher. The letters and numbers at the top of each entry—for instance, 3 + 260 a.m.—refer to the number of years and days after Malcolm's death. The asterisks at the bottom of each page, usually ranging from one to five, seem to be an assessment of her mood on that particular day.)

<u>4th August, 1978</u>
3 + 256 a.m.

A long and uncomfortable journey to Wales, with the three of us squashed into the back of the car. Gorgeous weather, though, as we drove out of Penybontfawr and up through the Tanat valley. Let's hope it stays this way for once, hey Lois? Paul of course says that it won't. He spent most of the drive with his transistor radio stuck to his ear listening to the forecasts. Every time they got worse he sounded happier and happier. "Rain!" he kept saying. "Rain, and lots of it! Thunderstorms! Strong winds later in the week! They're going to issue a gale warning!" On and on like that, he went, for three hours. Little creep.

(No no no. See the good in <u>everyone</u>, Lois. Negative Lois. Old Lois.)

Ben sat and listened to his tape recorder. He's found some way of plugging Dad's headphones into the back and now we don't get a word out of him. I wouldn't mind but all he ever seems to listen to is his own music. Is my lovely little brother becoming just a tiny bit egocentric? I don't think so. These tunes make him think of Cicely, I expect, and that is why he likes listening to them so much. And perhaps they make him think of Malcolm, too. I can hear echoes, faint echoes in the things that Ben writes of the music Malcolm liked to share with him.

You see, Lois, people don't die. In many ways they don't die.

I will watch Ben closely on this holiday. Why has he come with us, anyway? He is too old.

We arrived at the caravan site at 7 p.m. You cannot call it a site, though. It is just a field, a farmer's field, on Cilan Head. I have not been here for four years. Malcolm never came here with me, that is a pity. I had forgotten how beautiful it is. Beautiful and restful. The sky is blue, I am no good at describing things.

We pitched our caravan and put up the awning. Mum and Dad and I are to sleep in the caravan, Ben will be in the awning and Paul has put up a little tent all of his own. I hope it gets blown away in these supposed gales of his.

Bad, Lois, naughty Lois! No no no!

*   *   *

5th August, 1978
3 + 257 a.m.

Was awoken at 7:30 by the sound of rain hammering on the roof. It always sounds twice as loud on the roof of the caravan, I remember that now. So Paul was right after all, I'm afraid that he usually is.

Lay awake for a while. Mum and Dad were awake as well. They were also listening to the rain. Mum said it sounded pretty settled. Dad looked out of the curtain and said he had seen rain like this before and it wouldn't last. It carried on solidly for the next sixteen hours.

Finished reading "The Mirror Crack'd" and started "4:50 From Paddington." One Agatha Christie is much like another, I must say.

Paul stayed in his tent all day. I am afraid he is at that age when young boys spend most of the time playing with themselves. I popped my head through the flap at one point and said, "What are you trying to do, make yourself another tent pole?" but he just gave me a rude sign. He doesn't like it when I'm funny, none of them expect it from me.

Laughter is a great healer, Lois, as Doctor Saunders used to say to me. Mind you he was a miserable old sod if ever I met one.

In the evening Ben and I braved the downpour to walk to the phone box. He said he wanted to phone Jennifer. I stood outside while he spoke to her and as is the way with these boxes I could hear every word he said, not that there were many words to hear. I don't think it is possible to conceive of a couple who are less suited to each other. At one point he said "Do you miss me?" and then there was a little pause, and he said, "Well yes, I know it's only been two days," so obviously she had said she wasn't missing him very much at all. Well, it was a stupid question anyway.

Lois, Lois, be kind to your little brother. He was always kind to you.

On the walk back the weather got even worse and our umbrella blew inside out and flew away in the wind, and just after that I broached the subject of Jennifer. I reminded him that he said he was going to finish with her about six months ago. He said he was just waiting for the right moment. I said, "When do you think that will be, then, your golden wedding anniversary?" He said, "Well, it's all good experience, I'm putting it in my novel," and I said: "What's it going to be called, then, The Cowardly Lion, The Witch and The Wardrobe?"

Holy Baloney, Lois, but you're getting sharp! Not that Jennifer is a witch, of course, it's just that she is not the best he could do and only the best is good enough for my Benjamin. But I think he knows that and what's more I think he <u>will</u> do something about her, in his own good time and perhaps sooner than we expect.

*   *   *   *

<u>*6th August, 1978*</u>
3 + 258 a.m.

It rained all night and the wind <u>did</u> nearly blow Paul's tent away so perhaps there is a God after all. I would love to see the wind just whip the tent away and leave him lying there in the middle of a field surrounded by sheep with his pyjamas on and one hand clasped firmly round his Little John Thomas. Oh! It makes me laugh just thinking about it. While we were having breakfast I said to him, "Paul, you're not being unfaithful, are you?" and he said, "What do you mean?," and I said, "Well, I'm sure I saw you doing it with your left hand this morning." Mum and Dad were shocked to hear me saying such a thing but Oh! it was worth it just to see him looking so cross.

In fact despite the rain I'm feeling in a more and more cheerful mood and might even give myself five stars at the end of the day. Besides the rain is easing off I think. It really is lovely being here even though there's not much to do. Benjamin has still got his headphones on and I have finished "4:50 from Paddington." I started "The Murder of Roger Ackroyd" but I had only got about fifteen pages in when Paul poked his head round and said, "I suppose you know the narrator did it?" He really is the pits. Anyway I started

"Ten Little Niggers" instead although I see it is called "Ten Little Indians" these days and quite right too.

An hour later and the sun is definitely shining now. Dad has got the barbecue out and he's frying sausages on it, gorgeous, my favourite smell. We can eat outside for a change which will be nice as we have been rather squashed around that dinner table with all the windows steamed up. Mum is working hard in the kitchen getting everything ready. Go on, Lois, get up and help her, she would appreciate that. Oh, all right then, I will, if you insist.

7th August, 1978

five thousand years is a long time
    in anybody's book
  to be dead, and buried,
  in a grassy cromlech.
the muttering rain
    scalds me as I walk
  the dead paths
   in darkness
  among these quick and breathing
     souls
their bones like
   powder to my touch

8th August, 1978
3 + 260 a.m.

Ooh, that knocked me for six! A whole day and I can remember almost nothing about it. I certainly don't remember writing the above. It is horrid of Paul to talk about things like that over dinner when he knows how much it upsets me. Horrid horrid horrid.

I remember going for my walk but apparently I was gone four and a half hours. That must have been when the rain started again because Mum says I came back soaking. Now it is coming down in torrents, much worse than before, it feels like we shall be swept away.

What is a cromlech when it's at home?

Ben says it is a neolithic burial chamber. (He knows everything.) That rings a bell, too, because I read the other day in a guidebook in Abersoch that they have some of those round here. I must have tucked the word away at the back of my mind. Weird though, not to remember where I went or anything.

I'm feeling better, anyway. Nowadays these feelings always pass and that is a blessing, count your blessings, Lois.

But I have not been keeping my promise! I said that I was going to watch Ben closely and I've been doing nothing of the sort, and I can see now that he is really upset and not enjoying this holiday at all. I wonder if it is something in particular or just waiting for his exam results and being cooped up in here with the four of us and this wretched, wretched rain which is getting worse by the minute as I write this.

Oh, why do I worry about Benjamin so? Perhaps it is just what Dr. Saunders used to call displacement activity. But I know what the problem is, he has not been tested like I have, he has not seen the worst that life can do to you, he hasn't had to climb out of the depths. He has seen it happen to other people and heard about it but that is not the same. I know, Lois, I know that he is lucky in that respect, nobody should have to

Whoosh! There goes Paul's tent. I'd better stop.

Thirty minutes later, and well, we are all going to have to sleep in here tonight, the tent is down and the awning is leaking and two of the other caravans in the field have packed up and gone home. Mum nearly got blown off her feet when she went to throw the washing-up water in the bracken and just now Dad was trying to bail the awning out and hold the flapping canvas down and Paul started singing out of the window, "We're all going on a—summer holiday" and you should have heard Dad's language! You learn all sorts of new things about your family on holidays like this. Now where was I? Yes, I was saying that Benjamin is lucky, in a way, nobody should have to go through those things, and of course he has his religion, he has his Miracle, but I somehow don't believe in that. It's not that I don't believe it ever happened, I just don't think it has any substance, or any weight or something—oh dear, I'm not putting this very well, and now I'm going to have to carry over on to the next page, so what do you think, Lois, three stars or four? I just worry that

*   *   * $^1/_2$

9th August, 1978
3 + 261 a.m.

if he wants to write, if he wants to compose, all of those dreams that he carries about with him so transparently every day, there will be something missing, something he will never be able to, oh, goodness, I don't know, I can't find the words tonight, and that was hardly worth going on to a new page for, was it?

And now (4:20 p.m., next afternoon) two more things have happened, one of them funny and one of them not. Well, actually Mum and I seem to be the only people who think either of them is funny. Are we the only ones around here who still have a sense of humour?

The weather is unbelievable. Dad was up at 6:30 this morning, trying to put the awning back up and tighten the guy-ropes in the freezing wind and rain. So he was in a dreadful mood even <u>before</u> Paul and Ben had their latest stonking argument. This one was about Doug Anderton. Doug's on holiday in Portugal at the moment with some lucky girl or other, and Ben was hoping to get a letter from him before he left, but it never came. For some reason Paul

brought this up again today and said he wasn't surprised.
He said he always knew Doug would drop Benjamin like a
stone as soon as they left school. He thinks Doug is ruthless
and calculating. (But I know he only thinks that because
Doug embarrassed him once by printing one of his private
letters in the magazine. And a very silly letter it was too.)
Then he carried on twisting the knife by saying that Ben
was kidding himself if he thought any of his friends were
going to stay in touch. No one really stays in touch after
school, he said. And he even mentioned Cicely and said Ben
would probably never see her again either.

Ben didn't say anything back but I've never seen him look
so upset. I thought he was going to cry. He is still like that
now, just along from me on the sofa, and I can tell he is
thinking hard about something, trying to make a decision. I
don't know what it is.

I'm going to have to borrow an extra page from Ben's
pad, and paste it in afterwards, I think.

Anyway, now for the funny thing. Dad has just come in
in the most deplorable condition. There is no proper sewerage
in the caravan, just a chemical loo filled with urine and poo,
not to mince my words or beat about the bush. Every second
day Dad has to go to the cess-pit at the end of the field and
empty the contents of the loo into it. What a job! Only today
the wind was so strong that it blew him over. It blew him
right over while he was tipping the stuff out and the next
thing he knew he was covered from head to foot in the
family business, as it were.

Well, I thought his language was bad enough yesterday,
but now I realize that was nothing. He stood there in the
awning, dripping wet and ponging to high heaven, with the
wind still howling around like a force ten gale (which I
believe is exactly what it is), and he was screaming at Mum,
"This is supposed to be a f—king holiday, people are
supposed to relax on holiday, they're supposed to lie in the
f—king sunshine and drink cocktails, and here I am, soaked

*to the skin and covered in s—t, and we're in the middle of a
f—king monsoon . . ." and on and on like that for about half
an hour.*

*Well I'm sorry but I had to see the funny side. I became
completely hysterical, in fact. And that got Mum started, as
well. Dad was horrified. He couldn't believe we were
laughing at him in that state, only we weren't really, we
were just laughing at the whole terrible situation we were
in, and the way the holiday was turning into a complete
disaster.*

*Perhaps women are better at making a joke out of things
like that. Benjamin certainly hasn't seen the funny side. Just
now—about five minutes ago—he stood up and said, "Dad's
right. This is no way to spend a holiday. I'm getting out of
here."*

What does he mean by that?

*9:40 p.m. Well, now we know. Benjamin has gone. He
said he wanted to go home to Birmingham so Dad drove
him off to Pwllheli station and put him on the train. It's a
rotten journey, you have to make about three connections, I
hope he's all right. It's still teeming down out there. He's
probably done the right thing but I wish he hadn't left me in
the lurch, all alone here with no one but Agatha Christie for
company.*

*Come on, Lois, you can do it! You've been through worse!
What was it Dr. Saunders used to say?*

*

27

The storm raged on. Darkness fell and Benjamin could barely see more than five yards in front of his face. The narrow, winding lanes seemed endless. There were no cars any more, and he hadn't seen another walker for at least an hour. He was hopelessly lost. In the unbroken darkness, as the sharp arrows of rain drove stingingly into his eyes, he couldn't have said whether the mountains lay to his left, or the ocean to his right. Even these, the most obvious landmarks, had been obliterated by the elements.

After his father had put him on the train at Pwllheli, Benjamin had waited for the car to drive away and then swiftly disembarked. He was not going back to Birmingham at all. He was going to find Cicely.

He walked back along the Abersoch road for fifteen minutes and then managed to find a lift to Llanbedrog in a farmer's van. The weather seemed to be getting steadily worse, if that were possible, and he stopped for a while at the Glen-y-Weddw pub, hoping to allow time for the rain to die down a little. But it merely thickened and intensified. At about eight o'clock Benjamin began climbing the hill towards Mynytho. He was walking straight into the gale so it took almost an hour to reach the village, and by then it was quite dark. He continued on the road towards Botwnnog but soon plunged down a steep, single-track lane to the left, which he took to be the direction of the sea. Before long he realized that this had been his first mistake.

How long ago had he left the pub? Two hours? Three? And why had he not passed through Llangian or reached the grassy lowlands which led to Porth Neigwl? He had made a wrong turning somewhere, that much was clear. Surely this lane *had* to lead to a farm, or cottage, or village; surely there had to be some other living creature in this drenched and blasted spot, someone who could show him the way or even suggest a place to sleep for the night.

And then a living creature did jump out of the gloom. Three of them, to be precise, three terrified sheep running at full gallop down the lane towards him, their frantic bleating the first sound he had heard, apart from the wind and rain, since leaving the Botwnnog road. Benjamin leaped to one side, just as startled as they were by this freakish encounter. He looked back over his shoulder and quickened his pace, interpreting their sudden appearance as a bad omen. If even the sheep got lost on a night like this, what chance did he have?

After walking for another two or three miles, he came upon an empty barn at the side of the road, its broken doors flapping madly in the wind. He looked inside. There were a few scraps of straw on the earth floor; just enough to sleep on, if he gathered them all together. But it wasn't an appealing prospect. He was shivering violently, now, and didn't relish the thought of trying to sleep in his sopping clothes, with the wind pounding the walls of the barn and those doors banging all night. He threw his rucksack down on the floor and stood for a few minutes in the doorway, looking out into the storm. There was no sign of it fading. The blackness of the night remained absolute. It was easy to imagine that he was the last man on earth.

But then Benjamin felt a surge of hope: he glimpsed a pinprick of light in the distance. It had just appeared, he was sure of that. Somebody, somewhere, must have only recently switched a lamp on. In another moment it could go out again. He must head towards it as quickly as possible.

He grabbed his rucksack and began to run along the lane, but he was too tired to keep this up for long. He settled into a brisk, breathless stride and felt his heart thumping complainingly against his ribcage. The light vanished periodically and re-emerged again; Benjamin took this to mean that it was partly hidden by trees. And then a mountainous bulk rose without warning in front of him and the road began to trace a steep upward incline. The trees were to his right, a dense cluster of them; an unusual feature, on this peninsula, where the landscape tended to be sparse and unwooded. Now there was a thunder-crack, followed by a jagged flash of lightning which flickeringly revealed the ocean, heaving with massive and angry breakers, only a quarter of a mile to his left. This, then, was Porth Neigwl, or as the English called it, Hell's Mouth. He could not be far from Rhîw now. Buoyed up by this realization, he hurried onwards up the hillside with redoubled energy; the light had disappeared now but he was sure he could find it again. And Benjamin only had to walk a few more hundred yards when he saw what he was looking for: a rough wooden sign, nailed to a tree at the entrance to a long drive, bearing the two words "PLAS CADLAN."

He did not know it, but he was on the point of collapsing from exhaustion. He tripped and stumbled along the drive which for most of its considerable distance felt more like a tunnel, so low and tangled were the many overhanging branches. Torn from its tree by the buffeting wind, one branch struck him on the head and almost knocked him out cold as he passed by. Then the lamplight flared up again, much closer and to his left this time, and although it was blocked out at once by a row of unkempt rhododendron bushes, within another minute Benjamin found himself standing by a tiny wrought-iron gate. He pushed it open and it shrieked in the dark. He felt gravel beneath his feet, strode keenly onwards, then missed his footing and fell over almost immediately, landing in the middle of something angular and prickly: perhaps a miniature box-hedge. He stood up and tried to calm himself. There were scratches on his hand and he sucked on one of them, tasting warm blood.

Treading more carefully, he followed the narrow gravel path

as best he could, rounded three or four corners and came at last upon the house. His heart surged with joy. There were lights in two of the downstairs windows, and an oil lamp burned outside, illuminating a long covered walkway that ran the length of the house and led to a small cottage or annexe at its furthest end.

He had found it. He was there. The nightmare was over.

Benjamin hammered at the door and when it was pulled back found himself staring into one of the most frightening faces he had ever seen. A tall man in his fifties or sixties, his grey hair wild and unruly, his skin weatherworn like tanned hide, an astounding white beard reaching almost to his waist, stood on the doorstep glaring at him with manifest hostility and suspicion in his fiery brown eyes. The first words he spoke to Benjamin were in Welsh; and when they produced no response he barked:

"Well, come on then? Who are you and what do you want?"

"I'm a friend of Cicely's," Benjamin stammered.

"You're *what*?"

"Glyn! Glyn!" The reproving tones came from a small and motherly woman of about the same age who came padding up behind him. "Can't you see the boy's wringing wet?" She took Benjamin by the arm. "Come in, my boy, come in."

"I'm a friend of Cicely's," Benjamin repeated, as he stood dripping on the flagstones. It was the only thing he could think of. It was his calling card.

"I'm Beatrice, Cicely's aunt," said the woman. "And this is her Uncle Glyn."

The man glowered at him again; but this time, it seemed to be by way of greeting.

"Glyn, run and fetch this boy some whisky."

They gave him a tumbler of whisky, neat, and he drank it much too fast. Then they sat him by the glowing hearth in the kitchen and instead of feeling better he began to shiver even more uncontrollably. They gave him another glass of whisky, this time mixed with ginger and hot water. And then, presumably, they must have put him to bed.

. . .

When Benjamin awoke, he was dead and gone to heaven. There could be no doubt about that. He had never actually tried to imagine what heaven would be like, but he recognized it as soon as he saw it. Or heard it, rather, for the first thing he noticed about heaven was the sound: the sound of birdsong. He couldn't still be in Llŷn, because you never heard real birdsong on the peninsula: only the lonely wailing of gulls. But the birds here were singing in a mellifluous, unending chorale, to which the humming of bees provided a tunefully droning counterpoint. It was the most beautiful sound he had ever heard. Heaven felt good, as well: he was lying on crisp, thick, newly laundered cotton sheets. Sun was streaming in through the window in shafts of white gold, which rippled slightly as they passed through the white lace curtains which swung and drifted in a gentle breeze. Cool currents of air played on his face. In the background, waves broke softly on a distant shore.

Benjamin had never tried to imagine what heaven was like; but he knew, for certain, that it had one essential component, one criterion that simply had to be met. Cicely had to be there.

And here she was. Sitting at the end of his bed, gazing intently at him as his eyes struggled to open. She was dressed all in white, too, a loose white summer dress, and her hair was long and golden, she had grown it long again, and she was paler than ever and more slender than ever and the blue of her eyes seemed more fragile than ever before.

So it was true, then. Heaven existed; and he was the latest arrival.

"Hello, Benjamin," said Cicely.

Benjamin sat up in bed. He seemed to be wearing a nightshirt that didn't belong to him. "Hello," he said.

"You came to find me."

"It looks that way."

"Yes." Cicely smiled. "I knew that you would." Benjamin seemed surprised by this, so she added: "What I mean is—I knew that if anybody came, it would be you. Here—"

She took a cup of tea from his bedside table, and offered it to him. The tea in heaven tasted much the same as anywhere else, it transpired. A little too milky, if anything. All right, so this wasn't heaven after all. Benjamin didn't mind. Cicely kissed him on the forehead and whispered, "I'm so glad that you're here," and he knew that he was somewhere else altogether, somewhere even better.

The smell of fried bacon drifted out of the kitchen, through the cavernous hallway, up and around the ancient oak staircase and into every bedroom, bathroom, study, parlour, laundry room and attic in Plas Cadlan. It drew Benjamin, newly bathed and clothed, swiftly down to the kitchen, a room which never saw much sunlight, and where he found Cicely already sitting at the vast dining table with her uncle and aunt. They served him fried eggs, black pudding, coarse and delicious cuts of bacon and challengingly large slices of soft white bread.

"I'm afraid we are going to have to disillusion our niece," said Beatrice, beaming with satisfaction as Benjamin laid into his breakfast. "She's under the impression that you came all the way from Birmingham to see her."

Apparently, even in his state of near-delirium the night before, Benjamin had managed to offer some rambling explanation about being on holiday with his family near by. He now elaborated on this for the benefit of Cicely, who had been in bed at the time.

"I don't care where he came from," she told her aunt. "It's just so nice that he's here. Benjamin is the kindest and most thoughtful of all my friends."

"And is this your first visit to Llŷn?" Beatrice asked.

"Oh, no." At once Benjamin felt the need to stake some sort of proprietorial claim. "This is a kind of second home to my family. We've been coming here for years. Every year, to the same caravan site."

There was now a minor eruption as Cicely's uncle slammed his teacup down on the table and let out what could only be described as a snarl. It seemed that he was also on the point of speaking, but his wife warned him off by murmuring, "Glyn! Glyn!," and explaining to Benjamin:

"My husband has strong feelings about caravans. They are one of the many things that he has strong feelings about."

Shortly afterwards, Glyn muttered something about going to his studio, and left through the back door. Benjamin finished his breakfast and started to wash the dishes while Cicely dried.

"Did I make a *faux pas* back there?" he wanted to know, after Beatrice had disappeared upstairs.

"Don't worry about it. Pretty much every *pas* is *faux* as far as my uncle's concerned." She put down her tea towel and seized him around the waist. "Oh, Benjamin, it's *wonderful* to see you. You've no *idea*." He returned the embrace, but rather stiffly, as was his way. She drew back a little. "I'm sorry, I'm being frightfully tactile today, aren't I?" Resuming her drying, she said: "It's been so lonely here. I mean, they've both been great, but it's been four weeks now. I was starting to go out of my mind."

"Have you been *very* ill?" Benjamin asked.

"Oh, I don't know what happened. Everything just got a bit much, I suppose. I came down with flu or something and then I just couldn't shake it. It seemed to get worse and worse. I don't know if it was the exams, or that awful business with Mr. Ridley. I was mad to get involved in that. Insane. Oh—"

"Don't say it," Benjamin pleaded, and put a soapy finger to her lips.

"Say what?"

"That you're a terrible, terrible person."

"How did you know that was what I was going to say?"

Benjamin just laughed, and asked, "Well, do you want to hear what's been going on at school while you've been away?"

"Yes, of course I do."

And so he started to tell her; and it ended up taking most of the morning.

After lunch, Beatrice showed him around the house and the garden. She was especially proud of the garden.

"We were ready for that rain," she said, leading him across a small, well-trimmed lawn which was still notably wet underfoot, despite the afternoon sunshine. "I'm sorry if it spoiled your holiday, but for some of us it was a prayer answered. Anyway, they say it's going to be dry now for the rest of the week. What do you think of my buddleia?"

Benjamin said that it was very nice. As indeed it was.

"There's a special atmosphere here," he ventured. "It feels very different from the rest of the peninsula. Like another world."

"Yes. These bays," said Beatrice, gesturing at the ranks of bottle-green-leaved trees which climbed up the hill towards them and rose to a height of thirty or forty feet, "screen us from the rest of Llŷn and also provide us with shelter which other gardeners on the peninsula don't have. This is why I've been able to do so much here. Creating this garden has been the work of twenty years."

"I like your roses," said Benjamin, pleased to have found a flower that he could identify.

"In a moment we shall come to the herb garden. This walk-way is called Glyn's Walk. He loves the view of Porth Neigwl from here. These plants are among his favourites, too: forsythia, mallow, japanese azalea."

"Cicely tells me that your husband is a sculptor," Benjamin said, ducking to make his way between the plants, which grew close together on either side of the path.

"Do you think she's recovered?" asked Beatrice, ignoring this overture. "I find it so hard to tell, with Cicely. She is such a frail thing anyway. So pale."

"She seems in very good spirits," he said, non-committally.

"Your arrival has had a very salutary effect, I must say. I do hope you can stay a few more days. Note how the azalea here is covered with clematis orientalis. We have eucalyptus, as well. To your left. I had not realized that there was anyone among her schoolfriends of whom she was quite so fond. She has had some very unsuitable liaisons in the last few years. It would be nice to think of her spending time with someone suitable, for a change."

Benjamin heard a note of almost maternal anxiety in these words, and was intrigued, because he knew that Beatrice and Cicely were not blood relatives.

"Where's her mother at the moment?" he asked.

"In America. She has been there for two months now, in rehearsals. None of this might have happened, of course, if she had not been quite so . . . absent. However, that is not for me to say." They were now approaching an outbuilding, a low-roofed cottage from which the sounds of hammering and chiselling were clearly audible. "We must not disturb my husband," Beatrice said, walking on hastily. "He will be going to France next week. The civic authorities in Nantes have commissioned something for a most important public space."

From these hints Benjamin gathered that Cicely's uncle had a considerable reputation. She had never mentioned him before, but then she had always been offhand about her family and their various achievements, which to Benjamin seemed remarkable. Her father, he knew, was an architect, although he lived in London and rarely saw his daughter more than once or twice a year. Her mother (who had remarried several times) was a successful actress whose work kept her out of the country more often than not. It seemed to Benjamin that these people inhabited, as if by right, a world into which he would only ever be able to peer yearningly, his face pressed up against the glass.

"There," said Beatrice, turning to admire the view. They had walked as far as the wrought-iron gate, and could now see most of the house itself, the steep line of its high-pitched roof rising proudly out of the hollow in which it had been built. "It's a fine prospect, isn't it? The south-west gable never fails to delight."

Benjamin couldn't tell which gable she was drawing his attention to. Come to that, he wasn't too sure what a gable was. He didn't think that his parents' house in Longbridge had gables. He remembered his family, suddenly—almost for the first time that day—and found it bizarre, almost unthinkable, that their caravan was still pitched only a few miles away, on Cilan Head at the far end of Porth Neigwl.

"Is Plas Cadlan very old?" he asked, wanting to get the image out of his head.

"It was built in the late sixteenth century," said Beatrice, leading him back towards the front door, "and enlarged by the Victorians. We took it on twenty years ago, after it had been derelict for some time. It was an enormous task."

"I've always dreamed of living in a place like this."

"Of course. Well, perhaps you will, one day. Cicely tells me that you're going to be a writer."

"I hope so. Or a composer, maybe."

"Really? You have many strings to your bow."

This reminded Benjamin of something: a resolution he had taken earlier this morning, and which he was now ready to put into action. The time was right, at long last, to play Cicely one of his tapes. He found her sitting on a wooden bench in the back garden, high above the house, looking over the roofs and chimneys of Plas Cadlan and its outbuildings towards the sea as it swept into Porth Neigwl, placid and unthreatening this afternoon.

"Has Aunty been boring you?" she asked.

"Not at all. I love this place. It's magical—I feel like I've finally been let in on the most perfectly kept secret . . ." Cicely smiled, and clasped his hand as he sat next to her. It seemed the most natural thing in the world to sit together on the bench like this, hand in hand. How could they have moved so quickly on to this new level, this immeasurably higher plane, in just a few hours? "Cicely," he said, "is there a tape recorder in this house?"

"A tape recorder?"

"A cassette player."

"Yes, I think so. Uncle Glyn likes to listen to music while he's working."

"Do you think we could borrow it for a while?"

"I'm sure we could." She looked at him, her eyes bright with curiosity, as if she would never stop being surprised by him. "I'll go and ask."

Fifteen minutes later, they were sitting up in Cicely's room, on either side of the bed, with Glyn's portable radio-cassette player on the coverlet between them. Benjamin had fetched his rucksack and retrieved the tape which contained the series of pieces he had called *Seascape Nos. 1–7*. It was getting on for two years since he had recorded them. The tape was almost worn out, he had listened to them so often in that time.

"Are you going to tell me what this is all about?" Cicely asked, as he slotted the cassette into the machine.

Benjamin wound the tape forward about nine minutes, to the beginning of *Seascape No. 4*, then took a deep breath and said: "I write music, you know. Did I ever tell you that?"

"No," said Cicely, wonderingly.

"Well, I do. And I thought . . . I thought you might like to hear some of it."

"Yes. Of course. I'd love to."

"The thing is, the piece I'm going to play you . . . It's sort of—about you."

Cicely blushed, and asked: "But how can a piece of music be *about* someone?"

"Well, I was thinking about you when I wrote it. That's all I mean, I suppose. You inspired it, if you like."

"How . . . extraordinary. And when did you write it?"

"About two years ago," he said. He pressed the play button and soon heard the onset of extra hiss that signalled the start of the recording.

"But . . ." Cicely was thinking about this, and it made no sense. "But we didn't even know each other two years ago."

Then the music began and she fell politely silent.

Benjamin tried not to let her see how nervous he was feeling, in case it spoiled her enjoyment. He tried not to look at her as she was listening, in case it made her self-conscious. But some of the time, he couldn't help himself. They seemed like the longest four minutes of his life. The recording quality was terrible, he could admit that now. His performance was dire, too: all those bum notes! Why hadn't he played it again, until he got it right? How could he have listened to it so many times since, over and over, always so uncritically? And it seemed now to express nothing of his feelings for Cicely. Only the dimmest echo of the dimmest echo. He would need a symphony orchestra, and the lyrical gifts of a Ravel or Sibelius, to convey a fraction of what he now realized that he felt for her.

And yet, she was moved by this offering, he could see that. As it drifted on towards its ambiguous conclusion, he saw no loss of attention, no embarrassment on Cicely's face. Her lips were slightly parted and she was even swaying, very gently, to the rhythm. And then Benjamin tautened with excitement as the key moment had its desired effect: the one stroke, he thought, of real harmonic interest, at which precise point Cicely turned to him and said, over the closing chords:

"Oh—what was that?"

"Just a simple key change," he explained, proudly, "from G minor to D. Only you're not expecting it."

"No, I meant that noise. In the background."

"Noise?"

"It sounded like a cat."

The piece concluded and Benjamin switched off the tape.

"Yes, it was a cat. His name's Acorn. He was locked out of the room when I made the recording."

"I didn't know you had a cat. What sort is he?"

"He's not ours. He belongs to my grandparents."

Cicely told him how much she had liked the music, how touched she had been by it, and he could see that she was telling the truth. All the same, he was disappointed. He shouldn't have played it to her. It had been the wrong thing to do.

"I'd better take this back to Uncle Glyn," she said, picking up the tape recorder. "Oh, and by the way—" (she paused by the door) "—he wants us both to come out to the pub with him tonight. I've been here for four weeks and he hasn't asked me once, but now that you're here, he wants us both to go. It's the most amazing thing: I think he really likes you."

Benjamin was worried about this trip to the pub. Supposing they went to one of the places his family used, in Abersoch or Llanengan? But he had no cause for anxiety, as it turned out. Glyn was unswerving in his desire to keep away from holiday-makers, and the venue he had chosen was a good twenty-minute drive into one of the most remote and unvisited spots on the peninsula. They passed through Aberdaron, where the poet R. S. Thomas still lived and worked as the parish priest ("A great man; a very great man," Glyn informed them) and then wound their way slowly into the hills somewhere above Uwchmynydd. A few hundred yards off the coast lay the rocky outcrop of Ynys Enlli, Bardsey Island, once a monastic settlement and legendary place of pilgrimage. As they left the car they could just make it out in the blue, smoky dusk.

The building to which Glyn had brought them did not look like a pub at all. It seemed to be a small farmer's cottage, white-washed and partly thatched. Five sheep were nibbling at the thin grass outside the door, and there were no other cars parked near by, or any sign to imply that members of the public were wel-come. Inside there was no bar, just a pair of tables and an enor-mous oak cask set against the stone wall, from which the customers—if that was the right word—simply drew their glass-fuls of red, yeasty, foam-capped beer whenever they wanted. No money seemed to be changing hands.

There were three men already sitting at one of the tables when they arrived. When they saw Glyn they rose to their feet; there was much back-slapping, hand-shaking and exchanging of greetings in Welsh. The men said "Good evening" to Ben and Cicely, as well, but it was then made apparent, firmly but subtly, that they were expected to sit at the other table by themselves. This seemed to be the most sensible arrangement all round. At the four friends' table an elaborate game of cribbage began to take shape, interspersed with a good deal of conversation, some of it very boisterous, some of it conducted in quiet, earnest voices, with the occasional pointed glance towards the two English interlopers.

"I've seen these fellows before," Cicely said to Benjamin, sipping gamely on her beer and screwing her eyes up at the thick tartness of it. "They come to the house sometimes, usually after Aunty's gone to bed."

"What are they talking about?"

"Politics, I expect. They're fierce nationalists, all of them."

Ben was shocked. He had heard about the Welsh National-ists on the news. They burned people's holiday cottages down.

"Is your uncle a nationalist?"

"Of course he is. He's always giving quotes about it to the English newspapers and getting into all sorts of trouble. He supports the IRA as well."

Benjamin's eyes widened even further. For years, ever since the pub bombings or even before the pub bombings, he had heard nothing—whether from his family, his friends, the teach-ers at school, the politicians on the television—nothing but vili-fication and contempt being poured on the IRA. He had heard them being called everything from child-murderers to lunatics and psychopaths. It had simply never occurred to him before that there might be another way of looking at it. Glyn might be terrifying, but he was also Cicely's uncle, and she was obviously fond of him, so there could be no doubt, in Benjamin's mind, that he was essentially on the side of the angels. And yet this man supported the IRA! The people who had killed Malcolm and caused Lois such dreadful suffering. How could that pos-sibly be? Was the world even *more* complicated than he had imagined—weren't there even *any* arguments with only one side to them? How on earth did people like Doug keep hold of their certainties, their clearly defined, confidently held political posi-tions, in a world like this?

"The IRA hurt my sister," he said to Cicely. It was a simple statement of fact; the best he could do.

"How is she, Ben?"

He sighed. "Oh, not so bad. Quite jolly, these last few days, in fact. Mum and Dad are hoping she can go back to sixth-form college in the next two or three years, get her A-levels, then maybe think about university."

"It's been a long time, hasn't it? Nearly four years."

"Well, you know, there've been setbacks. You still have to tread pretty carefully around her. Just the other day Paul upset her again."

"What happened?"

"We'd put the table up outside the caravan in the evening, and we were all going to have some sausages. Dad had done them on the barbecue. And then—you know this terrible fight I was telling you about, between Steve and Culpepper, on the last day of term?—well, Paul started asking me about it. And he went *on* and *on*. He didn't want to know what it had been about, or anything like that, he just wanted all the gory details: 'Was his nose broken? How much blood was there? Did he fracture his skull?,' all that sort of thing. Well Lois can't handle that kind of stuff. It reminds her too much of what Malcolm must—must have looked like. So she flipped. She started screaming 'Stop it! Stop it! Stop it!' at Paul and then she threw her food at him and went inside and cried for about two hours. The next day she wouldn't get out of bed all morning, and we all went into Pwll-heli to do some shopping, all except Dad who stayed there to look after her. And apparently at about lunchtime she just got up and got dressed and announced she was going out for a walk. She was gone the whole afternoon. Of course we were all worried sick but I knew she'd come back, in the end. And she did. But she said afterwards that she didn't remember anything about it and she couldn't tell us where she'd been or anything like that."

Cicely took his hand and squeezed it. It was more than a gesture of comfort.

"I'm so sorry, Benjamin. Poor Lois."

He went to refill their glasses and then asked Cicely to tell him about her mother. He hadn't known that she was Welsh, for one thing.

"Well, she doesn't make nearly so much of it as Uncle Glyn. All her husbands have been from different countries and I think she rather likes the idea of having no nationality at all. Anyway, at the moment she's in New York and everything's America, America, America." Cicely lowered her voice. "The fact is, Ben, this whole Welsh business is all a bit of an exaggeration. Glyn and Mummy were born in Aberystwyth but they moved to Liverpool when they were small and spent most of their lives in England. He only got interested in Wales again when he heard about this house and found out that he could get it dirt cheap and live the life of a country gentleman. As for Aunty, her family are all from Tunbridge Wells. Of course that doesn't stop him from meaning what he says. You just shouldn't be intimidated by it, that's all."

Benjamin thought that Cicely was starting to look tired, and Glyn noticed this too, before very long. He said goodbye to his friends, who seemed to be settled in for the night, and took the two of them back to Plas Cadlan in the car. Benjamin sat in the front passenger seat.

"Well then, Englishman, what did you think of a taste of real Welsh beer? You don't get that in the tourist pubs or on your—" (he dredged the words up from the back of his throat like a ball of phlegm) "—caravan site."

"Don't call him 'Englishman,'" said Cicely. "It sounds incredibly rude."

"You are English, aren't you?" Glyn said, glancing at him.

"Of course."

"Well then, that's what I'll call you. You're not ashamed to be called an Englishman, I suppose?"

"Should I be?"

"Personally, I don't like the English. And funnily enough, neither do the friends I was talking to just now. Do you know why?" Without waiting for an answer, he went on: "I'll tell you, then: the Welsh have hated the English for as long as anyone

can remember, and they'll carry on hating them until the English
leave them alone and stop interfering in their affairs. They've
hated them ever since the thirteenth century, when Edward the
First invaded Wales and his armies slaughtered the women and
children and Llewellyn the Second was slaughtered too and laws
were passed which banned Welsh people from holding positions
of authority and English lords were put in place to govern them
and Welsh law was suppressed and replaced by English law and
English castles were built over the whole country and Welsh
people weren't allowed to live anywhere near them and Welsh-
men were continually sent off to the killing fields in France to
be slaughtered in wars which had nothing to do with them but
were mainly being paid for by Welsh taxes anyway. And then
they started to hate them even more at the beginning of the fif-
teenth century when Owain Glyn Dwr tried to lead the Welsh
to independence and restore to them a sense of nationhood, and
the English responded by turning the whole of North Wales
and Cardigan and Powys into a wasteland, burning the homes
and destroying the churches and even kidnapping thousands of
Welsh children and tearing them from their families and sending them away to England to be the servants of rich English
families." Glyn pulled over into a convenient passing space at
this point, and turned off the engine. His passion had been
getting the better of him and the car had been veering alarm-
ingly from side to side of the narrow road, so it was quite a relief
that he had stopped. "And all through this terrible time," he
resumed, "the Bardic tradition managed to keep the language
alive, the wonderful Welsh language which is the oldest language in these islands—did you even know that?—but then even
this, even our very language, our very identity, was taken away
from us in 1536 by Thomas Cromwell and his so-called Act of
so-called Union, which imposed the pale, sickly, enfeebled
English language on us and made it a crime even to conduct our
affairs in our own *language*, for pity's sake! That accursed Act
was no more an Act of Union than the one the English imposed
on the Scots in 1707, when they threatened to blockade all Scot-

tish trade if their terms were refused and forced the Scottish parliament to vote itself out of existence in return for a tiny sprinkling of Scottish MPs down in Westminster and a paltry bribe of a few hundred thousand pounds. 'We're bought and sold for English gold,' Robbie Burns wrote, and by God he was right! And then the English started doing to the Scots exactly what they'd always done to the Welsh, rigging the taxation system so that it was the hard-earned money of poor Scottish folk—weavers and miners—which was used to finance the imperial ventures of the English abroad. And so it remains to this day, with the North Sea oil revenues! And yet neither the Welsh nor the Scots have suffered so terribly from English rapacity and intransigence and ruthlessness as the Irish. Do you have any notion, have they taught you anything at all in that school of yours, about the horrors inflicted by the English upon the Irish during the reign of Elizabeth the First and the Protectorate of Oliver Cromwell? When Elizabeth undertook the plantation of Ireland in 1565, the country rose in rebellion, and her English generals competed with each other for the savagery with which they could butcher, hang, pillage, loot and massacre the innocent families of the native population. The lands of the victims and survivors alike were seized and given to Scottish settlers, and when there was another uprising in the 1640s it was crushed by Cromwell, and, after toying with the idea of total genocide, he decided just to transplant all the native Irish into the region bounded by the Shannon, and in the process thousands of them were either slaughtered or imprisoned or shipped out as slaves to the West Indies. For God's sake, after atrocities like that, does it surprise you that any Irishman of spirit still considers himself to be at war with the English, three centuries on? Does it surprise you that the Scots distrust you and the Welsh despise you? Do you think the native Indians of America, and the Maoris of New Zealand, and the aborigines of Australia and Tasmania will ever forgive you for all but exterminating them with murder and famine and disease? You don't fool the world, you know, not any more, with your oh-so-charming diffidence and politeness and English irony and English self-deprecation. Ask any free-thinking Welshman or Scotsman or Irishman what he thinks of the English and you will get the same answer. You are a cruel and bloody and greedy and acquisitive people. A nation of butchers and vagabonds. *Butchers and vagabonds*, I tell you!" At which point Glyn, who had been leaning forward in his driver's seat and clutching at the steering wheel until his fingers went white, sat back with a deep breath and demanded, "So: what do you say to *that*, Englishman?"

There was a long silence, while Benjamin pursed his lips, and chose his words carefully. "It's a point of view," he said.

Glyn started the car again and drove them home.

The following afternoon, an afternoon of cloudless, jet blue skies and tireless sunshine, an afternoon of impossible stillness where the buzzing of a fly amongst the heather could seem like an event of consequence, Benjamin and Cicely walked on the headland above Rhîw. The previous night, before going to their separate beds, they had kissed at the doorway to her room, and there had been no ambiguity about the kiss at all. Even Benjamin could decipher this one. And to make it even clearer for him, Cicely had whispered, "We've started something, now, haven't we?," before slipping into the darkness of her bedroom and looking back at him with one more quick and delighted smile.

He lay awake almost until dawn, his mind dancing with the knowledge of his new, unhoped-for good fortune.

Today they scrambled up towards the ragged escarpment of Creigiau Gwineu, which Uncle Glyn had told them was the site of a hill fort probably dating back to the Iron Age. It was hard to think of such things on a hot and silent afternoon, with the crested ocean rolled out before them on three sides. The descent from the fort to the clifftops was gentler. Benjamin took Cicely's hand and guided her along a sheep-path through the bristling gorse: he became agile and sure-footed in this place, realizing that the very texture of the ground in Llŷn was imprinted on his consciousness, from years of childhood walks, long bright evenings of happy exploration with Lois, his mother and father, his grandparents, even Paul. He didn't care what Glyn said: part of this peninsula belonged to him, in some sense.

Before reaching the edge of the cliffs they came upon a broad and well-worn path which clung low to the headland. Here they turned left and walked in the direction of Porth Neigwl. Just as the path started to curve inland, a wide, flat rock jutted out from the bracken. It was the perfect place to sit. There was just room for two people, provided that they wanted to sit as close to each other as possible.

Benjamin looked across the bay, this prodigious four-mile strand which had earned its name by luring countless seamen to their deaths over the centuries, but which this afternoon, once again, looked almost kindly. The majesty of the prospect, conse-crated now by the presence of Cicely, filled him with a mysteri-ous, indefinable gladness.

"This time last year," he said, "I was looking at a view like this with my grandfather. Just—" (he pointed across the bay to Cilan) "—just over there. And he said this extraordinary thing. He told me that no one could look at this view and not believe in the existence of God."

Cicely was silent for a few moments. "And do you agree with him?" she asked.

Benjamin was on the point of replying, when he checked himself. He had been about to say yes, unhesitatingly; but some-thing was stopping him. Some new layer of uncertainty. A rapid and complex chain of thought was set in motion, at the sudden end of which he said to Cicely: "Can I ask you something?"

"Of course you can. Anything."

"How can you forgive me?"

"Forgive you? Forgive you for what?"

"For writing that review."

"But Benjamin—that was simply ages ago."

"Yes, I know that; but still—it was so hurtful. So unkind."

"Not at all. I've told you this before: it was the best thing anyone could have done for me. I was never any good at acting. I was just doing it because my mother wanted me to, and because it fitted in with some stupid self-image I had. You cured me of that. That's what it was, literally: a cure. And I don't believe you did it out of malice. You were already writing music out of . . . out of love for me—I know that now—and I think that's why you wrote the review, as well."

"Out of love?"

"Yes, I think so. To show me to myself. That's what love *is*, if you like. It's a condition in which . . . in which people help each other to see the truth about themselves."

"Yes," said Benjamin. "Yes, you're right."

She had answered his question. In his new closeness to Cicely, he was already discovering a truer self: and that self was not sure, not sure at all, whether God existed or not. It seemed he was about to be saddled now with an even more doubting self than the one he had lived with before.

"I don't know," he admitted to Cicely. "I don't know whether I agree with Grandpa or not."

"Christianity isn't for me," she said decisively. "I think the Eastern religions have a lot to teach us, don't you? And anyway, I believe the same God is probably at the bottom of every religion. What does that make me—a pantheist?"

"A pantheist is someone who sees God in everything. I think my grandfather may be a pantheist, actually." Poor Grandpa. He was bedridden now, and in constant pain. Benjamin shook off the morbid thoughts that were beginning to press in on him. "All I know," he said, "is that I love this place very much, and that it feels very much bound up with . . . my future." Cicely looked curiously at him, not understanding. He didn't understand either. "My story will end here," he said, slowly, but that was no better. "Sorry: that sounds so portentous."

She leaned her head on his shoulder and for a while they said nothing. But she was thinking about his last words. "Where on earth will *my* story end?" she wondered aloud. "I don't really have a home. I don't feel at home in Birmingham; or anywhere else, to tell the truth. Perhaps it'll be America."

"Why America?" Benjamin asked.

Her voice faltered. "Because that's where I'm going next." She felt Benjamin tense rigid beside her, and turned to him with eyes full of sorrow for the pain she was about to cause him. "Oh, it's not for ever, Ben. Just for a few months."

"A few *months*?"

"Just while my mother's doing this play in New York. It's an off-Broadway thing, it might even close after a week or two. I miss her terribly, Benjamin. It's a good opportunity. We'll stay in Manhattan, and have weekends on Long Island . . ."

"What about your exams? I thought you were going back to school."

"Not until after Christmas." She stood up, and drew Benjamin with her. She pressed her body tightly into his and he could feel her quick breath, her beating heart. "Look, Ben, I've made lots of stupid mistakes with men in the past. You're not a mistake. You're the first one. The first and the last and the only. What's happened between us here, it's just the beginning, don't you see? We're going to have fabulous times together, you and me. Fabulous, unbelievable times. We're *so* lucky, so very very lucky, to have found each other. We're so *young*, Ben, we're so young and already we *know*! We're the luckiest people in the world, you and I! I'm not going to throw that away. Nothing on earth is going to make me throw that away. What's a few months, a few months apart, compared to what we've got ahead of us? It's nothing, Benjamin. Nothing at all."

He smoothed back the hair from her forehead, and said, "Will you write to me?," and she said, "Every day," and in her eyes he could see two oceans reflected, and in his eyes she could see the swelling of tears, but even through his tears Benjamin felt a monstrous, divine happiness consume him, knowing at last what it was to love and be loved.

28

When Benjamin let himself into his parents' empty house the following afternoon, the first thing he saw lying on the doormat was a letter containing his exam results. He opened it up and found that he had achieved the highest possible grades in every subject.

The telephone rang. It was his grandmother.

"Where have you been? We've been calling you non-stop."

"Sorry, Grandma. I've been out a lot. How's Grandpa?"

"A bit better. Sitting up today. He sends his love."

Benjamin told her about his grades. He was glad to have somebody to tell. After he had told his grandmother he phoned Philip and told him. Philip himself had done almost as well. He would be able to go to Bristol in the autumn, no problem.

"What about Steve?" Benjamin asked.

Philip sighed. "He failed physics. Failed it outright. And he only got a D and C on the others."

"So what does that mean?"

"It means no university'll take him to do physics now. He'll have to sit them all again next year."

"And Culpepper?"

"One A, one B and one C. But the A was in physics, so basi-cally, he got what he needed. He'll scrape through." They were both glumly silent. "Life stinks, doesn't it?"

After what seemed to be a decent interval, Benjamin said: "Well, anyway, *we* should celebrate. You and me."

"Yes—and Claire. And Emily. How about tonight?"

"Not tonight: tomorrow," said Benjamin. "Tonight, I've got some dirty work to do."

He hung up and looked through the rest of the post. Most of it was pretty boring stuff, but there was one thing that made him laugh. Apparently the strike at the Grunwick factory was over at last. The strikers had been defeated, according to the newspapers: but at least his father's holiday photos from Skagen had arrived, finally, almost two years after he had sent them off to be developed.

Benjamin's dirty work consisted of taking Jennifer for their last drink at The Grapevine. He told her the story of his family's catastrophic trip to Wales and she laughed a lot. She had a throaty, slightly salacious laugh and a reliable sense of humour. He realized now that these were among the many things he liked about her. Even so, when they had finished exchanging news about holidays and exam results, he put his Guinness down on the table with careful emphasis and said: "Listen, Jennifer. I think we should call it a day, the two of us."

"Yes," she answered, cheerfully. "Of course we should."

Benjamin was thoroughly taken aback by this. He had expected some weeping at the very least. "I just think," he explained, wondering if she had really taken in what he was saying, "I just think we've reached the end of the road."

"Come off it, Ben: we never even found the road, did we? We had nothing in common, for one thing. I never learned to tell my Debussy from my Delius or my Beckett from my Baudelaire. I was boring you silly."

"No you weren't."

"Be honest with me, Benjamin. We owe each other that, at least."

"You might have sounded a *bit* upset," he protested.

"With university to look forward to? According to the prospectus there are a hundred and twenty-six rooms in my hall of residence; and every one of them's got its own wardrobe. That ought to keep me busy." She could tell that he was finding it hard to see the joke, so she admitted, reluctantly: "Yes, of course I'm upset. But don't look so tragic about it. Don't worry, Tiger—you'll find somebody else."

Benjamin saw the chance to regain some of his dignity. "I already have, as a matter of fact."

"Oh?" said Jennifer, in an offhand way which pleasingly failed to convince. "Anyone I know?"

"Yes, actually: it's Cicely."

Her reaction, again, was the last he had been expecting: there was a sudden gasp, and then her face drew itself into an expression he had never seen before, in all the months he had known her. She was looking at him with fondness and reproach and, above all, solicitude.

"Oh, Ben . . . *no*," she pleaded. "Not her. Not you and Cicely, for goodness' sake."

"Whyever not?" he asked. (Almost wanting to add: "Everyone else has been out with her.")

"Hasn't anyone ever warned you about Cicely? Haven't you noticed what she does to people? The way she chews them up and spits them out?"

He shook his head. "You don't know her. You don't know her the way I do."

"That," said Jennifer, after a short laugh, "is the stupidest thing I ever heard."

But she was never going to convince him. Benjamin wasn't in the market for common sense any more. The door had finally been flung open, the door that would take him out of his old life and into an infinitely richer one. Nothing that Jennifer could say would prevent him from stepping through. And nothing that anybody could say would ever unmake those moments he had shared with Cicely yesterday, as they had stood together on the headland and she had made her promise and he had looked into her eyes: eyes in which he saw reflected, twice over, the clear blue waters and gaping jaws of Porth Neigwl; Hell's Mouth; the very maws of doom.

Green Coaster

But are there moments in life worth purchasing with worlds, and moments so charged, so full of emotion that they become somehow timeless, like the moment when Inger and Emil sat on that bench in the rose garden and smiled at the camera, or when Inger's mother raised the Venetian blind to the very top of her high sitting-room window, or when Malcolm opened up his jeweller's box and was about to ask my sister to marry him (because he never did ask her, I know that now), and is this one of those moments, as I raise this glass of Guinness to my lips and think to myself that surely life can't get any better, it can only be downhill from here, so how can I prolong this moment, how can I stretch it, how can I make it last for ever, because I have been to Paradise Place and nothing else can ever compare with that, *et in Arcadia ego*, as somebody once said, I forget who, but perhaps it can be done, perhaps if I don't move, if I just hold the glass here, two inches from my mouth, and don't even look across at the bar, where Sam is buying me another, then it will last, and no, I won't even turn my head to look out of the window, either, to look at Cicely, my beautiful Cicely, my beautiful girlfriend—it's true, I know it sounds incredible, but it's true, that's what she is—because I don't need to look at her now, I know that I will see her again in a few hours, and in the meantime I can imagine her, I can imagine her walking away from Paradise Place and through the

concrete precincts of the library buildings and across
Chamberlain Square and into Victoria Square, the sway of her
long back, the air of thoughtful distraction, slight other-
worldliness, the way that she is never aware how other people
are looking at her, turning towards her irresistibly, magnetized,
how can she doubt herself when other people look at her this
way, how can she believe that she is anything other than a very
extraordinary person, but she doesn't even notice it, her
thoughts are elsewhere, I don't know where most of the time,
but I will fnd that out, it is one of the many things I will find
out in the years of knowing and loving her that I have to look
forward to, and then of course if my imagination fails me I
always have memory to fall back on, because I have memories
of Cicely now as well, amazing memories, and none more
amazing than what happened between us this morning, but I
will come to that carefully, slowly, every detail must be
savoured, and it starts, well, I suppose it starts with the very
first thing I was thinking this morning, can I remember what it
was, yes, I was thinking about Dickie's bag, bizarrely enough,
but wait a minute, there is something that comes before that,
the thing I was dreaming about, as is the way with dreams I
can't really remember it, it slipped away just as I was waking
up, but I can remember the policemen, there were rows and
rows of policemen in this dream, and I have nothing against
policemen as a rule but the sight of these men filled me with
dread, or filled the person in the dream with dread, am I the
same person that I dream about?, that is one of the great
unanswerables, but I can remember this feeling of dread, and it
was to do with the fact that I couldn't see the policemen's faces,
though I'm not sure if this was because they didn't have faces,
or because their faces were hidden by their helmets as they
stood there, heads bowed, ready to charge, hundreds and
hundreds of them now I come to picture it, or am I simply
making that up, I don't know, the clarity of it is fading, anyway,
but it was a sinister image, I think they were about to charge
into a crowd, truncheons in hand, to break up some

demonstration or other, in fact of course that is where the image comes from, it's because I was reading Doug's article this week, Doug's article for the *NME* about Blair Peach and what happened in Southall, that would explain it, good, and it was a terrible article, by which I don't mean it was badly written, it was brilliant from that point of view, like all of Doug's writing, but the things it described were terrible, unimaginable really, I wonder if he was exaggerating, somehow I can't help hoping that he was exaggerating, although it would reflect badly on him, so anyway, getting back to this morning, that was when I woke up, in the middle of this dream, something must have woken me, I think it may have been Mum shutting the door on her way out to the school, she teaches there now, what is it, four mornings a week, she is always happier when she is working, it matters to me that everybody should be as happy as I am, even though that is scarcely possible because I am after all the luckiest person in the world, and then, as soon as I woke up, something irrelevant popped into my mind, quite irrelevant, the way it often does, and within less than the fragment of a fraction of a splinter of a second, less time even than the moment I am trying to stretch now, I had forgotten about the policemen and I was thinking about Dickie's bag, which I haven't thought about for years, two or three years at least, and come to that I haven't thought about Dickie either, since he left school last summer, and by that time we weren't calling him Dickie, of course, any more than we were calling Steve Rastus, his name was Richard Campbell, but in the fourth form, I think it was, we used to call him Dickie, it must have been meant rudely, we were somehow implying that he was fey or effeminate or something, though I don't know why he should have been singled out in that respect, we all used to camp it up in those days, pretend to be queer or gay or whatever you want to call it, but so much of what we did now seems inexplicable, including picking on Richard Campbell, but the even stranger thing was how we all used to make a big joke out of Dickie's bag, who started it, I wonder, well, I would guess it was Harding, that always seems to be the safest assumption, though from what corner of his twisted mind he retrieved this one I shall never know, but let's assume it was Harding, at any rate, who decided that Dickie's bag should become not so much an object of derision but—and it sounds crazy, I'm fully aware of that—an object of sexual desire, a sex object if you like, and the way it worked was this, Dickie would arrive in the form room every morning, carrying his bag, which was an ordinary Adidas sports bag, in black vinyl, a bit battered, but almost identical to a hundred other bags which people brought into school every morning, and then the first person who saw him would shout out "Dickie's bag! Dickie's bag!," like a sort of hunting cry, and then everybody in the room would run towards Dickie and grab hold of his bag and snatch it away from him, and then they would fall upon it (why do I say they? I took part in this as well, so *we* snatched it away from him, *we* fell upon it) and what followed I can only describe as a kind of gang-rape, as the bag used to disappear beneath a sea of bodies and there would be a collective orgasmic groan and we would all take it in turns to hump Dickie's bag, there is no other word for it, while its owner looked on despairingly, resigned by now to this obscene daily insult to which he alone, for reasons which he could probably never fathom, seemed to be condemned, and I thought about this little ritual in bed this morning and I have to confess that a smile came to my face, more than a smile, actually, I found myself laughing, chuckling to myself in bed, laughing at the sheer vindictive, childish fun of it, and I also found myself wondering, as I wonder about so many of my schoolfriends these days, what Richard Campbell is doing now and how he is getting on at university and whether he will look back on what we used to do to his bag in twenty years' time and laugh about it himself, because the alternative, I suppose, is that it will have marked his character forever and turned him into a friendless sociopath or perhaps even a murderer or at the very least ensured that he will never be able to have a normal sex life, but

that's all in the future and don't think I'm not going to come to
that, don't think I'm going to be neglecting the future, but
right now I'm thinking about this morning, the feeling I had
when I woke up and I forgot about my dream and I allowed
those memories of Dickie's bag to shimmer through my head,
and then it suddenly occurred to me what a strange, expectant
atmosphere there was in the house, how quiet everything was,
because it was after nine o'clock, and Mum had gone to work
and Dad had gone to work and Lois had gone to work and
Paul would be at school, although he hadn't even been sleeping
there the night before, now I came to think of it, he was
staying over at a friend's house, which meant that his bedroom
was empty, except that it wasn't empty at all, and I should have
been going to work as well, but there was a good reason why I
wasn't, which was Cicely, needless to say, Cicely had stayed the
night with us last night, she had slept in Paul's bedroom and it
was the second time she had done this, but there was a crucial
difference this time, namely that *there was no one else in the house
with us this morning*, we had the house *entirely to ourselves*, so no
wonder it felt strange and expectant, and no wonder I had
decided that I was going to phone in sick and tell Martin that
I'd be taking the morning off, but even so there was no time to
lose, every second we had alone together was priceless, so I had
to think what I was going to do, I had to think how I was going
to handle this situation, because we've been apart a long time,
Cicely and I, eight months, eight long desolate months she's
been in New York with her mother, whose play was a huge
success, unfortunately for me, and although we wrote to each
other every week and I flew over there to be with them for a
few days in January, it's still been difficult, being back together
again, I can see that she is finding it hard to adjust, and perhaps
I have been making it too obvious, at times, that I am aware of
this, perhaps I have been too solicitous, too tentative, it's part
of my character, after all, oh yes, I am developing a tiny little
element of self-awareness at last, and not before time some
people might say (like Doug, for instance), but it meant that I

was not at all sure how to proceed this morning, at first, so I
ended up taking what some people (like Doug, for instance)
might have regarded as the safest route, I went downstairs and
made a cup of tea and took it up to her, yes, tea!, I'm sure
Uncle Glyn would have had something to say about that, the
multiplicity of uses which the English have found for the
humble cup of tea, how many emotions we manage to hide
behind it, how many subterfuges we manage to disguise with
it, and I suppose tea is a legacy of colonialism as well so he
would really have had a field day with that one, I'm sure, but
who cares, who cares what Uncle Glyn might have said, I was
not thinking about him, as I carried our two mugs up the
creaking stairs, it's the eleventh, the eleventh one that creaks
most loudly, how well you get to know your own house after
eighteen years, I suppose it's not so surprising, and I was
thinking about what I was going to say to Cicely when I woke
her up, I was thinking about words, as usual, I am a great man
for my words, I have come to believe that you can do almost
anything with words but I am also beginning to learn, at least
God, I hope so, it would not be before time, beginning to learn
that there are some situations in which words are not the most
important thing, there are some situations which call for
something beyond words, and those are the situations that
tend to confound me, as a rule, and so it was this morning,
when I pushed open the door of Paul's bedroom and came in
backwards with my two mugs of tea and set them down on his
bedside table and I was still trying to think of what I would say
to Cicely after I had woken her up, trying to get the words
right, and I can't even remember what they were, now, because
it turned out that she was awake already, I soon found that out,
she was wide awake and the first thing she did when I sat down
on the bed beside her was to sit up, and she was naked, oh,
God! she was completely naked, I was wearing my pyjamas, I
must have looked ridiculous, there is nothing alluring about
pyjamas, but this didn't seem to bother her, because she sat up
slowly, sleepily, and she draped her arms around my neck, her

bare arms, her wonderful bare arms, I could think about those
for a while, couldn't I, but I can't, my mind is racing on, and
her mouth was half open and she planted her lips against mine
and I could feel the touch of her breasts against my chest and
in all the years I have known Cicely because, my God, we have
known each other for more than two years now, nobody could
accuse us of rushing things, it had taken us long enough to get
to this point, but we were there now, we were on the very
threshold of Paradise Place, and in all the years I have known
Cicely this was the first time I had seen her body let alone
touched it, and I put my hand to her breast and the softness
and the smoothness of it were indescribable, and meanwhile
this kiss, she was kissing me so tenderly, we have kissed before,
many times, there was no shortage of kissing when I went to
see her in New York, that's for sure, but there was something
new about this one, as if all the kisses we had had before were
leading up to this one, as if all the moments we had spent
together, and how many have there been?—another of the
unanswerables, nobody knows what a moment is, how long it
lasts, you can't measure it, can't talk about it, an infinite
number, I suppose, we are in the realms of infinity—as if all
those moments, anyway, were suddenly rushing together,
converging, fusing into this one great explosive moment,
which began with her draping her arms around my neck and
lasted for how long, I don't know, I have no idea at all how
long we were in that bedroom together, in Paul's bed, beneath
his stupid posters, one of them a big picture of one of those
girls from *Charlie's Angels*, wearing a bikini and grinning
blankly, and the other, unbelievably, a picture of Margaret
Thatcher with the slogan "Vote Conservative!" underneath it,
yes!, I lost my virginity twice, in effect, once with an item of
luggage and once beneath a poster of Mrs. Thatcher, not the
most auspicious start to a sexual career, I must admit, but I
can't say that I gave her much attention this morning, during
those ten minutes or three hours or however long it was
because I swear to you that I have never in my life seen, and

never will see again, I'm convinced, anything as beautiful as what Cicely showed to me when she lay back in the bed and pulled away the duvet and held out her arms to me, there are simply no words to describe it, well, all right, there are, but they belong somewhere else, they have been claimed by Culpepper's magazines, they don't convey the loveliness, let alone the *mystery*, yes, that's the word, the mystery of what Cicely showed to me this morning and what I reached out to touch, because after slipping out of those absurd pyjamas, I reached out to touch her and when I did, when my amazed fingertips made their first contact with that place, Paradise Place, her face changed, I was watching her face, and she smiled, and made a noise, a tiny noise, something like a whisper, and she stirred among the bedclothes but I was looking at her smile, and it wasn't that she was smiling with pleasure, or happiness, it was a smile that went somehow beyond these things, and oh, I'm not saying that I'm the world's greatest lover, far from it, just ask Jennifer Hawkins, for one thing, I'm not saying that I can transport a woman to the pitch of ecstasy with one touch of my fingers, but with Cicely this morning there was something about our feelings for each other, something about the things that had passed between us, over the years, something about the time it had taken us to reach this point, that made it very different, I mean different for her, because this was really my first time but it wasn't her first time and yet afterwards she said to me that it was, in one sense, she said that it was her first time with somebody that she loved, and perhaps that's why she smiled so mysteriously, that word again, I keep coming back to it, when I touched her, touched her between the legs, and then crouched over her, and smelled her, and then tasted her, tasted her with the very tip of my tongue, and I can taste her still, yes, the taste of Cicely is still on my tongue, not alone now, not unmixed, I can taste Cicely and Guinness, and oh, I hope the taste of her never goes away, but I shall stop now, think of something else, come back later to my first taste of her, it is too good to think

about only the once, and now I am going to imagine Cicely
again, walking across Victoria Square as she must be at this
moment, yes, imagination and memory, that's it, those are my
two weapons in the fight against time, my pitch for infinity, as
long as I have those I have nothing to fear, she is thinking
about me now, I know she is, unless of course she is thinking
about Helen, which is possible, that after all is the reason she
wanted to go home so quickly, she phoned her mother just
now, about fifteen minutes ago, and her mother told her there
was a letter from America for her, a letter from Helen, so
perhaps Cicely is thinking about Helen but I don't believe she
is, I believe she is thinking about me, but is she imagining me
or remembering me?, I shall never know, but here's an idea, I
could imagine her remembering me, or I could remember her
imagining me, and that way it could go on forever—which of
course is exactly what I want!—like a hall of mirrors or indeed
a Hall of Memory, yes, I like that phrase, I could use that, I
could put it in a poem or use it as the title of a chapter or a
tune or something, and what makes it so perfect is that I am
looking at the Hall of Memory right now, because I am sitting
in The Grapevine which I have noticed, only this morning, I
never noticed it before, but it is situated in a square called
Paradise Place, and straight through the window I can see
through to the civic square, with the Masonic Hall and
Municipal Bank on one side, to the left, and Baskerville House
to the right, and between them is the Hall of Memory, built of
Portland stone and Cornish granite, and topped with a
handsome white dome (I only know about the stone and the
granite because Philip told me, when he came home for the
holidays and we were walking around here, he was full of
information about all these buildings, seemed to have been
making a proper study of them, I was chastened, as usual,
because I am quite capable of living for years in a city without
noticing a thing about its architecture, without even thinking
that the buildings around me have been designed like works of
art and have histories to them, but Philip is becoming quite a

specialist in all this, and so he was telling me, for instance, about the Hall of Memory and how it was meant to be much grander than the one they finally built, in 1925, after the Great War most of the money they had set aside for it had to go towards housing instead, and in the end it only cost £35,000, and the figures are by a Birmingham sculptor called Albert Toft, and the day that it was opened more than 30,000 people queued outside to file through and pay their respects to the men who had died in the war, yes, Philip knew all of this, and it was wonderful, to walk around Birmingham with him that day and to see these familiar places as if for the first time, made new again by his knowledge and enthusiasm), and so today everything about my life seems to be changing, even the city is transforming itself around me, I am sitting in Paradise Place and looking into the Hall of Memory and suddenly it's as if everything refers to me and Cicely, everything is a metaphor for the way we feel, somehow the entire city has become nothing less than a life-size diagram of our hearts, and I could almost shout with the joy of it, I want to run out into the square and shout to anyone who will listen, *I LOVE THIS CITY!, I LOVE THIS CITY!,* but as you might have guessed I'm not going to do that, it's not exactly in character, and besides I don't have to move yet, I'm still locked into my moment and Cicely is still walking somewhere through Victoria Square, thinking of me, remembering, yes, I've decided what it is that she'll be remembering now, she's remembering the day, eight days ago, when I drove down to Heathrow to pick her up, and I have to imagine what she would have thought, or felt (felt, Benjamin, *felt*, concentrate on feelings for a change) when she came through the gate into the Arrivals hall and saw me waiting there, picked out my face from among the crowd, how anxious I must have looked, how transparent, my yearning and my nervousness, but all of that dissolved when I saw her eyes light up in recognition and her face break into a smile and she came towards me and put her bag down and brushed her hair away from her eyes, it is always

falling across her eyes, and then she hugged me, she was
wearing a suede jacket, I remember the texture of her suede
jacket, it had things dangling from it, what are they called,
tassles or something, like a cowboy, how on earth am I ever
going to be a writer if I can't describe clothes properly, perhaps
I should be a composer after all, so we hugged and then she
brought her lips up to mine, it was like everything was in slow
motion, I wonder if everybody was looking at us, it felt as
though they were, and, oh, to be kissing her again, I could
hardly believe it, it was three months since we had seen each
other, I had tried not to doubt her during that time, but once
or twice, it's inevitable I suppose, you find yourself wondering,
not about other men, I was never worried about that, but
feelings fade, it happens all the time, or so I'm told, so I've
read, but when she kissed me that afternoon I knew that
everything was all right, she is true, my Cicely is true, true to
the promises she made last summer, up on the headland, the
headland at Rhîw, I am so lucky, and then we drove home, it
was a long drive, the longest I have ever done in fact, and what
did we talk about?, we had been writing letters, long letters, so
we'd heard each other's news, anyway I didn't have much news,
there is not much to say about my job, it is just a job in a bank,
something to tide me over until I go to Oxford this autumn,
although lately it has become more interesting, I'll admit that,
now that I've been moved out of the branch and into the
regional office, but Cicely first of all wanted to know about the
strikes, people in America had been telling her about the
strikes, they had been reading about them in the newspapers,
she had heard it all second-hand, I don't believe Cicely herself
has ever read a newspaper in her life, but from what her
friends had been saying she had formed the impression that the
whole country was on the point of collapse, the British papers
were calling it the winter of discontent and it's true that the
weather had been incredibly bad and almost everyone in the
country had been on strike, at some point, but this picture they
were painting, rubbish piled high in the streets and corpses

rotting in the back rooms of funeral parlours because there was
nobody to bury them, I told her it was all an exaggeration, it
wasn't nearly as bad as that, but the Americans had been full of
it, apparently, they were convinced that Britain was turning
into a Communist state and we were on the verge of economic
disaster and the army was going to have to be brought in and
there was practically going to be a civil war, and Cicely had
believed all of this, I could see now why Doug had sometimes
been irritated by her, she is the very opposite of him, naive,
credulous in some ways, but that is one of the things I love
about her, she has the capacity, still, to be endlessly astonished
by the world, and Doug has lost that capacity, if he ever had it,
whereas I can play Cicely a piece of music, say (although not
one of mine, no, I don't think I will be doing that again, not for
a while), and she is invariably overwhelmed by it, taken over,
and then hungry for information about the composer, hungry
for the things that only I can tell her, which I suppose is
flattering to me, I mustn't pretend that that's not part of the
attraction, but as an example, while I think of it, of her naivety,
is that really the word, ignorance Doug would call it, but then
that misses the innocent quality of it, the wide-eyed
wonderment, whatever, the example that comes to mind is
when I went to visit her in New York and I asked her one day
whether Carter was still popular with the Americans, and she
didn't understand me, she had no idea who I was talking about,
she had been living in this country for four months and she
didn't know the name of the President, or at least she *knew* it,
she had heard it, but it had made no impression on her, it
would not automatically have occurred to her, hearing the
name Carter, that people were talking about the President, and
she did not know that James Callaghan was the Prime Minister
of Britain, either, but what does it matter, that's what I want to
know, what does it really matter if you don't know what's going
on in the world around you, what difference does it make, we
can't change things anyway, nothing that Cicely does or I do or
even Doug for that matter is ever going to change the world,

unless of course I write something that alters the course of musical history, or Cicely's poetry touches the hearts of a whole generation of women and changes their lives and makes her incredibly famous, because she's writing poetry, now, she only confessed this to me a few weeks ago, in one of her letters, and then I asked her to send me some of them, and she said that most of them weren't finished but then she did send me three, or two and a half, anyway, and they are good, really good, I am not just saying that because I am in love with her, she has an ear for rhythm and she uses words well and carefully, she is very exacting, very tough with herself when she writes, which makes her much better at writing than she ever was at acting, and makes me think that perhaps who knows one of these days we might both get something published or recorded, and we could become one of those famous artistic couples, except that I don't want to be famous, I don't want either of us to be famous, I just want us to live together and work together and be good at what we do, so that in forty years' time (yes, I am going to think about the future now, it is not just by visiting the past that I can escape the present, I can use the future as well, because as Eliot said, *Time present and time past / Are both perhaps present in time future, / And time future contained in time past,* and thank you Mr. Serkis for teaching me that, thank you King William's for introducing me to so much that now echoes and rebounds inside my head, and sustains me, I am grateful, really I am, whatever I might have said and thought about you in less charitable moods), in forty years' time we shall be living—where shall we be living?—oh, in a cottage, of course, or actually what I have always fancied is a converted mill, a watermill, down by the riverbank, somewhere in the country, not far from here, the Cotswolds perhaps or maybe Shropshire, less of a cliché, although the other possibility of course is that we have inherited Plas Cadlan, Glyn and Beatrice will surely have popped off in forty years' time and who else are they going to leave it to?, that's a nice thought, certainly, but I have got the watermill in my mind's

eye now so let's run with that one, yes, there we both are,
getting on for sixty I suppose, and have we got children?, God,
it's a bit early to start thinking about that, but yes, of course
we've got children, or have had children, rather, because they
will have left home by now and we are living alone again, quite
alone, but even after forty years we are so untired of each
other, so hungry to discover more about each other, that it's
actually a relief that the kids have gone at last, and besides, it
gives me more time to work on the new symphony, because
where am I in the cycle at this point, number seven or eight
I should think, the works of my late maturity, it was the
"Birmingham Symphony" that made my name and reputation
but these quieter, more reflective, more dissonant and complex
works are the ones that people will recognize, in the years to
come, as the real masterpieces, and of course my settings of
Cicely's poetry!, because that's the great thing about her
starting to write, now we can collaborate, so this is going to be
a true partnership, a true partnership of equals, and as well as
working together at the watermill, during the daytimes, when
evening falls we shall entertain, we shall give the kind of
dinners that people will never forget, people will spend
evenings at our house that will become treasured memories
(well done, Benjamin, you're really going for it here, you are
imagining the future of the future, and what people will
remember when they get there, back in their potential pasts,
my God, time present doesn't stand a chance against this kind
of opposition, it doesn't have an earthly), and just to take one
evening, for instance, who are the guests, well, obviously, there
will be Philip and his wife, and Doug and his wife, and Claire
and her husband, and Emily and her husband, which makes
eight, plus me and Cicely makes ten, a good number, but
should we have invited Steve?, why have we not invited Steve?,
is it because his future seems so uncertain, after what happened
last year, and I just cannot envisage where he is going to be in
forty years' time, or is there another reason, a nastier reason,
for excluding Steve from my little fantasy, you can never tell,

these things go very deep, and when Cicely and I went to visit him the other day there was certainly an element of hostility, I thought, of bitterness, even though he didn't hold me to blame personally, a gulf had opened up between us, a little gulf, if there can be such a thing, but I shall be optimistic about this, I am full of hope today, convinced that everything will be for the best, so of course Steve will be there, Steve and his wife, which makes twelve in all, which is an even better number, but do we have enough bedrooms to put everybody up in?, I don't see why not, we are talking about a bloody watermill here, for Christ's sake, we ought to be able to run to six bedrooms, so everyone is staying the night, and it gets to be about two o'clock in the morning, and we've finished the last of the wine and decided to leave the clearing up for now, so Cicely and I are upstairs in our bedroom, which is right next to the river, we can hear the noise of running water as we get undressed together, and then we fall into bed, very tired but happy, so happy, and not so tired either that we don't want to reach out and touch each other, it is not that we are at it like rabbits every hour God sends at the age of sixty-odd, no, but desire hasn't faded, yet, not by any means, we still sleep naked, for one thing (no pyjamas!, absolutely not!, no old man's stripey pyjamas for me at this age), and it only takes a second or two for Cicely to climb on top of me, tonight, I am hard and ready for her, just like this morning, and she takes hold of me and eases me inside her, yes, Oh God, yes, just like this morning, this morning in my brother's bedroom, that was exactly what she did, after I had raised my head from between her legs, from Paradise Place, where I had learned so many things, uncovered so many secrets, oh, Cicely, the taste of you, will it still be the same, will everything still be the same between us in forty years' time?, always, Cicely, always be new to me, that's all we must ask of each other, new like this morning, new like your body which I had never seen before but today I saw all of it, you gave me all of it, your beautiful young tall pale slender body, when you sat astride me I reached up and began to kiss your breasts and your hair fell across my face, the hair which you made me cut off all those years ago and I still have it, oh yes, I shall never throw that bag away, and this morning your blonde hair fell across my face, so that I had not just your nipple but some of your hair in my mouth too as you reached down and touched me and pulled me towards you and squeezed me inside you and then with your other hand you touched my cheek, drew my face up towards you again so that we could kiss, the softest kiss, the gentlest kiss you would ever believe, and in all the years I have spent trying to imagine how it would feel to be inside a woman, this was nothing like it, no, I had never even been close, because it wasn't just the sensation, it wasn't just the clinging of your skin against my skin, no, it was the generosity of you, the givingness of what you were doing with your body (that's it, yes! *Now I've found out that it's generosity that turns me on*), and, watch out, Benjamin, you are rushing on, rushing on towards the end now and you can hold back for a little bit longer, I think, don't lose this moment, don't, don't lose it, it may never come back, quick, think of something else, like that line, for instance, that line you just quoted, where did it come from?, it's both familiar and unfamiliar, it feels like something that's always been around in my head but I hadn't thought of it for a long time, and now I've got it, yes, of course, it's a song by Hatfield and the North, "Share It," how appropriate, everything is appropriate today, everything is coming together, but it's odd that I haven't listened to that record for so long, it used to be my absolute favourite, I've had a soft spot for them ever since I went to see them at Barbarella's, more than four years ago now, I have no trouble remembering the date, it was just two days before Malcolm died, and that reminds me of something that happened on Monday, three days ago, when I was walking through the cathedral square, with Cicely, as it happens, it was my lunch hour and until she goes back to school, in a week or two, she always comes to meet me in my lunch hour, and on this occasion we were walking through the square, hand in

hand, which is how we always walk these days, and we passed
this guy sitting on a bench, drinking from a can of something
or other, Ansell's I think it was, he had a red face and a big
beard and to be honest he smelled a bit, I just thought he was a
wino at first, but then I stopped walking and something clicked
into place and I looked back at him and then I turned, drawing
Cicely with me, and I went up to him and I looked him in the
eye and said, You don't recognize me, do you?, and he stared
back at me, he had this slightly glazed look to him, I think he'd
been drinking for an hour or two, and he said, No I don't—
who are you, you cunt? and I said, You're Roll-Up Reg, and he
said, I know who *I* am—who are you?, and I told him that he'd
come with me to Barbarella's all that time ago with Malcolm,
and when I mentioned that name it was as if some kind of
light-bulb went out behind his eyes, they went dark, and he
drooped forward on his bench, almost slumped, and when he
looked at me again he said, I remember you, you're the Tory
cunt, but there was no laughter in his voice when he said it this
time, and he didn't speak for quite a while after that but
eventually he raised his head and sort of looked me up and
down, took the measure of me, and said, You've grown up a bit
since then, haven't you?, and I didn't know what to say to that,
so I introduced him to Cicely and he shook her very nicely by
the hand and said, politely but very deliberately, enunciating
every word carefully, the way that some alcoholics do, It's an
honour to meet you, you must excuse me if I say anything out
of order, the fact is, I'm an uncouth and ill-mannered cunt, and
Cicely just laughed and assured him that whatever he said was
fine, and he turned to me and said, Are you giving it to her?,
and in fact the answer to that was still technically no, but I
don't think he expected me to tell him, anyway, because he
asked me next what I was doing these days, and when I told
him that I'd got a temporary job working for a bank and then I
was going up to Oxford he just laughed and said, So you never
did read *The Ragged Trousered Philanthropists*, then, and I knew
what he was getting at so I became a bit defensive and said,

T. S. Eliot worked for a bank, you know, and Roll-Up Reg said, Yes, and he was a cunt, as well, but I could tell he was only joking, and then we both went quiet and I was about to say goodbye and move on when he asked me, How's that sister of yours?, so I told him about Lois, as briefly as I could, saying as little as possible about the bad times and telling him that now, just in the last few months, she really seemed to have got her act together, and she even had this new boyfriend, a lawyer called Christopher, her first boyfriend since Malcolm, and completely different from him, too, the polar opposite in every respect, and Roll-Up Reg nodded and said that was nice, he was glad for her, but I could tell that I had depressed him by reminding him about all of this, and sure enough suddenly his eyes were full of tears and he sort of fell forward and Cicely grabbed hold of him and sat next to him on the bench, she had to support him, practically, he was leaning on her shoulder as he looked at me and said, It was my fault, you know, it was my fault they went to that pub, if it wasn't for me Malc would be alive today and he would have married your sister and none of this would have happened, they were going to go to The Grapevine and then I told them not to, I can remember the conversation now, I told him it would be full of cunts in suits, it was all my fault, I killed him, I killed him, and I had to kneel down beside him and say, No, Reg, No, I didn't know whether to call him Reg or Roll-Up actually, neither of them seemed to come very naturally, but I said, No, you're not to blame, no one's to blame for something like that, it's fate or destiny or God or something, and he pulled himself together and squeezed my shoulder and said, Yes, you're right, and Cicely gave him a Kleenex and wiped his face down a bit and he said again, You're right, son, you're right, it's God, and I said, Yes, it is, and he said, He's cunt, isn't he?, and I thought about what He'd done to Malcolm and what He'd done to Lois and what He'd done to the rest of us as a consequence and I said, Yes, He is, Reg, He's a complete and utter cunt, and I laughed and Reg laughed and Cicely laughed, too, she didn't know what it meant, for me, to say that, she doesn't know the truth about me and God, I've never told her the story of the miracle, maybe I will one day but not yet, and besides, there are other miracles in my life now, like the miracle of Cicely herself and how she made me feel this morning, so then we said goodbye to Roll-Up Reg, he sat up on his bench and he took us both by the hands, and he said God bless, he said God bless both of you, you cunts, and then we walked on, and it would be good, wouldn't it, if that was the last time I'd seen him in my life, there would have been a nice sense of closure about it, but as it happens he seems to sit and drink his Ansell's in the cathedral square most days, and I see him almost every lunch hour, not to speak to, though, we just wave hello or we make a bit of eye contact, but no, there will be no tidy rounding-off of that particular story, I'm sorry to say, whereas it was different with Steve, when Cicely and I went to visit him last Saturday, early in the afternoon, there was a definite sense of finality about that meeting, which did not start well in any case because Steve was out when we arrived, he was still at work and so we had to sit there for a while with his parents, Mr. and Mrs. Richards, and of course they hate Cicely because they think that she made their son unhappy, all that time ago, when they were in *Othello* together—it all started then, oh yes, everything started then!—because it was after that that Steve split up with his girlfriend, Valerie, who by all accounts was very nice, so you can imagine that the situation was pretty tense, as we all sat there waiting for him to come home, and I didn't make things any better because I was nervous, too, it's shameful to admit it but yes, I was nervous, we were in Handsworth and for years my family had brought me up to believe that Handsworth was a sort of no-go area, some dark outpost of colonial Africa which had somehow got transplanted to Birmingham, and they had managed to convince me that my car was bound to get broken into if I left it parked in the street, or we would come back to it after half an hour and find that it was sitting on bricks or something, but I have to say that I saw

very little evidence for these theories, not that Handsworth is
at all similar to Longbridge, no, you can feel the difference,
not just in the number of black people on the streets or all
the different languages you can see in the shop windows or the
different kinds of food for sale, it goes somehow deeper than
these things, yes, I admit it, it was like a foreign country to me
but I liked it for that very reason, and found myself thinking
how strange it was, what an indictment, that I could share the
same city with these people and yet I had had no contact with
them in all my eighteen years, apart from Steve, of course, and
how difficult it must have been for him, how very surreal and
disorientating, to have arrived at King William's and found
that he was the only black boy there and that we all made fun
of him and called him Rastus, God, we're a fucked-up country,
I'm beginning to see that, now, perhaps I really should have
been listening to Doug all these years, anyway, that's why I
had been feeling nervous, absurdly, but it didn't last for long
because Mr. and Mrs. Richards were very welcoming, whatever
they may have thought of Cicely, they made us tea and they
asked her questions about America, and they told us about
Steve's job, which does not sound like much of a job, I'm
afraid, he is only working in the local chip shop, but as they
said he has to get whatever work he can and save up towards
next year's fees because if he is going to retake his A-levels he
will have to go to sixth-form college, and they will have to pay
for that themselves, and they told us that he might get a
pay-rise soon because the shop is hoping to expand, they want
to put in a few tables and chairs at the back and turn it into a
proper little restaurant, and when I heard that I asked them
what the name of the chip shop was and they told me, and
when they told me I felt my heart sink but I didn't say anything
and just then Steve came in anyway, the shop had closed at
two-thirty, and he was so pleased to see us, he broke into this
enormous grin, he hadn't seen me since that terrible day last
year, the last day of term, and he hadn't seen Cicely for even
longer than that, he seemed especially pleased to see Cicely,

and she stood up when he came in and hugged him with real
affection, real fondness, he seemed quite overwhelmed by it,
Cicely has that effect on people, they forget what she is like,
and we didn't stay long in his parents' house, I'm pleased to
say, because I'm afraid I found it oppressive, it was a friendly
place, warm and tidy and full of lovely strange cooking smells,
but I'm afraid the smallness and the poverty of it depressed me,
yes, it's shocking, isn't it, but I realized then that Steve's family
were by far and away the poorest of all my friends,' it
embarrassed me, and it embarrassed me that I had my own car
parked outside, a Mini which was only two years old, which my
parents had basically given me, although I was paying them a
token amount towards it every week out of my wages, and as
the three of us walked towards Handsworth Park I felt
ashamed for having everything given to me so easily, my job at
the bank and my place at university and everything else, when
Steve seemed to have almost nothing, at the moment, and only
a year ago it had seemed that we were all in the same position
but perhaps that was just an illusion, perhaps the playing field
was never really level and life would always in fact be easier for
someone like me, I suspect that is the case, nothing changes,
nothing has changed, and I'll tell you something else that
hasn't changed, as well, he is still in love with her, yes, Steve is
still in love with Cicely, I saw it that afternoon in Handsworth
Park, it was obvious, obvious to me anyway, though I didn't say
anything to her about it afterwards and I think it's possible that
she didn't even notice, she often doesn't notice these things, it's
not that she takes it for granted that people will always adore
her, it's just that she lives her life at this pitch all the time,
always conducts her friendships at a level of intimacy which is
completely normal for her but not for most people, so she
doesn't realize how special she has made them feel, it was the
same with Helen in America, Helen obviously worshipped her,
had never met anyone like her, her father was in the same play
as Cicely's mother so naturally they were thrown together a
good deal, and it was fascinating for me, those few days in

January, to spend time with them both, God it was cold, that's
the main thing I remember about it, I have never felt cold like
the cold you get in New York in January, and there was one
night in particular I remember when the three of us were
supposed to be walking from Cicely's mother's apartment to
some cinema or other, and we literally couldn't make it, even
with all our coats and scarves and gloves and hats it was too
cold and the snow was too heavy so we stopped off at this hotel
instead, it was called the Gramercy Park, we went into the bar
and ordered whiskies and we never made it to the cinema at all,
we just sat drinking at the bar all evening, it was an amazing
evening, and an amazing place, full of these old actors, there
was this man there, I could swear it was Vincent Price, sitting
at the bar by himself most of the night and even he couldn't
take his eyes off Cicely half of the time, she draws people
towards her, somehow, is always getting into conversation with
strangers, and I was, yes, fascinated that evening to see the
quality of the friendship between Cicely and Helen, who was
from the West Coast, and so not like a New Yorker at all, I was
told, I don't know anything about America but apparently
there is this big divide between the East Coast and the West
Coast, and Cicely and Helen had known each other two or
three months now, so thinking about it they had spent far more
time together than she and I ever had, which might have
explained the intimacy between them, the sense of a private
language from which I felt excluded, private jokes, private
phrases, and not just in words, either, there were private looks
and private smiles, and I'm not saying it was the same with
Cicely and Steve that afternoon in Handsworth Park, I'm just
saying, well, what am I trying to say, exactly, that I felt jealous,
I suppose, on both occasions, I felt that I was being denied the
whole of her, I did not like sharing her with someone else, even
when I knew that there was nothing but friendship involved,
and when I knew that it was greedy of me to want to keep
Cicely all to myself, she is so special, so precious, everybody
should be allowed some time with her, everybody in the world,

but it's true, I can't deny it, "a hatred for you spat like a
welding flame," that was how I felt both times, towards Helen
in the Gramercy Park Hotel on that snowy New York evening
and towards Steve in Handsworth Park that bright Saturday
afternoon, the last Saturday of April, just five days ago, but it
seems a long time, already, as I said, there was this sense of
finality about it, this overtone of hail and farewell, I feel that
we have lost Steve, lost him to something, what can you call
it?, history, politics, circumstance, it's a horrible feeling,
actually, a feeling that our time together at school was a sort of
brilliant mistake, it was against the normal order of things, and
now everything is back to how it is meant to be, Steve has been
put back in his proper place and it is monstrous, not just to
think that this has happened, but to think *how* it happened, if
somebody really did screw up his chances in that exam, and the
worst thing is we shall never know, for certain, we can never
really know whether Culpepper slipped something into his
drink that day, taking his revenge for all the times Steve had
showed himself to be better than him, no, we shall never know
the truth about that or so many other things, and yet
somebody obviously thinks that Culpepper is to blame because
one night last year his car was torched, somebody came round
to his parents' house in the middle of the night and smashed
the car window and threw a petrol bomb inside, the whole
thing was completely gutted, it brought a smile to everybody's
face when we heard that, it just seemed like the least he
deserved, but again, nobody knows who did it, it seems that
secrets simply beget more secrets, and everything just gets
more and more unknowable, the disappearance of Claire's
sister is another case in point, I don't believe Claire will ever
get to the bottom of that, any more than I will ever know
exactly what made Harding tick or whether I will ever see him
again now that he's gone to Germany for a year without even
telling any of us which university place he has taken up, he is
lost now, lost to us, bent on some strange solitary course of his
own, but going back to Culpepper's car, my personal suspicion

is that Doug had something to do with it, by which I don't
mean that he went round there in the middle of the night and
threw the bomb in himself, but maybe he knows some people
who do that sort of thing and he told them the story, put them
up to it, if you see what I mean, but I can't know this for sure,
can I, we can never know anything for sure, and every time I
mention anything about it to Doug he just ignores me or
changes the subject, he did this very noticeably on Sunday,
for instance, yes, we saw Doug on Sunday as well, this has
been a great week for reunions, he was up from London for
the weekend with his new girlfriend, Marianne, and he was
full of stories about the Southall riots, he was there, of
course, right in the thick of it, I'm beginning to think it is
Doug's destiny always to be at the centre of things, just as it is
my destiny always to be offstage whenever the main action
occurs, always to wander away at the most important moment,
drifting into the kitchen to make a cup of tea just as the
denouement unfolds, he had written a piece about it and sent it
to the *NME*, not really knowing if they would use it, they have
used three or four of his reviews now but he is not what you
would call a regular contributor, so he showed me the
typescript on Sunday and today, I see, having bought the *NME*
on my way here with Cicely, they have printed it, amazingly, in
the *Thrills* section, not the full version I notice, they have cut
out all the stuff about his father, which is a shame, that was the
most moving part of the article, I thought, because his father
was also attacked by a policeman on a demo, and he was also
hit over the head with a truncheon and although it didn't kill
him like it killed Blair Peach, Doug thinks that his father has
changed since then, his personality has changed, he can't prove
of course that this has anything to do with the injury, but not
only does his father now get headaches, migraines, which he
never used to do, and not only does he find it harder to read
for long periods of time, but there is something worse than
that, Doug thinks, he says that his father has lost what he calls
the will to fight, because there are changes afoot at

Longbridge, apparently, this new chairman called Michael
Edwardes, who my father thinks is a hero sent by the gods to
rescue the company from the evil union barons, and Doug
seems to regard as the devil incarnate, he is closing down some
of the factories and setting new productivity targets and Doug
says that in the old days his father would have made sure
everybody was out on strike by now but instead he just seems
to be going along with it, and Doug thinks this is all to do with
the crack on the head he got down in London eighteen months
ago when he went to join the Grunwick picket line, but
perhaps the people at the *NME* thought that was too
speculative, or somethng, anyway, they cut it out, but it is still a
good article, very powerful, even someone like me, someone
who likes to think the best of the police, can see that there
must have been something very wrong that day, it was the
Special Patrol Group again, the same group that was involved
in the Grunwick demonstration, Doug told me, they are the
worst, the most violent and out of control, and the trouble
started after the meeting in the town hall was already under
way, the National Front were holding an election meeting
there, in the heart of Southall, a provocative place to hold a
meeting, it has a large Asian community, and thousands of
demonstrators had arrived to protest about this, most of them
peacefully, by all accounts, although an event like that is never
entirely peaceful, and sure enough some fighting broke out and
that was when the SPG vans started to arrive, and then Doug
and Marianne decided to get out while the going was good, so
they began to head off with a lot of the other protesters,
looking for a way to get to the station, and there was just one
road, one road which was not cordoned off and so they tried to
get down there, there was a big crowd of people where it
joined with the Broadway, mainly Asians, but they squeezed
their way through and then walked on for a bit but then they
heard people shouting behind them, so they looked back up to
the top of the road and suddenly all these policemen were
pouring out of the SPG vans, they had truncheons and riot

shields, and they were piling into the crowd, laying into them, indiscriminately, black or white, it didn't matter, and suddenly everybody was running, running down this street towards Doug and Marianne, and if they couldn't get down the street itself they were jumping over walls and fences into people's gardens, or trying to get through the alleys between the houses into the relative safety of the streets on either side, but the police were too quick for most of them, and Marianne says she saw this guy down on the floor, he was a white guy, and there were four policemen systematically kicking the shit out of him, he had his hands over his groin, and a woman went up to these policemen, a woman in her late twenties or thirties, and she said something like, Stop that, you ought to be helping him, and one of the policemen just ran up to her and whacked her in the face with his truncheon, felled her to the ground, and they both went to help her, they managed to carry her into somebody's garden and lie her down and put a handkerchief to the wound, because she was bleeding quite badly, it is all in Doug's article, all of these details, it is the best thing anyone has written about that riot, if there is any justice it will make him famous or at least mean that the *NME* will ask him to write more things for them, he is doing well, very well, it is only his first year as a student but Doug is going to succeed, I can see that, if any of us is going to succeed it will be him, and I was impressed with Marianne, too, it was a brave thing to do, to help that woman with her wound, in the midst of all that chaos and violence, they managed to stay with her until the ambulances began to arrive, and then they visited her in hospital the next day, she was all right, she survived, which is more than can be said for Blair Peach, poor guy, he was only thirty-three, a New Zealander, and he died from his head wounds in the early hours of the next morning, Doug is convinced that the policeman who did it will never be caught, an inquiry is being set up but he says it's bound to be a whitewash, the state always looks after its own, that's the kind of thing he says these days and Marianne smiles indulgently at

him, I think she shares his beliefs but she has more of a sense
of humour about them, and Doug told her on Sunday that this
was to do with class, it's always easier for upper-class people to
see the funny side of things, he said, because nothing is ever
really important to them, nothing is ever a matter of life and
death, and I can see the truth of that but it hasn't stoppd him
from going out with an upper-class woman, I notice, Marianne
has this fabulously posh accent and her father apparently has
an estate in Hertfordshire and another one in Scotland
somewhere, they are an odd couple in some ways but they
seem very happy together and it occurs to me, now, that Doug
has always had a thing about posh women, there was that
secretary he met in London the first time he went down there,
he was always boasting about the night they spent together,
you would think that nobody had ever had sex before or since,
he made it sound like *Emmanuelle, Last Tango in Paris* and *The
Kama Sutra* all rolled into one, well, perhaps it was, but I've
never been envious of Doug and I'm certainly not now,
because even he could see, even he could see on Sunday what is
happening between me and Cicely, how much feeling there is
between us, he said it was almost palpable, you could sense it
just being in the same room as us, and he took me aside at one
point and asked what on earth had happened when I went to
visit her in Wales, and I told him that I didn't know, it had just
happened very quickly, perhaps it was something to do with
that beautiful house, Plas Cadlan, or more likely all it needed,
for me and Cicely to realize that we were meant to be together,
was just to meet somewhere else for a while, somewhere away
from school and all its associated crap and nonsense, and as
soon as that happened we could just see, it was obvious, it was
as if the waters had suddenly cleared, and I told him that it was
a fantastic feeling, a weird feeling, actually, to be living your
life at this level of happiness, I felt giddy with the excitement
of it, I was having trouble sleeping at night, and I have
butterflies in my stomach, too, now that she is back, there is a
kind of urgency about life, suddenly, a sense that everything is

at stake, now, do or die, make or break, everything is
important, every moment, including this moment which to
anybody watching me from the other side of the pub must
seem totally mundane, just a young bloke in a suit raising a
glass of Guinness to his mouth but no, this is one of the great
moments of my life, I know that, which is why I am going to
stretch it, stretch it until it snaps or bursts, and there was the
same urgency about the way we made love this morning, after
Cicely had climbed on top of me, and I had entered her, at last,
at last!, I had found my way to Paradise Place, I looked at her
face and what I saw there, it was fear, almost, it was a kind of
excitement bordering on fear, fear of what?, I know, yes, I
know now, because I was feeling it too, it was fear of the past,
fear of how the past might have turned out, because we came
within a whisker, Cicely and I, of missing each other
altogether, we might never have found each other, if I had not
decided to walk to Plas Cadlan in the middle of that storm last
summer, and the thought of that, the thought that we might
never have reached this point after all, oh, it was almost
unbearable, insupportable, and it must have occurred to us
both at the very same time, because she grabbed my hair and
we lunged for each other, suddenly, all the tenderness was gone
and we were biting into each other's mouths so hard it was
almost painful and then Cicely began to shake and to make
these noises, I thought she was crying at first, it wouldn't have
surprised me, I felt like crying, in a way, but it wasn't that,
these were different noises, animal noises, as she began to rise
and fall on top of me, rise and fall, her whole body drawn up
into this pillar of flesh, and now she is moving faster, faster and
faster, her teeth are clenched and I can see the veins, now, the
blue veins standing out on her wrists as she clutches my arm,
squeezing me until it hurts and we are nearly there now, so
nearly, but there is one more thing I must think about before
we get there, one more attempt to stretch this moment and it
is something I have been putting off all this time, because I feel
so guilty about it, but I can't do that any more, I have to

confess it, it is about Steve, and my job, because after I had
been working at the bank for just a couple of months, the
manager called me into his office and told me that they were
moving me on, they were fast-tracking me, as he called it, and
I was going to be moved to the regional office in Temple Row,
as a Loans Officer, and I could hardly believe this, I had
already been moving through the ranks much too fast, I'd only
had to open the post for about three days and then I was put
straight on to the counter, the other people working there
couldn't understand it, they couldn't help but be resentful,
even though they were a nice bunch of people, really, a very
nice bunch, but it was all part of the bank's scheme, apparently,
to take bright young students like me and show us as much as
possible of how things operated before we went to university,
so that we became so fascinated, I suppose, that when we
graduated we would come straight back to work for them, well,
I have no intention of doing that, I can assure you, but it now
seemed that the next stage in this process was to transfer me to
the regional office and let me work as a Loans Officer and so
that's what I did, starting two days later, and now instead of
coming to Smallbrook Queensway every morning I go to
Temple Row instead, and I love it there, I have to say, it's my
favourite part of Birmingham, I love St. Philip's Cathedral,
which we can see out of our office window, and the Grand
Hotel beyond it in Colmore Row, and I love going to sit in the
square at lunchtime with Martin and Gil, I love the solid
dignity of all those banks and insurance buildings, what would
Doug have to say about *that*, I wonder, I can hear it now,
another one of those ten-minute lectures on selling out to the
establishment, but I don't care, it is good architecture, they are
fine buildings (and so is St. Philip's itself, which Philip tells me
was built in 1715 and is the first example of Italianate design in
the city, it was designed by a man called Thomas Archer and it
is the smallest cathedral in England, what a grand sight it must
have been, back in the eighteenth century, standing proud on
its ridge with long views down across Colmore Row, which was

then called New Hall Lane, towards the great estate of New
Hall itself, and it was then that the wealthy builders and
manufacturers put up their houses around the new churchyard
as well, and what is now called Temple Row began to take
shape, only in those days it was known as Tory-Row—there
you are, Doug, what a gift, run with it!—and on the opposite
side of the square, just a few years later, they built the Blue
Coat Charity School, to provide education for the city's poorer
children, yes, that building is handsome as well, it stands as a
monument to the enlightened spirit of those who designed it,
this city has been blessed, over the centuries, with good and
enterprising and compassionate leaders, there is the Cadbury
family, for instance, who built a whole village for their
workforce at the turn of the century, Bournville, it is called,
and they even made sure that everyone had a decent amount of
land so that they could grow fruit trees and spend their leisure
time gardening rather than going down to the pub, the
Cadburys were teetotallers and there are still no pubs in the
whole of Bournville, seventy years later, Philip tells me, but I
am just trying to distract myself, now, it is time to forget all
this local history and return to the unpleasant matter in hand),
so then, after just a week or so's training, it was announced that
I had become a fully fledged Loans Officer, and instead of
having to deal with members of the public over the counter I
now sit in one corner of a bright, open-plan office, with Martin
and Gil, my new colleagues and my new friends, which
reminds me, I told Martin that I would be in at two o'clock, it's
almost time I was going, but Sam has gone to the bar again so
it won't do any harm to have another swift half, and every day
we get applications from all over the city, small companies send
us their business plans and ask us for loans, anything from one
to fifty thousand pounds, to help them expand their operations
or buy new equipment or premises, and it seems ridiculous,
doesn't it, that just because I have a place at Oxford the bank
trusts me to make these decisions, I don't even have A-level
maths and I have never studied economics, but every day I sit

in judgement on these people, I play God with their hopes and
ambitions, and though I know I am trying to do the job fairly,
the bank always wants me to be strict, they don't want to lend
money out unless they can be sure of a return, and we usually
reject two out of three applications, and last week Gil handed
me a big file from the Handsworth branch and said, Go on,
Ben, you can do this one, and it was a fish and chip shop which
wanted to put in a few tables and chairs to make a little
restaurant area, for God's sake they only needed a couple of
thousand pounds but the figures didn't really add up and it
looked as though the business was struggling anyway and
they'd exceeded their overdraft limit for the last eighteen
months, so I said no, it was as simple as that, I just put a big
red stamp on it and then I found out on Saturday afternoon
that this was the place where Steve worked and if the scheme
had gone ahead he would have got a pay-rise, it wouldn't have
been much I dare say but it would have meant something to
him, so there you are, I've just managed to put yet another
obstacle in his path, without even realizing it, oh shit shit shit,
I'm a terrible terrible person, as Cicely would no doubt say, but
she doesn't say that any more, I've noticed, no, she is cured,
cured of her insecurities, I have done that for her, I am going
to allow myself to take full and wholehearted credit for that,
so I have achieved something, something already in my short
life, I have made another person happy and it turned out that it
was the easiest thing to do in the world, all I had to do was
follow my own strongest desires, my keenest instincts, and
look where it led me in the end, to my little brother's bedroom,
my little brother's bed, where Cicely and I made love this
morning, and yes, we are there, now, there at last, my lovely
naked Cicely is clinging on to me and I can feel myself gripped
by those beautiful, subtle, supple muscles between her legs,
rising and falling, rising and falling, and our mouths are locked
together, tighter and tighter, until, yes, really, it happened
today, Cicely and I looked for Paradise Place and we found
it together and when we found it we discovered that it was a

place full of laughter, not tears, when the moment came it was like a burst of light, a burst of white light as if I'd been staring too long at the sun, and then the sun came back into focus only it wasn't the sun it was a yellow dot only it wasn't a dot it was a yellow balloon, my yellow balloon, the one I lost all those years ago, my earliest memory, I could see it again, touch it again, it wasn't lost at all, and then suddenly I remembered where I was, who I was with, and I looked at Cicely and we were still for a hot endless moment and then we fell together on to the bed and rolled in each other's arms and then we laughed, oh, we laughed as though we would never stop, at last all the fear was gone, and the frustration was gone, and the longing was gone, and the missing each other was gone, and everything was funny, all of a sudden, everything seemed hilarious, like the fact that we had done it for the first time in my little brother's bedroom, and that we had done it on election day, because, yes!, there is a general election today, the fate of my country hangs in the balance, and that is hilarious, too, and yes I refuse, from this moment onwards, to worry about anything any more, to take anything seriously any more, there has been too much of that, we have all been too sad for too long, and nothing is going to go wrong ever again, not for me or for Cicely or for Lois or for anybody, it's all a joke, everything is a big wonderful joke, like that song which I have carried in my head for so many years—

Mirthless merriment, sickly sentiments
So commonplace, it would bore you to tears,
Give me non-stop laughter, dispel disaster
Or The Rotters' Club might well lop off your ears

—and no wonder people were staring at us on the bus into town as if we were mad, everything we saw, every time we looked out of the window made us burst into laughter and it was the same when we came into The Grapevine and the first person we saw was Sam Chase, Philip's father, I started laughing with gladness because I hadn't seen him for years either, and I knew that he was happy now too because his wife has stopped having her affair with Sugar Plum Fairy, I don't know how he put a stop to it but he did, Philip told me, and he was just sitting in the pub by himelf, reading a novel, it was *Ulysses*, actually, who would have thought it, and he seemed so pleased to see us, and he bought us drinks, and he watched us together and when Cicely went to make her phone call he said, That is the most beautiful girl I have ever seen in my life, and I said, I know she is, and that made me laugh, and when Cicely came back from making her phone call he said, You two are quite simply the two happiest people I have ever met, and that made us both laugh, and after Cicely had gone home to read her letter from Helen he said to me, Benjamin, he said, I'm not one for making predictions, and that already made me laugh, because we have all noticed, everybody who knows Sam has noticed that whenever he says he's not one for making predictions, it always means that he's about to make a prediction, and today he said Benjamin, I'm not one for making predictions, but this is a special day and today I'm going to make two, so I said, Oh yes?, and he said, Number One, and he held up his finger, Number One, you and Cicely will have a long and happy life together, and of course I laughed at that, because I know that it's true, and then he held up another finger and said Number Two, and then he pointed at the newspaper someone had left on the next table, it was a copy of *The Sun*, with a big picture of Mrs. Thatcher on the front page, Number Two, he said, that woman will never be Prime Minister of this country, and then we both roared with laughter and clinked our glasses and he said, Come on, son, I'll buy you another, and it seemed to me then that not only does God exist but he must be a genius, a comic genius, to have made everything in the world so funny, everything from Sam and his crazy predictions right down to the dark beery circle my glass has just left on this green coaster.

On a clear, blueblack, starry night, in the city of Berlin, in the year 2003, the restaurant at the top of the Fernsehturm continued to revolve. Sophie, the only daughter of Lois and Christopher, and Patrick, the only son of Philip and Claire, gazed through their picture window at the Volkspark Friedrichshain, more than three hundred metres beneath them.

Neither of them spoke for a while. They sipped their Riesling and looked out of the window and thought about Benjamin.

Finally Sophie said:

—What a mess they're making of that park. You can't even see the fountain in the middle. Who wants to look at a pile of scaffolding?

—It's like this whole city. One big building site. The same as London.

—I know. Why is the world so restless with itself, these days?

Then Sophie found herself looking around the restaurant at the other customers. There were a couple of men dining by themselves. One was taking out his glasses to study the menu, the other was tipping brown sugar into his coffee cup from a paper sachet. Their actions seemed banal: but how was anyone to know what storms, what torrents of ideas and memories and dreams were raging through their minds at that instant? She looked at their sad, preoccupied faces and thought again about her Uncle Benjamin, the rapturous joy he had known on that far-off day, and all that had happened since.

Patrick noticed the sudden shadow of melancholy in her eyes and said:

—Oh, come on, Sophie, don't look that way. It was a beautiful story. It was full of nice things: friendships, jokes, good experiences, love. It wasn't all doom and gloom.

—Yes. Yes, I know. It's not that, really. It's just that it was so long ago. They were all so young. And Benjamin and my mother went through so much.

—But look at her now. She's doing fine. Things could hardly be better for her. And for us.

—I know. That's all true.

—And it even has a happy ending.

—Except that it doesn't feel like the ending, to me.

—But stories never end, do they? Not really. All you can do is choose a moment to end on. One out of many. And what a moment you found!

And Sophie nodded slowly, and said:

—Yes. He was lucky, wasn't he, to have felt that way? Lucky Uncle Benjamin! To have known happiness like that, and to have held on to it, even for a moment.

—And lucky us, said Patrick. To be able to share in it, still, after all this time!

Then Sophie rallied, and saw that he was right, and after catching the eye of the wine waiter she turned back to Patrick and smiled her widest smile, full of hope and anticipation. And she said:

—All right, then: now it's your turn.

Author's Note

There will be a sequel to *The Rotters' Club*, entitled *The Closed Circle*, resuming the story in the late 1990s.

Acknowledgements

The following books proved informative, helpful or inspiring in writing this novel: Chris Upton, *A History of Birmingham* (Phillimore, 1993); Chris Mullin, *Error of Judgment: The Truth about the Birmingham Pub Bombings* (Poolbeg Press, 1997); Peter L. Edmead, *The Divisive Decade: A History of Caribbean Immigration to Birmingham in the 1950s* (Birmingham Library Services, 1999); Martin Walker, *The National Front* (Fontana, 1977); Mike Cronin (editor), *The Failure of British Fascism: The Far Right and the Fight for Political Recognition* (Macmillan, 1996); John Tyndall, *The Eleventh Hour: A Call for British Rebirth* (Albion Press, 1988); David Widgery, *Beating Time* (Chatto and Windus, 1986); Julie Burchill, *I Knew I Was Right* (Heinemann, 1998); Michael Edwardes, *Back from the Brink: An Apocalyptic Experience* (Collins, 1983); Jonathan Wood, *Wheels of Misfortune: The Rise and Fall of the British Motor Industry* (Sidgwick and Jackson, 1988); Bernie Passingham and Danny Connor, *Ford Shop Stewards on Industrial Democracy* (Institute for Workers' Control, 1977); Jack Dromey and Graham Taylor, *Grunwick: The Workers' Story* (Lawrence and Wishart, 1978); Michael Dummett (chairman), *The Death of Blair Peach: The Supplementary Report of the Unofficial Committee of Enquiry* (National Council for Civil Liberties, 1980); David Petrow, *The Bitter Years: The Invasion and Occupation of Denmark and Norway, April 1940—May 1945* (Hodder and Stoughton, 1975).

Section 1 of "The Chick and the Hairy Guy" contains quotations from genuine lonely hearts advertisements in *Sounds* (1973). Section 3 of "The Very Maws of Doom" contains quotations from the magazines *Woman* (1976) and *Take a Break* (1996). Section 18 contains quotations from *101 Ways to Improve Your Word Power*, by Hugh Enfield (The Dickens Press, 1967), *Word Power from the Reader's Digest* (Reader's Digest, 1967), *Twenty-five Magic Steps to Word Power*, by Dr. Wilfred Funk (Fawcett Publications, 1959) and *Word Power: Talk your Way to Life Leadership*, by Vernon Howard (Prentice-Hall, 1958).

Extract from *Watership Down* by Richard Adams. Extract from "Burnt Norton" by T. S. Eliot, from *Collected Poems 1909–1962* by T. S. Eliot. Extract from "Sonnet for Zulfikar Ghose" by B. S. Johnson, from *Poems 1* by B. S. Johnson.

Excerpts from "I Get a Kick Out of You" by Cole Porter, copyright © 1934 (renewed) by Warner Bros. Inc. All rights reserved. Excerpt from "The Remembering" by Jon Anderson, Steve Howe, Chris Squire, Alan White, Rick Wakeman, copyright © 1973 (renewed) by Topographic Music, Ltd. (PRS). All rights administered by WB Music Corp. (ASCAP). All rights reserved. Reproduced by permission of Warner Bros. Publications U.S. Inc., Miami, FL 33014.

The Rotters' Club, by Hatfield and the North, released in 1975, is available on Virgin Records (CDV2030). The section of this novel called "Green Coaster" was inspired by the song of the same name by The High Llamas, from their album *Snowbug* (V2 Records, VVR1008972).

Thanks for general help, advice and encouragement must also go to: Philippe Auclair, Daniel Coe, Janet and Roger Coe, Laura Cumming, Paul Daintry, Helena Dela, Charles Drazin, Artemis Gause-Stamboulopoulou, Simon Gidney, Tanja Graf, Andrew Hodgkiss, Tony Lacey, Barèt Magarian, Janine McKeown, Ivor

Meredith, Tony Peake, Pernilla Pearce, Nicholas Pearson, Guy Perry, Ralph Pite, Pip Pyle, Nicholas Royle, Dave Stewart, Richard Temple and staff at the Modern Records Centre at Warwick University, Tony Trott, Adama Ulrich, Francis Wheen, Conrad Williams and Gaby Wood.

Special thanks to Carlo Feltrinelli and his family for their generous hospitality in Gargnano, Brescia Province, where a large part of *The Rotters' Club* was written.

A NOTE ON THE TYPE

This book was set in Janson, a typeface long thought to have been made by the Dutchman Anton Janson, who was a practicing typefounder in Leipzig during the years 1668–1687. However, it has been conclusively demonstrated that these types are actually the work of Nicholas Kis (1650–1702), a Hungarian, who most probably learned his trade from the master Dutch typefounder Dirk Voskens. The type is an excellent example of the influential and sturdy Dutch types that prevailed in England up to the time William Caslon (1692–1766) developed his own incomparable designs from them.

Composed by
Creative Graphics,
Allentown, Pennsylvania

Printed and bound by
R. R. Donnelley & Sons,
Harrisonburg, Virginia

Designed by
Soonyoung Kwon